P9-CJH-318

Alberta Alone

Cora Sandel/Alberta Alone

Translated by Elizabeth Rokkan
Introduced by Solveig Nellinge
Afterword by Linda Hunt

DISCARD

Ohio University Press
Athens, Ohio

839.82372
S214aLb

To
A Norwegian passing through Stockholm
in the summer of 1936,
with gratitude for her flowers
and encouragement

Ohio University Press edition 1984
Printed in the United States of America.
All rights reserved.

First published in English by Peter Owen Limited 1965
Original title, *Bare Alberte*
English translation copyright © Elizabeth Rokkan 1965
Copyright © Cora Sandel 1939
All rights reserved

Library of Congress Cataloging in Publication Data

Sandel, Cora, 1880-1974.
  Alberta alone.

  Translation of: Bare Alberte.
  Vol. 3 of a triology; v. 1. Alberta and Jacob; v. 2.
Alberta and freedom.
  Reprint. Originally published: London: Women's Press,
1980, c1965.
  I. Title.
PT8950.F2B33   1983   839.8'2372   83-19323
ISBN 0-8214-0760-0
ISBN 0-8214-0761-9 (pbk.)

2/89

INTRODUCTION
A personal memoir by Solveig Nellinge

Cora Sandel's real name, Sara Fabricus, did not become known until several years after her first book was published. She was born in Oslo, in 1880. Her father was a naval officer and when she was twelve her family moved to Tromsø, in the most northern part of Norway, which is where *Alberta and Jacob* is set.

She decided early to become a painter and around the turn of the century left for Oslo, then called Kristiania, to become a pupil in Harriet Backer's Art School. When she was twenty-five, in 1905, Sara Fabricus left for Paris, taking with her 800 Norwegian Crowns. Her plan was to stay for six months but her visit was to last for fifteen years. She was determined to earn her living as a painter and worked hard at it until 1918 when she put down her brush, having finished her last painting, a landscape from Bretagne. In the spring of 1970, when she was nearly ninety, an exhibition was arranged in Stockholm of as many of her paintings as could be gathered together. She found it very strange to have her first exhibition so late, especially as she had given up painting so long before.

While in Paris Sara Fabricus had sent home a few sketches, articles and short stories in order to survive. She also admitted to having written down ideas, sentences and words on pieces of paper which she threw into a large suitcase. Writing never came easily to her and that she was for so long torn between her two major talents – writing and painting – was a continuous source of conflict for her until she decided to give up painting. She would never admit that both her talents were far above average but she chose to write – or, rather, writing chose her.

Her first novel, *Alberta and Jacob*, was published in 1926. By then she had left Paris: 'It felt like having one's heart torn out.' Those fifteen years left their stamp for life on Cora Sandel's personality. French taste and French ésprit always characterised her.

1

She was married in 1913, while still in Paris, to the Swedish sculptor Anders Jönsson and together they had one son, Erik. For his sake they tried to save their marriage but in the summer of 1926, as she wrote the last chapters of *Alberta and Jacob*, their divorce became a fact.

Cora Sandel had Swedish citizenship through her marriage and lived in Sweden before the war, moving there permanently in 1939. For several years she lived in Stockholm in the home of a good friend, a Swedish woman doctor, but later, in 1945, moved to Uppsala. She was sixty-five by then and for the first time had an apartment of her own. She lived there almost to her last years.

She was never keen to acquire lots of possessions. Cora Sandel and her character Alberta are alike in this: 'in their fear of dying of surfeit they'd rather die of starvation and are capable of running away from everything – even pension benefits.'

There is one fairly complete biography of Cora Sandel, written by her countryman Odd Solumsmoen. In this book (*A Writer of Spirit and Truth*) there is a typical footnote added by Cora Sandel who had read the book herself and approved of it before its publication in 1957. Towards its end Solumsmoen writes that Cora Sandel always followed the example of Alberta in not having too many belongings to worry about: 'Everything she owns is packed in trunks and deposited in various attics here and there.' Cora Sandel's comment (the *only* one in the whole book) states in three words: 'Not *quite* everything'. This reservation is characteristic of Cora Sandel, who always kept a certain distance. Although she was prepared to part with a certain amount of information about her private life she would never tell everything. 'I have always been of the opinion that no more needs to be expected of an author than that they should write books', she once said in a sentence which has become a classic. When asked by a literary magazine which was the most important experience in her life Cora Sandel replied: 'That I prefer to keep to myself.' The biographical data she once gave to her publisher could hardly be more concise: 'I was a child in Oslo, a young girl in Northern Norway, a grown woman in France and Sweden. I grew old during the Second World War, I had a son during the First and I live in fear that he will be sacrificed during the Second.'

2

When I first met Cora Sandel she was eighty-five years old. She was living in her apartment in Uppsala and made very few new acquaintances. There was a myth about her reserve, many stories were told at the university among the students who studied her work of how she always refused to see people. It is still easy to remember the calm sitting room with beautiful, beloved belongings – the stillness of the room and the things themselves in such contrast to the heavy traffic in the busy street outside. She used to sit on a blue sofa, above which hung a painting of Tromsø. She cut ice cold grapes: 'Grapes, like chocolate, should be kept in the fridge.' On the small table next to an easy chair were many of the new novels or collections of poetry which authors had sent her, or new novels and books of poetry which she had bought herself. In her bookshelves were many French books in beautiful leather bindings, several by Colette, her twinsoul, whose books she translated into Norwegian but whom she never met in person. 'I considered it too presumptuous to have friends arrange a meeting – Colette was forced to meet so many people anyway – although it could have been done while I lived in Paris.'

She had no television set and when, in 1963, *Krane's Café* was adapted for television, her Swedish publisher brought a television set to her flat in Uppsala so that she could see it at home. All her life she refused to be interviewed for television or the Swedish Broadcasting Corporation. When she was over ninety her Swedish publisher and I were allowed to make a long radio interview with her. Out of respect we hid the technician in the bathroom but she immediately caught on when she saw the wires and asked him in and gave him a glass of sherry.

Animals were always most important in her life. She even called one of her books *Animals I have known*. In her study all the animals from *Winnie the Pooh* sat in a row and it was, of course, Piglet, the small and frightened one, who had most of her sympathy. One of the paintings in her small breakfast room where we used to have tea is dominated by the green colour so characteristic of her style. It shows a garden in summer and in the lush grass a black and white cat is arching its back. If one looks closely one discovers that it is a wooden toy cat. 'I don't find it all that good,' she said, 'I would have liked a real cat for a model.'

To all those who even late in life feel that they have an unborn

3

novel inside them, Cora Sandel may represent a certain hope. She was forty-six when she published her first novel in Norway, under her pen name, Cora Sandel. Her real name was not known and no photo was to be had of the author. Her uncle wrote to her from Tromsø: 'I have just read a book by a woman who calls herself Cora Sandel. Everyone here says that it is you.' And he went on to tell her how he liked the book and how he always thought she would do something quite exceptional one day.

Alberta and Jacob is indeed an unusual book and with it she made a real breakthrough. It was to be followed five years later, in 1931, by *Alberta and Freedom* and the final volume in the trilogy, *Alberta Alone*, was published in 1939. It didn't come easily. Proofs were read and sent back to the publisher together with the next chapter – and all the time cables and letters were arriving imploring her to send more of the manuscript.

'One of the truly great woman characters in contemporary Scandinavian fiction' was how Alberta was described by the critics. The trilogy is partly autobiographical but, one wonders, can such a perfect whole be 'partly'? Cora Sandel herself says: 'In everything one writes there is woven in a thread from one's own life. It can be so hidden that nobody notices it, but it *is* there and it must be there, I suppose, if it is to be seen as a piece of living writing.'

Although the trilogy was a feat in itself several collections of short stories were written and published while Cora Sandel was grappling with her Alberta character. In 1927 came *A Blue Sofa*, followed by three more books of short stories. Her last novel, *Köp inte Dondi*, was published in 1958 and translated into English under the title *The Leech*. She did not publish much after that, only a last collection of short stories with the symbolic title *Our Complicated Life*.

Cora Sandel's own life was long. She was ninety-four when she died and she left an impressive legacy, perhaps above all, she had created Alberta. Cora Sandel said about the writing of *Alberta Alone*, the last volume in the trilogy: 'Every word came floating up from the unknown depths whence it rises anew, transformed, unrecognisable, like a dream, impossible to refute.'

Solveig Nellinge
Stockholm, 1980

PART ONE

The cart taking Liesel and Jeanne was at the top of the slope, standing still against the light wall of mist. They turned and waved, Liesel with quick graceful movements of her wrist, Jeanne with a broad swing of the arm and a high, piercing '*Au revoir*' which the wind blew down to them piecemeal. The children were lifted off, the baker swung himself up instead. A final gust of fresh bread on the breeze, the altered ring of the hooves striking the road as the horse began to trot. Liesel and Jeanne waved once more. Then they were gone.

'It's lifting. It's going to be fine. Just as I said.'

'It's going to be fine.'

'Soon it will be your turn. Sivert will be coming back a rich man, and you'll be off to meet him.' Pierre turned his head and looked at Alberta for a second.

Her heart gave a painful little jump. The words, 'Sivert, rich man', provoked her. What was disturbing about them? On the contrary she ought to—She laughed a little. 'Rich?'

'It's always a beginning,' Pierre said reprovingly. 'If he brings off this deal—and he will. You'll see how it goes afterwards. What a good thing the baker came this way, or we'd never have got Liesel to the train. Jeanne does enjoy going to town.'

There was an undertone to his voice, almost as if he were saying: 'At least I can do that for her'. He was standing a little in front of Alberta with his back to her, his right hand thrust deep into his pocket, as was his habit, so that his trousers were pulled askew; he was still looking upwards even though there was nothing to be seen any more.

Fond of Jeanne all the same, thought Alberta.

5

She felt chilled, and hid her hands in her sleeves. The early morning mist lay damply on everything, and the night had not yet released her: the long night hours when her heart punched out the seconds, passed, passed, passed, passed, and sleep descended only momentarily, loose and full of holes. What was the dream she had had? A bad one as usual? The times were gone when dreams had been a refuge, a land of promise. They had turned into a purgatory where she stood face to face with her own inadequacy, her disquiet and anxiety.

'Streets, shops, purchases, a meal at a restaurant—strange what a weakness women have for all that.' Pierre shrugged his shoulders, turned and looked in the direction of the sea, screwing up his eyes.

Strange? thought Alberta. No, it's not strange.

For an instant she visualised the narrow, crooked street of the town with its domed cobblestones, the low, dark little shops, the peasant women crowding everywhere with their baskets and their big skirts, the market place packed and noisy with men and animals, the heat of the midday sun beating down on it all. A longing to go from window to window, to stand rummaging amongst materials, perhaps to buy them, a truly feminine longing came over her; and a longing to sit under the trees outside the hotel, eating shrimps, released from the daily round.

She stood watching the children coming down the slope: the little girl leaping, arms and legs flying, the boy walking slowly with bent head, absorbed in stroking his finger along the stone wall. His tan was too thin, too transparent, reminding her of the coffee they used for the first wash of colour in the school drawing class at home. One longed for the next time, when it would be the real thing.

The dungarees she had made him were far from flattering, too long at the back, awkwardly cut. The woollen jersey he had on to protect him from the chill had felted into a comical shape from poor laundering. With torturing clarity she saw it all.

The little girl, on the other hand, came running boisterously, her tan healthy and complete, as if she had several summers'

6

sunburn in her skin, the one on top of the other. Her bare arms and legs stuck out of faded, but normal, well-cut clothes. Jeanne was clever, her child strong and tough.

In a moment Marthe would reach her father, throw her arms round him—

Then Alberta noticed that Pierre was humming. Involuntarily she turned towards the sound, so unusual was it. He was still looking down to where the sea lay behind the mist, and he was humming; one of the tunes one has always known but not where it came from, something or other out of an old opera. It was unheard-of behaviour for Pierre. Alberta could not remember hearing him hum before. He hummed nicely.

Then everything was drowned in eager children's talk.

The little girl clung to her father's arm, jumping up and down. 'Why didn't you look at me? Why are you looking the other way? I ran all the way down from the top and you're looking the other way!'

'Hm,' said Pierre, taken by surprise, and smiled his crooked smile, which consisted in drawing his mouth to one side. He made a movement as if to lift the child. Nothing came of it. His hands, which had been halfway out of his pockets, returned to the bottom of them. 'Another time,' he said.

'I may not run another time. But today *Tante* Alberta is going to look after us all day. And if there's not enough of the cold pancakes for lunch she's to give us soft-boiled eggs, and if the butcher doesn't come before dinner she's to give us yesterday's soup and something made with eggs, and fried potatoes. But if Jean-Marie brings any fish, she's to boil them fresh and ask Jean-Marie to clean them. He might as well considering the price he asks for it. But Papa is to have the cold chop as well, because he needs more. And at five o'clock we're to fetch the milk and the fresh butter, and afterwards we must be quiet and not disturb Papa, for we are to play up here round the house while *Tante* Alberta cooks dinner. And Papa is to send off he knows what by the postman, and afterwards he is to write his book. But we are to bathe at two o'clock, for then it will be high tide. And for our snack we shall have—'

Pierre put his hand over his left ear.

'Marthe, Marthe, Marthe, have you finished?'

'Now I've finished,' explained the child in all seriousness. 'Except that *Tante* Alberta must fasten the shutters in our room, because *Maman* forgot. And Papa is to be sure to take his medicine.'

'He's to be sure to, is he?' Pierre stood with an ambiguous expression on his damaged face. His scar was two white lips that would not tan, pressed tightly together in the black beard. His mouth—was it sad or defiant, contemptuous or patient, or a little of all these things? Pierre lived behind a mask, brown above his pallor, and angular, with deep saucers of shadow beneath the cheekbones and temples, the lower jaw crooked and wrongly-shaped from the sword-thrust.

For the time being he would go upstairs. He would say, 'Well, you must excuse me,' and go upstairs. And his type-writer would clatter until lunch. And until it was time to bathe. And until dinner time. Or he would disappear outside amongst the grassy slopes, his old beret askew on his head, taking pencil and paper with him. Both kinds of behaviour were in order. He was a man, a breadwinner, a writer of repute into the bargain. It was Alberta whom Marthe would nag all day long and talk to a standstill with Jeanne's decrees; Alberta's child whom she would tyrannize with her excess energy until there was trouble, and the day became dark with scolding and tears. Alberta would not scold. She was a woman and no more.

Tired out already by the coming day she faced it as best she could. A fear that had haunted her in recent years, of not appearing sufficiently motherly and domesticated, often drove her to simulate cheerful enterprise.

'I expect we'll manage, Marthe. Don't look sarcastic, Pierre.'

'Sarcastic?'

Pierre looked at her for an instant. His expression was blank. It was impossible to know what he felt and did not feel. He looked away again, and the slight irritation, which Alberta had unexpectedly felt, subsided.

A rent had appeared in the mist. Behind it the day lay

ready, clear and warm; a tarnished silver shilling of a sun, a scrap of very blue sky. The spider's web on the nettles glistened with dew like fine pearl embroidery. The slopes that ran down towards the sea became more distinct, then the white strip of sand and the long sandbank beyond, dark, hostile, exposed as far as the edge of the gunmetal sea that suddenly caught lustre from above and lay there like newly-polished pewter. A boat with slack sail resembled a shadow.

It would not be one of the days smelling of seaweed and salt, but of flowers and hay from far inland. The wind came caressingly in light, warm puffs, turning aside into one's ear, playing round it and moving on. The simple flora of the meadow curtseyed before it, a wasp was buzzing about already. After a few minutes only a little coil of mist was left up in the air above the surface of the sea. It floated away like smoke as it disintegrated. A mild warmth, full of promise, reached them.

The boy had paused a short distance away; he was standing with his back to them, picking lichen off the wall. The nape of his thin neck was exposed to the light. He looked round, with a strange little face that cut Alberta to the heart. She remembered what she had dreamed.

The boy had bought a large silver dish with a lid, a frightful object in Jugend style. It stood there, polished and shining, its contents steaming. Music was coming from somewhere, a thin, tinkling sound like a musical box.

It was the dish playing. A musical dish that played as long as there was anything inside it. An expensive and useless item, vulgar and ostentatious, that played weakly and tirelessly. Tot had bought it, he was proud of it—

No!

She could not help going over to him, tilting his face upwards from behind and examining it. The eyes that were much too blue met hers for an instant, then looked away to watch the dissolving mist. She flinched from uneasiness and longing, old hurts that were tender to the touch. Then the boy twisted away, and she was left empty-handed.

'Alberta!'

'Yes?' said Alberta. An expectation passed through her mind, fleetingly and gropingly; nothing that could be put into words, not even into thought. As if Pierre could help!

But Marthe, who had been watching all three of them, as only Marthe could watch, with bent head and eyes that jerked sideways and up and down, tugged at her father: 'Go in and write, go in and write. So that you can come with us when we bathe. Go in and write, go in and write.' She went to the other side of him and pushed.

For once Pierre was angry. The colour rose violently in his badly repaired face. He picked up the child with both arms and put her down again hard, as if he had a nervous compulsion to move something about. And he quickly hid his injured hand in his pocket, while his colour rose even higher.

Then he was just as suddenly himself, with his pale sunburn and calm voice, his expression blank and closed. It allowed none of his thoughts to escape, and shut off access to him: 'Mind your own business. Run along and play.'

So that's what his anger is like, thought Alberta; a flame that blazes up and which he masters. Fortunate for Jeanne. Very fortunate.

'What were you going to say, Pierre?'

'Oh, nothing—'

Marthe was standing where he had put her down, within hearing distance, still squinting up at them. Her lower lip pouted. Jeanne in miniature, although Jeanne never stood like that. She must have done so once upon a time.

'The sugar bowl is full of flies.'

Without having been indoors, Marthe announced this unpleasant fact, which no one dared challenge. The sugar bowl had not been put away; it was still standing on the breakfast table, which everyone had hastily abandoned when the baker's horse, neighing and irritable from having been pulled up so abruptly, stuck all four legs into the crest of the slope, spattering the pebbles downwards. There was every reason to believe that the flies had come in long ago. They came from the bricklayer's cowshed, and were a scandal and a public nuisance that Jeanne, armed with a rolled-up newspaper, fought with great energy and vigorous commands to her troops: 'There, Pierre! Hit it, Alberta! Take proper aim, Liesel. *Mon Dieu*, how clumsy you all are!'

If Jeanne had been at home—

'The bread basket is full of flies.'

Marthe stood, pouting and squinting up at them. 'The butter is full of flies.'

'Go in and put them away then. Don't just stand there talking about it.' Pierre took a couple of steps towards his daughter.

'I am to be out in the sun,' explained Marthe. '*Maman* said so. The spring was so poor, we must make the most of it now.'

They might have been listening to Jeanne, a Jeanne transposed back to childhood. Pierre's eyes wavered, met Alberta's, slid further on at once. 'Go in and put them away,' he said curtly.

He gave a swing of the shoulders, as if pushing away an incumbrance, and another of the head, as if coming up from a dive. He laughed his curt little laugh, that had nothing to do with merriment. 'Have you ever heard anything like it! Seven years old, and we might as well have the police in the house. We're under surveillance, Alberta.'

Over by the wall the boy turned his head now and again. It was impossible to tell how much or how little he understood behind that alien little face. It usually turned out sooner or later that he had understood an astonishing amount. He looked lonely. Alberta resisted her desire to go over to him again. She would be repulsed, she knew.

The sea on this side of the dark sandbank had become shining blue from the reflection of the cleanswept sky and the fine offshore breeze. Two deep chords filled the air, advancing and receding, rising and falling, growing evenly in volume. The tide was coming in. It was the same enormous breathing Alberta had heard once a year at Big Gap, when the brief summer was at its height. Here it was never silent; it merely alternated in strength according to the ebb and flow of the

11

tide. Eternally restful, it supplied a framework and a rhythm to everyday life.

The larks were already hanging, invisible and untiring, somewhere up in space. The gulls planed on their wings, almost grazing the slope and then screaming. And Alberta's dejection gave way. The day and the song of the sea had had their effect. Sun on the boy's neck, she thought. I ought to be happy. Perhaps the children will behave themselves.

For mist and driving drizzle had hung over the world for days on end, hemming them in. She looked about her. Today it was all spacious and open just as on the day of their arrival, when, although tired and numbed by the journey, it had struck her with such force that she had had to shut herself away from it and pretend indifference, until she had rested and collected herself. Here was everything she had sighed for vainly for years. Slopes, exactly as she had imagined them, with ragged grass and white clover, a scattering of lady's slipper and cinquefoil, an occasional long, flat rock sticking up, yellow with lichen: the kind of slopes one finds along the coast in many parts of the world, at home in the north too, familiar, dependable and clean. Below them the beach, an even, white border to the south and north, as far as the eye could reach. Beyond it the sea, beyond that the universe: clouds, sun, moon, stars. And if one had not learnt in childhood that the earth was round, one could hardly have avoided discovering it here. For the horizon was drawn in a protracted bow.

The day had acquired colour and taste. It was a day for idling, for roaming about. For brief moments, minutes at a time, she would be able to join it in her own way, through the mesh of the net she had woven herself into. All that was old and put behind her stirred itself, not dead, in spite of the years.

'I must help Marthe. *Bonjour*, Pierre. We shall eat at the usual times.'

She walked towards the house, against the wind, straight into its warm, scented embrace. The worn little path was firm and elastic, pleasant to the feet. Hoary plantain grew straight up out of it, and myriads of tiny clover leaves which could not grow taller or flower as long as human feet used it for their daily business, but grew there just the same, compact and lush. In a while the boy could take off his jersey. It was going to be as fine as anyone could wish.

She heard Pierre humming again, and paused. The same old opera, or whatever it was: 'Da, da, da, da, dadada—'

Deep down in her mind, far back in time, lay the same melody, cheerful, graceful, simple as if composed by a child, now awakening note by note.

'What are you humming, Pierre?'

'Humming? I don't know. Something I knew as a child I expect. Was I humming?'

But Alberta suddenly knew what it was: Mama in her shawl sitting at the piano between two lighted candles on the other side of the dark sitting room. A thick volume of old opera scores, yellow with age, which had been new when grandfather was young and which would not lean upright on the music stand, but slid down into a curve. It had to be given a push now and again. Mama gave it a push when she had a free hand, and played on: 'The White Lady...'

A glimpse of something so far back that it seemed to belong to another person's life, something she had heard or read. A quick series of reactions followed: I must have taken the wrong turning, when did I go wrong, where did I go wrong? I have come to the wrong place. And the strange, meaningless sensation that she had really known Pierre, this strange man in a strange country, always. Like a fleeting view seen through a rift in the clouds it all flashed past her and was gone. Pierre himself chased it away: 'Go in and write? Damned if I do!'

He puffed out his chest and looked round as if the sea and the slopes belonged to him, hummed another bar and fell silent.

Paper, pencil, the beret, I shall have to look after the children alone, he'll go at least as far as the Pointe du Raz, thought Alberta, unpleasantly practical again.

'Go in and write! Listen, Alberta.'

'Would you like to take something with you to eat, Pierre? I can find something even though Jeanne isn't at home. We have a cold chop, I can boil some eggs—'

13

Pierre shook his head, and Alberta immediately felt anxious in case perhaps there was something he wanted her to do, type a fair copy, proof-read, now that Jeanne was away. Alberta was not generous in such matters; she had more than enough on her own account.

'I'll take the children to the beach,' Pierre said.

'You?'

'Yes.' He looked at his wrist-watch. 'You have a good three hours until lunch, and a couple more afterwards, if you want them. I can warm the soup. There's no magic about that.'

'Cold pancakes and soft-boiled eggs,' interrupted Marthe instantly from a window below. '*Maman* said so.'

'The police again.' Pierre sighed. He looked at Alberta, clearly waiting for her to understand something on her own. When she simply stood there like an interrogation mark he came nearer and said quietly, emphasizing his words: 'You must *concentrate* on your material, use every opportunity to work with it. It's the only way. If you don't manage to add something, at least you can erase, tidy it up, create clarity.'

His hands were on their way out of his pockets again, as if he needed them to clarify what he was saying. Then he stuffed them down still further. 'Come along Tot, come along Marthe, fetch your things, we're going to the beach.'

'No, Pierre!'

Solicitude for this aspect of her well-being made Alberta uneasy and perplexed. She automatically searched in her mind for excuses behind which to hide and on the spur of the moment found plenty. 'The washing came yesterday. I promised Jeanne I would sort it and dampen it. We're doing the ironing tomorrow, Josephine is coming. Then there's the food and the children, and the rooms have to be tidied. On the beach I must try to do some sewing; Tot won't have any clothes to wear soon. And you have so much to do yourself—'

A look of boyish disappointment came over Pierre's face.

'I have!' He took a couple of steps away from her again, as if tired of this fruitless conversation with a dullard and wishing to emphasize that he would prefer to drop it. Alberta

14

scarcely had time to regret that she had involved him at all when he was back again.

'Even if Tot hasn't a thing to wear, what does it matter out here?'

'More than you realise.'

'Hm. And Jeanne, she—'

'She already does more than her share because she's so capable. Liesel and I—'

'Liesel and you! Listen, Alberta, you can't afford to be so fair and correct. You must—'

'Learn from Sivert,' said Pierre suddenly in a different tone of voice. 'There's much to be learnt from Sivert. He's all of a piece right through, he's imperturbable. Sivert does not let any opportunity slip through his fingers. And he'll reach his goal. You can be certain of that.'

'Yes, there are quite a few things to be learnt from Sivert.' Alberta could hear the coldness in her voice. She broke off. Marthe was standing there as if shot up out of the ground, her eyes like a little detective's. '*Maman* said that—'

'Have you put everything away?'

'Yes, I have put everything away.'

'Then off we go, children.' Pierre was already on his way down, walking slowly, his hands thrust down into his pockets, pulling his trousers askew.

He looked back. And there it was again, the glimpse of the man behind the mask, of someone she felt she knew, who wished her well.

'If it has really got to the point when you *have* to cook and sew, then cook and sew. In that case there's nothing to be done.'

He waved. He smiled. Not at her, but to her.

Automatically she waved back, looking as she did so from the one child's face to the other. Both were standing full of that unfathomable quality that children put up against all that is new and disquieting. Without a word they fetched their things from under the stairs: buckets and spades, and the old pudding mould over which they often quarrelled, and which Marthe carried tightly under her arm.

A notion struck Alberta that Pierre intended to play a game that would in the long run become too involved. 'Tot must take off his jersey!' she called, and felt as if she were letting all life's chores slip out of her hands. She heard the children start asking questions both at once about this and that, because children are so easily distracted by something new, as long as it is amusing.

Jeanne, she thought. Jeanne! We're doing nothing wrong. And yet it almost seems as if we're deceiving you.

For a while she wandered in and out of the empty house, up and down the stairs. Times without number she had longed to be there by herself, thinking that if she were granted that, however briefly—. Now she was by herself and merely felt irresolute and abandoned.

The house stood alone, naked and unadorned, without even a tree nearby, and turned its face to the sea to such an extent that it did not have so much as a small peep-hole or back door on the other side. Alberta liked it, with its white, rough-cast walls and its unpainted floors that smelt newly planed. It was a real house with two storeys and an attic, built to be lived in and for no other purpose. Since having a child she had noticed in herself a liking for stability, for dwellings giving protection against wind and weather and keeping in the warmth, instead of ones with skylights and other picturesque advantages.

She opened the large cupboard in the living-room and contemplated the washing lying in heaps inside, children's clothes and adults' all in confusion. A bathing suit belonging to the boy stuck out from the pile. Alberta remembered the rent in it and shut the cupboard.

She continued to wander about, tidying up, looking at Marthe's arrangement for trapping the flies. It was quite clever, Marthe would be practical. She went upstairs, made her bed and the boy's, fastened the shutters everywhere as Jeanne had prescribed. In Jeanne's and Pierre's room and in Marthe's little closet order reigned; the beds were made, the washing water thrown away, everything carefully hung up and laid aside. On Pierre's writing table stood Jeanne's photograph, stained and yellowed; one could see that it had been wet. It was the one he had kept in his breast pocket throughout the war.

On Jeanne's bedside table there was a snapshot of herself and Pierre arm in arm, so small it could convey no impression of the original Pierre to a stranger. Two slender, dark-haired persons were standing together, grimacing at the sun, Jeanne in one of the hazardous skirts of 1913, so narrow at the ankles that a normal stride was out of the question. The picture was not new to Alberta. Jeanne had brought it downstairs on one occasion to show them how ridiculous the skirt was. She had said: 'I have other pictures of course, but I've put them away. It would be unkind to have them out, don't you think?'

Marthe's big doll Mimi sat on its little chair looking straight in front of it with stiff, blue eyes.

Up in Liesel's room in the attic clothes were scattered about and the bed was only loosely covered over. Liesel always got up at the last minute. Alberta made the bed, threw the washing water out of the window so that it slapped on to the ground, put a pair of shoes neatly by the wall and hung up some clothes. Then she went down to her own room and sat on the bed.

The window was full of sky and sea, as long as you did not go right up to it. And all day long every corner of the house was filled with the thunder of the breakers, so that it seemed to sough and sing like a seashell. But sounds within the house echoed as if it were a drum, built as it was with only one layer of planking. Keeping one's intimacies to oneself is one of the luxuries of the rich.

Considering how her life had turned out, Alberta ought to have been overjoyed at being able to wander about like this in a house. But, as Sivert said, she was the kind who would never be satisfied; such people were a burden to themselves, and much to be pitied.

She listened to the sea for a while. Afterwards she found the folder with her papers in it, putting it on her little lop-sided table, that could not stand straight without a piece of paper

17

under one of its legs, then took it down to the table in the living-room. It was round and the folder looked just as futile and out of place on the one as on the other.

She put a rug over her arm and took it out of doors.

A group of people in a home. They are held together by external laws and forced apart by internal ones. The tension between them is expressed in a number of small events, apparently without significance, in reality a screen for fate, who spins her mysterious threads behind it.

It often seemed to Alberta that she was wasting her time, tampering with something empty and meaningless. Why should she expose these persons' lives? Of what interest could it be to others? They were as grey as everyday. But she was bound to them, as one is bound to people with whom one has once associated. She might ask herself: Why did I want to get mixed up with them? It made no difference; she was just as involved.

It was as impossible to subtract from or add to them as it would have been to do so to her surroundings. They were themselves, conjured out of a multiplicity of old scribbles, just as others were conjured up and took shape in her mind, in bits and pieces, by means of thousands of small details, brief, unfinished utterances, apparently insignificant actions.

It had all come so far that it amounted to a pile in a folder. It had grown in slow stages and as far as possible in secrecy. But suddenly, when she had begun to believe that she had achieved a certain amount of order and coherence, new material had presented itself, at times in such quantities that she became sickened and felt she could not face it. It had come from the wrong direction and been the cause of much disturbance: innovations and renumbering of pages. The task threatened to be endless, and the old glint had returned to Sivert's eye a long time ago when he asked after it. Or he might say: 'Have you done any scribbling today?' And then she felt as if he had handled her roughly, and she did not know which she detested most, herself or Sivert, or the pile of papers.

18

Taking all of it under her arm she wandered down the slope, but not so far that Jean-Marie would not see her and call if he were to come with the fish. She felt no inclination towards working on her manuscript, it all seemed more than usually stupid and pointless, a story that was none of her business, that she really knew nothing about.

Where the opposite slope shelved like a little meadow, just right for lying on one's stomach looking out over the sea, just right too for propping up the folder, should the occasion arise, she stopped and arranged her rug.

The day unfurled itself, warm and beautiful. The tide was coming in fast. Slowly, inexorably the enormous bowl was filled. Shining tongues licked the sand, advancing with a hiss and retreating with a sigh, gaining an advantage each time, leaving behind them a floating border of lace that merged with the next tongue. The creation was accomplished. A higher level of universal order is created by the incoming tide.

Some way out she could see Pierre and the children. They looked like small, dark figures in a composition, Marthe rushing off like a puppy that has just been let out, squatting by the pools and then running again. Pierre was holding the boy's hand. Alberta knew that he must have taken Pierre's hand of his own accord, thrusting his thin little one into it and holding it tight.

There they were, all three of them, squatting round a pool. And although she was not fond of the beach because of the sandworms that sketched their curlicues everywhere so that it was difficult to know where to place one's feet, and positively disliked the revelation of marine life, she longed to be down there with them and felt lonely. The wind was blowing away from her, she could hear nothing, but the small figures were excited. She wished she had gone too. Such a pool is like a little aquarium of strange, green light and curious fauna and flora; a closed world, where the seaweed grows straight upwards and is a mysterious forest trafficked by tiny crabs and occasionally a big one, by shrimps, little fish, much that is even unidentifiable. Pretty stones and snail-shells glint at the bottom like jewellery.

19

Pierre was fond of children, at least in the sense that, when he wished, he could amuse them hugely. Neither he nor any other man possessed that endless patience, that faculty of being able to hang about with them hour after hour, of answering precisely and good-naturedly the countless questions they use to hold you fast. And those women who really do possess it are usually elderly or a little simple-minded.

She saw Marthe take off her shoes and socks, jump into a pool and paddle round in it, waving her arms. In a short while they all went northwards. Tinti-Anna's house hid them from her.

She looked at the folder with hostility.

What was she to do with this unexpected three hours of freedom? Freedom was something she felt embarrassed about and could not understand. Once she had had plenty of it. It had trickled away between her fingers while she loitered through life, sight-seeing, a member of an audience. When it eventually dawned on her that she had looked about her enough, that she glimpsed coherence, that she had something to say about life, then that same life had seized her by the scruff of the neck and had not yet loosed its grip. It seemed to wish to emphasize thoroughly that it was now too late. She was picking her way indirectly as in the old days at home.

And Pierre?

He tried to help her, now and again. Something indefinable, friendship perhaps, perhaps not even that, perhaps something a little more, existed at intervals between them. It might well have been pure imagination too, a trick played on her by her longing for warmth. It came and went, as such feelings do. It would certainly be forgotten one day. Already on the journey out . . .

A man changes in the aura of his wife. The way Pierre had sat, leaning his head against the wall of the compartment, his eyes closed, had seemed frighteningly strange. Even his old beret, worn crookedly, seemed to belong to someone else whose joys and sorrows, duties and responsibilities, were totally unknown to her. This new person, Jeanne, slept beside him as a matter of course, as if she were engaged in some task, that of sleeping in a sitting position in a train, a task she had taken upon herself and was carrying out irreproachably. There was nothing loose or inert in that well-constructed face, framed by hair as neat and smooth as it had been at their departure. When the grey, merciless dawn came, Jeanne still sat there, just as presentable, with Marthe's head in her lap, a picture of complete repose.

A *père de famille* on holiday. That was as it should be. It was no surprise to her. Far from it. She had felt it as violence, almost like pillage. But what should have been different?

Nothing, Alberta assured herself, and suspected despondently that everything would be, whether on account of Jeanne or somebody else. Time after time she had pushed back her own hair, heavy with smoke and smuts, which fell uncomfortably into stripes between her fingers. The friendship between Pierre and Sivert was not to suffer, however, that had already been clear at the station the previous evening.

But it had altered. It was not her imagination. It had altered considerably. She quickly taught herself to behave towards Pierre as one does towards an acquaintance. She was flexible.

Even during the preparations for their departure she had been given a salutary ducking into everyday reality. She had been kept busy running about, sewing, pestering Sivert for scores of things. When she saw Pierre again, a busy man about to set out with his wife and child, she felt as sorry for herself as if she were quite helpless. I can't stand ordinary kindness any more, she thought. It goes straight to my head. She shook hands with Jeanne and said, 'Madame'.

But she needed Pierre, needed his quiet understanding, his support when necessary, the fact that he sometimes took her part against Sivert and made Sivert give in. It had become good to have Pierre there, not least against Sivert, not least—

He had remained friendly, no-one could accuse him of anything else, polite and friendly, kind and obliging. All the same—

Today he, who was always the soul of patience, had hummed, turned angry, gone to the beach in working hours, as if the postman, his publisher and Jeanne had all ceased to exist. He had suddenly referred to Alberta's shapeless manuscript as if it were something to be taken into account. Was this good or bad? It was disturbing.

Sivert must have said something. Sivert was odd in that way. He thought nothing of what she did; nevertheless he had to talk about it. It was impossible to make out what Sivert's intentions were.

She too had been out on the slopes occasionally with pad and pencil, had had difficulty controlling her temper when the subsequent inner restlessness had inconveniently affected her. She had had one or two short stories published in magazines at home and even been paid for them, small sums, that had disappeared into the ever-gaping holes. This was the official side of the matter, impossible to hide, never taken seriously by the world at large. On the contrary, it had appeared unwarranted, the last thing a wife and mother ought to undertake. It would have been preferable, for instance, to wash everything oneself, make all one's own clothes, turn the collars of Sivert's shirts inside-out when they were frayed. Jeanne did that to Pierre's; it was a great saving.

Alberta's scribbling was a burden that had to be borne, because she was made that way, for the sake of peace, and to avoid making mountains out of molehills. Only Liesel and Pierre supported her openly. Neither of them could read a word she wrote.

Could she not afford to be fair? Behave like Sivert? Pierre was a man too, that was why he could talk as he did. He understood a good deal, but not everything. And yet something in her profoundly and boastfully agreed with his male talk.

If only she could pull herself together and gain possession of both her child and her work! As things were, Alberta felt she possessed neither. There was still more she did not possess, and when life offered her a moment like the present, her longing welled up, flooding over everything else and paralysing her, as it had always done.

Sweetness and bitterness were mingled. Sivert, Sivert, can't we try to manage together? We have Tot. Tot! I owe him so many moments I would not have missed. But I have to look to find them. I always remember the bad things first and most clearly. I admit it.

Concentrate on her material?

She leafed through the pages in the folder, struggled for a while with the wind for control of her straying papers, and put them away again. It was all dead, approximate, loosely formulated.

Pierre and the children had reappeared on the other side of Tinti-Anna's house and settled there. Pierre was leaning on his elbow in the white sand, his head bent as if reading. It was probably one of the pamphlets which he carried round in his pockets, which came from Paris, and which Jeanne disliked. Tot and Marthe were digging with their spades. It looked a peaceful little group, and Alberta longed more than ever to join them. She scowled at the folder, then lay on her back with her face turned away from the others and towards the wind, looking up at the sky. A procession of solid, white clouds were sailing slowly before the off-shore breeze, all kinds of country and summer scents and sporadic sounds of work from up in the village in their train. There was a wet, slapping sound from the washing place over at the stream. The world was full of people with their affairs well in hand who were achieving something. What she had was flimsy and tattered, without a beginning or an end.

There were moments when it was different. They came like thieves in the night, at the wrong times. Images, word sequences, that immediately seemed serviceable, floated up from the depths of her mind. An unexpected clarity of thought seemed flung at her. She had sometimes been alone with it in the evening, when the boy slept and Sivert was at the *Dôme*; it accompanied her to bed, got her up during the night as in the old days, to jot down sudden ideas, sentences, single words. Even her body felt it, and became strong and supple from the back of her neck down to her big toe. Sivert was woken by the light and grumbled. She would think: If only I could wake up like this in the morning, knowing that she would not. Yet she would sleep with a strange certainty that everything would be put right in the end, even what was most difficult, painful and heart-breaking.

The next morning she would be dull and heavy. The day with all its demands stood waiting at her bedside. The boy would whine from the moment he opened his eyes. Perhaps it would be one of the days when his face was white as chalk and he ate paper, and she could not take him out because it was pouring with rain. The time came when there was war on top of everything else. The boy was not yet a year old. The value of money dropped like a barometer reacting to an earthquake.

And she would see the intoxication of the night for what it was, a flight from reality. The day was the morning after, when she paid for her foolishness and in a daze washed the child's clothes, stirred saucepans, watched the boy to see that he did not get hold of paper, and took him out as soon as she could. More than anything else, she felt she must get some colour into that white little face. It was white when she left with him, and white when she came indoors again. Or blue with cold. It hurt her so much to see it that she grew bad-tempered.

If by chance she was able to sit down with her scraps of paper and fit them in where they belonged, or make them the foundation of a new little structure, this was only uphill, boring, hopeless work. What she put together grew grudgingly, infinitely slowly. Yet she knew that if she continued to pile one stone on top of another for a while, unwearyingly and whether she wanted to or not, through hope and doubt there would come a moment when it looked as if there was a solution to the problem, and from then on it would be easier. Like a puzzle, it took a long time before you saw how it was going to turn out. The scraps of paper grew into pages, then into piles, and were put away in the folder. To expand them further—it was laughable, as Sivert so often demonstrated. But this was the only way that she could see. To what? From what? Oh—she would be able to buy something, take Tot to the doctor when she thought this was necessary, give him this and give him that, a better place in which to live, better living conditions; she would be able to abandon her antiquated winter coat. She could think of things like that without feeling a traitor.

The larks sang on, invisible in the enormous space, the sound of the sea grew louder, the sun was baking hot. Alberta kicked her sandals off her bare feet, turned her clothes up in one place and down in another, surrendered herself piece by piece to the wind. It felt good, good enough to send her to sleep; it satisfied her old hunger for fresh air. She was overcome by inertia. She had thought she would experience the day through the mesh of the net. She had become one with it through a large hole.

Erase, was that what Pierre had said?

Suddenly she was through her inertia and beyond it. She turned over the leaves, struggled with the wind for the pages, knew where previously she had only suspected, made thick lines, corrected, added . . .

She leaned the folder against the slope as if it were a desk.

At two o'clock the sea lay white as milk in the sun.

But if one went right down to it the blue of the sky bobbed and dipped as pale shadows in the swell. The seaweed and stones showed through clearly a long way out. The horizon was a thin line of shading. Gulls hovered at an angle on splayed wings, sweeping the surface with their wing tips, snatching at something, screaming . . .

The enormous bowl was brimful, its contents lying edge to edge with the shining white sand, rocking gently against it. The flowers of the oyster plant and sea holly were reflections of sea and sky. Everything was clean, soot-free. The creation was accomplished.

They were taking off their clothes in Tinti-Anna's little boathouse, which adjoined her living-room. It smelt of tar, sun-baked wood and pigs in there. For the pig lived next door too, on the other side. You could hear it grubbing in its trough outside, grunting, pushing itself against the fence.

The boy was standing without a stitch on, slender and slight, stunted by several years of deprivation. But he was a little brown, however shallow it might be. And he was exhilarated by what the new day had brought, telling Alberta all about it while she dressed him in the little bathing trunks which she had brought to propitiate local propriety. Marthe had stamped on a crab and killed it and *Ton-ton* Pierre had been cross with her. But *Ton-ton* Pierre was kind. He had carried Marthe, he had carried Tot, found a big starfish for each of them, helped them to make sand-pies. They had made lots, but the sea came so quickly and spoilt them.

Alberta got him out into the sun, Marthe was already wading. Pierre was crawling a little way out. His head was almost beneath the water, his arms appeared alternately in an even, fast rhythm, in a movement that came from the shoulders. A damaged hand was no longer of importance, the spray hid it.

Alberta, who had actually put twenty to thirty words on paper and had also erased a good deal, was seized with such physical elation that she ran straight out to swim without so much as looking about her. Behind her she heard the children, used as they were to having her at their beck and call, Marthe shouting, Tot setting up an injured howl. He's naked, she thought. He's in the sun and the fresh air, he has everything I've hungered to give him until I felt it in my own body, he has what he most needs. Let him howl—for a little while at any rate.

She was intoxicated. The endless sea, white in the glare, green as glass when she looked down into it, with each stone, each swaying alga and tangle of seaweed clear at the bottom; the bell of the sky above her; her own healthy body, thin and muscular, so brown that it looked as if she had a little white bathing suit on when she was naked, the unexpected speed with which she shot through the water, everything contributed to it. Now the feeling of unbelievable possibilities was with her again, of an existence lying parallel to the one she led already, but on another level. It was close to her. But she felt she would have to leave her mind and body in order to inhabit it.

She lay on her back and kicked up a column of spray. Water splashed over and about her, the sunshine was broken

26

up in it, her face and eyes were smarting with salt. The sensation it gave of power and delight was as strong as if her metamorphosis had already taken place.

An extra shower blinded her, she heard the splashing and snorting of a sea creature. Pierre was swimming past her towards the shore. When she could see once more, his legs seemed to be whirling behind him like propellers a good way off. He had said nothing as he went by. It made her uneasy, chilling her and reminding her of the old days at home, as if she had let herself be drawn into flippancy and suddenly come to her senses.

But shortly afterwards, when she reached the shore and emerged step by step from the salt sea into the sea of air, pulling down her wet, clinging suit, he said 'Bravo!' without a trace of irony. He and the children were sitting cross-legged in a row, Pierre brown and hard, his long muscles still shining and damp. He had buried his right hand in the sand as usual. At this time of day it was obvious that the bullets and bayonet thrusts that had disabled the man had struck a fine example of homo sapiens. The face that went with it must have been fine too.

'That bullet knew where it was going,' Eliel was used to declaiming, when the subject came up. He and Sivert had once tried to make sketches of Pierre. But Pierre had noticed, slung his beach robe round him and gone to sunbathe elsewhere. 'Idiots!' called Jeanne from the bottom of her heart, following him. 'Tactless creatures! He was in the war, this man, while you—!'

'Bravo!' Pierre repeated. 'One day you'll swim the Channel.'

'Don't make fun of me.'

'I'm not making fun of you. You've learnt quickly. When you began—'

'I'd never swum before. At home the sea was too cold, nobody thought of doing it. It did look hopeless at the beginning.'

She saw herself lying on her stomach in shallow water, while Liesel held her under the chin and Jeanne commanded, 'Up

27

with your legs! Up with your legs! Think of a frog. Up with your legs!'

'Nothing is hopeless once Jeanne takes an interest in it. It would be—.' Pierre's voice deepened. 'Poor Jeanne, if anyone deserves to succeed—. Did you swim, Marthe?'

'I did, but Tot didn't,' Marthe informed them. Her eyes and ears were alert to the conversation as she sat filtering sand through her fingers and toes.

'Come along, Tot, let's go and swim. The sea's nice today.'

Pierre got up and stood waiting, broad-shouldered and narrow-hipped, brown-skinned, slightly blue round the loins, silhouetted against the sky and sea. Alberta felt a pang of joy and despondency when the boy grasped Pierre's hand tightly in his thin little one and went without resistance. She always had to argue with him, persuading and reassuring. It was difficult to get him into the water, mistrustful as he was and unused to it all. When the question of how to deal with him was mooted, not even Jeanne would advise firmness. 'If it were Marthe,' she said, 'I'd just drop her in, and it would be over and done with. But this little one—!' The two wrinkles that did not suit her, would appear in her forehead. She seemed to be thinking: I'm glad I don't have any responsibility for *him*.

Now he was going with Pierre as if there were nothing the matter. They splashed and strode about at the water's edge, the boy laughing aloud. Now they were going in, the water was up to the boy's knees, then under his hollow little breastbone, now almost up to his neck. It was too much, he was going to cry. But when Pierre put him on his stomach and supported him in shallower water he tried eagerly and ineffectually to swim. When he returned to the shore and Alberta wrapped him in the bathrobe he was beside himself with pride and happiness. 'Tot swam,' he said. 'Tot swam with *Ton-ton* Pierre.'

'What a clever boy!' Alberta rubbed him in the cautious manner that made Sivert so impatient. 'Take hold of him properly,' he would say. 'He's not made of glass.'

It seemed to her that his little heart was beating faster than

28

it should; she rubbed even more cautiously, changed his bathing trunks and took out the biscuits and chocolate that were part of the ritual. Marthe was there at once: 'We're to share the extra one. *Maman* said so.'

Alberta shared it out. 'We'll write to Father and tell him Tot swam,' she said.

'He didn't swim. Besides, my Papa was there. When my Papa is there it's easy.' Marthe put down what was in her hands and ran into the water a second time, firm and brown in her faded red bathing suit, ruthless and superior. She swam around near the edge of the water, splashing to draw attention to herself. She was a year older than Alberta's child, could read, write, do sums, was used to the water from former summers and made of sterner stuff. Probably the same as Jeanne was made of. It was strong material.

Tot burst into tears. He stamped his feet, threw away his biscuits and chocolate and bellowed, while Pierre hauled his child back to the beach and gave her a well-aimed slap on the bottom. His hand managed it very well. 'And that's for you. Nobody asked you for your opinion.'

'But it's true. He didn't swim.'

Howls from Tot.

'He didn't swim.'

'Be quiet.'

'He *didn't* swim.'

Marthe suddenly arched her back and put her hands behind her to protect herself; another slap was on its way. She stood up to it for a moment, then threw herself on her knees in the sand, as if the slap had sent her there, and looked up at Pierre inquiringly, used as she was to receiving chastisement from Jeanne. Then she made up her mind, threw things about and howled too.

Alberta and Pierre looked at each other like two people who have caused a fiasco together. Then Pierre's expression turned blank: 'Pick up your chocolate. And the biscuit. Put your clothes on. Stop howling, you've got nothing to howl about. Hurry up.'

He bent over the boy: 'You swam, Tot. *Ton-ton* Pierre

knows you swam. Next time you'll swim even better. Get his clothes on him, Alberta. We'd better go home.'

Pierre looked disheartened. He disappeared behind the large rock where he dressed and undressed. Alberta took the children, still crying, each in a different key, into the boathouse. The day was darkened with scolding and tears, as all days were, sooner or later. And yet the boy was not quite as outmatched by the robust little girl as he had been when they arrived, and there had been perpetual friction. He had been so unused to other children that she had felt raw herself.

'Walk in front, children,' commanded Pierre when the procession moved off. As clearly as if she heard or saw, Alberta felt how the two sniffling children were immediately changed from opponents into hostile conspirators with common interests and a common front. They continued to walk, each on his own side of the path, but with their thoughts and ears directed the same way.

'I can't stand her when she's spiteful,' Pierre said, when there was sufficient distance between them.

'She was only telling the truth. And Tot *is* too sensitive.' All the elation had gone out of her. She was still trembling from the blow that had hurt the boy. He had conquered his fear. It was no small thing. Then Marthe had come along and—

'Some truths are worse than lies. It's brutality, no less.'

'She's only a child, Pierre. Children are brutal.'

'I expect you're right.' Pierre's voice was so toneless that Alberta thought: It doesn't take much to depress you. Then she remembered how little it took to make her depressed. She fell silent. Besides, the children had slackened their pace. Marthe was pulling a piece of sea holly to pieces, walking more and more slowly. Alberta could see her listening under her sunbleached dark hair.

Nothing was said for a while. The children were dragging their feet. Marthe dragged her bathing wrap demonstratively behind her as well, as if trying to provoke more of Pierre's unaccustomed anger. It led nowhere. Tot's kneebones seemed painfully large in contrast to his thighs and calves as he walked. It is not true that love is blind; one sees twice as clearly.

Sensitive? More than that. Suddenly, without apparent reason, the boy could become bad-tempered and whining. Jeanne called it nervousness. Sivert said he was spoilt and took after his mother. For Alberta it was an exhaustion she shared. She could not bring herself to scold him. The boy seemed to find life itself difficult; he saw that this was how it had to be. His mind was composed of memories of city air, winter dampness, cold, disturbed sleep, itching bug bites, insufficient food: vague anxiety about everything and nothing.

Marthe had spent most of the war in Dijon, with Jeanne's parents. She had toddled on lawns under tall trees, had milk from their own cow, eggs from their own chickens, fruit from the garden, sat on the laps of kind old grandparents, played naked in the sun. Jeanne had a whole album full of pictures, in which the cow, the chickens and everything else were visible. Not once had Marthe been snatched up out of sleep and carried down to the cellar, not one day had they been short of butter, firewood or sugar for her, even though the whole of the old avenue up to the house had been sacrificed because the army had needed big logs. Jeanne had sat, thin, but beautiful, seemingly incandescent with patient waiting beside a large hearth with a blazing fire, knitting warm clothes for Marthe, for Pierre, for unknown soldiers. This too appeared in the photographs. Pierre was in some of them, home on leave and in uniform. But there was not one in which he did not turn his face partially or wholly away. He had received the ugly cut on his cheek almost as soon as he got out to the front.

'Hurry, Marthe. Run. There's the postman. Ask him if there's anything for us. Off you go.' Pierre's voice was full of relief; something was happening, something innocent, about which they could talk easily to each other.

Marthe ran. Tot began to walk faster.

'We'll put them to bed early, shall we?' Pierre said quietly.

'As early as we can,' Alberta too spoke quietly. Her thoughts went abruptly to Jeanne.

Up at the house Marthe called: 'A telegram for *Tante*

31

Alberta. She has to sign for it. *Les Modes* for *Maman*, letters for Papa. And the newspapers. And a telegram for—'

Alberta was already running up the slope.

* * *

'That's all, Pierre.' Half a chop, two fried eggs, some fried potatoes. If only Jeanne had been home. Or Liesel. 'You can't have had enough.'

Alberta gestured apologetically towards the simple still-life on the table. The lamplight on the cloth, the bowl of dahlias, the background of wide, darkening sky through the open windows, the gusts of mild air from outside flapping the curtains, would have been becoming to a luxurious meal. Their cigarette smoke rose in beautiful whorls and rings, the ceaseless noise of the breakers was like a heavy accompaniment to the larks and gulls. But on the table were two plates, two cups, a couple of small dishes and the bread basket, all of them empty.

'If only Jean-Marie had come with fish.'

'Good heavens, Alberta!' Pierre pushed away his cup and leaned his palms on the table, shutting his eyes as he did when he was trying to collect himself. The gap left by the amputated fingers straddled defencelessly, painful to see. 'When will you stop talking about food? Mending, washing, food, mending, washing, food, like a parrot. What was I trying to say?—now don't interrupt me—get it all out of your system as quickly as you can. You can cut it down and polish it, put in new material and make alterations later. Break into the action, get to the important part. You'll have to rewrite it plenty of times as it is before you find a tone that doesn't seem too grating to your ears. In the meantime things may occur to you that you had no idea were in the material. And it doesn't have to be sent to the publisher's tomorrow. For God's sake organise yourself so that it won't—'

Pierre stopped. His fingers curled, he clenched his teeth, baring them slightly, and went on talking, now fast, as if the seconds mattered, now slowly, with difficulty: 'Get it out of

32

you while you still see it fresh. Something may happen one day to make it all seem ridiculous, and you won't be able to face it any more. If there's anyone who has the right to come after you with a whip and say: 'Write this and that, thus and so, have it ready by such and such a time . . .'

He's talking to himself, not to me, thought Alberta. But he's talking. He hasn't gone down to the beach as he usually does in the evenings. He's forgotten his hand, forgotten the cut in his face, exposing them both to the lamplight. He looks like a symbol—no, two—of human beings' ill-treatment of each other and of their struggle to survive in spite of it. If Sivert had been sitting here he would have forgotten him too, until Sivert decided that that was enough and said something to put a stop to it. He would not have forgotten Jeanne. He would not have talked like this, but gone out, asking whether she would like to go with him.

Alberta had to make an effort to follow him. As soon as the conversation left ordinary matters she felt giddy, that same giddiness that had lain in wait for her all her life as soon as anyone broached subjects she tried to hide. Besides, Sivert's telegram lay open on the mantelpiece demanding attention. From both she sought refuge in trifles as if they were small rocks to which she could cling for safety.

'I can smell mussels, can you?'

'The tide's going out,' Pierre replied curtly. 'Now listen to me. I may not get the opportunity to tell you again.'

Alberta acknowledged the reprimand and felt her eyes grow larger. 'I am grateful, Pierre.'

'If only there were any other course for you to take. But I can't see anything else for it, you will go this way sooner or later in the belief that it will lead to control of your life and your child. Perhaps it will. You do want to control everything yourself, Alberta.'

'I want to, yes,' answered Alberta ruefully, a little defiant and derisive. A thought sequence passed rapidly and vaguely through her head: The moments when you want to and must do so are few, those when you want to and cannot are number-less. Victory goes to the latter.

33

'You more than want. When I saw you for the first time I had the impression of a person in disintegration. Now—'

Is it possible? thought Alberta. She saw herself as someone at the bottom of an abyss.

'You might need support. But one day Sivert will . . .'

Is it only Sivert you want to talk about? Only about Sivert? She was gripped by loneliness, Pierre and Jeanne would go off one day. She would be left with Sivert.

'He's completely absorbed in his own affairs. That is his strength.'

But now Pierre seemed to feel he had rowed out too far. He added quickly, 'You know how much I admire Sivert. He is my friend, he is an artist. I—we ought to have drunk his health this evening. I don't grudge him his success. Nor you. Now everything will be easier.'

Alberta sat twisting a teaspoon between her fingers. She thought: We were talking about me. Say more, say things that make me feel better. Sivert, Sivert all the time. He doesn't even see me. I have turned myself into a doormat for him, and it has led nowhere.

'You must assert yourself beside Sivert, Alberta, let him see that you, too—. I felt I wanted to say this to you.'

Pierre got to his feet, walked up and down, leant against the mantelpiece, the ornament of the room, and absently read the telegram again.

'You must come to terms with Sivert.'

Alberta again felt reprimanded. His words were surprisingly hurtful. She suddenly saw herself and Sivert in the years to come. It was endless. 'We haven't quarrelled.'

'No, no. But you must accept him as he is, be patient with him.'

'I did accept him as he was and I was patient, to the point where we almost lost our lives, Tot and I. Yes, Pierre! If fire broke out he would save his canvases first.'

'You must be patient and accept him as he is until you have achieved something, until you are equals. Then Sivert will see you differently, and everything will work out all right.'

'Then Sivert will hate me,' Alberta said giddily. She bit

her lip hard. One did not say such things. One only thought them in moments of depression. Gratitude for what Sivert had, in spite of everything, managed to give her and the boy lay hidden beneath much else, ready to flame up in and out of season. Often she was too tired to acknowledge it. Now it was there like a warm wave, released by her bitter words. Pierre was a friend, he felt and understood. But it was Sivert who worked and paid, Sivert who for years had brought with him a kind of life and excitement merely by coming home with a wet canvas in each hand, or a package of food, or money from the pawnbroker's. It was in Sivert's arms she ought to belong.

'I don't know what I'm saying,' she said.

Pierre did not reply. The murmur of the sea and the untiring refrain of the larks became intrusively distinct. How many could there be up there in the sky? How long were they going to keep it up? It was some time since sunset.

'Since you have to stick together,' said Pierre.

The word divorce had never crossed Alberta's mind, yet Pierre's words made her feel as if a door had slammed in her face.

'Yes, you're right, we have to stick together.' Her voice was hard. She went on twisting the teaspoon and thought: That's what he was getting at. Now he'll go.

But Pierre blew a smoke-ring and picked up the thread where he had dropped it. 'Don't let yourself be paralysed by the bad days, when nothing happens. Something is lying there, turning into something, something you don't know how to grasp. You feel a wastrel and a criminal. If you try to help, you catch hold of an arm or a leg and everything is at a dead-lock, like an embryo lying in the wrong position. Yet you must go on tugging and pulling. Life demands it, one must live.'

Jeanne demands it, thought Alberta. He didn't go. He still has something to say to me.

'Then you have to turn the whole thing round and try another approach. That one is wrong too. The day you feel yourself grasping the head, then delivery begins in earnest, the day—' Pierre paused, lighted another cigarette with the old one, continued: 'When evening comes you may have no more

35

than ten serviceable lines. But ten lines that open up for the rest.'

He stood looking at her with the same expression. Then he laughed. 'It would be better for you if you were able to cook and sew. But you can't.'

Through her giddiness Alberta thought of the distressing fury she could feel when Sivert brought out his 'Have you done any scribbling today?' Here was the explanation. Sivert's tone was too similar to the one he used to the boy: 'Have you had a nice time today?' It was painful to write, it was not a game. She had to be far advanced with her material before it ceased to distress her with its shapelessness, its reek of raw matter, of stillbirth. Pierre was right to talk of embryos. It took a long time before these lumps from the depths of the mind turned into something she could bear to expose to the gaze of others. Here was Pierre, who had written several books of distinction, corroborating the truth of it.

'All in all it's a luxury for the rich,' Pierre said, still talking about writing. 'But at any rate see to it that you get something out of you while you're still capable of accepting what you produce, while you're still naive enough to do so. We can fear our own work finally, shun it, flee from it like the plague, find incredible excuses for avoiding it. Hurry up and get something down before you reach that stage. Earn money, earn money, buy yourself peace in good time, peace to be yourself. Here you are, wasting your time! Even the washing-up—'

'I haven't touched the washing-up.'

'Good.'

At the same moment a bed creaked upstairs in the echoing house. A child suddenly cried. Alberta and Pierre looked at each other guiltily. '*Voilà*. Is it yours or mine?'

'Mine, of course.' Alberta was already on her feet, hurrying out into the passage and up the stairs, which were in complete darkness. 'Have you any matches?' Pierre called after her, 'In case you need them?'

'Yes, thank you.'

Up in the bedroom the fading twilight fell in stripes through the shutters. Alberta pushed them open. The sky with one

36

pale star and a piece of ink-black sea became visible. She could see to walk.

Over in the cot the cries had turned into screams, which became more angry after her arrival. She glimpsed a tangle of naked legs and sheets; the blanket was on the floor.

'What is it?' Her voice grated on her ears. She tidied the bed and rearranged the blanket.

'It's the sea. I don't want to hear the sea.'

'You must go to sleep, then you won't hear the sea.'

'It's the sea that stops me from going to sleep. I don't like being by the sea.'

'But in the daytime you love the sea. Then you like hearing it.'

'Not at night-time.'

'Now Mother's going to turn the pillow, and then you'll go to sleep.'

'Mother must sit with me.'

'Nonsense,' said Alberta. But the pillow was hot with fever, and the boy's body burned to the touch. Quickly, stealthily, she put her hand on his chest, under the nightshirt. It beat too violently inside there, she knew it did, and nobody would get her to change her mind. It distressed her almost to the point of loathing and disgust. It was too much; it was one of the things that gave her nausea, the feeling that she could not bear it because she was in any case quite helpless. It turned her own heart into a hard, hammering little lump.

'What were you feeling for?'

'Nothing. Now little boys must go to sleep.'

'Sing to me.'

'Sing to a big boy like you?'

'You said I was little just now.'

'Not so very little.'

'Sing about Colin, then I shan't hear the sea.'

'But it won't hurt you to hear the sea. It's nice to hear the sea.'

'The sea's not nice. The sea's wicked. Sing to me.'

The boy's small hand, sticky and hot, lay in Alberta's, gripping it tighter now and then as if to assure itself that it

37

was holding her. Unwillingly, cross with herself for her unwillingness, thinly, a little out of tune, and as softly as possible, she sang. The melody hit on the wrong notes continually and distressed her with its inadequacy. Were those footsteps on the path outside? Pierre was probably walking up and down out there, smiling to himself at how badly she did everything.

'Fais dodo, Colin, mon petit frère,
Fais dodo, tu auras du lolo—'

'Sing louder!'

'Maman est en haut, qui fait du gâteau—'

'Louder!'

'Papa est en bas, qui fait du chocolat.
Fais dodo Colin, mon petit frère,
Fais dodo, tu auras du lolo.'

It was ridiculous from every point of view to be singing to a boy nearly six years old, ridiculous to sing as badly as she did, ridiculous too that little shift of emotion which generally accompanied the naive song. A song about childish poor man's comfort, of the happiness of a full stomach; two children, one bigger boy, one smaller, a cold, miserable room, a candle burning low in a candlestick. Nobody was making anything for them; outside the world was full of similar rooms. Soon all the candles would have burned out.

'I don't expect he cared for milk when he could have chocolate.'

'I don't expect he did. Now go to sleep.'

'Perhaps it was only something his big brother thought up to get Colin to sleep. I expect he only got milk really. But there's nothing nice in milk. They had as much milk as they wanted, didn't they?'

'I'm sure they did.' Alberta recalled with bitterness the days when they had by no means had as much milk as they wanted. It was a good thing the boy did not remember them.

It was at last quiet in the bed. The child's hand still clung to hers immovably. She turned her head and looked out.

38

The darkness of the late summer evening was falling fast. The last trace of red along the horizon had been erased, the larks were silent. Only the breakers continued their eternal motion, up with a hiss, back with a sigh as if for the whole world's grief and distress.

The lighthouse at Penmarc'h had been lit. She could not see it, but its beams swept the surface of the sea, soundlessly and as regular as a heartbeat. The offshore wind must have met an air current that threw it back again. It came in, filling the room with spicy air, and was gone again. Now and then it smelt of the ebb-tide.

Now she could hear Pierre's footsteps clearly on the path outside. There they were—now he stopped—and went on again, wandering without purpose, moved a little way away, again came closer. There was a puff from his cigarette. She was seized with fear in case he might disappear for good, and go off on one of his usual evening walks along the beach. Carefully she began to disengage her hand.

'You put me to bed too early.'

'What do you mean?'

'You and *Ton-ton* Pierre want to sit and talk to each other.'

'Grown-ups always sit and talk to each other when children are in bed.'

'This evening you will talk more, because *Tante* Jeanne is away. And *Tante* Liesel is away, Father is away, everybody is away. Then you will talk a lot. You will talk about things that the others must not hear.'

'Tot!' exclaimed Alberta in despair.

'Father wants me to be called Brede now.'

'Mother wants you to be called that too.'

'Why do you say Tot then?'

'We called you that when you were little.'

'Sing about Martin too.'

'No, now you're going to sleep.'

'I shall tell Father you put me to bed too early. You put Marthe to bed too early as well. I shall tell *Tante* Jeanne. Marthe was silly and fell asleep, because she's a girl.'

'You fell asleep too.'

39

'I was only pretending. I heard you talking. Sing about Martin.'

'Will you go to sleep if I do?'

The boy considered for a moment. 'Yes,' he said.

And Alberta was in for it again:

> *'Danse Martin, vieux camarade*
> *Pour amuser les petits et les grands . . .'*

This song generally made her feel emotional too. The eternal tragedy of man and beast lay behind it, the tramping along the high road, fatigue and hunger, courage in spite of everything. This evening she felt nothing. She watched her son tensely. He lay peacefully, his eyes closed.

The song was finished, she began to withdraw her hand.

'Did he have a ring in the bear's nose?' came instantly.

'Is this going to sleep?'

'Are all bears called Martin? Do they all have rings in their noses?'

'Not the ones who are wild and live in the forest.'

'How do people catch bears?'

'I'll tell you in the morning. Go to sleep.'

'I shan't if you go.'

'You're very naughty,' exploded Alberta. She leaned her head against the bedpost in utter dejection.

'Sing to me again, then I'll go to sleep. You put me to bed too early.'

And Alberta went on singing. About Marlborough, about the three little lambs, about the art of planting cabbages:

> *'Savez-vous planter les choux*
> *à la mode, à la mode,*
> *savez-vous planter les choux*
> *à la mode de chez nous?*
>
> *On y plante avec les doigts,*
> *à la mode, à la mode,*
> *on y plante avec les doigts*
> *à la mode de chez moi.'*

She felt like a second-rate hurdy-gurdy, going on and on. She could no longer hear the footsteps outside.

She wanted to go downstairs to Pierre.. This one evening. She was sitting with her child, wanting it. Pierre would have gone on talking. He had things to say to her, things he had kept hidden until now, and there had been no occasion to say them before. He had the occasion this evening. Miraculously all the others were away. The house was quiet and strange on account of it, solemn as if in anticipation. Only the boy was present, seeing to it that she did not talk to Pierre. She was not even allowed to do that, to talk to Pierre.

When she came downstairs the only sign of life came from the moths whirring round the lamp. Alberta carried the lamp out to the kitchen, cleared the table in the half-light, and carried the dishes out, clattering them unnecessarily and carelessly, and punishing herself by lighting the primus. It started smoking immediately and she felt savage with hatred for it. She pumped wildly, the smoke got worse and worse. On the floor by the water pump two black snails stretched their horns towards the light, moving their slimy bodies slowly and tenaciously. She found a twig and threw the snails out of the window, the one after the other, with an angry, accustomed, firm gesture. The kitchen had an earthen floor. In the evening it seemed to breed vermin and creeping things, especially round the water pump, which stood there looking as if it belonged to some village square.

The primus burned at last with a little flickering, ragged, evil-smelling flame, an insult to the fresh air from outside. She stood holding the palms of her hands against the sides of the kettle, just as she used to stand with the coffee kettle at home long ago, keeping a watch on the temperature. There always seemed to be a temperature to watch, and certain habits stay with one to the end of one's days. When she had stood like this for a little while the heat moved from her fore-arms right up into her shoulders, the old, painful, soothing sensation. It kept its value in the winter.

41

She did the washing-up, the whole day's crockery and sauce-pans. On the wall, where the towels hung, Jeanne had written in a large, clear hand: Glass, China, Kitchen utensils, Hands. Alberta used the glass one for the china and the kitchen one for her hands, hung them up again any-old-how and shrugged her shoulders at her own childishness. The moths came tumbling in, dashing themselves in confusion against her face, the smoke from the primus still hung, noxious and disgusting, between the walls. It seemed to her at this moment to be the air of life, a suffocating aura that enclosed every breath of fresh air and in which everything decisive took place.

Had it not been exactly the same, worse even, that afternoon last winter when she—when Pierre—?

He had visited them several times, Pierre Cloquet, *Prix Fémina* and *Croix de Guerre,* married and the father of a little girl slightly older than Tot, one of Sivert's many acquaintances from the *Dôme* and one of those who had been 'out there', all four years of it. They compelled a rather oppressive feeling of respect, one tended to feel uncertain and perplexed, more insignificant than usual in their taciturn company. This one had, in addition to everything else, a face like a mask and was a writer. Why had Sivert wanted to drag him home?

But the times were past when she and Sivert got on better alone. A third was usually welcome, as long as he fitted in, and she and Tot had a few clothes on. Gradually she came to like his strange expression, blank, apparently concentrated on something in the distance, and his low, monotonous voice. He suited their surroundings, he seemed to belong.

That afternoon nobody would have been welcome. With black fingers and hair on end, wearing one of Sivert's old painting smocks that she had inherited for household use, she stood struggling with the primus. It was smoking so badly that soot was falling all over the place. Tot was on the pot. He had a cold and she dared not take him across the yard in the November rain; the Spanish influenza was at its height, especially among children. And all of a sudden there was Pierre standing in the doorway with Sivert, who also had a cold and immediately demanded a clean handkerchief.

42

Alberta could not supply him with one.

'Why not?'

'But Sivert, you know very well why not.'

'Oh Lord!' Sivert struck his forehead. The laundry had not been paid for. 'Damnation. But a few handkerchiefs? Such small things. Is it necessary to—?'

'They have to be boiled,' answered Alberta curtly. 'It's difficult enough to boil everything else as it is.'

As she said it she happened to look Pierre straight in the eye. And his were no longer blank, they were those of a confidant, almost of an accomplice, not those of a judge, and not merely sympathetic. There was an all-forgiving irony in them, kindness. It had been a fleeting and unbelievable moment. A current of life went through her, years' forgotten warmth shifted. It made her think of someone raised from the dead who gets his first glimpse of the light again.

He and Sivert busied themselves with money, digging loose change out of their pockets and pooling the results, and left in haste to fetch the laundry and new cleaning equipment for the primus. Alberta had time to tidy herself and her surroundings while they were gone, and everything was so normal again that she must only have had one of her foolish moments. Sivert brought out his latest pictures, he and Pierre discussed politics and art, as usual. Pierre sat there as he normally did, looking at her absently now and then, talking about Jeanne and little Marthe, his permanent subject of conversation. Alberta finally managed to get a cup of tea on the table.

He had been alone in Paris at that time, attempting in various ways to start writing again, even to the extent of sending his wife and child away for a while. He had a half-finished manuscript which he had begun before the war, a continuation of the book for which he had been awarded the *Prix Fémina*. The publisher wanted it, as he had gone as far as he could, and further, during the war years. It was imperative that Pierre should deliver it. But he achieved nothing, according to Sivert; he fled from it, to cafés, to friends, to revolutionary meetings in Montmartre. Alberta never heard

43

him mention either his work or himself. 'Poor devil,' Eliel used to say.

It was after that day that she had begun to feel there was support in Pierre, and started to count on him, to reach out to him in her thoughts every time there was something the matter. She was happy when he came, and desolate when he left. Somebody cared a little as to how she felt. She was no longer simply the eternal culprit, who deserved what she got, and serve her right.

Disintegration, had he said? A strong word. It struck home. He had used it without hesitation, without even searching for another. She herself had sometimes wondered what this inner and outer composure that she inhabited really was? Passivity or courage, self-renunciation or self-control? Disintegration?

Whatever the reason for her composure, her old restlessness had returned. She caught herself thinking about her appearance, looking in the mirror, a thing she had almost forgotten about. One evening when Sivert had been at the *Dôme* and the boy was asleep, she had taken out her papers: not the short stories she pieced together in an emergency, the others, the pile in the folder. A long time had passed since she had last looked at them. A cold defiance had loosened its grip on her.

Then came the journey here. And Jeanne. But Jeanne in Dijon and Jeanne here were two different things. And two different things the simple knowledge that Pierre had a wife, and spending the days in her company.

The boy, Alberta and Liesel—at times Sivert and Eliel— that would have been for better or worse, like everything else in life, but she would have been able to calculate more or less in advance how things would turn out. But Jeanne . . .

Alberta's heart sank at the thought of how empty it had become, how little there was that could be called her own, in the life that was hers. Without Jeanne no Pierre.

She had gone outside to sit on the bench in the dark. The dew was falling, but the earth beneath it was warm from the sun. The stars had come out, boring into the disc of the sea with thin swords that were broken by the swell, carried in

44

fragments to the shore and lost in the faintly luminous border of froth along the low tide line. Even now that it was dark she could see clearly how emphatically the curve of the sky pressed down on the surface of the water; the eye could follow it all the way round. Two enormous sections had been fitted together with geometrical accuracy. Penmarc'h lighthouse signalled life, death, life, death, with unfailing precision. Everything conformed to the natural law, eternal, serene.

Pierre had gone. He had lost patience, she supposed, even though it was their only chance. And what did she expect of him? Assert yourself beside Sivert, come to terms with him, work on your material continually, peg away, keep going. A kind observer's wise reflections, the good, sensible advice of a friend. He had crossed the chasm he himself had created between them and given it to her, in order to bring her out of the lethargy into which she had relapsed, to rouse her.

She had managed to write a little today. Pierre had helped her to look after the children, feed them, put them to bed, relieving her in every possible way. And yet—

Was that all you were after? she thought, and was suddenly as embarrassed as if she had compromised herself without redress. For deep inside her there was an obstinate murmur: You were really after something else, really, really. You've been observing and watching and thinking. It can't only be out of interest in my wretched writing of which you're completely ignorant.

A figment of the imagination; ordinary friendliness, that had gone to her head. It had been too much for her. But tomorrow Jeanne would be here. In a few days Sivert would arrive. She would be sober then, if not before.

She had leaned over Tot at dinner-time, standing there with the telegram, and said, 'Father's coming home soon, and *Ton-ton* Eliel,' happily and enthusiastically, as such things ought to be said. But her heart had been anxious. It was not only to the good that Sivert was coming, not only to the good that he was coming with money. Plenty of money.

Tot had given one of his convulsive jumps for joy. They could not really be described as jumps either, for he did not

45

leave the ground, merely moved his arms and legs energetically and in vain. 'Father's coming,' he shouted. It had made her wince like a false note.

Sivert—? Tot—?

The day Pierre came and told them that Jeanne had found a cheap house in Brittany for the summer, big enough for at least two families, Sivert had been all enthusiasm. So had she. The Spanish influenza was raging for the second time. Pierre would not advise them for or against it. He was not so sure that the sea would be good for the boy. 'You ought to ask a doctor.'

'The sea?' echoed Sivert. 'What could be better than the sea?'

Alberta agreed with him. Everything in her reached out towards this new possibility. All the same she thought they should ask the doctor. For many reasons.

'Nonsense,' said Sivert. 'These Frenchmen spoil their children. Have you ever heard of a child who couldn't stand the sea?' Alberta had not. Nor had Eliel. 'Damnation,' he said. 'If a person can't stand the sea, what will he stand? Nothing.' Liesel hesitated; she had certainly heard of it. Alphonsine was exceedingly hesitant. But Eliel and Sivert said in chorus: 'Frenchmen and womenfolk!'

A short while ago Tot's heart had hammered like that of a frightened little animal. Her own hardened and stuttered as soon as she thought about it.

She started. Pierre had come up so quietly in his sandshoes that she had not heard him. He felt the ground with his hand and said quietly, as if he did not want to wake the children, 'Don't sit there, the dew is falling. I hope you left the washing-up, Alberta?'

'I couldn't leave it for Jeanne and Liesel. Coming home to dirty dishes . . .' She got up obediently.

'But Josephine? What about Josephine?'

'There's enough for her to do as it is,' said Alberta in an experienced tone of voice. She thought of Jeanne's face and of what she would have said if she had found the kitchen sink full.

46

'I ought to have helped you.' In the dark she could see how Pierre made a fumbling gesture as if to take his damaged hand out of his pocket. He was haunted by the memory of the time when he had had the use of two hands and done what he liked with them. 'To be honest, I lost patience. Is the tyrant asleep now? You sat up there for more than an hour, a full hour by the clock and let yourself be bullied. I left.' She could see his shoulders move as if in apology.

But Alberta, who at once felt more cheerful and full of gratitude because he had come, managed to ask a difficult question in the same quiet tone of voice. 'Is it the heart that can't stand the sea, Pierre?' She could hear the uncertainty in her voice. Curious, how easy it is to talk beside the point in everything one says.

'It's well known that the sea doesn't suit everyone,' Pierre said evasively, and his cautious words seemed to open her veins. All her strength ebbed away. She had worried over this, hinted it to Sivert, aloud and in writing. He had replied and written, 'Nonsense', and much else besides. She had stopped worrying, or pretended to herself that she had. But what others see acquires terrifying reality, gives one confirmation.

'I grew up by the sea myself. It suited me as a child. Sivert too.'

'It needn't be anything serious. Tot may well grow up strong. But if I were you, Alberta—I'm telling you for the tenth time, find yourself a living. You're wasting your time like this, and it's not as if you're good at it, you're clumsy.' Pierre said the final sentence in his usual voice, as if wanting to break the low, intimate tone on purpose.

'I'm not as clumsy as all that.' Years of drudgery with tasks that she really could not master, and carried out as if she were all thumbs, had made Alberta sensitive on this point. She had at least taken up the struggle, with honesty and goodwill. She did not really demand appreciation for anything whatsoever besides these things. She replied with irritation, 'What do you know about it?'

'Quite a lot. More than you think.'

'Of course, you have Jeanne.'

'Yes, of course, I have Jeanne, I have Jeanne. That explains everything, doesn't it?'

Alberta said nothing. Now *Pierre* was irritated. They were difficult, these men from the war. He was usually the first to give Jeanne the credit on every occasion: 'Thanks to Jeanne. Jeanne's magnificent. Jeanne's splendid. She manages everything. I wouldn't get far without her.' How many times had Alberta heard it all? 'Marthe will be pretty, but she'll never be like Jeanne. All of them were after her at home. There was nobody who didn't know who Jeanne Fauvel was.'

Jeanne here and Jeanne there. Yet one must not imply that she belonged to Pierre. But Alberta knew very well that it was not the words, but the tone. She regretted them.

And she was punished. Pierre yawned. He explained that he had walked quite far while she was sitting upstairs, and was tired. They had better go to bed.

He preceded her to the house, stopped to let her enter first, fastened the door securely, asked politely whether she had matches, whether there was enough oil in her lamp, whether she had water upstairs, something to read. She must be sure to tell him . . . with such icy, correct kindness, that there was no escape. She could only take what she deserved and pretend not to notice.

And worst of all, when they had reached the landing and were about to go to their rooms, Pierre said, 'Perhaps I tend to interfere more than I should in my friends' affairs. Forgive me. Goodnight.'

'Goodnight,' answered Alberta, utterly discomfited.

'Non, ce n'est pas vers toi que je me tourne, mon enfant.

'Tout ce qui bat en moi de vrai et de meilleur, le Dieu, la part de l'âme, cela ne te concerne pas.

'La question palpitante, que je suis, mes actes, leurs dessein, tu es né pour les contredire, puisque tu dois les dépasser, et toi, que j'ai porté dans mon ventre neuf mois, tu ne seras jamais devant moi, devant mes yeux mouillés, contre les baisers de mes lèvres, qu'un étranger, qui part en emportant mon sang.'

48

Alberta put the book down and picked up another. Her eyes were smarting from reading too long in the poor light. She tried to find composure, failed, and went on opening book after book. They belonged to Liesel. Books written by women.

'J'ai un tel besoin, si vous saviez, de bras autour de moi. J'ai besoin qu'on s'approche, qu'on me vienne en aide. Personne n'est venu.'

She sat upright in bed. The night was painful and restless. Someone to share with! To share, if only in the wind chasing round the house in the dark and pausing to sigh among the four or five trees beside the brook in the little valley a short way off; in the waning moon that had risen and was erasing the flickers of light coming through the mist from the lighthouse. Someone to say things to . . .

She was roused by a disturbance in the house. When she was properly awake she could distinguish the hurried tapping of heels on the stairs, doors opening and shutting, voices.

Jeanne and Liesel were back. They had come in the middle of the night.

She heard Jeanne: 'That's the chocolate, here's the material for your shirts, that's for Marthe's nightdresses. Did you take your medicine? Did you have the chop? Of course not, they're asleep, nobody'll hear. Won't you have something to eat? I'm ravenous. Here are *your* parcels, Liesel. And everything has been all right here? We dined at the Hôtel de l'Epée. It was expensive, but there you are. It's only once. Did you manage to get what you wanted sent by the postman?'

She heard Pierre's voice now and again, mumbling and indistinct. He was talking as quietly as he could.

Through the mist the dawn was breaking.

* * *

Jeanne moved about the house, brisk and efficient. Up and down the stairs went her tapping heels. She always finished her share of the chores in good time. Afterwards she would sit

49

with her handwork, indoors or outside on the grass, according to the weather.

With beautiful regular stitches she would sew some well-made, absolutely correct garment for herself, for Marthe, or for Pierre. At her side would be more work, cut out and tacked. Soon she would embark on that too. She finished them incredibly quickly.

Alberta usually sat there too with one of her extraordinary pieces of sewing, supposedly a garment for the boy. Although she cut them out according to the right measurements and used a good pattern they always turned out oddly as did everything of that kind that she undertook. There was something hopeless about it. She wanted to be able to do this at least, it was necessary that she should. But life went on and on, and nothing that she embarked on turned out as she had intended. If Pierre came by he might look at her ironically, or with irritation, or with slight amusement. It all depended on what kind of a day it was.

Jeanne was not a silent soul; but neither was she particularly informative. In her slightly too high-pitched voice she would talk about ordinary subjects: Marthe, the difficulties of the times, the necessity for housewives to find something to do as well.

She had friends who had begun to take up weaving. Or they sewed and embroidered and sold the results, tried painting on parchment, or journalism. Their husbands had come home from the war and had failed to get their jobs back, they were disabled, blinded, crippled; or they had not come home at all. Life was quite different from what it had been before, and impossibly expensive.

She assured Alberta kindly that Tot was browner and more lively. 'Oh yes, of course he is, Alberta. The country might have suited him better?' Jeanne shrugged her shoulders. 'Possibly. Very likely.' If she had seen him at an earlier stage than at the last moment at the station, she might perhaps have advised her against it. But here he was and it was much better for him than Paris. She asked Alberta's advice concerning colours and thread, talked fashion, literature, cooking. Of

Pierre she said: 'If only he could pull himself together and get out a longer work. It's so important.'

On top of her workbasket there usually lay the most recent issue of *Les Modes de la Femme de France*, a publication about which Pierre teased her. He accused her of being a member of *The Honeycomb*, a supplement in which subscribers exchanged experiences and philosophical reflections, over pseudonyms; and of getting advice from 'Enigma', who read horoscopes at five francs apiece.

'Be quiet,' Jeanne said. 'I'm not so stupid. If I didn't take *Les Modes* Marthe and I couldn't look as we do on almost nothing.'

Jeanne had all the good qualities you could think of. She was useful, respectable and trustworthy. She meant well, nobody's intentions were better. Nevertheless to be with Jeanne was like ceasing to live.

She could arrive full of plans, energy and busyness, always with a thought for others; slender and beautiful, in gay, practical clothes, lovely to look at. It was just that there was never a moment's peace. What was quiet and essential in one withered and died.

'Don't forget your strengthening medicine, Pierre. Then you must lie down for a while. You'll work all the better for it. Marthe, you've scratched yourself; don't touch anything before I've put iodine on it. You ought to look in on Madame Poulain, Alberta, before she sells the rest of those sandshoes, she only had a couple of pairs left. If you're going, would you mind buying a reel of cotton for me? Has anyone seen the paper? There was something in it I wanted to read to you. It's so true, as he says, that man who writes that we must not imagine peace has come yet, it is only a new phase of the war. I don't think Tot ought to be in the sun for such a long time, Alberta. It's different for Marthe. Who's going to shell the peas? You or Liesel? I did them last time. Whoever does them must remove all the withered pieces from the pods and we'll boil them up for soup tomorrow.'

Jeanne, so good-humoured, so full of activity. What would have become of a great many things out here, without Jeanne?

Getting supplies was difficult, vegetables and groceries had to be fetched from Audierne, eight kilometres away. Thanks to Jeanne everything went amazingly far. But tasks one had happily forgotten, anxieties one had pushed aside in one's consciousness, apprehension for tomorrow usually followed in her train.

The clatter of a typewriter came from the open window above. If it stopped, Jeanne noticed at once. Her sewing dropped into her lap, and she sat with upraised head, in her forehead the two small wrinkles that did not become her, forgot what she was talking about, absent-mindedly quietened the children.

When a few minutes had passed and there was still no clatter, Jeanne got up and disappeared inside the house.

Alberta looked down towards the bricklayer's cabbage field. Blue-green as verdigris it dipped steeply into a depression. In the middle of the field stood Liesel's painting parasol, and beneath it was Liesel.

She, too, had a good ear for the typewriter. As soon as Jeanne had gone she put her things down and came plodding through the tall cabbages, which reached up to her thighs. She pushed them aside with her hands as she walked, plucking a couple of large, mottled caterpillars off her skirt on the way up.

'She plagues the life out of him, Albertchen. At least we don't do *that* to Sivert and Eliel.'

'We shouldn't get very far with it either.' Alberta raised her voice and spoke naturally, as one has a right to do when saying things anybody may hear. 'How can you stand those caterpillars! There's one on your shoulder. It's revolting. Now it's climbing on to your hair!'

Liesel picked off the caterpillar coolly and threw it over the stone wall. 'Plenty of things are revolting. Painting is revolting too. I was bored with it a long time ago. If it were not that I had to—'

She sat down and threw her arms round her knees. People usually disappeared in the course of time. They whirled round in Alberta's range of vision for a while and were gone; she could think of many. Liesel was still there, as gangling as a

52

schoolgirl in the short dresses that were now the fashion, her handsome face drawn and thin, a little too freckled to be attractive, and with a suspicion of early furrows running from the sides of her nose down to her mouth. Her coil of plaits was not firm and shining as it used to be, but tended to hang askew and get untidy. It was beginning to be obvious that for Liesel the years were passing, grey and without lustre.

'You really must buy yourself that new brush, Liesel, with hair like yours. And now Eliel is coming back.'

'Hair?' said Liesel. 'Eliel?' she said. 'Look at my hands, Albertchen. Thin, loathsome winter hands, although I'm in the sun all day, Before, when I went to the sea, it made me prettier. But it's this eternal influenza. I'm going to cut my hair when I get back to Paris. Nobody has long hair any more. As for Eliel—does he care what my hair looks like?' And she whispered again, 'If I were Pierre, I'd speak my mind one day. He works from morning till night. She goes about it the wrong way. There ought to be limits.' Liesel coughed.

'You caught a cold on that trip during the night, Liesel.'

'Yes, I did,' Liesel said. 'But I saved the price of a room at the *Lion d'Or* and got two tubes of cobalt blue instead. And Jeanne obtained peace of mind. Everything was in order and respectable here. It's true that Pierre had been idle, the washing had not been touched, and you had put the children to bed in the middle of the day. But the worst had not happened.'

'Who can possibly know?' said Alberta with irritation.

'That sort of thing hangs in the air, Albertchen. You wouldn't be able to deceive Jeanne for as much as a day.'

'I won't listen to this nonsense, Liesel. Is it *you* who thinks up such rubbish?'

'Why else should she decide to come home as soon as the last train had left?' said Liesel undaunted. 'It came over her all of a sudden. We combed the town for a farmer who was going this way. We might have been sitting in a vice, there was so little room beside him. All the way from Quimper to Pont-Croix, and then we walked.'

'She was thinking of Marthe, naturally.'

'You don't believe that, Albertchen.'

53

'Talk out loud,' whispered Alberta. 'Otherwise they'll notice.'

'Of course they won't. But why are you sitting here? *She* can look after the children. *She* can prepare the meals. She sits here in any case, and she's made for that sort of thing. You should see about finishing whatever it is you're writing.'

'Sssh,' Alberta said, from that hidden dread of many things that she could not always explain to herself. 'I work now and again. It's just that one can't do it as a matter of course, Liesel.'

An exchange of words could be heard through the open window above. It was mostly Jeanne who was speaking, insistently, persuasively. Now and then she paused as if to give Pierre the opportunity to reply. He did so briefly and quietly.

'Talk out loud, as if nothing's the matter. Here she comes.'

Jeanne came, silent, with the two unattractive wrinkles in her forehead. She sat down and bent over her work as before. Her mouth was sad and tired.

The typewriter started again, a light, nimble clatter that made Alberta feel that if only she had a typewriter . . . Jeanne's forehead smoothed out. She bit off a thread and said, 'It's so much better for his own sake . . .'

'But he does work, Jeanne!'

'If you can call it work!' Jeanne drew more thread from the reel and narrowed her brown eyes short-sightedly as she re-threaded her needle. 'If you can call it work! He could write them all into a cocked hat if only he'd pull himself together. Short stories are all very well, and he must write them if we're to live. But if he doesn't get that novel out soon . . .'

Stitch after stitch she sewed, regularly, beautifully. They all lay in the same direction, each one as small as the last. The movement of Jeanne's little finger each time she drew out the thread was perfection.

Her beauty would last. It lay in the perfect structure of the cranium, the unassailability of her teeth, the abundance of her hair, her even, golden complexion: in a healthiness that defied everything. In spite of wrinkles and furrows Jeanne's beauty would make an impression to the end, and continue to smoulder in the deep-set eyes far into old age. Jeanne with white hair would be a magnificent old lady, one of those one looks at with astonishment, who are slender and chic, vital and active until death.

From each earlobe there dangled a tiny pearl. They were beautiful against her skin and her dark hair. Pierre had put them on her the day he was given the *Prix Fémina*. Madness of course. But a man must be allowed a little madness now and again.

Sometimes the machine would stop again. Footsteps would come rattling down the stairs. Pierre would stride past them, his hands in his pockets and his beret demonstratively awry, as if it had been thrown on his head. He would look neither to right nor left.

In dismay Jeanne would mutter, 'Would you believe it!' with sudden tears in her eyes. Marthe would notice immediately and come to put her arms round her neck, kiss and caress her. *'Petit maman,* don't cry.'

'He must get some exercise, Jeanne,' Liesel might say.

Alberta would sit, uncertain whether to try to console Jeanne or not. On occasion Jeanne had looked up at her with a strange expression and said, 'It's the war; he came home so changed.' To this Alberta had nothing to say. The women had stormed the hospitals; Liesel had offered her services, had no qualifications and simply came home again. But she had offered. Alberta had merely existed, while darkness enclosed her and her small world. She had perceived it as darkness, not being able to cope with it in any other way. Through the washing and the wakeful nights she had watched it thickening endlessly. The years had passed, one after the other. She had felt as if she and the sickly child were on a rock out at sea, with the tide coming in and night falling. The Spanish influenza came. Children died like flies. But Sivert had not been threatened in life or limb, and this was undeniable.

Nor had Eliel. There had been a period when they wanted to go to war too, coming home with serious expressions to

55

tell her about other Scandinavians who had enlisted. 'If we have to experience this, we want to be in it,' they said. 'It won't last long, and it won't be repeated in our lifetime.'

Alberta and Liesel went round for days on tenterhooks. Then it was rumoured that one of the Swedes from the *Dôme* was in hospital somewhere in the provinces, with one leg amputated and the other in danger, after only one day of this experience that would never be repeated. A Norwegian had lost his sight, a Dane was dead. Sivert and Eliel did not mention the matter again.

Since her trip to Quimper Jeanne had begun to harp on matters which she had only hinted at before. If the machine stopped she might say, turning down her mouth as if sucking in the corners hard: 'It was unanimous, they gave *him* the prize.'

Alberta and Liesel knew this. 'Yes,' they said.

'For his *first* really *big* work. *I* had never questioned his talent. When he gave up the law and wanted to do nothing but write, it was I who stood by him. He became involved in a literary côterie in Paris, one of these cliques, you know. My parents wanted me to break off the engagement.'

'Oh?' Liesel and Alberta exchanged glances. It was not like Jeanne to make such confidences. Yet there she sat, making them.

'Naturally. It's a gamble to be an author, isn't it? An insecure kind of life. Even his mother was against him. Not I. I believed in him. We had been engaged since we were children.' For a moment Jeanne was almost breathless. 'When the telegram came, saying that he had been given the prize—what a triumph! I had had a hard struggle, I can tell you. They wanted to marry me off to the son of a landed family at home. I come from the Dijon district. But I held out, of course. And after a victory like that they all gave in. We married, were happy for a couple of years. And then the war came.'

She paused, and closed her eyes for a second, gazing inwards at her heroically survived martyrdom. She had the right to do so. She had been heroic, victoriously fighting out the long, tenacious struggle with anxiety and hopelessness,

56

which was what the war had meant to women. Alberta suddenly lost her thread, her hand trembled. She saw what it must have been like to have Pierre 'out there' those four long years. For some reason Jeanne's words pierced her like awls.

The machine started again. Jeanne fell silent, But immediately afterwards it stopped. She dropped her sewing. Marthe, who was making a pattern of pretty stones in the grass, being a little too demonstrative about it while clearly following the discussion, turned her head.

'Pierre!' called Jeanne.

'Jeanne!' exclaimed Liesel softly. 'Jeanne!' said Alberta.

Footsteps on the stairs, strides taking at least two steps at a time. Pierre went past them, his hands in his pockets, his beret askew. He was in great haste. Tot, who was sitting on the ground, looked up. Marthe scattered her stones and snail-shells and ran to Jeanne. But Jeanne pushed her away. 'Go and play!'

Then the words suddenly tripped over one another. 'His friends—didn't I get out of bed, even when they came came in the small hours, even when I was pregnant? Wasn't I just as good-tempered when they had raided my larder and turned everything upside down? As if I were not one of the côterie, I as well as the others! All I ever heard was: Kind Jeanne, marvellous Jeanne, just the kind of wife a writer should have. I'm not allowed to see what he writes any more either. I, who used to read every word before anyone else.'

She got up and ran into the house, Marthe following. Then Liesel nodded three times at Alberta, sucking in her cheeks as if she had had something confirmed. Originally it had been one of Eliel's affectations. Liesel had caught it from him.

'*No*, Liesel,' Alberta said involuntarily. 'Oh no, Liesel.'

She put her hand to her breast as if to defend herself.

'*Yes*,' said Liesel.

At lunchtime that day Pierre was exquisitely polite to Jeanne and Jeanne more than usually solicitous towards Pierre, but more subdued than usual. She did not bother to help clear the table, but went upstairs with him.

57

In a while the others heard her sobbing and Pierre talking quietly and soothingly.

Tonight, thought Alberta mechanically. Tonight . . .

The night came and was indeed one of those when she had to put her head under the blankets in order to avoid hearing Jeanne's intense, effusive whispers, her silence and contented sighs, the creaking of the bed in their room.

* * *

The path up to the village went through the bricklayer's farm-yard. Children swarmed in and out across the threshold, apparently dropped into the world as frequently as the laws of nature permit. Their mother was coming from the fields carrying a large basket of cabbages on her head for the cows. They were kept indoors at mid-day because of the sun and the flies. She herself resembled a large, slow-witted animal going about its business. Her pale, round eyes were quite empty, without conscious expression, and she was pregnant yet again. Her heavy belly swayed before her like a large drum; she moved in an even, patient jog-trot.

People said the bricklayer hit her on Saturday evenings, for then he was drunk; hit her and made her pregnant, if she was not so already and he was not dead drunk. He had not even been away at the war, as he was already lame. There had therefore been no intermission.

Some of the children had their father's fretful, crafty expression beneath red eyebrows, others their mother's listless, stupid one under white ones. Judging by this family, the laws of heredity were simple and clear.

'*Ann amser zo brao,* fine weather today,' said Liesel and Alberta, as was the custom. The day was indeed fine: an offshore breeze, a sea like milk, boats out on it, moving banks of cloud, warmth; the pleasant sounds of work in progress, of threshing and whetstones on the farms.

The woman did not reply. She did not seem to be aware that they were speaking to her as a human being. She jogged on

58

in her clogs and disappeared into the barn, with a shoal of her offspring crowding after her like frightened animals. Their stockings were wrinkled, snot ran from their noses. One had his trousers unbuttoned; they slapped against his little black rump. The others pressed themselves against the wall and stood there with their fingers in their mouths, scowling at Alberta, Liesel and the children, as if they could be suspected of anything.

A sympathy akin to irritation, a desire to do something brutal, to seize this sluggish creature and shake her, came over Alberta: Hit back, kick, put up a fight, take your children and leave.

But it is difficult to leave with one child, let alone several. All the collective degradation women have to suffer tormented her every time she passed this farm.

She felt Tot's hand gripping hers more tightly, saw Marthe inspecting everything about her with the arrogant air of the well-brought up child, caught sight of the expression in Liesel's face against which she was helpless, and quickened her pace. 'We must hurry.'

'We're not to speak to those people,' Marthe said reprovingly, when they were out on the path once more. 'They are not *comme il faut. Maman* says they have lice, and that we must never play with them, because then we'll get them too. They are *malpropre,* dirty people.'

'Dirty people,' repeated Tot, who did not usually imitate Marthe.

'They are people you should be sorry for, poor people, who have learnt nothing and don't know any better.' Alberta raised her voice harshly and looked down into her son's face. The bricklayer could not have been as poor as all that, since he was the only bricklayer for miles around. She felt strongly that her explanation was unsatisfactory. The boy's eyes met her own for an instant, and then looked away as usual.

'It's their own fault if they're poor,' Marthe insisted. 'They should not be poor. Lazy people are poor.'

The boy repeated, 'Lazy people are poor, lazy people are poor.'

59

'I expect other people are too.' Alberta could hear the irritation in her voice.

But the boy went on repeating, 'Lazy people are poor, lazy people are poor.'

And she let the children have the last word, the convenient word that people prefer even in childhood. Involuntarily she looked across at Liesel, who was walking alone, her face old and pathetic. Shortly she said, dropping her voice: 'And someone like that can have children, Albertchen. Full of children. An idiot.'

We ought to have gone by the road after all, thought Alberta. Liesel's remark was quite natural. But behind it there lay a morbidly developed sensitivity for certain matters. It increased with the years and could occasionally bring Liesel quite out of balance. She had bouts of weeping, convulsive sobbing that would not stop. It was then that Eliel would shake his head and say, 'Women! They're all the same.'

'I can't bear to see it, Albertchen, the way those children are brought up. It makes me feel ill.'

'She's so wretched herself, Liesel. One can't expect anything else.'

'I don't mean that either, I mean—' Liesel stopped. Marthe was obviously listening. It was not the moment for going into the subject more deeply.

At Josephine's and Jean-Marie's house only Jean-Marie's mother was at home. Through the open door they could see her busily polishing the table while keeping an eye on the pig, which was loose outside, and the chickens. The wall of the house was bright with dahlias, the old-fashioned, round kind one had such a desire to hold as a child. Fuchsia and pelargonium crowded each other behind the window panes. They looked pretty in contrast to the white-washed little house with its border of grey stone and its light blue window frames. Alongside was the outhouse, the black and white flank of a cow visible in the doorway; behind it all the cabbage field, blue-green as verdigris. It was pleasant on the little farm; it was all as neat and tidy as one could wish. It smelt of the cowshed, pigs, the sea, flowers from the country, in a warm

60

blend. There was even a tiny fig tree, slanting and distorted by the wind from the sea, the shadows of its glossy leaves flickering above the well. A curious feeling of being at home was unavoidable here; Alberta was always reminded of certain words: At home we live in a village, Mademoiselle. We have a cow and a pig, potatoes, cabbages, the sardine fishing . . . Today the sea is as white as milk in the sun . . .

'*Ann amser zo brao,* Tinti-Marianna.'

'*Zo brao ann amser.*' Tinti-Marianna put down the cloth, dried her hands and came out to the doorway with them hidden under her apron as decorum demanded. 'Came in time, Josephine? Hens plucked yesterday. Good!'

Tinti-Marianna spoke French as a Negro might. Freckles were scattered over her thin, brown face. Stripes of pale red could be seen in her grey hair through her head-dress of white tulle. Her round, blue eyes seemed spun into a net of wrinkles. 'The gentlemen are coming, the gentlemen are coming. Good! Tinti-Marianna pleased, the ladies pleased, the little gentleman pleased.' She nodded in the direction of Tot, who was vainly attempting to approach the pig. 'Jean-Marie at sea. Fine weather. Fish this evening. Good.'

'Good,' said Alberta and Liesel, nodding. 'Good, Tinti-Marianna.'

'Do you wish you were Josephine, Albertchen?' asked Liesel as calmly as if she were asking where Alberta was going. They were out on the path again.

'Don't be ridiculous.' Alberta laughed. After a pause she said, 'Not that I were Josephine, but perhaps that I resembled her. Although—I don't know, Liesel. One wants to be oneself, in spite of everything.'

'Hm,' Liesel said.

From the open country they turned into the narrow lane that led up between outhouses and dung-heaps to the centre of the village, where the main road passed through, and the church, the priest's house, the mayor's house and the inn were situated. The sun beat down on the little square, not a leaf moved in the elms along the churchyard wall, and the shadow beneath them was heavy and blue.

61

Fully grown trees were normally only to be found far inland. Here eight of them stood in a row, thanks to the houses which sheltered them on all sides. Each time Alberta saw them the effect was always one of overwhelming luxuriance. An old, never quite satisfied longing would seize her for precisely this kind of summer, for warm abundance, such as she had experienced on brief holidays in the inner fjords as a child. On the journey out, when in the morning the train had steamed among green hills alternating with rich deciduous forests, she had been on the point of calling out that here was the place to stop, here the moment of time they should seize. Here was the murmur of bees, quiet breezes through the foliage, wild strawberries that could be plucked without changing your position, perhaps someone who would come and say that it was late, and call them home to a meal out of doors, under the trees. Jeanne was sitting crocheting in silence, her face kind and beautiful. She had looked up and smiled at the children, who had settled down, each in some-one's lap, their wide, shining eyes reflecting the green light from outside. The fatigue of the journey was dispersed by it. Alberta was reminded of the rowan tree above the shoe-maker's roof; this was what it had symbolized year after year in another life. The park at Versailles belonged with it, and other parks, in the life that had followed.

'Quick, Alberta,' whispered Liesel.

Madame Poulain's door was open as usual. Alberta and Liesel tried to hurry past. For what was there to say to Madame Poulain? But the children walked slowly, dragging their feet. Before they had rounded the corner she was standing on the doorstep.

'*Mesdames*! One moment! And the little ones? Are they to go past my house?'

'Another day, Madame Poulain. Someone is coming by the train. We—'

'The gentlemen. I know. But only for a moment. I have had *news*.' Madame Poulain's eyes were full of tears, they were brimming over already.

'Oh!' said Alberta and Liesel. 'Oh, Madame Poulain!'

Marthe was already inside, and had taken up her position in front of the shelf of dolls. They were small and cheap, and stood in their cardboard boxes as if in open coffins, staring stiffly into thin air with stupid eyes. They were made of calico or the kind of material that comes apart at the touch of a raindrop, stiff with sizing. At home Marthe had Mimi. Mimi was as big as a baby, could shut her eyes, had thick ringlets of real hair, hats, frocks, coats, three changes of underwear. Jeanne had made all her clothes. She was put to bed at night and dressed in the morning, usually on command; the rest of the day she just sat. But in front of Madame Poulain's dolls Marthe was lost in contemplation, lifting the small dresses, carefully touching the ringlets which were not attached to their heads, but only to their hats, so that it was simple to establish that the dolls were bald.

Jeanne was in the habit of saying, 'Not one *sou* will I spend on those rags. You are not to buy a hoop for Tot, Alberta, I'd like to make that clear. Give him one to take to the Luxembourg Gardens in the autumn. He won't be able to roll it on these slopes; it's not healthy to run too much near the sea, it strains the heart. And Marthe will give me no peace.'

Madame Poulain was looking for something in a drawer. Now and again she brushed the corner of her eye with her finger. 'One of his friends has been here . . .'

'Oh!' said Alberta and Liesel again. They would have liked to find words, but it was difficult.

'Yesterday, *mesdames*. He has been a prisoner ever since. He saw my boy fall, just managed to take what was in his breast pocket, then everything went black. He knew nothing more until he woke up and found himself a prisoner. A grenade, *mesdames*. He assures me—he says my boy was dead before—before—'

Madame Poulain changed the subject. 'Here is the photograph of me. This is my daughter-in-law. Just imagine, she has gone into Audierne today again to get a mourning veil! As if I haven't got good enough veils here in the shop. But of course it's the new doctor, I know that. He's young; he

63

survived it unharmed. She is young too, of course, and pretty. And it's three years since my boy disappeared—'

Alberta and Liesel looked at the worn wallet Madame Poulain was holding as if it were alive, and at the two photographs she had taken from it: the young fiancée who had married him as soon as the order came to mobilize, because she insisted; Madame Poulain herself, a pleasant middle-aged woman without a trace of white in her hair and a cheerful expression on her kind, understanding face. Now her hair was as white as snow. Alberta hesitantly mumbled something to the effect that it was better to know for certain.

'For certain? Yes, I know I shall never prepare him for burial, never put a pillow under his head, never even know where he lies. And that it is no use hoping any more. Before I had hope, in spite of all the things they said. Now they tell me: It is only his body that is gone, Madame Poulain. Only? You know yourself, Madame, how much we love that body from the first moment we handle it. It is a part of us; if there is anything wrong with it, we too are ill, if it is happy—oh, you know how it is, Madame, you have a little boy yourself.'

Her words affected Alberta as only the truth can. Helplessly she looked at Madame Poulain, powerless to contradict her. She turned, looking this way and that inside the little shop. Sewing things and knick-knacks, cheap toys, cheap soap, cheap perfume, doubtful brands of hair-oil. She wished she could say something comforting, but found nothing beyond reaching out her hand to Madame Poulain across the counter. And she began negotiating the purchase of a reel of white cotton.

'Thank you, Madame. It helps me to talk to you, Madame. You are so understanding. The others say: His soul is in heaven. The parish priest was here yesterday and said so. How do we know? However much of a priest he is, he does not know more than we ordinary folk. We have to be chastened, he said. Why start the whole business, I said, when it's all such a failure and can't be improved? What sort of a God is that? And my daughter-in-law in Audierne today again! It is only we mothers who do not forget, Madame. He is growing, your little one. Mine was not so robust either when he was small, he was quite delicate. Yours will grow big and strong later on, like mine.'

'Do you think so?' asked Alberta eagerly, suddenly involved. 'Do you think so?'

'Of course. Wait until he is thirteen or fourteen. Mine had such bearing, Madame, a way of carrying his head, such shoulders. It all came at that age. You ask whether I shall go there? Yes, Madame. It will be my first journey and my last. I come from Audierne, so did my husband. We have never been the kind to move about. We had the boy, you see. Anything we managed to save went to him. He spent a summer in England for the sake of the language, and another in Germany; he had almost finished training to be an engineer. We did our best. And when you think that he might have been shot by his German friend! They wrote to each other often. Yes indeed, Madame. He was a fine boy too, like mine. I even have a photograph of him. I say again: what sort of a God are they talking about? I didn't start this shop until I was widowed; it took half an hour in the wagon with the furniture, and I never thought I'd make any more journeys. His friend described the place to me as well as he could, but everything is in such confusion there. People can't find their own farms any more. I shall have to lay a wreath on the ground. Or on any one of the crosses. If it is not my boy it will be some other mother's son. The cotton, Madame, here it is. And the little ones? What are the little ones to have today, my angels?'

Madame Poulain looked round and took, in spite of Alberta's protests, two rubber balls from the shelf. '*Spoil* them? They *ought* to be spoilt. They can never be spoilt enough. One day you are left regretting all the things you never did—yes indeed, Madame.'

When they were outside again, Liesel said, 'How you talk. Everybody thinks a thing like that is beyond me.'

'Oh, Liesel! Don't start on that now, please,' Alberta said under her breath.

'No, there's no necessity to start on it. Here they come,' replied Liesel curtly.

A little way off two men were walking towards them along

65

the road, the one tall, the other short and thick-set. They were carrying suitcases, and coats over their arms, and approached quickly, at a brisk pace. In silent agreement Alberta and Liesel sat down on the stone wall to wait. Tot pressed himself up against it. His little face was stranger and more unfathomable than ever. In the middle of the road Marthe jumped and skipped demonstratively with her new ball. They would have preferred not to have taken her with them, but Jeanne had said, 'The stove is smoking. And we have more than enough with the kitchen and laying the table, Josephine and I. If we're to have Marthe hanging about—'

Alberta's heart still thumped a little with excitement when she was about to meet Sivert again after they had been parted for a while, if only a few hours. And she could still sag with disappointment after their first exchange of words. She still felt this anticipation, more consciously, more impatiently insistent than before. Were they never to grope their way to something different, Sivert and she? Was this journey's end for them? It could not be possible.

Fond of him? Of course she was fond of him. Life had welded them together, they were two people close together in the infinity of that relationship. Something that must have been yearning for him ran, hidden like a rootstock, beneath all their dissension and ill-humour.

There he was. The suitcase he was carrying was brand new, that was the first thing she noticed. It shone with nickel at each corner. And what else was different? He was tanned and handsome, but he had been so before he left. He was in new clothes, from top to toe in new clothes, the visible confirmation that they were over the worst for the time being, perhaps for good. But there was something else too, something indefinable.

The clothes fitted him, the hat suited him. It suddenly made her deeply happy to see it, and brought him closer. Aspects of Sivert that she had struggled to perceive seemed to become real as a result. Affection welled up in her. Why not stand shoulder to shoulder, why disagree? We have a child together, now we shall have a following wind. Let us set sail like good friends. But deep down there lurked a familiar, hurtful

66

thought: It's difficult enough when we're poor; it will be worse if— Rubbish.

'There's Father. Run to meet him, give him a hug.'

The boy gave one of the strange leaps that did not take him off the ground. Only now did he seem certain as to who was coming. Now he had reached Sivert, who put down the suitcase, took him by the arms and lifted him up. 'Let's have a look at you, boy! Brown as a berry, eh? Swimming like a fish?'

'Ouch!' the boy exclaimed. His arms were hurting.

'Hmm.' Sivert shook his head. 'Alberta's damned sentimentality again. Can't even stand being touched. We must play another tune now, there must be an end to spoiling and coddling.'

He patted his son on the head in a fatherly manner. 'We're a big boy now, called Brede. Brede Ness. I shall have to look after you a bit more, I can see. Now you shall go swimming in the sea with Father. Hello, Alberta, hello, Liesel, nice of you to come and meet us. And there's Marthe too. Hello, Marthe.'

'Tot *can* swim,' came breathlessly from Tot.

'That's good, boy, that's good.'

Sivert's conversation was friendly and just as it should be. There could be nothing the matter with her. Yet his eyes glittered, the old glitter that Alberta could not stand at one time, and kept having to forget afresh in order to make progress. It could disappear for long periods at a time. Now it was back, forcing itself up from the bottom, confident and watchful.

She must get away from it, past it. He must be different.

'Sivert!' She gave him both her hands. 'How splendid you look. And how handsome you are.'

She meant it. He looked handsome and well-dressed, he cut a fine figure. And this new quality about him . . .

'Hm, yes,' said Sivert. 'It was about time,' he said. 'I haven't spent much on myself the last few years. I thought it was my right for once.'

67

'Yes, of course.' Alberta was amazed at his tone and the words, even though what he said was quite correct. Sivert had not been reckless about clothes, or anything else; circumstances had forbidden it in any case, and nobody had accused him of it. He seemed to be waiting for accusations.

'*Hei paa dig*, Alberta, how are you?' It was Eliel, tall, slightly stooping, handsome as a peasant, with his too-white teeth in his strong, tanned face. 'We shall all have to deal a little more roughly with that boy, if we're to make a man of him. Well—what do you think of Sivert? What airs he's putting on, isn't he? Look at his clothes, look at his suitcase. Yes, I must say—Damned beautiful out here at any rate. Enough to make a man wish he were a painter.'

'Welcome back, Eliel.' Alberta gave him her right hand, leaning down to handle the suitcase with her left. She was struggling with a completely new feeling of uncertainty towards Sivert. What he had said about looking after the boy, and Eliel about dealing with him more roughly, made her heart beat anxiously, as if she glimpsed a conspiracy. The suitcase stood there solidly in the middle of it all. It was nice that he had had bought that, at any rate, nice that they could buy things.

'What a handsome suitcase.'

'It is quite handsome,' said Sivert. 'I thought I should have a decent one.'

'Yes, of course.' Pleasure in the development of Sivert's concern for his outward appearance mingled so strangely with Alberta's feelings. He seemed to be thinking about something else all the time.

They had sat down on the wall to rest, he and Eliel. They swung their legs with their hats pushed on to the backs on their heads. Eliel had had his success last year, and it could indeed alter a person. Now Sivert was sitting here and was altered as well, in that utterly unexpected way of his. There was something nonchalant about his newly clad person, something daredevil, which had not been a part of his personality before. He shoved his hat even further back and looked at the sea with an expression of boyish defiance which made her

68

uneasy. He seemed to be meditating mischief. 'Damned beautiful,' he said. 'This has to be done big, if it's to be done at all,
no niggling.'

I'm even impatient of his happiness, thought Alberta, full
of contrition. She sat down beside him with the boy. 'Come
along, Tot. Let's sit here with Father.' Sivert's gaze returned
from the distance and he took the boy on his knee. Alberta
asked him where his new canvases were, had he not brought
any with him? They could not be in the suitcase? He had
worked at such a rate when they first came out here that he
had used up all his material by the time he left. He had been
forced to borrow from Liesel. Somewhat carelessly Sivert
replied that Castelucho could send what he needed—if he
needed anything; he had not made up his mind yet. Surprised beyond words Alberta said nothing. Would he not be
needing canvases? Sivert? Diligence itself?

There had been changes for Liesel too when Eliel's large
group was sold, such great changes that it was incredible that
she had agreed to them. On the other hand—it was not easy
for Liesel. As the war years passed she had been sent less and
less by the family in the photograph, and now they sent nothing. The war had taught one geography, if nothing else. There
had used to be some mystery about Liesel's fatherland, as
there is about the Balkan states, and nobody had really
bothered to find out where she came from. Then the day came
when everyone realized she was from Estonia. During the brief
period of Bolshevik rule her family had fled in panic and were
still living on sufferance with poor German relations, even
though their country became independent later. Liesel
struggled to make a living out of her painting, meanwhile
pressing Eliel for every *sou* she could, cold-bloodedly, almost
with *schadenfreude*. 'It's good for him to part with it,' she said.

Now she was sitting on the grass border below the wall, her
arms slung round her drawn-up knees, her usual position out
here, cross-examining him methodically: Yes, he had locked
the door properly and given the key to the concierge; she had
promised to water the flowers and look after the cat. No, he
had done nothing about the mattress yet, he had had other

things to think about. There was no hurry, surely, so why talk about it now? Yes, yes, there was a new pane in the attic window. *Cleaned* the place after him? No, he hadn't. Surely there would be time to do that when they got home?

He spoke as if it was a long time since he had given these things a thought. Liesel did not look at him, merely continued asking her monotonous questions, sticking out her lower lip after each reply. She was watching a pile of clouds moving slowly across the sky. Not a muscle moved in her face when Eliel suddenly leaned forward, put his arm round her shoulders and shook her a little. Could they not talk about something else? Even at the Versailles people were not discussing their troubles any more. Why be worse than they were?

With a spacious gesture, the confidence of a peasant, he drew Liesel's head closer. Alberta was reminded of the way one draws a horse's head to oneself, in a gesture of confident mastery. There was also something of the capricious colt in Liesel's sudden toss of the head in order to free herself.

From her position out on the road Marthe watched them from under her eyelids, running about with her ball with the sole purpose of hiding this fact.

Sivert pushed his hat on straight, took Tot's hand and seized the suitcase. 'Come along. A bathe before lunch, what do you say to that, Eliel? After all that train dust? Here's the whole Atlantic waiting for us.' He threw back his shoulders and took a deep breath, nonchalantly drew out a new gold watch, looked at it quickly and put it back into his waistcoat pocket. The effect was all the more surprising since it had no chain. As if by magic it appeared and then was gone. Did I actually see that? thought Alberta. But Tot exclaimed, 'Father has a new watch, Father has a new watch. Tot wants to see it.'

'You may see it when you say "I" and remember that your name is Brede. Brede Ness.' Sivert nodded down at the boy. 'Then you may look at the watch as much as you like. Then Father will teach you how to tell the time.'

Josephine waited at table, clumsy and attractive in her Bigouden costume, red-faced and eager to do everything

70

correctly. Eliel and Sivert watched her. She was new to them, having returned from a visit to her parents since their departure.

'Damnably picturesque,' Sivert muttered.

'Sculptural too,' Eliel assured him. 'Such solidity, don't you think?'

When she poured out for them or offered them a dish they teased her: 'Ring on your finger? Husband or sweetheart? Is there hope for anyone else?'

'Jean-Marie's wife,' whispered Alberta informatively.

Josephine glowed, herculean and healthy, without urban scruples. 'Husband, *messieurs,* husband, come back to me safe and sound from the war. I can assure you he is not one to waste his nights.'

And when a moment of amazed silence followed this remark: 'I could very well do without it. It means nothing to me—but for him! You know what men are!' The age-old feminine refrain, which they believe raises their status and gives them superiority.

Fresh silence. Josephine looked perplexed. It was evidently no use. She gave up trying to make herself understood by these city folk and fell silent. With a somewhat strained expression Jeanne brought up the matter of the sale of Sivert's big composition. She also asked him how things were in Paris. 'Tell us, Sivert.'

And Sivert told her, ready and willing to be cross-questioned by her and by Pierre, who was in high spirits in his quiet way and listened attentively. At other times he could look so astonished when he was in company. It came over him sometimes, making Jeanne's eyes and hands uneasy. Now her gaze moved incessantly between him and Sivert, full of confidence, of excessive satisfaction. If he notices it, it will be too much for him, thought Alberta.

'Everything is as usual on Montparnasse,' reported Sivert. 'Except that the girls get more and more like the boys, all of them with their hair cut short.' He didn't mind. It suited them. Yes, the composition had been sold. He would have made money on it a couple of years ago, but one had to be satisfied

71

with things as they were. It had gone to his home town. One of the city fathers, who had seen it on exhibition at home, had come on a trip to Paris and decided to be generous. Came to the studio one day and initiated the transaction. Yes, he had said he was coming. But there you see, one shouldn't really be out of Paris. However lovely it might be here Sivert had not thought of staying long this time either. Heaven knew what it would look like when it was hung. Objects of that size were not suitable for private collections; though it was said that many people had been able to build amazingly large and beautiful houses during the war.

'The neutrals,' said Jeanne. There was silence for a moment. Her voice had been colourless, yet running over with bitterness and contempt. Pierre resumed the conversation. 'It was exhibited a couple of years ago, wasn't it?'

'In the spring of 1917,' Sivert informed him. 'It found a buyer none too soon, I must say. I sent it home with a friend. If I had been at home myself—' Sivert shrugged his shoulders, used to accepting life's difficulties.

'*Eh bien*, Alberta?' It was Pierre. His sudden question made them all look at her. Then they looked away again, and Alberta smilingly drank with them, when they drank a toast to Sivert. But the wine lay like vinegar on her tongue. She remembered all too clearly the occasion when the composition had been sent off and what subsequently happened.

Strangely enough it had arrived in Norway safely. There were all sorts of reasons why it should not have done so: hundreds of complicated formalities, mines in the North Sea, submarines. Sivert had driven to the station with it as if seeing off a person. Rolled up, long and cylindrical, it stood up by his side in the cab. It meant well-being and a future; it meant everything. It was going home. At home pictures were selling like hot cakes.

The cab fare had been begged as a loan from three different sources. It had been that kind of a day.

For a long time they had heard nothing. Then news came. It had arrived, had been included at the last moment in an

72

exhibition held jointly by some of his friends. Newspaper cuttings arrived. Sivert was praised. He was given one of the more generous stipends.

And he had wanted to go home, by himself, alone. At home artists were not only selling their work, they had commissions enough for themselves, their children and grandchildren. Art was being sold as never before. He could not consider taking Alberta and the boy with him, for many reasons. One was the difficult journey. She did not wish to undertake it either. But she had realised for the first time that she could not rely on Sivert. Not that she would allow him to leave her and the delicate child, with conditions as they were then. Besides, he might have been torpedoed.

She suggested as much. Sivert laughed and said 'Nonsense!' The outcome was that she used harsh words, repeating them over and over again, behaving as she had behaved only once before and had never imagined she would again. And Sivert did not go. But this was one of the things that stood between them.

'*Skaal*, Alberta! Didn't I say Sivert would come back a rich man?'

'*Skaal*!' Alberta suddenly drained her glass and held it out for more. Pierre smiled crookedly in admonition before pouring her the wine, doing so awkwardly with his left hand. She was usually cautious with wine, and this was cheap and treacherous, bought up in the village. The glass she had emptied had already gone to her head.

She nodded to him in confirmation. Yes, she would like some more. Then she put down the full glass untouched, suddenly quite sober. Through the murmur of the others' voices, through the quickly alternating mixture of French and Scandinavian which had come about in their conversations, she heard Sivert say quietly, almost defensively, 'Of course I've been working, working like the devil. You work all the better for a love affair, you know that. *Skaal*!'

'True enough. *Skaal*, brother.' Eliel drank deep, while Pierre and Jeanne smiled politely at the strange words they did not

73

understand, and went on talking about the Treaty of Versailles, what was being said in Paris and what they were saying abroad.

But what had Sivert said? It was very unlike him. He was not the kind of person whose feelings and thoughts you could guess at. On the contrary. He had presumably thought and felt much that she had never suspected in the course of the years. Some people gave themselves away continually. Sivert never did. It was new for him to mention feelings at all.

She looked across at Liesel. She was never sure how much Scandinavian, and Norwegian in particular, Liesel understood. She was sitting sucking in her cheeks, feeding Tot piece by piece with Jeanne's celebrated apple cake. She was not looking at anybody. Perhaps she had not heard.

'More apple cake? No, Marthe. We mustn't spoil your digestion. Can a child eat as much as it likes? Perhaps your Vikings can, Eliel, but here we have to look after our stomachs. Marthe's is as regular as clockwork. Why? Because I have given her healthy habits.' Jeanne wiped her offspring's mouth energetically. 'Are you really going to have more wine, Pierre?'

She looked imploringly at Pierre, who filled his glass and emptied it. 'It's sweet of you, Jeanne, but I don't think anyone has yet seen me drink more than was good for me.' His voice was absent-minded and monotonous, his expression blank. It was one of the moments when it looked as if Jeanne's occasional remarks might be true: 'He's not concerned about anything any more. He's not affected by anything. It wouldn't matter to him if we were dead.'

What was Pierre thinking about when he sat like that? Did he not think at all? He had not only injured his face out there, he had not only lost three fingers. According to what he had told Sivert once something had been shot out of his brain, he had an empty space in his grey matter. As he was sitting the emptiness would open out; he literally saw it and progress was blocked.

He was supposed to have said, 'Three fingers. Well, I can't

74

shoot any more. If only they had gone a little earlier and not at the very end perhaps I'd still have been fit for something.' This was Pierre's sickness, that he believed he was fit for nothing. But his machine clattered from morning till night, and Jeanne would not hear of any empty space. *'Une idée fixe,'* she said. 'Just get over it. The doctors say so too.'

Now she got up quickly from the table. 'I think everyone has finished. You help Josephine, Marthe. We'll have our coffee outside.' The wrinkles had appeared in her forehead. Her voice was high-pitched.

'I'm afraid the sea isn't altogether good for the boy, Sivert.'

Alberta was standing with her back to the window in their bedroom, watching Sivert unpack the new suitcase. New underwear, new socks, tie and bath-robe, a shaving set she had not seen before; books in yellow jackets, which he placed on his bedside table without more ado. He put a large, angular parcel, clearly meant for Tot, on one side. He handed another to Alberta; it was small, oblong and hard. She could tell that it was a box and felt a pang of remorse and emotion: That I could mention it at this moment. I could have waited. It's not pleasant for him. He has thought about me, he's giving me something I haven't had to ask for.

'Thank you, Sivert.' She fumbled with the narrow red ribbon, unable to open it in her haste. There were so many things she needed. She hoped Sivert had not been extravagant. She felt a sudden rush of joy at the thought that perhaps he had been precisely that.

'Not good for him? The sea? What rubbish. Nothing could be better.'

'He gets so easily out of breath, he sleeps less and less.' He's still afraid of it, was on the tip of her tongue, but she stopped herself in time. 'Have you a knife, Sivert?'

'He's as brown as a berry.' Sivert searched his pockets. 'He's never looked as healthy as he does now. You coddle him too much. But naturally a boy ought to be brought up by his father, or he'll be mismanaged. I see more and more how unevenly he's developing.'

'Pierre says—'

'Pierre! In the first place he's a weakling himself, in the second place he's a Frenchman. You must admit they're not as hardy as we are at home.'

'Jeanne says so too.' Alberta's throat constricted. She felt her impotence as if it were a physical defect.

'Jeanne and Pierre!' said Sivert.

'There's nothing wrong with their child.'

'No. But they do tend to coddle her. This business of her stomach. A healthy child can eat whatever it likes and whenever it likes.'

'The sea *isn't* good for Tot,' said Alberta vehemently.

'Now listen, Alberta, you *look* for excuses to make life difficult for me. It's always been the same. I've thought so plenty of times. Isn't the sea any good either? Here I am, doing my best; I provide you with this, that and the other, and it's never right. I believe you do it on purpose so as to give me no peace. I took it to be typical woman's nonsense, along with much else, but—'

'You have come to the conclusion that it's not so typical after all.' Alberta was suddenly enraged. Her anger and resentment flamed up into her forehead. She spoke quietly but her voice was like ice.

'Yes, I have come to that conclusion. One does draw one's conclusions. Let me tell you something. Other people don't share your attitude towards me. Some people feel quite differently.'

'They haven't had a child by you,' answered Alberta. 'To be your friend, Sivert, can be bad enough. But to have a child by you is God's retribution.'

She did not know herself where she found the words. They came tumbling out, spiteful and over-solemn, in this same cold, quiet tone of voice. She did not recognise it; she had not possessed it before.

Sivert had found the knife that had gone astray among the things on the bed. He put it down roughly beside her on the window-sill. 'God's retribution,' he repeated with emphasis. He too spoke quietly, with icy deliberation. 'I shall not forget that,' he said. The words struck her like daggers, piercing surfaces in her mind that were sensitive and fearful; surfaces that gave her pain long afterwards if touched. Slowly she left Sivert and the unopened little packet. She bled with remorse and sorrow for herself and for him, for the fact that they scarcely met before they brought out the worst in each other. Their child was no bond uniting them, he was a symbol of dissension. And yet she had to believe that both of them meant well.

Downstairs Josephine was talking to Jean-Marie, a cheerful, loud-voiced exchange in the local dialect, impossible to understand beyond the brief introductory phrases about the weather that were essential to good manners. The children were with them. It was impossible to slip past unobserved. Alberta ordered her expression as best she could.

Jean-Marie had put the basket of fish down on the steps. In amongst the seaweed a few plaice slapped their tails languidly, a heap of sardines glittered like silver in the sun. He, Josephine and the children were standing in a ring round the catch looking at it; but it was impossible to tell whether that was what he and Josephine were discussing.

Jean-Marie was wearing his handsome reddish-brown sailor's tunic, loosely cut and open at the chest. It was made of the same stuff as the sails of his boat and suited, far better than one might have expected, his light chestnut hair, pale blue eyes and countless freckles that no amount of sunburn could hide. He was no charmer, but at least he had changed since the days when he had plodded round in his shirt sleeves and unbuttoned waistcoat, armed with a feather duster, in a fourth class Paris hotel, and was only called Jean. A basket of fish on his head suited him better than a bucket in his hand, or the occasional chamber pot. A person's background contributes something too. Sea and sky are more flattering than dark, unaired staircases. He and Josephine had a robust, natural matter-of-factness about them which almost made them a handsome couple. He swept his blue cap off his head and said, '*Ann amser zo brao.*'

'*Zo brao ann amser.*' Alberta hoped they would let her pass.

77

Then she saw that she could not behave so strangely. She stopped and looked at the fish. 'Splendid, Jean-Marie. Kill it, Josephine. Don't let it lie there like that.'

Jean-Marie had not displayed the slightest astonishment at seeing Alberta turn up with a boy almost six years of age, nor at the information that the shortest of 'the gentlemen' was the father. He had explained at once that he for his part had married when he was home on leave during the war, and that he was quite satisfied with the result. Josephine lived up to his idea of a good wife in every respect, and he expressed no regrets for the lost fancy of his youth. 'The shortest one?' he had said. '*Bien*. One must have someone.'

Now he was looking at Alberta with some surprise as he praised the fish and emphasized their qualities. 'We caught mackerel too. But I said: The ladies are expecting their men. Then there's nothing like a good meal. Look at this.' He weighed a large plaice in his hand, turned the corpse-pale stomach upwards and slapped its tail reprovingly. 'Steamed, with a good *hollandaise*, or plenty of parsley in the butter. Here, Josephine.'

Josephine took it all into the kitchen. The harsh sound of a knife cutting into the live fish, the helpless slapping of cold, wet muscles reached them outside. Sivert came down at the same time, and the children turned their excited faces towards him and the parcel he was carrying. He put it down, struck his hand with his fist, lifted the boy so high in the air that he gasped from fun and fright, then did the same to Marthe, who screamed with delight. Then he shook Jean-Marie's hand jovially, told him to put on his cap, and embarked on a conversation about the fishing, the weather, the old days in Paris, and the war. There was no lack of topics, and Sivert was clearly not one to allow his conduct to be disturbed by an unpleasant exchange of words. He looked cheerful and elated, even trying to draw Alberta into the conversation. 'To change the subject, when is it high tide today? We had to walk almost a kilometre before lunch, Eliel and I, to have a swim.'

He turned secretive about the contents of the boy's parcel. 'What do you think is inside? Try to guess. No, you must open it yourself. Use your fingers.' Trembling, clumsy with excitement, the boy started untying the string.

Unlike Pierre, Jean-Marie did not mind talking about life in the trenches. He did so without bloodthirstiness, almost with conviviality. Once he had been buried in a crater by a grenade and was dragged out half dead; a couple of times he had been wounded. As far as one could see it had left him with no external or internal scars.

'The German soldiers?' Jean-Marie shrugged his shoulders. 'Poor devils like ourselves, Monsieur. They probably wanted to go home to their wives and their work just as we did. If only we could have talked to each other, come to an agreement to send the Kaiser and Poincaré out to fight instead; there would have been some point in that. We threw boxes of sardines across to them, and packets of cigarettes. If there happened to be fresh water nearby we arranged times for going and fetching it. When the officers weren't looking we signalled all kinds of messages to each other. Once they lighted small Christmas trees on their side of the wire. It was beautiful. We had fun too. You have to find something to do. One day we carried a top hat along our trench. They thought the President was visiting us and shot at the hat. That gave us a good laugh. Afterwards we lifted it up so that they could see the pole and the bullet holes. I expect they laughed too. Did we *shoot* at *them* later?' Jean-Marie shrugged his shoulders. 'What the devil were we to do, Monsieur? If there was an attack it was in earnest.'

But even Jean-Marie would not comment on the use of bayonets. 'Filthy,' he said curtly.

'Well, Alberta? Going out for a walk?' Sivert glanced at Alberta, who was still standing there for the sake of appearances. His eyes seemed never to have glittered more than at that moment.

'Yes,' said Alberta. She turned and went. Sivert's cold, threatening words suddenly seemed unimportant beside his carefree behaviour now. That too was unlike him. It was something new that he had brought with him, something more dangerous, more cunning than the obstinate manner in which he bore a grudge. For a second she thought: I must pull my-self together and pretend; I mustn't let them stand here and see—

But she could not manage it. With her mind at a standstill she walked blindly down the path. She heard the boy say, 'Where's Mother going?' heard him rustling the stiff paper, and Sivert's reply, 'I expect she'll be back.'

When had she begun to be afraid of Sivert? Perhaps she had always been afraid, and simply forgotten about it in between? Now she was lying there, so afraid that her heart stood still for sudden, painful moments at a time. He was asleep at her side, breathing evenly and calmly. Over in the cot it had been quiet for a long time too, as if Tot was less restless when both of them were there. He had been scared out of his wits when Sivert had taken him into the water that afternoon, his strange little face distorted, not daring to make a sound. But afterwards he had danced his curious little war dance, and stood stiff with the convulsive effort to put a brave face on it while his father rubbed him energetically with the towel. For Sivert to look after him physically was also new. Previously he had contented himself with shaking his head at Alberta's decrees.

She raised herself on her elbow and looked out at the room. The pale glimmer, like moonlight, that fell in stripes through the shutters flickered and was gone, flickered and was gone, as the Penmarc'h lighthouse revolved its beam. It was some time since the rocking and creaking of the bed in the attic had ceased. Alberta had heard it and thought: How can she? How can she in this house, where you can hear every sound, if for no other reason. But I'm the only one who knows how much can be heard, for I'm the quietest of them all.

The last time Sivert was here she had curled herself up into a defensive ball, raised a wall of silence, told him lies, because of the echoing house and the boy in the same room. The child kept them apart; it was no longer possible to forget that he was there and might be lying awake. She would do the same thing now, if necessary. So far there were no signs that it would be.

Someone was snoring upstairs. It was Eliel. The only other sound was Alberta's hammering heart against the background of Sivert's breathing and that of the sea. The tide was coming in. It would be high water in the small hours.

She could still hear Josephine's well-meaning *'Bonne nuit messieurs, bonne nuit mesdames, au plaisir.'* The last plate had been dried and the last snail thrown out. Josephine had curtsied and pulled the door to behind her, as if shutting them solemnly in, three couples in all. The slightly disconcerted faces, Eliel's ready laughter that elicited no response and died away at once, the awkward evening that followed— Alberta wished she could erase it all from her memory.

When she had started to take Tot up to bed, Sivert had interfered: 'I'll do it.' It might have been attentiveness on his part, unexpected relief from her chores. She knew it was something else, something vague and undefined.

Later on—they had been in bed for a while, and Sivert had just put out the light after looking through his yellow books, cutting the pages here and there and yawning—she had managed to say: 'I spoke too harshly today, Sivert. I'm sorry. I didn't mean it.'

Reluctance to say this, mingled with panic, compulsion and fear, forced the words to her lips. She had meant what she said.

'Yes, you have a sharp tongue,' said Sivert lightly. His tone let it be clearly understood that her apology was of no importance. And he turned over on to his side. In a moment he was asleep.

Over on the window sill she could just glimpse the packet. It lay there, small, oblong and merciless. Neither she nor Sivert had referred to it. Tot had not referred to it either when she had said good night to him. An unopened packet was not one of the things a child could normally tolerate. He must have been told.

The stairs creaked. Cautious footsteps were coming down. They passed the door and continued downwards, stealthily, nimbly, pausing now and then. Alberta would not have heard them had she not been awake. It was Liesel, for Eliel was still snoring. She must be barefoot, she was so quiet.

There was the front door opening, now it was closed, for a moment there was no sound, then the footsteps crept across the gravel in front of the house and were silent again as they reached the path. And now Liesel had her sandals on. She had gone out. She was not going to a certain place.

Suddenly Alberta was struggling with her bathrobe in the darkness, trying to find the sleeves, groping under the bed for her own sandals, fumbling and clumsy in her fear of waking the others. A tremendous feeling of anxiety came over her, relief too. She was not all alone in the depths of the night; and now there was something for her to do. What could be better for a soul in need?

The moon, in its last quarter, hung low and crooked just above the horizon, like a badly slung, ill-treated light. The air was kind and soothing to the eyes. Evenly and without pause the huge sweep of the lighthouse beams swept the surface of the sea and the sloping land. In the illumination of one of them Liesel came into view and disappeared again. She was sitting on the grass hugging her knees, not very far away. Alberta's tension left her. It was replaced by fatigue. What had she feared?

At the next swing of the beam she saw that Liesel was swaying backwards and forwards. Her face was tilted upwards, her eyes closed, her lips pressed tightly together as if she were in pain. Alberta hesitated, halfway across to her.

'Is that you, Albertchen? Are you out too?'

Liesel's quiet voice was larded with something else, bitter, resigned scorn.

'I heard you go downstairs. I was awake. What's the matter, Liesel?'

'The matter? The matter? There you stand asking what's the matter, you, who cannot rest either.'

'There could be many reasons.'

'Could there be many reasons? No, you know very well there's only one reason, one single reason. Come along, let's

82

walk, let's walk fast!' Liesel got to her feet and ran forward, her bath robe flapping behind her black in the darkness, tripped and almost fell.

'We can't see the path, Liesel. The lighthouse only makes it more confusing. I'll fetch something to sit on.'

'Sit!' exclaimed Liesel contemptuously. 'With the restlessness I have in my body! I could fly on the sea.'

But when Alberta came out of doors again with a couple of coats she had found hanging in the hall and the tablecloth from the sitting-room, Liesel agreed to sit down. 'Eliel's raincoat,' she ascertained, spreading it out on the ground. 'My old coat,' wrapping herself in the second garment. 'What have you got there? It feels like the tablecloth? Why didn't you take—?'

'I didn't want to take Jeanne's rug,' said Alberta brusquely. 'It's lying on the armchair, I know.'

Liesel helped her to wrap herself up in the tablecloth. They crept together on the coat and said nothing for a while. Of course Alberta knew what was the matter; she had known it all along.

She looked over at the house. There it stood, unreal, faintly luminous in the light of the crooked sickle that was the moon. The door looked severe and solemn. Inside the boy and Sivert, Jeanne and Pierre, Eliel, Marthe, were asleep. Who were they all? Did they really exist? Were they more alive than the doll Mimi who shut her eyes as soon as she was put down? It was as if she sat looking back at a past existence, a door closed for ever. Only at the thought of Tot did Alberta feel a faint emotion, as if she had been away for years: guilt, pity, longing, sadness, something indefinable. But each time the illumination from the lighthouse swept across the house it became threatening, intrusive, almost gloating: Don't delude yourself. I shall keep everything that is mine.

Liesel gave a big sigh of relief. 'I'm glad you came, Albertchen, it's a good thing somebody came.' The sentence had a familiar and painful ring, reminding Alberta of another difficult moment.

'I'm glad I heard you, Liesel. It was good for me to get out of doors too.'

'There, you see, we *must* get out at night now and again, and we're not the only ones! Albertchen!' Liesel gripped Alberta's arm. 'Now, at this moment, the world is full of women who can't rest, who are up and about while a man lies snoring. There are so many of us. In Paris I sometimes pace up and down the passage outside like a madwoman. Sometimes I think I *am* mad.'

'Now Liesel!'

'I *hate* men.' Liesel hid her face in her hands and coughed.

Alberta did not contradict her. Not at this moment of candour and at this time of day. Her view was neither strange nor incomprehensible; it was the kind of feeling that came and went.

'Is that how it is again? he says, when all I want is to put my arms round his neck. Is that how it is again?'

Alberta could not stop herself thinking: Then why on earth *put* your arms round Eliel's neck? More than once she had felt like asking why Liesel did not look for someone else. She was still young, good-looking, when she occasionally went to the trouble of smartening herself up, still pursued as soon as she appeared in public. Her relationship with Eliel was somewhat of a mystery. They had no child to bind them together. They both strained at the yoke, Liesel in words: 'He's not worth bothering about; he's a miserable egoist'; and Eliel, as far as one could judge, in deeds. All the same, there must have been something between them, old, strange feelings that neither of them would admit to possessing any longer. Eliel, for instance, could simply have gone home during the war. He had not done so.

But even in the dark and at a time beyond reality Alberta could not bring herself to ask. Did she herself know why she did and did not do things? Should Liesel know any better? Life was not simple and lucid, it was full of contradictions. Liesel accompanied Eliel like a cowed but still rebellious animal, suffering when he chased other women, kicking out when he condescended to show her affection, grumblingly, almost greedily accepting her daily bread from his hands. Where was the tender, self-forgetful Liesel who had said, '*Ach*, family life wouldn't suit him, Albertchen. Artists have to be bachelors, especially sculptors.' She and Eliel were not legally married. Yet all the compulsion and pressure, wrangling and animosity that it can bring with it were there just the same.

'I'm unjust too. It's my own fault that I'm not normal.' Liesel took her hands away from her face, and her voice was icily calm.

'Of course you're normal!'

'No, I'm not. I've been damaged.'

'What nonsense! You must forget all that. You—'

'Forget? Did you say *forget*? When I've been—put outside.' She spoke in the same cold voice, calmly and monotonously, even though she seemed to be spitting out her words. 'Unable to give or receive happiness, dead as a stone internally. They shattered me, they destroyed the nerves. Oh, Albertchen — all the ugly things boys say to you when you're growing up, the crudest things that we didn't even understand — the day comes when you do understand, and it's all true.'

As if on cue the beam from the lighthouse swept over Liesel's face. The grimace with which she spoke appeared like a weird still from a film and was gone again. 'It's not strange for a man to get tired of you and want someone else. We must be reasonable, mustn't we? But if only I had a child Eliel could do as he liked. Then I'd be all right again, I know I would. All that has gone wrong would be wiped out. Imagine that there should be a penalty for what I did! It's enough of a penalty in itself, but no one who really knows dare say so, for fear of being sent to prison.'

Alberta said nothing; a gasp escaped her, too slight to be heard. She remembered how she had sat with Liesel feeling that she had escaped some disfigurement, a blemish on her body; remembered that her aversion for doing the same thing had been mainly concern for her body, an instinctive fear of harming it, a terror of being maimed and defiled.

But how would Liesel manage, alone with a child? She ought to know what she was talking about, too; she who had been Alberta's help and refuge in all kinds of difficult situations, prepared to go to any lengths for Tot, though often at her wits' end to know what to do.

'Eliel's child, Liesel? Would you really want that? When you are not so very fond of him any more? A child is a tie. And there are other men. Are you so sure you—?'

There came the question. Of its own accord? It's time had come.

'I'm not sure of anything,' answered Liesel sharply. 'That's just the trouble. What can one be sure of in life? I refuse to —you know very well what I mean.

'Shamming!' The cold scorn in Liesel's voice defined the limit of the feasible. 'Shamming. If you do that you must feel affection, love, as they call it. I shammed for a long time. In the end I shouted at him, I became spiteful, foul-mouthed, hysterical, according to him. Besides, there is no-one else for someone like me. I'm the kind who will put up with anything from the one person it happened to be. We are *faithful,* Albertchen, on top of everything else. To be faithful when you are happy is easy enough, it comes naturally. We're the kind who are faithful in spite of everything, without knowing why, like a dog. Genuine fidelity, in other words. Wait and you'll see—' Liesel raised her hand to check Alberta, who had opened her mouth to protest. 'But at least I could have a child. Some people are still able to—'

And suddenly, without transition, Liesel sobbed: 'He might have been nearly seven years old. When I'm old and still childless perhaps, I shall be saying twenty-five, twenty-six. If I had another child I would believe he had come back to me.'

Alberta sat in confusion and distress, alternating between sympathy and a desire to contradict her. She could find nothing to say. 'He,' Liesel had said. So it had been a boy? Like Tot? This fact gave it a fearful clarity, bringing it close, terribly close. Fidelity, on the other hand—what had that to do with it?

'A little Eliel? That might not be much fun.' The words dropped out unexpectedly. Alberta listened to the jocular undertone in her voice with disquiet. This was no joking matter. It had clipped Liesel's wings, hindered her growth.

But getting her to laugh was a well-tried means of diverting her attention. Alberta turned to it instinctively from many years' habit. In spite of everything Liesel's laughter was not so far below the surface as one might often think. There it was already, bubbling beneath her sobs. 'It might not be much fun, but I'd lick him into shape, don't worry.'

Her face appeared in the light of the beam, in close-up, the corners of her mouth quivering between tears and a smile, the teardrops hanging from her eyelashes and her hair falling in disorder over her forehead. 'If only success didn't make them put on such airs, these men of ours. That's what happens. Just like boys. Sivert's already in full bloom, that's obvious. Yes, let's just laugh at them, Albertchen.'

'They ought to know we laugh at them, they take themselves so seriously,' she said shortly afterwards, with a wicked glee, a hidden rancour that Alberta recognised. Then Liesel dried her face and her voice was calm and resolute. 'Eliel would never stop me from doing what I thought right where a child was concerned. He could just try.'

'It's a matter of money, Liesel.' Alberta suddenly felt insignificant. Liesel was strong in her way, if only in her stiff-necked clinging to Eliel. More than once it had seemed like cowardice, like an incomprehensible lack of pride. With a tight expression round the beautiful mouth that was no longer as red as it used to be, but had acquired a tendency to look a little blue, she remained in the clammy air of his studio, whatever happened. It almost looked as though he gained amusement from seeing how much she would put up with. She seemed to put up with everything. Until suddenly one day she was again good enough for Eliel, who was a confoundedly good sculptor, but not much of a man. Alberta had seen many like him on Montparnasse as the years went by. 'Our men are unfaithful too,' Alphonsine had said once. 'I'm not saying they aren't. But not in such a primitive way as yours from the North. Forgive me for saying so. But then—' Alphonsine laughed—'Unfaithful? They are *merely* primitive. They don't go any further than that.'

87

'Money, yes indeed.' Liesel sounded tired and defeated. 'Money.' She sighed. Alberta at once felt the pressure of the trap she was caught in herself and had always dreaded; the struggle with things which were simply too much for her. She did not have them in her grasp, nor in her head. We know too little about how we ought to live, and we exist as haphazardly as savages, having children and unable to take it in. Once we have them we are bound in chains stronger than iron. Fidelity, said Liesel. Surely the word was too grand, even if one called it canine fidelity.

The crust of moon, now minute and wrapped in mist, was about to disappear behind the inky blue surface of the sea. Raw vapour rose as if extracted from the ground, making the stars indistinct. There was a change in the weather, a suspicion of damp in the air.

'I suppose we ought,' said Liesel. Slowly they walked up the slope. Suddenly Liesel's head was on Alberta's shoulder. It bored in between shoulder and throat, looking for a place there, like a child. 'Tenderness, Albertchen. Tenderness! That's what we need more than anything. It keeps us alive. Men's tenderness, children's tenderness. Work is all very well, it's as necessary as food and drink; I wish I had some proper work to do. But it's not *enough*. Don't tell me it's enough. We need so much tenderness, far more than the men. How else should we dare to commit ourselves to all that's so difficult? That's how nature has arranged things to get her own way. As long as we're given tenderness we can put up with anything. But that's what these fools will never understand.' Liesel rolled her head from side to side, butting with it.

'No, they don't understand,' Alberta said, feeling that she knew it all even better than Liesel.

'Fall in love with many of them?' Liesel raised her head and tossed back her heavy plait. 'We could do that too, if only it were not so depressing. But it is depressing. So we hang around and are good to come back to when the others are tired of them.'

She loves Eliel all the same, thought Alberta without surprise. In herself longing for Sivert, fellow-feeling and mother

88

love lay side by side with fear and animosity. In love with many of them? Her thoughts went to Pierre, and then suddenly to Tot: perhaps he had kicked off the blanket?

They reached the door. Tacitly they took off their sandals. Of course Liesel dropped one of hers on the staircase; it fell down a couple of steps, making a disproportionate amount of noise in the sleeping house. But no-one was disturbed; everything was silent and continued to be so.

'I talk about nothing but myself, but it was good of you to come, Albertchen, good to talk,' Liesel whispered guiltily on the landing, smoothing the palms of her hands down her body, as if smoothing something away from her.

'Good night,' whispered Alberta.

'Good night.' Liesel did something she had done only twice before, in a moment of desperation in an attic, and when Tot had come into the world. She kissed Alberta.

Inside the bedroom there was warmth from the two sleepers, from their breathing; warmth and fresh air, thanks to the windows which were always kept open. In the flash through the mist from the lighthouse Alberta groped over to the boy's bed to feel whether he was properly covered, then groped to her own. A small remnant of warmth left under the blanket welcomed her and enclosed her. Sivert's breathing was as regular as clockwork.

A yearning for everything to be right and inevitable between them was insistent in her mind. Her disquiet had vanished. Liesel had talked of tenderness. Alberta would get the better of herself, open the box, thank Sivert, make good the wrong she had done as far as it was in her power. She lay watching the dawn erase the alternation of light and darkness, noticed that the lighthouse must have been extinguished.

But after she had been lying like this for a long time she suddenly raised herself on one elbow and said aloud: 'That's right, sleep, you great oaf.'

Of which Sivert remained totally oblivious.

*　　*　　*

89

Cold, driving rain shut them in for three days. As fine as smoke it filled the air, laying a damp film over everything, indoors and out. Tot's teeth chattered when he came up after his bathe; Sivert saw to it that he was not allowed to escape.

Alberta struggled with the primus and got warm milk into the boy as quickly as she could. 'Stuff and nonsense,' Sivert said, accepting a cup with alacrity, rubbing his hands together. 'Foul weather, but it's splendid I must say. Nothing like the sea.'

He had installed himself at the small upright table in the bedroom, and drew there, supporting his sketch book between it and his knees; he wrote letters there too. The present had been a fountain pen. 'I thought it might be useful for when you did your scribbling,' he had said when Alberta thanked him.

'Of course it will, Sivert, it's a lovely present.'

For the time being he borrowed it himself for his correspondence, while the boy played on the floor for hours with the aeroplane he had been given. That did not worry Sivert. He was wonderfully patient, and in this respect far better suited to looking after children than Alberta. Sivert always managed in some way or another; hindrances or disturbances did not exist for him, and he never had a moment's boredom.

Alberta was in the sitting-room with Jeanne, sewing. Even when they were silent for long periods at a time she seemed to be unable to think. Time merely passed. She had felt for a long time that Sivert's mere presence extinguished her true existence. Jeanne's presence did not improve matters.

Marthe was tramping up and down the stairs. She had built some kind of many-storeyed house out there with stones and shells left by the tide. Jeanne had forbidden it and told her to play in the sitting-room with Mimi, but Pierre had said, 'Let her do it. It amuses her. It doesn't make any difference to me, I assure you.'

A little further off the typewriter clattered in fits and starts with oppressive silences in between. If they lasted Jeanne's sewing would sink into her lap as usual, and she sat with wrinkled forehead, about to lay it aside. As if it suspected

90

this, the typewriter would spring to life again. Among the other sounds Alberta could tell when Pierre tore out the paper and rustled a new sheet as he put it in.

'He has become so morbidly self-critical,' Jeanne worried. 'He has a mania for throwing away. Pages the others would have given years of their lives to have written go into the waste-paper basket, I know it. If only I could save some of it. But he's always too quick for me and burns it. If that smoking stove is used for nothing else . . .'

Then she relaxed again, and started talking about the things women usually discuss amongst themselves. Having Marthe had been a difficult business. When one was narrowly built——yes, Alberta was not so broad either, but it had been a question of Jeanne's life, hers and the child's. Thank God she had been at home with her parents, and had had her mother at her bedside day and night.

Unpleasant memories floated up in Alberta's mind. Incoherent and dissatisfying as dreams they lay in wait in her consciousness ready to surface at the slightest opportunity. There was something the matter with them.

The worst had been the cold. When everything that could be hung had been hung round the stove, a corner screened off where the warmth could pause for a little on its way out of the room, she had achieved a temperature of eleven degrees centigrade . . .

A little child lying asleep, radiating peace. But someone else lying awake . . .

Every time the child had fallen asleep, warm and satisfied, holding one of her fingers tightly in his tiny hand, she had felt a new, mysterious understanding of hidden matters. Time stood still, all demands were silenced.

But when he screamed endlessly, an injured, angry, protesting scream, Alberta felt united with all bad-tempered, bitter women who had had more than enough of it. Children and mothers have rights; it began to dawn on her to what extent they were ignored and neglected.

To Liesel, who came regularly to help her in whatever way she could, she said, 'I should have done as you did.' But deep down she did not mean it. When the child fell ill and Sivert had refused to go for the doctor, when she realised that he thought it would be just as well if the whole business were brought to an end, she had been provoked to malice. Foot by foot she had driven him out of the door with words as merciless as those she had used when he had wanted to return home. It was the first time she had attacked him; it had been an unfamiliar and terrifying experience. And the first time she had seen him as he used to be, someone she really disliked. This feeling came and went. He had fetched the doctor. The danger passed, the days began to go by, no one can stand living in perpetual enmity. Better times came. But nothing hidden is ever really forgotten.

'You had Tot in hospital, didn't you?' Jeanne's voice was kind and sympathetic. 'It's not supposed to be so bad, according to what they say.'

'No, it's not so bad,' said Alberta, and meant it. Her emotion when they laid the child beside her for the first time stirred again in her mind, a sympathy that on the instant had filled her eyes with tears. There existed nothing more helpless or more dependent on human good-will. She had never taken an interest in babies. Suddenly she was holding one in her arms, one that was hers, so tiny, so strange, yet so familiar, so inevitable.

Her first coherent reflection had been: Now I am truly vulnerable. Now I can be hurt as never before.

With it came distrust. No child was more open to injury, none more threatened in life and limb. From the first moment all the world's wickedness was lying in wait: insensitive hands that picked him up too roughly, footsteps and voices that might frighten him. As soon as the child was brought to her, dressed and ready, she saw that the correct concern was lacking. They treated his vacillating little head so recklessly; they did not always put a hand beneath to support it. Neither did anyone seem the slightest bit interested in what all the painful little grimaces might mean, as if it was sufficient for a child to be born, changed and fed. She promised herself that if only

92

they escaped without accident things would be different. We, she thought, as if she had been thinking it for years.

Sivert came and went, sat by her bed, brought news from the world outside, and looked at the boy with an expression which Alberta considered critical and out of place. And she was left alone again with the new, alarming thought that she was the one who was shackled for life by this ostensibly light, yet indissoluble bond.

When she came home she soon realised that she and the child had really been well off where they were.

'Of course it's not the same as having one's mother there.'

'No, of course not.' Alberta was filled with wonderment. Mama? Mama in that contingency? Impossible, unthinkable. None of all this would have happened if Mama had been alive. Alberta would probably have stayed at home to this day like a second Otilie Meyer, only more ugly, less kind, stubborn in her spinsterhood. She did know as a rule what she did *not* want. She would never have fallen into the trap there; it had been too obvious, too grossly constructed. An oddity, ageing early, a 'discard' as Eliel put it? Slightly deranged?

Her affection for Sivert, latent and shackled as it was, suddenly flared up. Whether to Sivert or another, her surrender had been neither a miracle nor a horrifying experience. Something utterly complete had taken place, releasing new warmth, enabling nature to blossom. It had been a step further, away from bondage, towards full knowledge of life. They tell lies and talk nonsense about this as about so much else. One day one experiences it oneself and it assumes the right proportions. Alberta's distant memory of a night with another was wrapped in unreal mist. Life's tangible realities were gradually erasing it. It was Sivert with whom she had lived after all, Sivert by whom she had had a child.

'What are you thinking about?' said Jeanne. 'You look so pensive.'

'Oh, nothing,' answered Alberta, caught off her guard, because she really had been thinking for a moment. 'Nothing, Jeanne. And you?'

'Oh, me!' said Jeanne gloomily.

'If only it would stop raining.'

'If only it would.'

They fell silent. Tot's aeroplane was still whirring across the floor upstairs, Marthe tramping on the staircase, the typewriter clattering. The panes were running with wet.

Amongst the pictures shifting ceaselessly in our hearts, the film we watch at intervals, Alberta suddenly saw herself whirl round in confusion, holding an impossibly small glass in her hand. *'Faîtes pipi,'* said a voice. 'Where, where?' she stammered helplessly. 'There!' came the impatient reply. 'Try, make haste.' She was pushed into a narrow room with white tiled walls, a high ceiling like a shaft, it *was* a shaft, it was the bottom of the world. A moment later she handed over the full beaker. One masters astonishing situations when forced, discovering oneself to be incredibly resourceful . . .

She was sitting up to her neck in water in a bath tub, forsaken by God and man. They had closed the door and gone away, as if she were quite capable of looking after herself. Suppose they forgot her? Suppose the pain came back before she was safe in bed? With sinking heart she stared at the door.

There they were! She breathed again.

But it was only a hand which snatched her clothes from the chair on which they were lying, placed some kind of white linen robe there instead, and closed the door again. She called. Nobody answered. She was a prisoner, with no chance of flight.

What was happening was inevitable. Outside night lay over the city; the profound, late hours of the night, when cars are infrequent, lonely wanderers suspect. Far, far away, in another world, lived people she knew who were close to her: Liesel, Alphonsine, Sivert, Eliel — shades, left behind in an earlier life, incapable of helping her. Nor had they any suspicion of how bitterly forsaken she was in this machine composed of curt, white-clad persons and shining tiled walls, which had her in its clutches and would not release her again until she was transformed, one become two, or until —

94

She was not afraid, but uneasy, as if there were some danger of the air giving out . . .

What was that?

It was a typewriter that paused and stopped. Jeanne lowered her sewing, the machine did not stir. Alberta, always ready to feel anxiety over matters about which she could do nothing, sat an the edge of her chair, an old habit of hers, as if Pierre was about to get into trouble, and it was partly her fault. It suddenly seemed as though she and Jeanne had been the custodians of this typewriter for an eternity.

'The short story,' said Jeanne. 'It *must* go off today, the postman will be here in three quarters of an hour. And these famous articles about this, that and the other that he's begun to write. We shall never get back to the book, I don't suppose. He promised me—'

'Yes, but Jeanne—'

Jeanne did not answer. She put down her sewing, got up, went upstairs. Nothing could be done for Pierre. There were her heels tapping across the floor of his room.

Ill at ease, Alberta sewed large, unsightly stitches, so unsightly that she started without hesitation to unpick them, a rare event. If only the everlasting rain would stop. It forced them all so close together that it was suffocating. That was the scraping of a chair. And what was that? Oh, Tot's aeroplane. Wasn't the typewriter going to start up again? No—Pierre was coming down!

His footsteps came tumbling down the stairs together with rattling, rolling stones. Alberta heard Marthe exclaim, 'He's tramping on my drawing room! That's my dining-room! The bedroom's one big mess! *Maman*!'

Pierre stood in the doorway. His blank expression searched the room: 'Is my beret here?'

'Are you going out, Pierre?'

'Yes, Madame, with your permission or without it. You are sewing, Madame? An admirable pursuit given that you can master it to perfection.' Pierre wandered round her in search of the beret, paused by the fireplace, raised the pile of newspapers lying on the mantelshelf, rustled the pages, suddenly laughed his curt, sad laughter: 'Magnificent. Capital, Just listen: "Bettina has entered the Beehive. Dear Bees, I hope many of you will welcome her; she loves you. She belongs to the rose-red clan, loves dancing, pretty clothes, art and sports, loves laughing, singing and running—" '

Jeanne entered the room. Her face frozen, she went across to take the magazine from him, but Pierre lifted it up high so that she could not reach it, and relentlessly read on: ' " Blue Butterfly, if you wish I can provide you with details concerning Rouard, the baritone, if you will send me your home address and a photograph." Ha ha, thank God the war spared Rouard, the baritone! As long as he's alive, there's hope.'

And Pierre seized the beret which had in fact been lying under the newspapers, threw it on his head and rushed out. They heard him snatch something from a peg in the hall, saw him heave his raincoat over his shoulders as he strode down the slope, turn into a shadow in the drizzle and disappear.

Jeanne sank down on to a chair and for a moment she looked so tired that for once Alberta felt she was the one to be sorry for. Marthe was there at once with her arm round her mother's neck and her *Petit Maman.* Jeanne pushed her away: 'Go and play.'

'He's spoilt it all, my dining-room and my drawing-room too. My drawing-room was chic. Papa is wicked.'

'If that was all he spoilt!' Jeanne stared stiffly in front of her and repeated, 'wicked', as if the word had only just acquired meaning for her.

Then she pulled herself together. 'He's not wicked, he's ill. Build it up again, Marthe. You have all the stones still, you must remember how they went.'

'My dining-room,' whimpered Marthe, 'When I think of my dining-room.'

'Off you go,' said Jeanne angrily. 'I will not listen to one word more.' Marthe disappeared.

'I shall become wicked too, I suppose.' Jeanne sobbed a dry little sob, hastily dried a single tear. 'That's how I got him back. Like *that*! He used to be so considerate, so good. He always listened to what I said, asked my opinion on everything. Nothing could have been more foreign to him than spite and sarcasm. He was hard-working, he was—'

'But he still is, Jeanne.' Alberta could no longer refrain from attempting to plead Pierre's case. She wanted to say. You only make things worse, but stopped herself in time. 'But he is hard-working,' she repeated.

Then Jeanne looked her coldly in the eye and said. 'What do you know about it? Nothing. But where Pierre is concerned. You and Pierre!' Her voice was on the instant so barbed that Alberta involuntarily rose to her feet.

'Sit down. It's quite safe to sit down. I'm not the revolver type, I don't carry a dagger. If you think I'm so scared of you—'

'I think nothing.' Alberta listened to her low voice, ice-cold above a violent inner tumult. 'Nothing, Jeanne.'

But Jeanne brushed her hand across her face as if brushing away the remnants of intoxication, of an aberration. 'We shall all go mad soon. You must forgive me, Alberta, Everything plays on my nerves so. It's this rain too. I—I beg your pardon.'

'It's of no account, Jeanne, no account at all,' said Alberta, as Jeanne went quickly past her on her way out of the room.

She sat down again. Her heart hammered and thumped. She jerked the thimble off her finger and let it disappear into the muddle in her work-basket, as if to divest herself of something, to make herself lighter, more mobile. She felt herself ringed by evil, dangerous forces. If only she could do as Pierre had done! Put on her coat and go. Never come back. Drown herself rather than stay here a day longer.

There was a whirring across the floor above. Someone in a sou'wester tramped past the window. It was Jean-Marie with fish for dinner. In that case it was time for Tot's snack, for the honey that Alberta got inside him by trickery in his milk on these raw, damp days, without either him or Sivert noticing it. It took a great deal of honey to make it taste.

She went out to the primus with the feeling she had had on so many other occasions in life, a feeling of acting under compulsion, of being a pawn in a game that was being moved in

97

accordance with certain rules, whether she wished it or no.

Jean-Marie, his wet oilskins glistening, was standing at the kitchen dresser, cleaning mackerel. With a deft movement of his hand he removed all the guts at once, rinsed the fish under the pump and put it in a dish that was standing ready. '*Voilà, voilà*! Now all you have to do is put them in the pan. Josephine said you had better boil them since the stove is smoking and she's not coming today. *Ien eo ann amser*, it's cold today,' he said, looking at Alberta to see if she understood, and laughing.

'Yes, it is cold. Thank you, Jean-Marie.'

His expression changed to one of wonderment. He looked at her a little more closely, bent over the fish again, wrapped the insides up in newspaper and prepared to leave with it. At the door he paused for a moment with his hand on the latch. Then out it came.

'I don't think he understands what he is about, this husband of yours. A contented wife doesn't look like that. If Josephine were to go about with a face like yours—*ma foi*, I'd say to myself, you are a blockhead, my friend.' And Jean-Marie went out of the door, shaking his head. Alberta was left speechless.

Eliel came down from the attic and threw himself into one of the basket chairs. 'Disgusting weather! If I'd known what it was going to be like I'd have stayed in Montparnasse. You come here to sun yourself and enjoy it and then it turns out like this. Liesel? She's in bed, says she has a slight fever. This damned weather again, I suppose. Apropos the weather— has Pierre gone out? Almost two hours ago? Quite right too, damn it. But what about Jeanne? And the little girl? It's so unusually quiet indoors. You can only hear the boy. Clever little girl, Marthe, I must say, swims like a good 'un. You've been too soft with the boy, Alberta, you must put a stop to it.'

'And you must see about marrying Liesel,' answered Alberta angrily, amazed at her own sally. 'Don't force her to force you.' But she was thinking: Why am I interfering? It must be the oppressive atmosphere that's making me so foolish. Now I suppose he'll ask what I mean by it.

But Eliel said, 'All right, and when are you and Sivert going to get married?' His voice was remarkably gentle. He sat looking at the floor.

'The boy will grow up—' said Alberta. The uneasiness she always felt when she thought about the future gripped her. She did not like looking ahead.

Eliel looked up. He was drawing in his cheeks as if amused at a child's naiveté. It was a habit of his, the one he had passed on to Liesel.

And Alberta suddenly felt even more uneasy. If there was only one way of putting a difficult situation to rights, and if this too had to be surmounted, and if the result did not prove to be tenable—what then?

Eliel got to his feet. 'Aren't we going to eat today?' he asked, looking at the clock. 'Isn't it time to—?'

As he spoke Jeanne's heels could be heard on the stairs. They tapped into the kitchen and were silenced by the earth floor out there. Tacitly Alberta followed her and began peeling potatoes, while Jeanne lighted the primus. Marthe too lent a hand; 'Yes, *Maman*. I will, *Maman*.' Nobody said a word beyond what was necessary for the preparation of the food. Alberta knew that for some reason Jeanne was greatly worried about Pierre.

They had held back dinner for a long time. Sivert and Eliel were getting ready to go out into the early, overcast twilight to search, when Pierre suddenly appeared in the doorway.

Alberta could not remember having seen him in such high spirits before. He was elated, loudly teasing Jeanne who, agitated by the long wait, hung round his neck without scruple, groping for him. She seemed to be feeling to see if he was in fact alive, but it was perhaps just to verify how wet he was. She laid her head against him over and over again, repeating that he was wet through.

'There, there, there,' Pierre said. 'I am alive, *voyons*, I shan't melt because of a little rain. Have you been waiting? I do beg your pardon.'

He held her close, patted her hair, hugged Marthe. It was clear that the hours of walking had done him good in every way. He and Jeanne disappeared upstairs, Jeanne eagerly insisting that he must change.

And, just like a man, Pierre ate as if he had not seen food for a long time, clearly relishing being back home again, calling for wine and getting it without any objections being raised. He, Eliel and Sivert discussed long walks that they would take, the three of them alone, 'without women and children', as soon as the weather permitted. In any case, a change would not be long in coming. Pierre could feel it in the air, see it in the movement of the clouds, had talked to a fisherman he happened to meet. Those people knew what they were talking about. In these parts bad weather lasted for three, six or nine days. This was a three-day bout. It would clear during the night.

Pierre was so exhilarated that he forgot his hand. He rubbed them both together several times.

'*Oui mon ami, oui mon ami,*' said Jeanne, amenable to anything, filling his glass herself, making no mention of his work. Eliel and Sivert exchanged whispered remarks now and again: 'He did that very well. That's the way to treat them. About time she learnt a lesson.'

Liesel sat drawing in her cheeks in Eliel's fashion. She did not say much.

That evening Alberta was on her way down to fetch a book. On the stairs she met Jeanne coming up. Jeanne was carrying a lighted candle and a jug of hot water; a suggestion of vapour betrayed that she had just been using the primus.

With her hair falling forward on to her shoulders in two plaits and in a charming nightdress of crepe de Chine and lace she looked more beautiful than ever. The candle flame was reflected in her black eyes as they looked calmly into Alberta's.

A young wife on her way to her husband, perfectly within her rights.

Only when she had gone did it strike Alberta that neither

of them had uttered a word this time either. They had only looked at each other.

* * *

'This Freud, Liesel, do *you* understand him?'

Alberta was out of her depth. Names buzzed in the air. There was Freud and there was Einstein. She noticed them in the newspapers, noticed that books were being published about them and by them, and that was all. Since Eliel's and Sivert's arrival she had had an uncomfortable impression that Freud was behind everything they said and did; he seemed to be ubiquitous. He inspired fear, if only because Sivert and Eliel had in some way managed to appropriate him as an authority on their side. One evening they discussed him with Pierre. Pierre said: 'He has discovered new territory. To go further and treat this territory as if it were mapped, a region in which we can travel without more ado—*parbleu*! It can be dangerous to establish mysteries. Besides, in this as in so much else, it was the poets who understood about it first, and always have since time immemorial. It was their field. If science comes along now and steals it—very well!' Pierre seemed to be saying: Let them steal it, and the trouble and risk as well. Then we'd be rid of it.

Jeanne looked up anxiously, wrinkling her forehead. 'Is that the man with the dreams? The man who only sees nastiness in everything? Nobody has the right to dream any more. If you think it's respectable to dream that a chimney is being swept, you are mistaken. It's highly improper. Some of my friends accept it all as if it were Holy Writ. It's terrible to run into them nowadays. But it's the fashion. It was the same with Bergson before the war. Pierre, you don't really mean that writers will ever become superfluous?'

'They became superfluous a long time ago,' said Pierre sullenly, and suddenly retreated into himself as only he knew how.

Alberta said nothing. She was cautious in such matters, not least in Sivert's presence.

101

'Freud? They dug him out of Dr Freytag's crate,' Liesel informed her. 'Do you remember when they dug out Nietzsche?'

Alberta remembered it very well. 'When you go to Woman do not forget your whip.' She and Liesel had heard the quotation to excess.

'I wish we were rid of the whole crate,' Liesel said. 'Those books aren't any good to Sivert and Eliel. They ought to have been handed over to the police, but Eliel refused.'

The books had been left with Eliel when the mobilisation order had come. Dr Freytag had just completed his qualifying examinations. His French citizenship was in order and he was to start practising in the autumn. 'Austrian, but French in heart and soul,' he used to say when he introduced himself. As a doctor he was sent straight into the field. Since then nothing had been heard or seen of him. One rumour on Montparnasse had it that he was discovered to be a German spy and shot, another that he had simply disappeared like so many others. The years went by. Eliel had begun to look on the crate as his own property long ago.

When Alberta had asked Sivert recently to tell her something about Freud, he had said, 'That's not so easy on the spur of the moment. He throws new light on the mind, completely new light. It's of great value, especially for an educator.'

Alberta had walked away. Sivert's tone of voice had said more plainly than words: It is enough for me to know about it. His reference to his task as an educator made her start, his nonchalance wounded her in an unaccustomed way; as if Sivert had demeaned himself without the slightest necessity for it.

She was sitting on the grass with her sewing. Sometimes she sewed with such violence that it seemed like flight. The stitches succeeded one another rapidly and awkwardly. Two ugly little trousers were ready, and she was mending the old ones. But once in Paris Sivert could stump up. She and the boy were going to have decent clothes, at least for the street. Surreptitiously she tried to catch a glimpse of what was in

Jeanne's workbasket. Alberta thought: *That* dress, *that* coat; not so bad, not too expensive either. Something in that style might suit me. She felt an insistent longing to be beautiful while she was still young, a longing to see Tot in nice clothes.

Jeanne had not cancelled her fashion magazine, although she had threatened to do so the day after the scene with Pierre. 'I'd better give it up, if it irritates him so much. But just now, when I have to make clothes for Marthe and myself for the autumn—no, it's out of the question. He is so changed. I shall have to stop leaving my things about on the mantel-shelf.'

Jeanne did not sit quietly any more. She would suddenly rush into the house or over to the village, taking the children with her. She went by the road to avoid the bricklayer's house, and assured Alberta that it was nice to have Tot with them. Both she and Pierre were very amicable, perhaps even more amicable than before. It sometimes struck Alberta as incredible that she should have said things to him that one does not say to anybody, that it was he whom she had asked for advice, from whom she had sought support: this stranger with his efficient, beautiful wife, his model child, his blank expression.

Between him and Jeanne was the same knowledge of each other as between herself and Sivert, as between all couples; and the same intimacy when the occasion arose. Alberta bit off her thread and clenched her teeth, promising herself to be more reserved another time.

If she were left alone for a while, Liesel would come up from her painting in the cabbage field. No great alterations were made to it, only that sometimes Liesel had figures in the foreground, sometimes none. Alberta said, 'Don't you think you'd better start on something else, Liesel, instead of standing there among those disgusting caterpillars?'

'I've put a lot of work into it,' Liesel replied. 'It binds you. And it's the kind of thing that might sell. White clouds and the sea, a boat, simple and easy to understand. The clouds are the best; I shan't touch them. It very probably would be better to stop, but I can't. I'm not like that. I'm on the wrong tack

103

with my painting in any case, Albertchen. Once I was just getting hold of something, and even got a picture into the Autumn Exhibition, do you remember? Then I lost the thread.' Liesel shrugged her sloping shoulders resignedly.

It was one of the days when she preferred simply to sit. Inert and pale, with dark rings under her eyes, she would settle next to Alberta and whisper: 'Not this time either, not this time either. If there's no change soon, I don't know what I'll do. I'll go away from it all, go on the streets—'

'Nonsense, Liesel. One doesn't go on the streets.'

'And not I,' said Liesel, with that ring of bitterness that so easily came into her voice. 'Especially not I, Albertchen. But I'm on the prostitute's side. Either they're unnecessary, and if so they're a disgrace to us all; or they are necessary, and in that case they should be given ordinary respect like other members of society.' Liesel spoke as if challenging the world. She jutted out her lower lip with a contemptuous, hard expression, that ill accorded with the rest of her personality.

Alberta glanced at her sideways. Liesel was getting more and more into the habit of making unexpected remarks at unexpected moments. 'You ought to rest today, Liesel. And what made you think about prostitutes?'

'I often think about prostitutes. I think about a lot of things. Life is unjust. One sees it more clearly every day.'

Unjust? The word immediately sent Alberta back to the time when Tot was small. The summers had passed, nauseating and heavy. However they struggled through them, the feeling that injustice was being done towards herself and the child increased. The winter had its claims. With the spring there came a fierce obsession, the desire to see the boy playing in sunshine in a meadow, to cease being perpetually anxious, perpetually nervous. It was a drag to go to the Luxembourg Gardens: dusty streets all the way there, dusty streets all the way home again. And what good did it do him? Sitting low down as he did in his little push-chair, close to all the dirt whirled upwards by people's feet, she might just as well have dragged him behind her along the cobbles. Usually they ended up under the trees on the Avenue du Maine, among

104

other mothers with tired faces and small, pale-faced children. When she occasionally took the boy to a park, he was seized with a kind of dumb wildness, and could scarcely be kept away from the lawns. It had been just the same when they came here. He had lain full length on the grass, clawing on to the ground, refusing to get up again, giving Marthe the opportunity to exult spitefully, 'He hasn't seen grass before, he hasn't seen grass before.'

'If I didn't have to try to earn money, and if I were not so stupid and useless, and if the war had not come and made everything so difficult—I'd have liked to be the kind of person who tries to put it all right. You know, suffragettes and that kind of thing. It sounds dreadful, but . . .'

They were far from all that, Liesel and Alberta; their hands were full with their own small affairs. And Liesel spoke as if in apology. After all, one gave up being a woman in the accepted sense, attractive to men, charming, if one went in for something like that; one became as it were sexless. Merely to think about it was to break with so much.

Instead Liesel mounted her hobby-horse, the one she rode perpetually. 'Some of them want to abolish the penalty. I've read about it. I suppose they think that would be the end of the matter. But it would only be one more convenience for the men and a penalty for us in any case, since it's penalty enough in itself. They can't ever have been through anything themselves; I suppose they're old maids. I'm sure they mean well, but—

'They can't have had children, at any rate,' Liesel said, jutting out her lower lip. She turned a pale, freckled face with large eyes towards Alberta, a fanatical face. 'Can you understand how it is that now, when masses of people have been shot and they're crying out for children everywhere, they don't *help* women with this problem and look after the children if necessary? Can you understand it?'

'No, Liesel.'

'The world is so awry, it will never be put right again. I agree with Madame Poulain, why start the whole business if it's to be burdened with so many drawbacks? It shouldn't be

105

allowed. It's nothing to laugh about, Albertchen. But why are you sitting here? Take yourself off, now, while Jeanne and the children are away; go down among the rocks and stay there till dinner-time. What was it Pierre said the other day— that one has duties towards one's characters? I must say that if I were a writer . . .'

You're as good a writer as any of us, thought Alberta. You once rewrote Eliel until he was unrecognisable, at any rate. She said: 'I'm not a writer. But you're almost a painter; all you've got to do is pull yourself together. Rest today and find a new motif.'

'I'm nothing,' said Liesel wearily.

The fine weather had returned. Heavy with calm the sea lay in the sun, milk-white, with small rocking blue shadows here and there and a thick blue streak for horizon. A slight mistiness in the air gave warning that the summer was coming to an end.

The men were carrying out their plans for long walks. They walked to the Pointe du Raz, to Penmarc'h and Douarnenez, coming home at sunset, stuffing themselves with food while they recounted their adventures, promising generously to go into Audierne the next day for more provisions.

Alberta could not help feeling let down and badly treated on these occasions. They might have taken me, she thought; I've been able to keep up since childhood, and I'm not the sort who never stops talking. As if she were the only one to suffer! How Jeanne's anxieties had increased, for instance. 'It's all right, I'm sure it does him good,' she sighed. 'But it would have been even better for him to have finished his work. It doesn't matter to the rest of you. But the book, the book, when I think of the book! If it were ready, he could do what he liked,' she added, frowning.

But Alberta admitted to herself: I miss Pierre. He takes no notice of me any more, and yet it's empty and aching without him. He's the one who makes life worth living here.

Their trips down to the beach were not the same as before either. Jeanne's considerate activity was more irritating than ever. And Tot, who could go stiff with fear when Sivert was looking after him and made no discernible progress where daring was concerned, was perverse and obstinate with Alberta.

'Everything has become so horrid, Liesel.'

Liesel admitted that it could be more pleasant. It was a pity about Jeanne, but she had the worst of it. She probably regretted it in her fashion, she was more friendly these days.

'Yes. That only makes it worse.'

'She's not happy,' Liesel said, 'the way she takes things.'

'She doesn't have to be unhappy because of me.' Alberta noticed the slight hesitation in her voice. 'He's so incredibly kind and patient most of the time. If he were not fond of her— He doesn't even look at me.' She stopped. Now she had certainly revealed something, to Liesel and to herself. She sewed feverishly.

'He daren't look at you,' stated Liesel calmly. 'Not any longer. And is he fond of her? She may have cause, even if he is fond of her. Besides, is that a necessary reason? She's the one who plagues him, that's sufficient. Since the day we went to Quimper she hasn't been able to hide it. It broke out then. I can't understand why you didn't notice it long ago.'

'I did and I didn't. What was I to notice? We did nothing wrong, we never have, never exchanged a word that—'

'That's not necessary either. I noticed it a long time ago, I noticed it on the train journey.'

'Now you're exaggerating, Liesel.'

Alberta blew hot and cold. Liesel alternately fanned her unrest and choked it. A not entirely foreign idea played in her mind: He has a child, I have a child. So it's impossible, even if—even if— She killed it in the usual way: Fond of Jeanne. Deep down very fond of Jeanne. If it came to the point, if something were to happen, the end of the world for instance, he would choose to be with her and Marthe at the last, as I would want to be with Tot and Sivert. In love with Pierre in *that* way? Love another woman's husband like *that*? Of course not. It's just that I've made a mistake with Sivert. Why can't you be different, Sivert? So that I could find peace with you? So that I wouldn't have to stop myself from almost

107

searching for somewhere else to go? My own fault, that every-thing is not as it should be? Yes—but not mine alone. Ours. And nobody's.

Her thoughts centred on Sivert, on all that was new about him, on his passivity, night and day. She had lied to him the last time he came. She would do the same again, put on an act perhaps, stop bathing. Some things were unthinkable, as matters now stood. But the inmost possibility of everything coming right between them lay in their embraces at night.

If Sivert made no approach he must have a reason for it, a new reason. Supposing someone else stood between them already, what then? Then there would be herself and Tot. Would she be in despair? No—as long as it would be possible to put the rest of her life in order. They would have to marry for the boy's sake, and then divorce again. The idea made her feel a little giddy. But that Sivert should have another, that he was not alone? Good, so far as she could see, good.

Suddenly she dropped her sewing. In astonishment she followed her line of reasoning. Her life, which had been a narrow little patch, broadened out. She saw that it was spacious beyond the enclosure, so frighteningly spacious that it took her breath away. But it was open and free on all sides for those who had courage and vigour, something to journey with. Everything was possible, as long as one dared and was strong.

'What are you thinking about now?' asked Liesel.

'I don't know. There's so much to think about nowadays. I'm becoming nervy, I scarcely get any sleep.'

'Go and *write*. That's what you ought to do. Write badly, if you have to, but earn some money.'

'What do you think is the matter with Sivert, Liesel? There's something.'

'He *has* earned money. It always goes to their heads.'

'There's something else too.'

'Something or other always comes with it,' said Liesel wisely. 'If I were you, I'd put my energies into turning my writing to account. Every line you've put together has been

108

printed. But as long as you go on producing short pieces and paying Sivert's paint bills with the fees—'

'That's not true, Liesel.'

'No, I know you've bought shoes for Tot and paid for shoe repairs and the instalments at the grocer's, and that there was no other money in the house, and that you had to.'

'I had to. You would have done the same in my place. It's only fair for both parties to—'

'If I were in your place and had a child, I wouldn't sit sewing. I'd earn money and leave it to others to sew. Oh, Albertchen, if I were you—with a little boy who needed me.' Liesel tilted her head backwards and shut her eyes as if to look into a dream world in peace. 'You are foolish, foolish, even more foolish than I.'

Alberta hung her head. Now they had come to a point which she could not quite explain to herself. Someone who has not even contributed one complete, undivided feeling to the household has incurred great liabilities, very great ones. Sivert had picked her up when she had gone under.

'I'm afraid,' she burst out. 'That's why I sit here pretending.'

'Afraid of what?'

And now Alberta failed to understand how her reply could cross her lips. 'I'm afraid of Sivert.'

Liesel did not answer immediately. After a while she said: 'One more reason.'

One of the young wives from the farms came by with her little child. It had just started to walk and was at the stage when it refused to do anything else. If she took it up on her arm it kicked to be put down again. Foot by foot they plodded along. Her bent back looked so patient, as if it had grown this way once and for all. It was the third child she had taught to walk, her fourth year of marriage. She looked up and smiled, not wearily but humbly. It struck Alberta how stooping most women's work was. Man stretches: he rows, or reaches out for stones or planks. He is often bent beneath burdens, but woman bends over almost all her tasks, except when she hangs up washing. Perhaps that is why she likes doing it; then she too stretches, giving pleasure to her body. She spends years bent over small children . . .

'Listen, Liesel, I think I'll go down for a while all the same. With my papers.'

'At last a little common sense,' said Liesel. 'But get away before Jeanne comes back, or it'll come to nothing.'

With her folder under her arm Alberta walked quickly downhill in the direction of the cliffs. Like a mountain landscape on a scale for children they broke into the white stretch of beach a little to the north of Tinti-Anna's house. Panic seized her, an irritating eagerness to begin. Writing was something for people who could do nothing else. Some of them earned a living by writing, not just the genuine writers, others too. They produced nothing of importance, but they lived by it, it seemed. The thought that she might be left alone with the boy was far from new; before he came into the world it had lain in wait and had since reappeared at intervals like an attack of pain, a cramp in the region of her heart.

Towards the end of her term she had thought she would try seriously. An unexpected calm had come over her when she moved in with Sivert. She had sent strange letters home, fabricating their contents in order to divert the attention of the world from what was happening. She had taken devious routes more than ever before; the autumn had come and with it people from whom she had every reason to hide. She had been calm all the same. With Sivert they had a roof over their heads, the child and she. That was the most important thing, although the roof was not very satisfactory and needed replacing as soon as possible. She had intended to earn her living and help to provide for their needs. The worst would be over when the baby was born. In her imagination she saw herself writing successfully. Nothing was lacking. And Sivert *could* leave her. Such things did happen.

He had probably thought along the same lines. He had said once: 'The two of you have my pictures, you know.' Alberta replied: 'Don't talk like that, Sivert.' But before an artist's work turns into money and clothes and food he may have been in his grave for a century or more. It was impossible to forget this.

The worst had been far from over. It had not merely been a matter of learning about the needs of the infant's body, recognising and feeling them as if they were her own. It had been a matter of satisfying them in the face of the impossible, of struggling to do so night and day. Bad times came, so bad that her mind shrank from remembering them; it flinched as the boy had done when they bathed him in front of the stove. His tiny shoulders had contracted with cold, his mouth became square with pathetic, helpless crying, his eyes older, experienced, upbraiding. Alberta caught herself wishing foolishly that she could fluff out her feathers like a hen, that she resembled an animal: furry and warm, they never failed their young. Every woman, including Alberta, had the right to memories other than these.

Sivert had been unable to get anything painted and gradually became thoroughly tired of the whole business; it was unavoidable. His mouth tense, more reticent as the days went by, he helped with the shopping, the meals, even the washing, doing it efficiently, as he did everything. But he had no rest at night, and the line full of napkins intruded into the motif wherever they hung it. 'I thought I was a painter,' he muttered one day, 'not a washerwoman or a maid.'

Alberta herself was more wretched than she could have imagined anyone could feel. When they finally fetched a doctor to the boy she had her own bill of health written up at the same time. She was anaemic and her milk was too thin. She had to eat such and such, rest, avoid this and that, try to go away with the child for a change of air.

'Yes,' she said, looking into the wise eyes of the elderly man, knowing that they saw through her and everything in the studio, knowing that the days would pass just as before. Shortly afterwards war broke out. Everything they ought to have had disappeared little by little: butter, sugar, money, coal.

The second winter—no, she would not think about it. She

111

had sometimes said when she prattled to the boy: 'Tough, that's what we are.'

She came down among the cliffs, found a place where there was a natural bench in the warm granite wall, seated herself comfortably, turned the pages of her manuscript. Duties towards imagined characters? In that case they ought to be different from the ones with whom she had involved herself, a capricious, easily offended company, who never said or did anything when she sought them out, but attacked her at night, beside the primus, at the child's bedside, and were gone again before she had time to turn round; who tried to arrest her attention when the living, who had every right, had already done so, and who expressed themselves vaguely, in banal phrases and without profundity.

Concentrate on her material? Alberta's material was fluctuating and billowing: a cloud formation illuminated now from this side, now from that, and which then disintegrated and disappeared; a mirage, that vanished and was all of a sudden there again; a whirling nebula containing glimpses of voices, accents, faces, gestures, landscapes, streets, interiors, all of it appallingly like everyday life. If a thread lay hidden in it somewhere, it was well hidden.

Ten lines that open up for the rest, Pierre had said. Alberta's misfortune was that almost any line could do that. She could approach her theme from one direction, or from another, or from yet a third. Then she had countless lines, paper piling up, full of words: ill-behaved words that would not sound right together, would not be subservient, but had a frightful tendency to appear over and over again in proximity, to steal from each other. Words like 'suddenly', for instance, the most intrusive of them all. They resembled precious stones in that they were independent of their setting.

Sivert had colours and broad brushes, he could work backwards and forwards over the canvas, hinting here, emphasizing there. Without getting in his own way he could create a lucid frame within which to work. Alberta lost one glimpse for each that she was given, grasping at dots instead of outlines. Out of two hours' day-dreaming perhaps one or two sentences

112

would be released. Haphazard external impressions interfered, confused her, broke off the thread. She wished she were deaf and blind, wished she lay ill in bed, shut off from the outside world so that she could concentrate. The result was that she fled from it all.

Except in the strange, rare moments, when it seemed to her that this imperfect thing with which she had no patience— there *was* something to it after all. It was not yet in print. It was still possible to handle it, to approach it more closely, encircle another piece of fog.

Alberta stopped turning the pages. What business had she here? She was playing truant from the things she was capable of doing, although with difficulty and badly, for something uncertain and elusive. She sat twisting her fountain pen and looking at the sea. The tide was coming in. With long, lazy tongues the water licked at the land, creeping up behind and beneath the seaweed that grew round the smooth, slanting rocks, lifting it, rocking it, letting it float and dip, releasing it again, seizing it more greedily the next time. A wisp of cloud sailed across the sun; the enormous surface of milk and silk was changed at once into molten metal; the sand to the south and north dazzled the eye excruciatingly, as if the light were thrown down on to it by a shade; the screaming of the gulls took on a deeper tone. The wisp sailed on, the world lay there again, dissolved in heat haze, the sun was burning hot. A day for idling, for wandering; for living relaxed, without thought, without worry; a day from which to return renewed.

Alberta leaned back against the granite wall and closed her eyes; she kicked off her sandals and let the folder slide off her lap. She heard a thud and a suspicious rustle of paper. Out of pure cussedness she did not look down, but continued to sit stretching her toes in the light, burning layer of sand that the wind took with it everywhere as soon as it blew. She thought: If a puff of wind comes and takes something with it out to sea, there's no harm done. A moment of dejection, the kind that drains away all one's strength, had come over her. Shortly she felt burning tears trickle from under her closed lids, down her cheeks and into the low neckline of her dress.

She gave way to them and found relief. She looked up for a second, but nobody was there, she could weep freely. She gave way completely and sobbed without so much as drying a tear. I must stop going out alone, she thought. I shall have to stay near the house minding my own business. Soon it will be time to bathe. I must go home, look after Tot, it's my duty. Liesel can do it instead of me, and she does it better, but she shouldn't waste her time. I shall let myself drift on just the same in the current I have thrown myself into. The only person who can clear up the mess I have made of my life is myself, and I haven't the strength, the resources, the courage.

She could hear the sound of the sea more clearly when she shut her eyes. It was good to sit still, to listen to it, giving rein to her tears and her misery. Many years ago she had sat like this, listening to the teeming sound of the sea as the tide came in, while her tears flowed and a great, soothing emptiness melted away the rebellion in her. Her longing for life, her disappointment in it, the sea was suited to both. She had ended up composing poetry that time. Poetry!

If only it were really good for Tot to be here, she would stay willingly. They could live together in this white-washed house, she and he; perhaps she might even pull herself together and write—Alberta's train of thought did an about turn and she guided it elsewhere. Her longings would have plenty of time at their disposal, all kinds of longings. Once impossible, always impossible.

She remembered first hearing the sea on the journey out. They had changed trains for the second time, and suddenly found themselves out in the open. It seemed to Alberta that she had not been out in the open like this since she lived at home, in the north. The station had not been roofed in. There were a few tiny coaches, and a locomotive of amazingly simple construction which stood spewing out black smoke against the wide sky.

Dragging suitcases and travelling clothes, dulled after sitting up all night, she dazedly picked her way amongst sleepers and rails, gaining a confused impression of her surroundings, which were new and yet profoundly familiar. Sivert was

114

carrying the luggage too. Liesel was looking after the boy. He hung back and stumbled over the rails, overtired and cross. Liesel helped him up patiently, laden herself with her easel and bag of paint brushes. Eliel was not properly awake yet; he flew into a rage over a dog, which for unfathomable reasons decided to bark at him and him alone. 'Devil of a cur. I'll damn well give you something to remember.' Eliel kicked out at the animal into thin air; the dog was already far away. He stumbled over one of the rails too, which made him even angrier. Jeanne walked, correct and beautiful, beside Pierre, who was also struggling with his burdens. She had Marthe by the hand.

It was then that something reached Alberta. It filled the air, it was everywhere, lying behind and about all other sounds. She could not quite make out what it was.

The little train smelt of stale tobacco and bowled along with them as if running along the ground. She sat, so tired that she was quite bewildered. But once when the train stood still the air was filled with a roaring, an enormous, monotonous song on two notes. It rose and fell, came and went like a breath from somewhere in space, taking her back years in time. Involuntarily she got to her feet.

'It's not the first time you've heard the sea, surely?' said Pierre.

'The first time for many years.'

From now on she listened at every station. The roar increased in dimension, closed round her, limitless and secure, an embrace. It was then that the expectation, the faith that here beneath the enormous dome of the sky almost everything would come right had stirred in her strongly; in spite of Jeanne, in spite of the fact that Pierre was different. And here we are, all of us miserable, sobbed Alberta to herself.

Pierre, for instance.

'He's ill,' said Sivert one evening after a walk to Penmarc'h with Pierre and Eliel, when they had evidently talked together intimately. 'No doubt about it. He says he's no longer interested in his characters. That's not the talk of a healthy person. He says there are days when he feels dead. Nothing

115

stirs in his brain. But he has a wife and a child, he's up to his ears in debt. He wishes he had never come back. Besides, he knows very well that he's not as he should be. He says he can see it in his handwriting.

'No, he's finished. If he were not, it would surely be just as natural for him to write as it is for me to paint. He has come to the point where nothing can be expressed any more, nothing can be said. He stands outside himself, he says, watching himself, unable to take himself seriously any more. So you see, Alberta . . .'

Sivert's report, thought Alberta. But he interprets things too literally. In part that's what must make him dangerous . . .

'He's too old for competition, he says. Old? He's still in his thirties, thirty-seven or eight. If you start feeling like that at his time of life there must be something wrong.'

Sivert walked about, undressing and making his comments. He had come to the conclusion that on many matters Jeanne had plenty of excuse. To be sure she was a family nuisance and an infliction, but it was not easy for her. If Sivert was not entirely mistaken, it was she who had arranged all the advance payments—

'Alberta! Has it come to that?'

Alberta started as if stung. It was Pierre, in the flesh, blocking out the sun. She had difficulty distinguishing his face, from the way he was standing and blinded as she was by her tears. Yet she knew it was the real Pierre standing there looking at her right through that strange mask of his. He had slung his jacket across one shoulder, his hands were in his trouser pockets. He made a movement as if to withdraw them, but drove them down again.

'Oh, it's you?' she said stupidly. He was in fact standing there. As an initial measure she laid the palms of her hands against her swollen, blotched face, looked at him again through her fingers, and then with bent head began to put her disarranged person to rights, pulling her dress straight, grubbing for her sandals and putting them on. As best she could she dried her eyes, wiped her nose, smoothed her hair. It was one thing for him to appear, another the moment he had chosen.

116

Pierre was busy picking up sheets of paper and putting them in a pile. He displayed great precision, studying the page numbers carefully, finding his way with their help. They had been struck out frequently and new numbers put in their place. Alberta felt exposed, body and soul. Everything embarrassed her, from her ugly handwriting, countless crossings out and dreadful scribbled numbers to her own condition. If only she were not looking like this. She was no backfish any longer, and crying did not become her. Jeanne, on the other hand—. It was a good thing Pierre was incapable of understanding her scribble.

When Jeanne cried there was something pearling about it; as crying it was perfect. Round and bright the tears rolled down her cheeks and hung in her long eyelashes, without spilling over into a devastating flood.

Pierre stood holding the pile of papers under his right arm, took out a handkerchief and dried his forehead with his left hand, stuffed the handkerchief down again and swept his beret off his head. 'Supposing a gust of wind had come along instead of me.'

'It wouldn't have mattered, Pierre.'

'All right. Not today. I can see that. But perhaps tomorrow.' He put the papers into the folder and tied the ribbon. *'Voilà.* Saved for posterity for the time being. But I might not come along another time. Is there any room for me?'

Alberta had put herself more or less to rights; she sat dabbing at her wretched face. She smiled her thanks, knowing that it was a foolish smile.

'Here—' Pierre took out cigarettes, put one in her mouth and lit them both. 'It always helps a little. Well—here we are, Alberta.'

'Here we are.' Alberta had to laugh at her own foolishness. 'I thought you were at La Pointe.'

But Pierre explained that they had not walked more than half-way there. Eliel had had a blister for the last couple of days, and now it had worsened, so that he had been forced to go to the chemist at Audierne and have it dressed. Afterwards

117

he and Sivert had sat eating pancakes at Mère Catherine's, although their lunch packets had been more than sufficient and the tour had not materialized. They would probably arrive soon, though Eliel's foot was bad. Pierre had walked back along the beach. It was longer, but cooler.

'And there you have a tidy manuscript.' He nodded in the direction of the folder, which was lying on a small shelf in the cliff looking ridiculous. 'I wish I had as much.'

'Don't laugh at me. I don't suppose there's anything there that can be used.'

'It's raw material, at any rate. And if you've got the raw material out of you—' Pierre shrugged his shoulders. 'Just squeeze out what you know, even though it may come out untidily and sound false. You always know something, and one thing leads to another. Afterwards you can put it in order, over and over again as if each day were the last and the accountant was to come tomorrow. What are you doing when it comes down to it but juggling with your experiences, building with them, but differently from life? Remember, you can do this only so long as you can take yourself and your life seriously. If you can't do that any more—I expect I've said this before, but you're the kind of person one has to din things into. I don't suppose it's really any use talking to you at all. But I'm glad I ran into you today.'

'Are you?'

'I was rude to you the other day, rude and churlish. Not to you alone; I've apologised to others as well. I behaved badly. But—send a man to hell and then demand of him that he shall sit pottering with the same things as before—' The words burst out of him, he threw his cigarette butt into the sea. 'To come home having saved your skin isn't everything. And the Lord preserve us, I'm told I'm ill, I'm given medicine, I must learn to pull myself together. Damn me if I'm not just as healthy as anyone else. I'm healthier, because I'm no longer blind. I can see so clearly that it makes my eyes smart. Shall we go, Alberta?'

'I suppose we must.'

'I mean go away from it all. You would have nothing against it either. But you daren't. You'll never get away.'

Alberta glanced at him sideways. There he sat, fortuitously inclining towards her again. But he was talking about himself, and that was new. And his concluding words lacerated her to such an extent that she wondered for a moment whether he had said them in order to observe their effect, to study her. He had leaned his head against the cliff and shut his eyes, but that proved nothing, he had ears. She forgot about it just as quickly as it had occurred to her. His face was almost as it must have been before it was cut to pieces and distorted : a calm, strong face, a good one too. A person who could afford goodness, who did not need to look fierce in order to look manly. Boundless fatigue had, like death, wiped out all superficialities and brought out the essentials.

'You think I'm mad.' Pierre opened his eyes, looked at her, smiled crookedly; his expression was blank. 'Now you think I'm mad. But many madmen have been more right than the righteous.'

'I think you're unhappy.'

'Listen, get rid of this mountain of paper before it suffocates you. You must steal a march on yourself. So that you don't find yourself one day standing like a cow in its stall expected to furnish a certain quantity of—literature.'

The word had a bitter ring in Pierre's mouth. 'Literature. They think it has something to do with a mission, don't they? If you're fortunate you'll go down to your grave on that assumption, without having noticed that people grasp nothing beyond what they themselves have experienced. If it was any use telling them anything in print the world would be a different place. They have been told quite often. All the same—if only I were given a little breathing space to take a look at myself and my ideas, I suppose I'd try sending them a few more packets of truth. When you've been out there, it doesn't look quite the same as before. *Enfin*—let me tell you one thing, if you're going to enter the miserable business, then keep at it so that the devil himself can't catch up with you. So that you can defray the expenses of a few years in hell, if

119

the worst happens, without straightaway falling into another one.'

'Pierre—'

But Pierre changed his tone. 'Jeanne was splendid. She always has been splendid. Without her—! Simply coming home to a wife and child for us out there was — — that somebody should be sitting waiting for you, without letting you down! If anyone is worth sacrifice—'

Not to have let you down was the least she could do, thought Alberta, horrified. She remembered the crowds of soldiers leaving the railway station. *Les poilus,* overgrown with hair and dirt, caged birds and other strange objects hanging about them, cats and puppies on their arms, animals that had sought refuge in the trenches and attached themselves to the men who were now bringing them to safety. She remembered their eyes : disorientated, full of wonder, eyes such as one might imagine the dead to have, if they really do wake up again in the beyond, or men coming up from a mine.

Pierre had not been like that, she knew. He was not the kind to permit his misery to come to the surface; he had not been an ordinary infantryman either. He would most certainly have made himself presentable so far as he could, and adopted his mask.

She remembered the severely wounded on stretchers. All traffic along the pavement in front of the station had been stopped. White bandages from head to foot, deathly pale faces, bloodless membranes for eyelids. These men had been strong and healthy, among the strongest, the healthiest.

Not to have let you down was the least she could do, she thought again.

But Pierre went on talking about it. 'She wanted to make use of her small dowry all the time. I tell you, Jeanne—'

He picked up a handful of pebbles and began throwing them into the water as if aiming at the invisible cigarette stub. 'But when a man is at war and may be killed at any moment—! She has her parents, it's true. They're good people, and we borrowed from them. But you can't go on like that for years. I wrote to the publisher, I promised anything, a continuation

120

of the best-seller, even a war book. A war book! I! He took
the risk. Now I'm trapped, a more or less honourable man.'
Quite a large stone flew far out, incredibly far considering that
it was thrown with the left hand.

'Supposing you wrote something else?' said Alberta
cautiously.

'The book *sold*,' Pierre said. 'People want to hear more
about the characters. If there's anything I really hate—.
Besides, they're dead. Fictitious persons can die too. Jeanne
said once, 'Surely you can let the war come and change them?'
Clever of Jeanne, wasn't it? But when they're already dead?
When I can neither see nor hear them any more?'

'You'll soon come through it. You work so much, after all.'

'It may look like it.' Pierre suddenly spoke in the tone of
voice that meant he wanted to shut himself in. Alberta took
care not to look at him. She sat watching the rocking seaweed.
The sea released it no longer, but kept it perpetually on the
move. In a little while it would have disappeared. In a little
while they would have to go home.

'It didn't work out here quite as we had expected, eh,
Alberta?'

'Nothing ever does, surely?'

'There's something in that. I work? One flimsy short story
after the other, soup on sausage sticks. There are days when
I can't see clearly, can't react properly; but away it must go,
it's been promised, the postman will be here any minute.
It's not work, it's prostitution, one might as well be a whore
in a brothel. Here you are, go upstairs with this one and that
one. It's humiliating, you haven't the time to make even the
smallest claim on yourself. Sometimes at night—'

'At night?'

'I get up occasionally, and scribble in a notebook. It relieves
me for a while—I've laid an egg. I don't know yet what it will
lead to. Not to where the creditors imagine, I can predict that
much. I manage to get off one or two brief articles of the kind
Jeanne dislikes. She's afraid of—poor Jeanne. Every day I say
to myself, you have *her*, your child, food on the table, what
do you lack? Write and be glad you're alive, that you have

121

arms and legs, that you're not a helpless cripple—are you crying again? Now listen, Alberta—'

'I cry so easily. It's only my nerves.'

'You have good reason,' said Pierre curtly. 'It's just that I'm not used to seeing you, and—I don't like it. And here I sit complaining when I ought to be trying to help you. That's what happens when one makes one's apologies. Now listen, *ma petite Alberte*—'

'If you say *ma petite Alberte* you'll make it ten times worse.' Alberta hastily withdrew the hand Pierre had taken. She forced a laugh through her tears, though by this time she was really crying, and it was smothered by her sodden handkerchief.

Then Pierre's hand was on her shoulder, shaking and patting it encouragingly, at once reminding her over-whelmingly of Jacob. Now it was round the other shoulder, drawing her slightly—

'Mother!' said somebody above their heads.

The next moment Tot was holding her tightly round the neck, looking at Pierre as if he were thinking: This is my business, not yours.

'Is that you? Where have *you* come from?'

Everything was unreal and strange. Tot was not an affectionate child. It was a long time since he had responded to a caress, let alone given one of his own accord. It was in fact a long time since anyone had caressed her. A child's arm round her neck, a hand shaking her shoulder, it was too much, too good to be true. Sivert's caresses were not in the same category. Simultaneously she felt as if she had arrived at an open, exposed place in life, where a disquieting wind blew and from which she could see the numerous paths that crossed it in all directions. She dried her tears and clung to Tot, the fixed point in her existence.

'I've come from over there,' pointed Tot. 'We're there and we're going to bathe. *Tante* Liesel said you were here.'

'Have you been here long?'

'A little while.'

'And you said nothing?' Alberta looked in bewilderment

122

from her son to Pierre. He was sitting studying the boy.

'I said something now.'

'Yes, now.'

Tot stood there, still holding her by the neck, and said for the first time, as far as she could remember, 'I' about himself. 'Come along then, we'll go and bathe. Come along, Tot.' Pierre got to his feet.

'I shall hold Mother's hand,' Tot said, refusing to let Alberta go.

At Tinti-Anna's Marthe was splashing about at the edge of the water in her bathing suit. She informed them that Jeanne and Liesel were inside the boathouse. They had Alberta's things with them, and chocolate and biscuits. Everything was back to the accustomed routine.

Alberta sat down for a moment in the warm sand, knowing that she did so in the hope of having the child's arm round her neck again. It came too. She laid her cheek against it and felt warmed by it through and through. The ice is cracking in me, she thought. I must have been frostbound.

And then she sat naked and bereft, cold to the marrow. Someone had jerked Tot's arm away from her neck. She turned round and looked up into the glitter in Sivert's eyes. 'We can't have that kind of thing,' he said. 'It's not proper.'

'Are you mad, Sivert? Are you out of your mind?'

Alberta was enraged. She looked from Sivert to the boy who was standing there, the expression on his face stranger than ever. 'Are you mad?' she repeated.

'On the contrary. I know very well what I'm about. I've learnt a good deal recently, about the upbringing of children amongst other things, and particularly that of boys. Matters that there's probably no point in discussing.'

Eliel, who was limping about on one foot with the toe of the other bound up, drew in his cheeks. It made Alberta even angrier.

'Oh, hold your tongue, Sivert. Have you been reading something again that you haven't the capacity to understand?' The malicious words scorched her tongue. She was about to stretch out her hand to the child, but changed her mind. It must not

123

develop into an open quarrel. She met Pierre's blank expression, and knew that if she were to find support anywhere it would be from him. He had seen, understood, he would speak to Sivert. She clenched her teeth. Now there would probably be much to resist. Now things were beginning to look serious.

Jeanne and Liesel came out of the boathouse, Jeanne lovely, slender, attractively tanned in her dark blue bathing suit, Liesel suspiciously thin and round-shouldered in rust-red, sweetly feminine and a little ungainly. She sat down in the sand and said she would only sun herself.

'Are you back already?' Jeanne exclaimed, looking about her in surprise.

'Sivert and I got a lift with a farmer from Audierne.' Eliel held out his foot. 'We came by ambulance.'

'And Pierre?'

'I came by the beach. You haven't asked Eliel what he's done to his foot?'

'No. I don't suppose it's so very serious. But I'd like to ask what's going on here. You all look so strange?'

'Only natural events, Jeanne. Quite natural. We are as we normally are.' Pierre opened his left hand as if letting a bird fly.

PART TWO

. . . two green horses, two green dogs, green as copper . . .

Alberta was looking at them from the side. Strongly illuminated from above they stood out in relief against a wall of green leaves, which were lying in shadow and appeared blue.

They resembled casts.

But when she patted the dog nearest her they all turned their heads and regarded her with gentle, beautiful animals' eyes.

She was sitting on a bench asleep. Their departure hour was seven. She awoke. It was twelve, the horses and dogs were gone, it was too late. Anna Sletnesset sat there; she laid her hand sympathetically on Alberta's. But it was too late and the road in front was thick with dust as if carpeted with felt. It was straight and endless, she knew it stretched out for ever, stretched out beyond what she could see.

The thought of it oppressed her, it took her breath away. Dust settled over her face. She tried to brush it off, her hand was full of something greasy and stiff, and she realised that she was struggling with the dirty window of the compartment. It must have blown open. There was the throbbing rhythm of the wheels, there Eliel's snoring, there Liesel's dry little cough, scarcely audible above the din of the train. Had she dropped off for a long time or only for a moment?

She wiped her face and bent anxiously over Tot, who was lying with his head in her lap. He was sleeping quietly. What a good thing.

A glimmer of light filtered in, outshone the small lamp in the ceiling, revealed faces. Slowly they came into view, coarsened

125

or hollowed, each according to its cast, by the night on the train. All of them were sitting as before, apparently jolted right down inside their clothes. When she had looked in other directions for a while, she could no longer avoid looking at Pierre. In the grudging light she felt rather than saw that his eyes never left her.

In embarrassment she raised the blind.

The dawn was greying. A narrow brook flowed solitary and intricate among the meadows, carrying the weak light of the sky through the dark landscape, then disappeared at the edge of a wood in the distance. A bird flew up out of the bushes at the side of the track; its piping could be heard for an instant. A landscape without distinction which one passes on a journey and immediately forgets; and wonders where it came from when one day it re-appears in the memory, more distinct than any of those looked at more carefully. Meadow, wood, air and water: these life-giving four.

Cautiously, so as not to wake the boy, she stretched up to the draught from the half-open window, and eagerly breathed the air from outside. It tasted of dew and grass, tasted of all she needed most bitterly and had once weaned herself from believing in. She closed her eyes.

When they had travelled out, and she had encountered the same air for the first time after the endless night in the train, she had felt her features soften, as if an astringent mask had fallen away. A dream had plagued her during recent years, recurring time after time. They were being immured, Tot and she; she could hear the clatter of the trowels, feel the air thicken—until all of a sudden she heard nothing, screamed, thrashed about and woke Sivert.

Now the boy was going to fill his lungs day and night with air as fresh and strong as this, even fresher, even stronger. It would fill his blood with oxygen, assume solidity in his muscles, glow in his skin, his eyes, his lips, at last, at last. A few more hours, and it would begin to force its way into the slender body, transform it, perform its miracle. The bad dream would lose its sting. And she too—

She dropped the blind and looked down at the child's face

in her lap. It seemed paler and thinner than ever in the grudging light and somehow twice as dirty as Marthe's. His black hair lay flat and lifeless about his forehead, one of his legs had fallen from the seat and hung down in full view of the adults, pathetically thin in the calf. Bothered by the sight Alberta leaned forward, brought it carefully into place again and drew the blanket over it.

Marthe was bursting with health as she slept under the railway soot. Her mouth pouted as waywardly as ever, ripe as a fruit. If she awoke, Jeanne only had to whisper to her a little and give her a pat or a smack, whichever was necessary. And Marthe would sigh and go back to sleep.

Alberta had hungered to see her own child like this, greedy for food and sleep, hungered for it for the sixth year. Getting him out into the sunshine and fresh air on a beach had been like carrying him to a new birth; at last he would be born after the full period of time, noisy, naughty, like other children.

But the things one longs for seldom happen. Other things happen instead.

Again she met Pierre's eyes; she could see them clearly now. There came the same sudden brilliance in the air about her, the light-hearted, sweet delirium, that she had felt repeatedly of late. It was as if gravity disappeared, she no longer denied it to herself. Then Jeanne's glance crossed hers. Calmly, without shrinking, Alberta parried it. She could look Jeanne straight in the eye, Sivert too. She had deceived neither of them.

Jeanne was no longer asleep. Perhaps she had not slept at all. Again and again Alberta had felt her eyes on her. Slowly the grey light chiselled her form, showing that Jeanne had altered since the previous time they had sat together in the train. She continually changed her position, and there was an expression round her pretty mouth as if she were clenching her teeth spasmodically. Alberta had words ready on her tongue: Don't take me seriously on top of everything else. What I get has nothing to do with you, and what you have nobody can take from you. It was unnecessary to add it all up; you could have spared us that with safety. What could I

127

have done to you? No-one could be less dangerous. In a few hours I shall be out of sight.

One does not say things like that. They throb through one's brain with the rhythm of the wheels and get no further.

Jeanne started up and looked about her. 'Pierre, you're not asleep. You haven't slept at all.'

'Yes, of course I have.' Pierre too started up as if dragged out of deep slumber. He rearranged the blanket over Marthe, who was lying between them, and they sat as before, leaning their heads against the wall, their throats outstretched, unsteady and uncomfortable.

'You're not asleep. I can see you're not. I've seen it for some time. You must change places with me, or you'll be fit for nothing tomorrow.' Jeanne's voice was sharp and high-pitched.

'Today, you mean. Don't wake Marthe. I'm quite all right.'

But Jeanne was already on her feet, making the child sit up, disturbing the whole compartment. 'Rather than know you're sitting like this. Take my corner. No one needs it as much as you.'

Marthe began to cry, Liesel stood up, prepared for anything, and shook Eliel. Jeanne gestured impatiently and deprecatingly. Pierre said: 'Certainly not.' Eliel looked about him uncomprehendingly, pushed himself more comfortably into his corner and snored on. Liesel shook him once more. That was his voice, high-pitched and aggrieved, rough with sleep: 'What? Snoring? Me? Of course not.' And he resumed his snoring.

But Jeanne had her way. She took Marthe, whimpering, on to her lap again and gave her a smack, both with a violence that did not disturb Marthe in the slightest . 'You are naughty, *Maman*,' she said, turned over to make herself more comfortable, and went to sleep.

It was yesterday evening's dispute that had flared up. Pierre had argued that the women should each have a corner, but then gave in to the pressure of opinion and took the fourth himself. But during the night he and Eliel had changed places. Jeanne could not get over it, not over that either.

128

'You who have been to the war,' she said, firing her last shot. It was directed at Pierre, but levelled at Eliel.

Alberta looked across at Liesel. She was sitting with her back partly turned towards her and her face in towards the wall. She had folded her arms tightly about her and drawn up her shoulders. In spite of the heat inside the compartment she looked as if she were frozen.

Happily out of it all, Sivert was sleeping quietly behind the overcoat he had hung up. One of Sivert's gifts was that of staying out of things on certain occasions, a talent which sometimes drove Alberta to rash, ill-considered action. Had she not once gone over to him in public and pulled his chair away when she thought he ought to get up and he had made no move to do so?

The train stopped with a jerk. Eliel yawned, shook himself a little, and drew the blind back from the window in the door. It framed a section of a station building and people going past. Neither the house nor the people were typical of Brittany any more. Outside it was a lovely day. Liesel leaned forward, looked out, coughed her little cough. Her stooping shoulders, her long, supple neck, her head with its coil of plaits thoroughly askew after sitting up all night, were silhouetted for a moment against the lighter background.

Alberta felt a deep pang of longing for the sky and the sea, for fresh air. But the boy began to whimper.

'Do think of the children.' Jeanne was holding up a section of blanket protectively in front of her daughter's eyes.

'*Pardon.*' Eliel dropped the blind. The compartment again became dim.

'Children fall asleep again quickly,' said Pierre.

'Can you guarantee that? He is nervous, this little one. And it's quite enough to have one of them crying, don't you think?'

In distress, Alberta leaned over her child. Dulled and distant from sudden, limitless exhaustion she attempted to quieten him. He continued to fret for a long time as if in physical pain. It was fortunate Sivert was still asleep. *He* slept like a log.

129

Automatically Alberta looked for Pierre's gaze and found it. It was in position, it was waiting for her. For a second they looked at each other.

The hours passed. They were approaching the city. Once when the train stopped a crowd of people with bright morning faces joined it. With light luggage in their hands they ran alongside the row of carriages, off to the capital on a brief visit. It became crowded. The children had to sit on the grown-ups' knees and went on nodding there. The blinds were right up, the faces of the adults exposed mercilessly to the daylight. They wore the disorientated expression that comes of a night awake; a stamp of disolution, of guilt and homelessness. Thus do criminals look at each other, with evasive eyes, brief, twisted smiles, when they have given up and been caught. Eliel looked as if he had woken up after a spree, with his coarse, thick features. Pierre's scar was ugly in the darkening stubble on his face, two naked lips meeting at the wrong place. Alberta noticed it and thought: If there were any question of coming close to it, coming close to it now . . .

She had known for a long time that it would feel perfectly natural. With alarm she realized how quiveringly close she was to giving herself to him. It lay just below the surface, in spite of Tot, in spite of Sivert, in spite of everything. If she were free, if she had control of her life, of her child; if Pierre were free, with no child, she would have no doubts at all.

When did it come? How did it come? When did it start to grow? It only seems as if such things happen suddenly. One day it was there, in the atmosphere, obvious to everyone.

Was it when she had realised that Pierre had talked to Sivert about the episode at the beach, and perhaps about other things? And Sivert had come upstairs and sat down, looking at her with the glitter in his eyes.

'What are you looking at, Sivert?'

'At you.'

'Is there something the matter with me?'

'That depends on one's attitude.'

Was it when, driven after a while by the uneasiness and

130

embarrassment of sitting there with Sivert, she had gone down-stairs to the sitting-room and received a shock? For Pierre was there, and she had not known. Immovable as a statue he had stood leaning against the mantelshelf and simply looked at her, he too. They had both stood looking at each other. Alberta did not move, said nothing. The feeling that if she made a remark or a movement something fatal would happen, nailed her fast, paralysed her tongue. She smiled momentarily out of sheer bewilderment. Pierre did not smile back. She came away giddy, leaving the room with bowed head and hammering heart, as if she had been scolded. She went out. When she came home she walked straight upstairs as if dream-ing and looked at herself in the mirror. Why? Was it to find out whether she already bore some visible evidence or not?

Sivert? It had happened that Sivert had tossed his head, behaved with authority and a proprietary expression when anyone took an interest in her, however fleeting. This simple mechanism had functioned through the years without breaking down; only the occasions had become fewer and fewer. She had never given him any grounds for it.

He had no grounds now either, not according to his way of thinking. And it would be wrong to say that he was taking it seriously. He took it sarcastically and rather maliciously. This time they were equals. Alberta knew very well that he went to meet the postman up in the village, and that he re-ceived letters with an unfamiliar handwriting on the envelope. She ought not to have been afraid of him any more. But she was, so much so that her heart sometimes stopped short; and she scarcely dared exchange normal conversation with Pierre in the hearing of them all. She had become adept at avoiding meeting him alone.

Once when they met on the stairs he had said, 'Alberta.'

'Yes, Pierre,' was all that she replied. She listened to her voice, its busy tone incredibly easy and light. She had hurried past without pausing. Talking to him might open a door to her strength, the little she had, so that it would drain away like blood from a severed artery, leaving her helpless. And what should she say, for her part? Now I have arrived. I took a long, stupid path, but I found the way here at last. I am grown-up and I know what life is and what I am doing, and that I want to be here. Here I can unfurl into a person.

She must not say it. She had entangled herself to such an extent that she had cut off any retreat. He too, as far as she could see.

Time and again she had said to herself: If he were not so tired of everything, if Jeanne did not nag him as she does, if we had not met just at this time, he would not even have noticed me. If everything were as it should be between me and Sivert I would be invulnerable. We're in the grip of circumstances; they're playing with us, duping us. And if only Jeanne had not become suspicious and Sivert full of malice, then— then—

It was no use. The same dark desire was in her still. If she followed it she would go away with Pierre. For good, for evil, for anything whatsoever with Pierre. At any moment and travelling light.

She gritted her teeth. She must not give it rein. Everything passes, life wipes out its own traces. One day this feeling would have left her as blossom and foliage leave the tree. She would do without it. A plant dies without sustenance. She looked up, met Pierre's eyes, allowed her own to rest there briefly, moved her glance slowly away, while the pain the thought had given her died, as acute pain does. They had the present, a bloodless shadow of a present. Today, in a couple of hours, each of them would be going in his own direction. Afterwards it was impossible to predict anything.

It had begun to pour with rain. It drummed on the roof and drove against the window panes. A couple of the other passengers were talking to each other. Sivert and Eliel were bending forward, elbows on knees, enjoying themselves. Isolated words reached Alberta: 'Yes, so help me . . . my opinion too . . . would be no alternative. Listen to me, old chap.'

They were dazed no longer. There was that cheerful nonchalance about them that had been so striking on their arrival in Brittany. Sivert sat slapping his hand repeatedly with his new gloves, another unfamiliar gesture. It was as if the proximity of the city was going to their heads. But when had anything gone to Sivert's head before?

When he glanced over at Pierre he had the same slightly malicious expression as when he looked at Alberta. It did not appear in his features, it lay beneath much else in his eyes and wedged itself up from the bottom in grey glimpses. The next second his thoughts were elsewhere. He gave himself an extra slap with the gloves and looked resolute. Pierre presumably noticed nothing. He seemed to have forgotten Sivert's existence.

The suburbs appeared. Small, ugly villas, fine old houses behind walls, new banal gardens and old ones full of shadows and mystery, ivy in cascades, glistening with rain. This headlong journey back to streets and noise struck Alberta as sheer madness. They ought to have stayed out there, found some means of putting up with each other. Tot's heart had beat unevenly, but was it any better for him to be anaemic? It was not late autumn yet; the evenings were mild. Far out the sea glittered with moonshine; close to the land the moon itself rocked in the swell. Like an enormous balcony jutting out towards the universe the ocean lay there day and night. At high tide it surged stronger than ever, offering itself to the equinoctial gales. They would come.

Sivert had got the idea that Alberta ought to write. Before, when she had referred to the subject, he had not answered : an unequivocal manner of expressing his opinion.

'I'll look after Brede,' he had begun to say, 'if you want to scribble.

'Well, you have a pen,' he added.

'Aren't you going to paint?' asked Alberta to gain time and decide what attitude to adopt; perhaps also to show that she was not blind.

Surely she could see that he was not painting? He was doing some sketching, but Castelucho had not sent either canvases or paints. He occasionally took out the sketches he had made earlier that summer, whistled, and put them back with their faces to the wall. Everything pointed to Sivert's early return to

Paris. It was remarkable how light-heartedly he and Eliel regarded the journey in and out, twice each way during the course of the summer, as if there were no question of money or inflation.

'Penny wise, pound foolish,' he had said once, when the matter was raised. 'Working capital,' he said. 'If you have it, you must take risks. That's one lesson I've learnt.'

The day the storm came Sivert had been lying out on the slope near Jeanne. 'I have something to read, so I'll stay here until it's time to bathe. You go if you want.'

He took from his pockets the exhibition catalogues, art brochures and other pamphlets that he always carried about with him. Among them there inadvertently came letters which he quickly stuffed back again. He offered to look after both children if Jeanne had anything else to do.

'Oh, I!' said Jeanne. 'I have no talent. I'm just a simple housewife. You go, Alberta, as your husband suggests.' She looked up and sniffed the breeze, which was heavy with sea-weed and salt. 'I shouldn't be surprised if we had a storm before nightfall.'

Alberta left them. It all seemed odd and disquieting. For obscure reasons she did not like the fact that Sivert and Jeanne together watched her go. It had nothing to do with jealousy; it was an inexplicable uneasiness of another kind.

From the window above the typewriter clattered like some warning ally, or so it seemed to her. The atmosphere was stifling and her head was heavy. She did no work to speak of. She sat in her accustomed place, leafed through her manu-script, struck out here and there, moved pages from one chap-ter over to another and back again, while her thoughts re-volved round very different matters, vacillating like a swing between insane possibilities and cramping heart-sickness.

She must have sat there for a long time. When she looked up a rust-red stripe lay along the horizon, and everything else was the colour of lead, sea as well as sky. The silence, the boundless metal surface without a ripple, the screech of a soli-tary gull that seemed to be the last one in flight from the earth, struck Alberta with sudden anxiety. She went home

134

quickly, as if pursued. On the stone steps outside the kitchen door Josephine's clogs stood as usual; but their appearance was not as usual. In the nauseating light that grew paler minute by minute there was something significant and sinister about them. All summer Alberta had seen clogs standing in front of the doors of the houses. All it meant was that one could not cross the floor in them; they clattered noisily and spoiled the wood. Josephine glided round the house in her stockinged feet, nimbly and noiselessly, up and down stairs. Her clogs were attractive out of doors.

Now they revealed their true essence all of a sudden and appeared to be a warning, fulfilling a mission. They stood pointing towards the house. They said: In, not out again.

One attaches no importance to such impressions; they occur fleetingly and one passes on. Afterwards, when something terrible has taken place, they surface again.

An hour later the storm was upon them: a tremendous storm, that tore down slates and fences, altered the beach completely, threw mountains of seaweed up on land and brought with it a downpour that washed away roads and paths in the course of a few hours. It isolated them from each other. Only infrequently and at close quarters could they hear each others' voices and footsteps. They heard the rattle of the shutters, the heavy gusts of wind that were hurled against the house, then heard it give at the joints, sodden and buffeted. From the upstairs windows they watched the sea coming towards the land in row upon row of moving mountains, grey as rock, to be shattered against the beach. The spray hung at a great height beneath the lowering, turbulent sky; foam floated in the air, a rookery of white rags. They slapped against the panes or fluttered past, rising and falling on the storm, as far as the village and beyond.

It lasted for six days. Josephine had to spend the first night on the chaise-longue in the sitting-room, as it was impossible to open the outer door. In the morning Jean-Marie came to fetch her, bringing butter and four plucked chickens tied to his back. Arm in arm, he and Josephine crept over the crest of the slope and disappeared. For six days they were shut in, except for one afternoon when it abated a little, and Sivert and Eliel went out to fetch supplies, bent double, navigating before the gusts like ships at sea.

Liesel's influenza worsened. Usually nobody took it seriously; it was one of the things to which they had all become accustomed. When they had said: 'You ought to go to a doctor, Liesel, and get something for that cough,' they had done what they could. She stayed in bed while the storm lasted, eating nothing, her eyes glittering with fever, her hands clammy and hot. Even Eliel said, 'That cold's a nuisance. It can't go on like this.'

On the morning of the fifth day Sivert decided to return to town as soon as possible. He began taking out his belongings and packing them in the shining new suitcase. It was then that Alberta was seized by one of her attacks and announced suddenly: 'I want clothes and things too, nice clothes, nice things.'

'Of course,' Sivert said, and sounded as if caught unawares. 'But after all, you can't have them out here.'

'I want to go to Paris and buy myself some decent clothes,' said Alberta, sinking lower in her own estimation with every remark.

'Well,' said Sivert slowly—he was standing at the table rearranging his belongings repeatedly, as if composing a still-life—'Well, you can come with me if you like. There's no longer any epidemic, so as far as that's concerned . . .'

It had sounded like a threat. Uneasiness crept over her, but she shook it off. As a preliminary measure she started to look over Tot's and her stockings. All summer they had both of them gone without. She could not remember what was usable and what was not. Perhaps she could throw away the worst pairs and escape darning them.

Jeanne was upstairs with Pierre; she was there for a long time. The storm reigned, nothing could be heard. But later on, when she and Alberta were preparing lunch together in the kitchen, Pierre came down and wandered in and out singing to a tune of his own:

> *'Je souhaite dans ma maison*
> *une femme ayant sa raison*
> *un chat passant parmi les livres . . .'* [1]

He did not continue, but returned to the first line: *'Je souhaite dans ma maison une femme ayant sa raison.'* In spite of the weather each word could be heard clearly, so loudly did he sing. His expression was hard, his mouth twisted out the words. He remained briefly in the sitting-room and then went upstairs again.

Jeanne's hands trembled as she chopped up parsley at the kitchen table. She put the knife down, went across and lifted the lid of the pan of potatoes. When she came back again her hands were calm. Without altering her expression she chopped the rest. But the atmosphere in the house had become almost impossible to breathe.

The explosion came later, as they were eating. She got to her feet, pushed her chair back violently, and gripped the edge of the table so that her knuckles whitened. Her words tumbled out pell-mell. She referred to her expectations during her engagement and throughout the war, her struggle and her anxiety. 'Shall we talk about Mondement?' shouted Jeanne. 'About Soissons and Chemin des Dames and La Fère? I know a bit about those places. I was not present, and yet I was there. Or shall we talk about 'House X'? I know that book by heart. I can repeat whole pages of it, word by word. You wait for years. One day you find yourself sitting there with a child, waiting. There is no horror one does not experience. But what are you in the end? Are you so much as a comrade? No. A housekeeper, a nursemaid, a—a—a—'

'Be quiet,' said Pierre. 'Be quiet now, Jeanne.' He went over, put his left hand over her mouth and his right, his wretched, fingerless stump, which he hid so carefully, round her shoulders. He did that for Jeanne. He said: 'Come along, we'll go upstairs. You're saying things you don't really mean.' His voice was low and tender.

[1] Guillaume Apollinaire

137

But Jeanne shouted: 'That Alberta! What's she sitting staring at, that Alberta! With eyes like that!' And burst into tears. Pierre began to force her to go upstairs. Then Jeanne threw herself on his neck exclaiming, 'I don't know what I'm saying, I don't know what I'm saying, I don't know what's the matter with me. Forgive me!' Then they left. Her sobs and Pierre's low voice could be heard for a moment from the staircase between two gusts of wind.

Nobody said anything for a long while. The door out to the kitchen had been ajar the whole time, Josephine, who had come back again during a lull, was out there, and Jeanne had shouted so loudly that even a hurricane could not have drowned her. The scandal was complete. The thought hammered in Alberta: She was adding up the bonds, the ones that cannot be broken, the ones that sooner or later would draw him back again if he were to leave her. You cannot free yourself from them.

Pierre came downstairs afterwards and tried to explain it away. He did not say much, and he blamed himself: 'My fault, my fault entirely. Here I am letting my nerves run away with me, without thinking of Jeanne's. The soldiers weren't the only ones whose nerves were disordered by the war years; the civilians' were too, the women's above all. Even Jeanne, who is so brave—she's not more than human. All she wants is what's best for me.'

He paced up and down for a bit. Then he said: 'We've decided to leave. Our stay here has become meaningless, we're getting nothing out of it. Marthe is missing school to no purpose. But there's nothing to stop the rest of you from staying. The house is paid for for the next three weeks, and . . .' He stood staring at Alberta as if in distraction, with wide, tired eyes. He supported himself against the mantelshelf.

'I had thought of leaving in any case,' said Sivert. 'I think Eliel has too. But perhaps Liesel and Alberta would like to stay.'

Alberta stared into Pierre's staring eyes and said no. She was thinking that that slightly tender conscience, which comes

138

of not loving wholly and unconditionally was something they had in common, he and she.

'Not much longer now, a quarter of an hour, the ticket collector says.' Sivert, who had gone out into the corridor, came back to report. He began rearranging the suitcases so that it would be easier to pick them up, brushed his clothes, made a new crease in his hat, and sat down ready. Jeanne started to busy herself. Undaunted by crossness and opposition she rubbed engine soot off Marthe's face with cotton wool and eau de Cologne. 'We are on a train, *mon enfant,* we are not at home.' Marthe stopped complaining. She repeated emphatically: 'We are on a train, we are not at home,' pouting and docile under the ordeal, while Jeanne rubbed and rubbed until she shone.

Alberta was reminded bitterly of the bottle of eau de Cologne she had wanted to buy at the last moment in Audierne, and had not done so because Sivert had thought that was carrying virtue a little too far. It had been the same on the journey out. In the morning Jeanne had unpacked various attractively and practically arranged toilet articles and provisions and prepared to refresh her family. She handed Pierre ready mixed mouth wash in a bottle and nodded in the direction of the place to which he should go, as if he were incapable of finding the way on his own. She offered Alberta eau de Cologne, and Alberta washed her son's face and put him in a rage. It was obvious to everyone that the process was quite new to him and that he was thoroughly opposed to it. He stood there in his unsuccessful dungarees with his hostile little face, exposed to the tender mercies of Jeanne's secure, motherly eye. Sivert did not improve matters by saying, 'Aren't you going to shake hands with the little girl?' The boy squirmed and simply said 'No'. Marthe looked at Sivert with the calm disdain children display towards adults. Jeanne said, 'Don't bother him.'

'Alberta!'

It was Jeanne. She had turned and was handing her the bottle and the packet of cotton wool, now as then. 'You can't possibly use the water in the W.C.; take these.'

Something in her eyes made Alberta put extra warmth into her voice as she replied, 'Thank you, Jeanne.' She was not Jeanne's adversary, and had no intention of being so. It would be good if that were clear.

Sivert intervened. 'I'll do it. Come here, boy.'

Alberta relinquished the articles, went outside and stood at the window in the corridor. They would soon be there. Factories and working class districts slid past, glimpses of wet asphalt, slum children playing, people stopping to look at the train. The white-washed house on the green slope suddenly stood in front of her more clearly than those she was looking at. White clouds, piled up like eiderdowns, were sailing above it, the clogs were standing at the kitchen door, dwarf clover grew along the little path. The live lobster, which, to Alberta's horror, Jean-Marie had taken out of his tunic and handed her as a parting gift, extended its black claws slowly and with hesitation. She dared not touch it, Josephine had had to intervene. The pot was brought, the most frightful execution took place, the bright red lobster was brought triumphantly in to supper and greeted with ovations from the men. She heard the sound of the sea, heard Madame Poulain's parting words: I've been thinking. I've come to the conclusion that the creation is far from complete. It is wrong to tell us it is, and that God found that everything was good. If He exists, He must be in despair over how incomplete it all is, especially mankind; for we have many talents but not enough sense to make use of them. I am only a simple woman, Madame, I cannot instruct anyone. But this is my belief.

'What are you thinking about, Alberta? That we shall soon be there?'

She started. Pierre was standing beside her, looking at her.

'Yes, something of the sort.'

'It always ends with an arrival. Was that our purpose in leaving? It is written somewhere: *Le vrai voyageur part pour partir.*'

'Is it?' said Alberta giddily. As if the words had removed covering layers in her mind she realised how much she loved

140

travel for it's own sake: the thump of the wheels, the changing, curving lines of the landscape, the furrow that seems to
make a circular movement around you, arriving at strange
places where everything is fresh and new as it only can be
when you have never been there before and will not be staying
long.

She smiled, not daring to look at him. Immediately afterwards she did so in astonishment, for Pierre said, 'No, it's not
the dome of the Pantheon. But what can it be? In weather
like this you can't distinguish the one from the other.'

At once words began tumbling hurriedly out of her own
mouth; she was not sure what they were, only that they were
unexpected, stupid, and far too numerous: 'No, it's not the
Pantheon. It's, let me see, it's — — no, it can't be the Pantheon, I'm sure of that.'

She went on repeating it, breathlessly and at random.
Jeanne had put her head in between them, her black eyes
looking from her to Pierre and back again. 'Fancy being able
to say so with such certainty, Alberta. You must know Paris
very well. Even for us it's difficult when it's overcast. We're
provincials, but all the same . . . How unfortunate that it
should be raining. Not a cab to be had, I don't suppose. Sivert
and Eliel have promised to rush on ahead and do what they
can. Have you the tickets ready, Pierre? Can you be quick
about getting a porter? Don't let everyone else go in front of
you, even if they are old ladies. You're much too unselfish
about such things. Think of tomorrow. You have to call on
Monsieur Chollet at nine o'clock. You must be rested and in
good spirits, to give him the impression that—After all, young
writers spring up out of the ground like mushrooms these
days, and some of them have talent. You must go to bed at
once, have a bath and go to bed, eat your supper there and
have a good night's rest.'

'Don't worry, Jeanne. A lot of money has been placed on
me. If it's to bring in any profit the best thing is to put in more
while I'm still alive. No one knows how long someone like
myself can keep it up. Now's the time to put me in a position
to produce.'

141

Pierre's voice was quiet and cold. Alberta stood embarrassed at being a party to their conversation, irritated that she had let herself be drawn into a foolish piece of play-acting which had been nothing but a fiasco. What had been the point of it? What had they to hide, she and Pierre? Jeanne was still talking in a high-pitched, nervous voice. 'Why do you always have to harp on that? It's unjust of you. They have been most obliging. They could simply take your manuscript, force you to hand it in. They're running a business, not a — a —'

She paused. When she had said 'take your manuscript' Pierre had laughed, that curt, almost silent laughter of his. It always made her unsure of herself. He stood looking at her, his eyes blank. More words came pouring out, low and faltering: 'If you're given another respite—a chance to get this piece finished—you can apply for the stipends, you can— as soon as you've produced something new.'

'Why not beg on the doorsteps?' Pierre neither raised nor lowered his voice. He looked at Jeanne a second longer, turned, gave Marthe his left hand and went towards the exit. Jeanne closed her eyes and slowly shrugged her beautiful, tailor-made shoulders. A jerk that made them all stagger passed through the train. It stood still.

Now there was nothing for it but to descend and get away from the mob. In front of the station the violent and un-accustomed combination of drumming rain and the noise of the street engulfed them bewilderingly. At great danger to life and limb, their coat collars turned up and shaking the rain off themselves, Sivert and Eliel ran hither and thither in the road after taxi-cabs, were stopped and sent back by the police and ran again. Marthe was carrying Mimi, wherever Mimi had come from. Jeanne buttoned Pierre's raincoat up to his neck and told him he must not move; all he had to do was stay quietly and shelter. Pierre acquiesced, was kind to Jeanne again, patting her on the cheek and smiling crookedly and absently as he watched the traffic with disorientated eyes. A reflection of old tenderness and of the soldier's wonder-ment at life behind the front was visible for a moment in his face, making Alberta feel an intrusive and somewhat ridiculous figure. A new, devastating thought slid into her mind: They have furniture and a home, he and Jeanne, a small world of their own, a shell they have built round themselves. It does not consist merely of chairs and tables, of objects that can be seen and touched. For better or worse it lives, it is a living web, it exists or goes under with the people who inhabit it. It was in the Rue Notre Dame des Champs, near the Rue de Rennes. Sivert had been there, but never Alberta. She held Tot's hand more tightly.

Sivert and Eliel had found cabs. Jeanne, Pierre and Marthe took the one. In a daze, Alberta felt them take her hand in turn, heard herself saying *au revoir* and how pleasant the holiday had been, first to the one, then to the other.

'I shall be terribly busy to begin with,' explained Jeanne. 'Must get Marthe off to school, make clothes for her, help her with her homework. She has missed almost a month. Then there's everything to be got ready for the winter. But later, in one, two, three weeks—I suppose you take Tot to the Luxembourg Gardens now and again, Alberta?'

'Yes, of course, Jeanne.'

'Then we'll see each other there if not before. I always go near the big fountain.'

'So do we,' answered Alberta mechanically. She watched the car drive away and mingle with the countless others moving down the street. Not even Marthe's little hand waving from the back window distinguished it from the rest any longer. Numbly she allowed herself to be packed into the other cab. She had a profound certainty that nothing of what had just happened could really be possible; that all the things they were saying and doing were not really as they seemed.

They sat squashed together, luggage everywhere, outside and inside the vehicle. They did not say much, only yawned now and again. Tot stared out, his intensely blue eyes wide from fatigue in his blackened little face that no washing had improved. Past them rushed rows of houses, people, traffic, all of which had the peculiar property of being exactly as they had left them. Rain dripped from umbrellas, from gutters and awnings; from chestnut trees which, confused by city life, were

143

flowering for the second time with small, scattered, pathetic flowers; from plane trees, their bark peeling in flaps, and from trees like the ones belonging to a Noah's Ark, round at the top and unnaturally dark. The air coming through the open window smelt of hosed streets, a unique mixture of vapours impregnated with water.

Only Sivert seemed to be entirely at ease, rested and cheerful. He was still slapping his hand with his gloves. After a while Alberta felt as if she were being whipped; she cringed, waiting for the next stroke. He was as brown as tanned leather and contrasted almost shamefully with the pale people on the pavements. Every year he and Eliel acquired the same solid, even patina. It made them look younger and handsome as peasants. Their eyes and teeth glittered competitively. This time the sea air had deepened the beautiful basic colour by several shades. The china blue of Sivert's pupils contrasted so surprisingly with his skin and his black hair that it was unpleasant.

At the Parc de Montsouris they put down Liesel and Eliel. Liesel took leave of Alberta with a limp, hot hand. 'When I think that Eliel left it all in one big mess. You're lucky, Albertchen, to be going to a comparatively tidy home.'

'Comparatively?' said Sivert. 'And I even scrubbed the attic stairs.'

'Yes, Sivert's the man with his papers in order.' Eliel giggled. 'Besides, Liesel can move to a hotel. There's nothing to stop her, it would be better in every way.' He commandeered his final piece of luggage and kicked the door shut. '*Hei paa Er*. We'll see each other at the Dôme, Sivert? As usual? *Maa saa godt.*'

He put his things down and waved. Liesel waved too, a couple of small gestures. The last Alberta saw of her she was standing upright, her arms hanging down at her sides and a dull, bewildered expression on her face.

At a good speed and with plenty of room they drove on to the Rue Vercingétorix. Sivert was humming in quiet snatches. When in obedience to his instructions the cab turned into the

144

courtyard, rounded the little shrubbery in the middle and stopped at the door of the studio, Sivert swung into *forte* and finished on a strong, long-drawn out note. Yet again Alberta's heart was constricted by inexplicable fear: fear of his strength, of his repose, of aspects of his character that she would never really fathom. Yet again she felt her absolute dependence on him as highly dangerous; it came and went, alternating with very different feelings, with old devotion, almost sympathy.

While he settled up with the driver she looked up at the walls of the houses round about. They looked as if they were about to collapse on top of her, so high were they. She had not remembered that the air was *so* heavy. She ought to have stayed at the seaside with the boy. Unconsciously she squeezed his hand so hard that he cried 'Ouch!' and drew it away. What were these potted plants that were standing in the way round her legs? The flowers had stalks that were far too long, as if they had been stretching towards the light. Behind her she heard the concierge: 'Here I am with the keys, Madame, and the most recent letters. *Mon Dieu,* how sunburnt you are! And Tot! Tot! Do I see any difference? A great difference, Madame, a great difference. He is not plump, he never will be, he is tired after the journey, *voilà.* A whole night on the train, *n'est-ce pas?* But wait until tomorrow when you take him out on to the street. Then you will see children who have not been to the sea. I shall say nothing about Monsieur. He is magnificent. Monsieur is always magnificent, with or without sea air. Is everything as it was when you left? I hope so, Madame, I hope so. I can answer for the flowers at any rate. They have not lacked water. Today they are outside, as you see. Nothing does them so much good as a shower of rain. We have had such a heatwave. The summer is sultry in Paris. We have not one single case of the Spanish sickness left in this *quartier,* thank God. I was at the chemist's only yesterday . . .'

Madame Morin bent down, helpfully moved fuchsias and pelargonias so that the entrance was free, rattled her bunch of keys and opened the door.

'Thank you,' said Alberta, suddenly recognizing her own

145

plants, whose existence she had forgotten. 'I can see they have been well looked after. They've grown.'

On the threshold she paused. Through a haze of fatigue she recognized the interior again too. Was that how it looked? And how unused it smelt. Quickly she went to and fro in the large, rather dilapidated room, opening windows to let in the air. It was tidy, everything was in its right place, the floor was clean. Sivert was not the man to leave a thorough mess like Eliel. In that respect she had much to be thankful for. She vainly attempted to feel something more for this, their home, Tot's home.

She heard Sivert's relieved, 'Well, that's that,' when the cab had gone, and the boy's footsteps sounded across to the corner where his toys were. She looked down at the letters in her hand. The one was a *pneumatique* for Sivert; the other had Australian stamps all over it and was from Jacob.

Jacob? She could forget him for long stretches at a time, until all of a sudden he would remind her of his existence in one way or another and heighten her feeling of having deserted her own destiny. When did she take the wrong turning? Where did she take it? The only persons she recognised at all times as part of her life and knew she was close to, were Jacob and Tot: this odd little stranger she longed for and did not know how to win.

'Magnificent?' repeated Sivert with irritation, putting the last suitcase down on the floor and wiping his forehead. 'Magnificent? What does she mean by that? A pretty irrelevant expression, it seems to me. Is the good Madame Morin beginning to be impertinent?'

He put the *pneumatique* that Alberta handed him quickly in his pocket, as if he already knew who it was from and what it contained. In passing he asked about Alberta's letter.

'It's from Jacob.'

'Fancy that.'

But Alberta suddenly realised what was strange about the room. Two brand new cushions lay on the divan in the corner, on top of the ones she herself had stitched together at great pains and with limited materials. She stood looking at them for a second. They were attractive, and made the place brighter. She recalled occasions when she had had a desire for many well-matched cushions. A wild notion prodded her, but did not seem to accord with anything else. She said nothing, put her letter aside, and began to unpack what they needed for their immediate use.

*   *   *

Although the days had long since turned into weeks, looking upwards still gave her the same feeling. The houses seemed to be leaning over her threateningly. They bordered closely on the remains of the low old studio buildings, their enormous brick walls rising upwards, the lower half covered with ivy, the upper with advertisements for Byrrh, Dubonnet, Pneus Michelin in giant letters, Man-size bottles paraded up there together with the inescapable apparition made out of car tyres and a cigar, that had once frightened Tot so much.

Out in the street, beyond the gate and the low house belonging to the concierge, storey was piled upon storey: identical windows, all of them open, washing on lines, bird cages and window boxes, a rectangle of the ubiquitous flowered wallpaper visible on the inner wall of the narrow rooms; women going to and fro, leaning out, carrying children on their arms, sewing something, polishing something; high up a balcony running along the length of the façade, above that attics under the steep roof; and when she tilted her head back as far as it would go, the sky, a grudgingly measured, crookedly and badly cut sample, in so far as one could see that the material existed at all.

Behind much else in her consciousness Alberta had, since her return, been reluctant to admit that she had lived here for years with her child and that she would continue to live here for an uncertain length of time. Tot was breathing in the same air as in previous years: the heavy city brew of exhaust and food smells, exhaust and scent, exhaust and tired vapours, exhaust and dust. It hung in the streets unaltered from year to year. If it was scattered by a shower of rain, a few hours of

147

fresh night breeze from the country, it oozed back just as quickly, tenacious and satiated, from the houses, the cars, the people. Once, a long time ago, she had inhaled it like a stimulant. It was one, but, like most stimulants, it was a slow poison too.

When she had finished tidying up in the morning she went to the milk shop and the vegetable and fruit barrows. Tot went with her and helped her to carry the things, unapproachable, undaunted by the cries that greeted him on his way. 'How he has grown.' 'He's brown.' 'Yes indeed, and more robust.' 'All the same I'd give him cod-liver oil in the winter, if he were mine, cod-liver oil from Norway.' '*Oh là là,* the damned war, not a child who isn't marked by it, except for those of the rich, they always manage of course, all they have to do is leave in good time.' 'Come here, Tot, and say good-day and you shall have some grapes. They're not bad for him, Madame, on the contrary.' 'He has a serious air, that little boy, it makes quite an impression on one just to see him.'

Every comment was well-meaning, every one cut Alberta to the quick. 'Thank you,' she would say. 'Thank you Mesdames. Shake hands nicely, Tot.' She nodded and smiled to the neighbourhood children, who stopped in their play to watch the boy. He had had a couple of friends among them when he was small; they had come into the courtyard to play. It had always resulted in tears and been brought to an end by each new epidemic. There was no trace of them any more, and Madame Morin said: 'Boys of his age in here, no Madame. Toddlers are a different matter. He would learn bad habits, and I would get into difficulties with the tenants. They're working folk, they need quiet. You can imagine yourself how it would be if there were shouting and screaming here, fighting and throwing of stones. Now he is pleasant and well brought-up, approved of by everyone. My cousin from Saint-Denis comes to spend a day with me every autumn. I'll ask her to bring her boy with her, he's nearly six years of age too.'

Too well brought-up, thought Alberta, impotent and guilty. And so am I. I ought to fight for this, struggle and not give in. He needs friends again, kind ones, not too rough, not too

148

pliant either. I dare not let him run loose on the streets. A good thing that idea has not occurred to Sivert. A good thing he . . .

For Sivert, on the contrary, said: 'The boy will probably find someone to play with. I daresay a solution will be found.' He seemed to be saying, 'Don't interfere. I have my plans.' Paralysed in the face of the mystery of Sivert's plans, which were perhaps completely out of her range of vision in any case, Alberta could not bring herself to ask further questions.

She would sit beside the shrubbery in the middle of the courtyard, sewing, shelling broad beans, or doing some other task, while the boy pottered about, in and out of the open studio door. She could see straight into the corner which did duty as a sitting-room: two divans at right-angles, bookshelves on the wall above them and a table in front, draperies and cushions, two new ones in Hungarian embroidery amongst them, looking bright and luxurious; at the end of one of the divans Tot's corner with his rocking horse, bought after a struggle, the chair and table that Sivert had made some time ago, the box with old objects that the boy himself had collected and put away. Out of doors strong, baking sunshine lay like a flaming puddle between the houses for a brief while, then began to move, creeping upwards along a brick gable, sliding over at an angle to the next and the next, higher and higher as the day progressed. Indoors the air had something clammy and mildewed about it that Alberta never managed to dispel. Every time the boy disappeared through the door she was on the point of calling him back, but stopped herself so as not to nag.

Minute by minute she had to force herself to sit there at all. Longings passed through her in unnerving confusion: the longing to be a peaceful woman, looking after her husband and children competently without yearning for anything else, watching them prosper and grow about her, receiving diffident, rough caresses for reward, pats like blows, embraces endangering life and limb; the longing to be back in possession of the old, modest freedom that had once been hers, to use it properly and sensibly, making room in it for Tot, for the future, for interests beyond the immediate, for knowledge;

149

the longing simply to get to her feet, take the boy by the hand, and go. Where? Out into the city. Down into the Rue Notre Dame des Champs to where it joined the Rue de Rennes. What business had she there? Whatever happened she would not reveal anything, confess anything, she would grit her teeth above her secret. Nevertheless she wandered about down there in her thoughts, imagining sudden meetings on corners, words casually spoken that made life good and candid.

She brought herself home again. There was a scent of box from the low hedge surrounding the shrubbery, which consisted of three aspidistras and a skinny fan palm, grouped in pots round a deformed acacia. She tore off a leaf now and again, crushed it between her fingers and inhaled the astringent perfume, which became so strong in the sun and reminded her of Versailles. Smoke blew down from nearby chimneys, black nauseating coal smoke; and the woolly, pale wood smoke, that had hung thick in the kitchen as soon as they lighted the impossible stove, making her eyes smart, smelling of burning undergrowth and Lapp camps, came back to her, one of the things in life she had not appreciated sufficiently at the time. She remembered the smell of hay and flowers, seaweed and salt, pleasant working sounds, drifting clouds, Jean-Marie plodding over the hill with a basket of fish on his head the second day and turning out to be the Jean of long ago. She had not been surprised, nor had he. For much had happened, and life was no longer surprising except perhaps where Sivert was concerned. Jean-Marie had told her about his wife, a splendid wife in every respect, away for the moment because of illness at home. She would be ready to come and help them later if they needed anybody—

'Tot!'

The boy looked up from what he was doing.

'The mirror is pretty now.'

'It's the sun,' he said briefly and continued with his play.

It was the sun. And it was just as well he no longer ran indoors every time a window, swinging on its hinges in the house at the other side of the street, threw reflections into the far end of the studio, into Sivert's big mirror. Emeralds and

150

rubies caught fire along its edge. When the boy was small he had been seized with that mute wildness: each time it happened he had stood on tiptoe trying to catch the splendour with his hands; then refused to go out again, and sat down, his face radiant, waiting for it to happen again. 'It's pretty,' he would say to himself. 'Tot thinks it's pretty.'

There was no need to regret it. It was good for him to be out of doors, good that he was growing bigger and more reasonable. But values always slipped between her fingers before she had time to come to her senses and realise that she possessed them. She must have lost the ability to grasp the fleeting moment during the endless years of the war. And yet every second became precious, acquiring value of its own as soon as she thought back to the first night when the bombers could no longer be expected, to the deep, unaccustomed peace of the morning after with its atmosphere of resurrection and new life, of limitless possibilities.

'Why don't you come and help me for a while, Tot? Here, take some beans and we'll see who can shell them the fastest.'

'You shell them the fastest, and you like doing it. I don't.'

'Are you sure I like doing it?'

'It's what mothers do.'

'That's true,' said Alberta. The boy suddenly seemed to resemble Sivert in a way that was almost horrible: Sivert's ability to dash cold water over one's enthusiasm and extinguish it effectively and at once. It was not right that a child should be so like an adult. The thought worried her, as if she had been unjustly severe towards Tot. She put the things down to take him in her arms, but did not do so. One can be reserved in one's love for a child, just as in other relationships. Since the episode on the beach he had withdrawn into himself again, twisting mutely away from her, refusing to agree to her suggestions but doing so when they came from Sivert. She could have put up with a great deal if only he had been different.

She caught herself down in the Rue Notre Dame des Champs again. Pierre had found a solution satisfactory to all parties. What solution? What indeed? But something had to happen. Her longing was so great that surely no-one could

151

long so much without something happening. She must be liberated, or else die.

The men from the studios round about passed by now and again. 'What a good little boy he is, Madame. You don't often see such a quiet child. He looks a thoughtful little soul.' And they patted him on the head.

The models came, squatted down and tried to talk to him. 'What a sweet little boy. Oh, what blue eyes you've got, I've never seen anything like it, blue as the sky.' And they turned to Alberta. 'I'm crazy about children, utterly crazy. You're fortunate, Madame: a husband, a beautiful child, peace and quiet. As for us—He's a bit thin, but very sweet,' they concluded, and hurried on.

Madame Morin came. She was a large, masculine person, feared by her neighbours, brusquely friendly towards Alberta. The fact that Alberta had settled here, had a child and stayed, in contrast to the rest of the women-folk who frequented the studios; and that she looked after the boy instead of simply putting him outside to play, had given her standing. Madame Morin addressed her as Madame Ness, although an occasional letter would arrive for Mademoiselle. She even held her up as an example: 'If only everyone behaved like Madame Ness. She's *comme il faut*, a good mother.' Oh indeed, thought Alberta.

Now she had spent the summer in the country. This made her highly respectable, an ornament of the whole courtyard, a person Madame Morin took pleasure in conversing with. 'You're right to take advantage of the sun, Madame, right to keep Tot out of doors as much as possible. Now that he has become stronger you must keep him that way. Not all mothers look after their children like you. But then we do have a little bit of green here, it is a great advantage. I don't draw a bucket of water that doesn't end up out here: water for scrubbing the floors, for washing the dishes, both of them are excellent for vegetation, I assure you. The summer is so dry in Paris. *Enfin*, one does one's best. And Monsieur is still working out of doors? He is industrious, I grant him that.'

152

'Yes,' said Alberta. She thought she detected a slight under-tone in Madame Morin's voice, as if she had really wanted to say something else. Had she not made some remark the day she came in and noticed the two new sofa cushions? If Alberta had had a confused notion that, in spite of everything, perhaps they had been meant as a surprise for her, this had been thoroughly dispelled.

'Nice to see that Monsieur thinks of Madame,' commented Madame Morin.

'I was expecting guests,' Sivert said, as off-handedly as only he knew how. 'So I bought them. I thought a little colour would be an improvement.'

'Well, well, Monsieur wanted everything to look its best in Madame's absence. An interior is judged according to the woman who lives in it. That's how a husband reasons. It's charming, it's touching.'

'My word, how she does poke her nose into things,' said Sivert angrily in Norwegian, rattling canvases against the wall and pretending he was no longer following the conversation.

'We shall have to put her in her place soon, to stop her getting too meddlesome,' he said when she had gone. Alberta trembled for a couple of days in case he should attempt such a thing. But nothing happened, and she breathed more easily. Madame Morin could not be put in her place; she occupied the place she already had with justification. When the shortage of fuel, butter, sugar, milk and proper flour had been at its worst, and Sivert had come home empty-handed from the queues, she had saved the situation more than once. 'A child must not lack for anything. We adults can manage,' she would say, putting small paper bags and packets on the table, or placing a bucket of coal inside the door. Perhaps she did stand with arms akimbo expressing her humble opinion about one thing or another, since she had looked in anyway. But Tot got soup, warm milk, porridge, warmth from the stove. It would be impossible to dislodge Madame Morin.

The attention excited by the cushions was irritating to all concerned. Alberta felt she was being pitied for her simplicity, it made her want to shout: 'They're there with my full

153

approval; I like them.' It made her think uneasily: Supposing it's serious between Sivert and this other woman—then, then—

At once she saw Jeanne, heard her saying, 'Sit down. It's quite safe to sit down. I'm not the revolver type, I don't carry a dagger. If you think I'm so frightened of you . . .' She saw Marthe, sound, healthy and secure, and guided her thoughts elsewhere.

Liesel whistled when she saw the cushions. She said: 'He's starting to buy things. We recognize that symptom, thank you.'

Sivert was out of doors, painting. Sometimes he came home to lunch, sometimes not. There was no need to wonder whether he had company on these expeditions; there was much to betray the fact. The *pneumatiques* he stuck in his pocket, whistling, betrayed it. On the canvases he brought home Alberta saw Paris again, a city pale with moist air, a city of light coloured stone, autumn colours and sunshine against a heavy, pastel blue sky. Was Sivert's latest work good or bad? Something of Cubist geometry and ascetic colour appeared here and there in his flamboyant palette; the effect was as if a stranger had shared in the picture. He himself was pleased. 'At last I'm beginning to find my own style,' he said.

He was, and always would be, surprising. Did he not take Alberta and the boy unasked to Galeries Lafayette one day? Tot was given plenty of new clothes, Alberta a dress, coat and hat. When she went over to look at the price tickets and let them fall again because they seemed to her fantastically high, Sivert had said: 'Try it on. You can try it on, after all. It's expensive, but never mind.' she had come home with things she had not even dreamed of possessing.

'It's too big an outlay, Sivert. I'll take the bus down and change it.'

'If you're pleased with it you're to keep it,' Sivert said. 'Then at least you'll have something.'

He said nothing to the effect that now he would not have to listen to nagging about clothes for a while. On this occasion Sivert was generous throughout, merely slapping himself on the hand with his gloves before putting them down. 'I'm glad

154

you found something you liked,' he said, when Alberta finally thanked him and hung the clothes neatly behind the curtain in the attic. She wished it could have been possible to say a little more, but it did not seem to be.

It was a long time since she had owned clothes she liked wearing, clothes that suited her and suited each other. When she went to the Luxembourg Gardens in the afternoon with Tot she looked like a comparatively carefree woman, with all her affairs in order. Tot was a well-dressed little boy with a vanishing layer of sunburn on his strange small face, with thin calves and large knees sticking out of small nautical trousers, a checked ball under his arm and a hoop. Mothers of a different category from the ones on the Avenue du Maine, handsome women with beautiful embroidery, often in mourning, talked to him and to Alberta, graciously inviting him to play with their children. Occasionally he would agree to throw his ball. When it was discovered that he was Norwegian, the ladies would ask, leaning forward with anxious faces: 'Norway is a friend of France, isn't she?' Alberta assured them that she was. She smiled with them at the children and held her sewing as naturally as possible.

A gnawing feeling that time was passing and something quite different ought to be happening possessed her day and night. It was an old acquaintance, the kind one never manages to shake off. She often looked round her involuntarily, and sometimes felt a pang at the sight of a back, a way of walking, a contour. Ha, ha, Alberta, you've gone round staring at shadows before, she thought. Even Jeanne was nowhere to be seen, although Alberta consistently stayed in the part of the Gardens where she had said she was to be found.

On the way home they walked along streets abandoned by the sun which resembled dark chasms between the houses. The air was thick with petrol vapour and food smells. Tot dragged his feet and whined, as if the shadow and the waning day oppressed him. But in spite of it all Alberta could feel herself moving in the light, weightless fashion of those in love.

When she opened the studio door stale air struck her. Not

155

until the cold weather came would there be any kind of ventilation through the few panes that it was possible to open. She left the door wide open, and the long evening began to pass.

Sivert came home briefly for dinner, though often he would not appear even then. 'I must be off again,' he would say, 'But if you want to go out, just go. Tot's old enough now. It's time he learned to be alone in the evening occasionally.' Sivert looked at her sideways; she felt as if he were studying her.

'I shouldn't dream of it.'

'You're indulging the boy.'

'I'm only thinking of the possibility of fire.'

'There won't be a fire.'

But Alberta pictured Tot alone in the big studio, where the darkness unfolded itself out of the corners like black mist, remembered how he would sometimes wake up, frightened and restless, and said no more.

It was when he was finally asleep that her longing became unbearable. She wandered up and down the courtyard, through the branches of the acacia sketched in the gravel by the nearest street lamp, watching the play of living shadows in the lighted windows on the opposite side of the street, a theatre of silhouettes in friendly, unfriendly, indifferent, sometimes affectionate inter-action: good performances, taken individually, under uncertain and temperamental direction. Until, little by little, the shutters were closed everywhere and the performance was over. This happened early in the evening. The actors were working folk.

She sat down with a book in the corner that was the sitting-room. Sivert had bought a considerable number of new books. Under different circumstances she would have devoured them, lived through them, perhaps been changed by them. Sivert was no fool. He could unexpectedly rise to a higher level very successfully, bringing home literature that made her wonder how he had found it at all. It was one of the characteristics that had always brought out her former affection and her regret for what ought to have been and never was. Now she put the book down without knowing what she had read. It did not occur to

156

her to write. She went outside again and wandered up and down. It was quiet in the narrow streets, dark in the studios. Nobody lived in them besides Sivert and Alberta. Dark at Madame Morin's. From the Avenue du Maine came the jangling of tram bells, the senseless, angry hooting of motor cars. Alberta's footsteps crunched unnaturally loudly, as if somebody were walking at her side or immediately behind her.

She had experienced loneliness, the will to live, blind desire, the play of blood and nerves in walking and breathing, affection, gratitude, a sense of duty, understanding, but never before this unconditional longing for another, as if she herself were only a half, lost and astray. Against this feeling she could now weigh and measure the life she shared with Sivert. It had withered rapidly, losing the first buds early. The boy had monopolized her, there had been no way of avoiding it, and one receives according to what one gives, in this as in much else.

Sivert first became passive, later indifferent. He had once been fond enough of her to pursue her, but he probably had not imagined things turning out as they did. She herself had been satisfied, she supposed, until the needs of the child had destroyed the framework. Things could look like this when the horizon had widened and one had progressed round them.

Beneath all her pondering, for and against, there was hope. Pierre would find a solution, make a move in one direction or another, turn up again at the very least. Tomorrow she would know. The post would come, a telegram would come. Now, in a little while, it would come. Telegrams were delivered even at night.

Nothing came. The uneventful moments linked themselves to each other, endlessly, pitilessly, as they had done so many times before. She was worried by suspicions that the man expects the woman to act in such a situation: to take the responsibility, even the initiative. She would not be saddled with that, not even for Pierre. Jeanne had won him back, and this was the most suitable, the most fortunate, the only reasonable solution. Won him back? She had never really lost him, he had only been tired. And here was Alberta taking it all seriously, longing with every drop of blood in her body to such

157

an extent that she felt it in her face, her breast, her lap; peering into the past and the future and believing herself to be in the grip of the power that governs the world and upsets fate. Ridiculous.

But when she awoke in the early hours, her head heavy, half unconscious with veronal, her pillow was wet with tears. She sat up in bed, stretching out her arms in the clammy, airless darkness, as if other hands were ready to grasp hers, to draw her with them, if only she could find them.

Sivert slept, his breathing regular as clockwork.

She heard *about* Pierre, in snatches and inadequately.

Liesel came, pale, somewhat out of breath but, according to herself, stronger and more energetic than before. She inspected Alberta's new clothes, feeling the material. 'Nice. Suspiciously nice. A silent apology, or else an advertisement for his generosity. Difficult to tell yet. It's that Swedish artist. Sivert and Eliel are equally mad about her, but Sivert has priority; you know how men are. They sit at the Dôme with her, paying for one drink after the other. She's the type who can take plenty—doesn't get drunk on half a glass of wine like us. It's called priority, isn't it, Albertchen?'

'I expect so, Liesel. So it's the Swedish artist? You see, I know nothing about it. What's she like otherwise?'

'Not Sivert's type, I shouldn't have thought. Expensive to run, fox furs and lots of rings. They say she has money. And she sings. Men have a weakness for that type. She's in the habit of bursting into song when they're sitting with her at Leduc's so that everyone turns their heads to look. If somebody comes and plays outside she joins in with soprano and alto and God knows what. Apparently she's studied singing. And we're not like that, Albertchen. I have some of it from Eliel and some of it from Alphonsine, whom I met the other day. She asked after you. She's married her mechanic now, and lives in Vanves, in a villa with chickens. When she's in town she eats at the usual places. We're to go out to see her one day. She has got quite fat. Marushka is back on Montparnasse. She still seems to manage, heaven knows how.'

Marushka was somewhat of a mystery. She got nothing from Russia any more. On the other hand two relations had landed themselves on her, two destitute refugees who had arrived in Paris after an adventurous journey through Sweden, Norway and England. Marushka kept them, painted, was as chic and well-dressed as before, but did not look well. 'Either she's burning the candle at both ends or else she's been as stupid as I was. No-one can tell me there's nothing the matter,' said Liesel.

The little medical student from Canada that Alberta knew, the one who had been expecting a baby by Foresti the painter, was up and about again, thin as a ghost in her white smock. In bed for nine days. Liesel had visited her at the hospital where she worked. The child was being fostered at Vincennes. She was worried about it because she could not afford to pay very much. She had said: 'If I have to go on the streets, then there's nothing else for it.' But all she said about Foresti was: 'Such a fine person, in his art, in every way, if only he didn't drink.' 'They always say that about their revolting men,' said Liesel. 'Of course she never hears from him. Potter is supposed to be back.'

Potter? thought Alberta, in distraction. Wasn't Liesel beginning to remind her a little of Potter, expressing herself in the same brusque, hard fashion, only not quite so cynically? Perhaps once upon a time Potter too had been young, gentle and charming?

Jeanne was beside herself because Pierre was always going off to meetings on Montmartre. He seemed to have become a thorough Bolshevik. His book was not finished yet.

At last. Alberta felt her heart flutter. At last we're getting to what is important. She devoured the words, pretending only moderate interest.

'Oh, Liesel? How are Pierre and Jeanne anyway? Who is she afraid is going to steal him from her now?'

'You,' answered Liesel dryly.

'I?' Alberta laughed a false, ringing laugh and was suddenly weightless, full of sweet dizziness. 'Surely she's given up by this time. I'm stuck here. I don't even see him.'

159

'That's no guarantee. Eliel says Jeanne wants to take him home to Dijon again. If you don't do something, Albertchen, she'll get her way.'

'Now, Liesel.'

'I'm going to speak my mind,' Liesel announced. 'I'm not keeping my mouth shut any longer. I'm tired of it, so why not speak frankly. It's a pity you and Sivert have a child and Pierre and Jean too. It takes money to arrange such matters, and that makes it difficult for people like ourselves.'

'How you do talk, Liesel!'

'Yes, yes,' said Liesel in a tired voice. 'Yes, yes.' As if she was saying: The world must go its own way without me.

She did not stay long. A new restlessness had seized her, an uneasy busyness. She was off to Colarossi's to sketch or else home to cook the dinner. Alberta watched her go, thinking that she had become alarmingly thin inside her clothes at the back. She thought: Liesel must pull herself together and go to a doctor. I ought to tell her in such a way that she understands it's imperative. And she forgot her for her own affairs again. If she had fought to keep a little calmness and presence of mind, it was dispelled now. Everything dangerous was again let loose. She tossed between two parallel lives and was pummelled weak and senseless. Her daily existence could not be the right one.

She took out the letter from Jacob. It was easy to find in her handbag. Through the brief contents she attempted again and again to see him as he must look now. But the picture he had sent her once, standing on the deck of a ship, got in her way. It had erased the memory of him as he was when he had left home. She remembered broad shoulders in a new seaman's tunic, remembered his lifting his sea-chest now with the right, now with the left hand, and that he had whistled and talked to Papa as one grown man to another. But his face was missing. And nothing was left of the schoolboy, or of the many anxieties of their years together as children, besides a pair of red fists sticking out of outgrown sleeves.

Now Jacob had sheep, not many by Australian standards, but he hoped for more. During the war he had threatened to enlist. Then he had had no sheep, but merely sheared them for others and was sometimes out of work. He no longer said, 'I'll stay for one more year'; he said, 'for several years'. He told her about the sheep, about the house he had built himself with another fellow, about how they looked after themselves, what the war had meant for people like him. And as a postscript: 'If that man not marry you or you want to marry him, come over here with the boy. If I get married, you and he can live here all the same. I'm all right, not a rich man, but you would not go without. I'll go and send money for the ticket if you want. That big boy of yours, I often think of him. Give him a good kiss from his uncle. Keep cheerful dear, take good care of yourself.'

Jacob's Norwegian became less Norwegian and more English with every year that passed. He had not found land in Norway, but sheep in quite another part of the world.

'Do you remember you have an uncle, Tot?'

'I have an aunt too.'

'An aunt, a grandpapa and a grandmama in Norway. And an uncle in Australia.'

'Australia, where's that?' The boy did not look up from the piece of wood into which he was hammering nails. She could hear that he was asking out of politeness, a child's politeness, that can be far more chilling than an adult's.

'It's far away on the other side of the world. It takes several months to get there by boat. Uncle Jacob has sheep, lots of sheep.'

'Does he?' said the boy, just like Sivert. Shortly afterwards he asked: 'Is a grandpapa only Father's father?'

'No, Mother's too.'

'But you have no father?'

'He's dead.'

'Dead? What's that?'

'It's—it's—it's falling asleep forever.'

'Can't anybody wake you up?'

'No.'

'I see.' The boy hammered away at his piece of wood and fell silent.

When he was a few weeks old Alberta had written about him to Jacob, telling him the truth without wrapping it up in explanations: I have had a child, Jacob, a little boy. Jacob had replied: That's all right, Alberta. If you need me, let me know. A cheque for five pounds was enclosed in the letter.

At home in Norway they knew about it too. She knew they knew about it, though she did not know who had passed on the information. For a time she had ransacked her brain, trying to present the matter in a way which would break the news while keeping them at a lifelong distance. But she had never sent the letter, and she soon became indifferent to what they thought of her up there on the other side of the war. They were no longer able to send travellers to descend on her. Events had proved even stronger than Aunt. She no longer heard from anyone in Norway.

Marry? She and Sivert? They must, for the sake of the boy. Everything would be better if they did. Sivert must be of the same opinion. It must happen before the boy started school; there would be expense and inconvenience. Would it be dissolved afterwards . . .?

'Come here, Tot, let's read our ABC.'

'No,' Tot said and went on hammering.

And Alberta, who wanted to prepare him on this point, to give him some literary superiority, and really had managed to get him to learn a few of the letters, bent her head over her sewing again. She ought to exert her authority in a good many matters. The reason for not doing so must have been her paralysing uncertainty about Sivert.

She ought to work at something lucrative. It became more pressing with each passing day. In thought she scrutinized her inefficiency thoroughly, found nothing but her writing and turned from it despondently. Never had it seemed more ridiculous, more distant, more impossible than now.

She applied herself to household tasks, mending and darning far beyond what was profitable and reasonable, cooking in new and more thorough ways, even baking in an upturned cake box on the miserable primus. Then she would have

162

periods of doing nothing as if addicted to a vice for which she despised herself.

Occasionally she was seized with savagery. This was her life, it really was *her* life, these uniform days that passed, one after the other. It was no longer something that occurred; it was a drain she could less and less afford.

Then she would catch sight of the boy's head as he bent over something, and thought: I shall never leave *you*. As if somebody had proposed that she should.

One day she was able to tell Sivert that Pierre had been there. She felt as if she were telling him that a spirit had manifested itself. It had been brief and unexpected as a vision. She was sitting outside the door. Suddenly Pierre was standing just inside the gate, then coming towards her round the shrubbery. She had no time to be surprised, no time to blush or turn pale. Mechanically she stroked Tot's hair; he had immediately come to her and clung to her as he seldom did. Pierre had stood looking at him the short while he was there, they both looked at him. Pierre asked her how she was. Very well, thank you, and he? From her confused brain she produced a conjecture about his departure to Dijon. Pierre shrugged his shoulders, he was not sure. A couple of times she noticed him glance, wearily and ironically, at her sewing, and it gave her confidence. All the same, the atmosphere quickly became raher oppressive. 'Sivert isn't at home,' Alberta informed him. 'Well, never mind.' Pierre patted Tot on the head, said something about just wanting to look in, since he had been in that district, and left. He left! Only then did Alberta realise that he had altered; or he had let the mask fall for good, one of the two. At the gate he turned and called out a greeting from Jeanne and Marthe, as if remembering something urgent at the last moment. Then he was gone. Alberta was still bewildered, restless in her arms and hands, as if something had been torn away from her by force. Instinctively she hastened to tell Sivert about the visit, to minimize its importance and steal a march on Tot. 'Fancy, Pierre looked in.'

'Did he?' Sivert replied. 'That fellow? What's he fooling about with nowadays?'

'Fooling?' Alberta instantly regretted taking up the challenge. Sivert's eyes met hers briefly, and a mixture of triumph, inquisitiveness, satisfaction was in them. Satisfaction?

'Yes, fooling. Surely it ought to be possible to slap together that everlasting book in a hurry, when he has spent so much time on it; an experienced fellow like that. But he's lazy, that's the trouble. He's not the only person to have gone to the war. A man ought to be able to pull himself together and make a new start.'

'You yourself have sometimes said he was ill.'

'Depends what you mean by ill. There are people who hide behind the notion that they're ill, run away from life into illness,' stated Sivert categorically. 'But of course, in this old-fashioned country they just pander to such cases. It'll take centuries before they catch up.'

'Catch up with what?'

'Oh, various matters.'

'What an authority you've become.'

'I keep up to date; I've studied one thing and another during the past few years.'

'Dr Freytag's box?'

'Amongst other things, yes. To change the subject, I may bring a visitor here one of these days. A Swedish girl who paints, a very pleasant acquaintance. You might perhaps wear your new dress. And I suppose we ought to offer her something to eat?'

Alberta paused on the way from the primus to the table. She almost dropped the dish with the ham and lentils. She was about to protest. She was not unfriendly, but the situation was a false one. She had a desire to call out, 'It's no good this way, we must tackle it differently.'

'Very well,' she replied. 'When will you be coming?'

'I thought Thursday, at about half past four. See that Tot looks decent, won't you? He could wear his new clothes too, perhaps? I meet her at the Dôme. We're going to look at some of my pictures.'

164

'Will it be the first time she's been here?' asked Alberta as indifferently as she could.

'Ye-e-es, no as a matter of fact she has been up before. I value her opinion highly. A wonderfully talented person. A strange person. She originally studied singing. Then she became obsessed with the idea that she wanted to paint. But there, she has other obsessions too.'

'Oh?'

'A strange person, as I said. For a woman, at any rate. Remarkable. I've never met anyone like her. No coffee for me, thank you. So if you're not having any—'

'I *am* having some,' said Alberta, pumping her enemy the primus so hard that it smoked.

'Well, well. How is it you can never learn to deal with that poor primus?' Sivert took over, and succeeded, in this as in everything else. Then he began to inspect his pictures, displaying some of them along the wall, and putting others away. As if quite by chance he went across and rearranged the sofa cushions, trying out different effects. Silly Sivert, thought Alberta, with sudden affection.

When the gate moved on its hinges her heart began to hammer. She heard footsteps and voices, pulled herself together and went to the door. Sivert and a tall stranger with so much fur round her shoulders that she resembled a returning trapper, were just rounding the shrubbery. She felt their eyes on her. She thought mechanically: No worse!

'Come in,' she said. 'I'm so glad you could come.'

'Yes, I'm so glad too, to be meeting Sivert's wife. We've talked about it so often. But some things never seem to come about here in Paris. There is such an enormous amount to get through. Fru Ness knows how it is. But what a pleasant place to live in, how attractive those plants are. This is the way to live, not in an ordinary, banal hotel.'

A powerful hand took Alberta's. And Alberta felt as if it was quite normal that they should touch each other, as if it was inevitable. She pressed the hand hastily and preceded them indoors. She heard Sivert say: 'Yes, it is pleasant, don't you agree? Isn't that what I told you, my dear, this is how you ought to live.' The rapid, accustomed 'my dear' at once seemed to her more decisive than an open embrace. With trembling hands she rearranged the tea table.

She had bought a tart and some nice little cakes, made delicate ham sandwiches, brought out the best cups, flowers and fruit. But the stranger would eat nothing, she never ate between meals. She could scarcely be persuaded to take a cup of tea without sugar, with a cigarette which she herself took out. She smiled indulgently at the things Alberta offered her, as if at a children's party. 'It'll soon be aperitif time,' she said. 'You should have remembered, Sivert, that I never take tea and that sort of thing. Such a pity Fru Ness has gone to all that trouble.' Abstractedly she looked at the boy, who was watching her shyly, threw away her half-smoked cigarette and immediately lighted a fresh one. 'What a sweet little boy you have.'

Sivert struck himself on the forehead. 'What an idiot I am! I'll run round the corner for a bottle of Dubonnet. Or would you prefer Byrrh? Italian vermouth? Amer-Picon?'

'What I'd really like at this moment, Sivert,' said their guest slowly, staring at him, 'is an ice-cold absinthe. And that you cannot get me.'

'Nobody else can either. It's been illegal since the beginning of the war.'

'What of it? If we were to give up what is illegal, what fun should we have? I drink absinthe every day. In that way I at least avoid that kind of complex. You look shocked? My dear, you can always find someone who can get hold of it. But hurry up and show me your pictures. We're going back to town again soon, aren't we?'

Sivert threw out his hands, powerless where absinthe was concerned. They both left the useless tea-table and began to inspect Sivert's pictures, which he lined up along the wall. Alberta listened to the stranger as she expressed her opinions, and had to admit that she did so clearly and wisely, without hesitation or deviousness. She listened to Sivert's respectful, almost grateful, 'Do you think so? I suppose I've seen it myself, but—. Too anecdotal? Not constructive enough? Merely sketches, preparatory work? I understand it from your point of view. But don't you think that—? Well, I'm glad you think so. Thank you.'

This is how they suit each other, thought Alberta involuntarily, as if she were marrying off a young, inexperienced Sivert. At the same time she could not help feeling exceedingly embarrassed on his behalf, if only for the fact that he was so small by comparison with her.

She was tall and well-built, with restless grey eyes which contrasted oddly with the childish bow of her upper lip. Her profile was clear-cut and strong, she was beautiful. But her complexion was sallow, her hair lank and dull. She looked as if she had lived through a good deal.

She was smartly dressed. Alberta had seen the same type of clothes at Lafayette and had an idea of the price; they were the kind whose price tags one did not even bother to read. She had taken off her fur; it lay in a heap on the chair she had left, teeming with tails and paws. And Alberta felt even more sorry for Sivert. He was so innocent where women's clothes were concerned. They all seemed to him to cost far more than they ought, and that was that. Suddenly she seemed to hear Potter: 'Men don't think with their brains, dear, they think with something further down.' No—Potter had said the heart. She did not deny men brains. It was Alberta's black soul that did that.

'Taking her home—oh, isn't that a dirty trick? She's hard up for a man, he wants to clean his body, that's all.' The way Potter had talked on many occasions. Alberta felt as if she had her sitting here on the divan, whispering the hard, brusque sentences in her ear. Again she rearranged the tea-table, to give herself something to do and to get away from the nastiness of her thoughts. What right had she to remember them? She wished Potter had never expressed an opinion on anything.

Alberta felt humiliated by the whole situation, by her own state of mind, by the new dress she had put on, the table she had taken such pains over. If Sivert and this woman wanted to live together, why not come to the point without mincing

167

matters? The situation was difficult enough as it was. But men seemed to have a mania for inviting their paramours home. Alberta pictured Liesel pouring out coffee for well-built, well-dressed Swedish girls who talked terribly loudly, had use for Eliel for a time, and took him. Or acted that way. Eliel also acted that way. He seemed purposely to heap Liesel with indignities.

Alberta went outside, leading Tot by the hand. Fortunately he went with a good grace without adding another defeat to the number. Madame Morin was standing in the courtyard, inspecting the shrubbery. They embarked on an animated conversation. Alberta did not have to listen to the vivacious exclamations from indoors every time Sivert turned a new canvas round. She talked at random about this and that, about the weather. Suddenly, the sound of singing came from the studio. A deep, rather rough, but true voice moved up and down in operatic recitative and then dropped into speech. Madame Morin leaned over: 'That's the one. Now she's singing. She was here when you were away too. Not to my taste. Women like her cause nothing but trouble. Be on your guard. You know what men are—No, this year the box hedge is not as it ought to be. I've watered it, I've pruned it, but what can you expect? It was scorching all July and August.'

Sivert and his companion had come to the doorway. He looked at Alberta, who went towards them with a toss of the head, saying effusively, 'Must you go already? How kind of you to come. It was a pleasure. Sivert has talked about you so often. Do come again very soon now that you know the way.'

Again she had the powerful hand in hers. Red fox furs and restless grey eyes flickered in front of her. 'Charmed to meet Fru Ness, charmed to meet your sweet little boy. It's very pleasant here, I think, so peaceful and pretty. Well, now I'm afraid I must rush off, Sivert.'

'I'm coming, I'm coming,' Sivert slapped his hand with his gloves. 'Good-bye Tot, good-bye Alberta. I shan't be late.' His eyes seemed to be apologizing for the situation.

She was left behind with the silent little boy. When the gate banged shut he said: 'That was not a nice auntie.'

'Oh yes, Tot, of course, a very nice auntie.' Alberta turned and looked into the sitting-room corner. Each little detail had cost her willpower or persuasion, fumbling and bother with needle and thread, maintenance, cleaning, resignation. Something had inspired her, something she had wanted to create in here. It had never turned out as she wanted. Now the new cushions led their own threatening life on the divan, and the ashtrays were overflowing with half-smoked cigarettes with a strange aroma.

A feeling of intense loneliness and helplessness seized her; and of pity for Sivert.

When he came home she had been in bed for a long time, pretending to read. As he got into bed he said: 'That reminds me, Jeanne wished to be remembered to you.'

'Jeanne?' Alberta propped herself up on her elbow and shut the book.

'Ran into her on the way down. She's leaving for Dijon tomorrow with Marthe. They're letting the apartment for the winter. She would have come up, but has had so much to do. Hoped to come to Paris just before Christmas, and would look in on you then.'

'Oh?'

Alberta failed to say more. Jeanne was leaving, Marthe was leaving, the apartment was being let. But what about Pierre? Had they ceased to take him into account? He was not dead, nor had he disappeared. He lived and breathed a few *quartiers* away. Her head swam. Then she noticed Sivert's sidelong glance, quick, cunning, his eyebrows slightly raised. 'I suppose Pierre is leaving too. In a few days. It's the best thing for him. He wished to be remembered to you too, by the way. Just caught a glimpse of him.'

'Thank you. So they're leaving?' It was possible to say such things coldly and quietly.

'Yes, they're leaving. Things are getting worse instead of better with Pierre here in Paris. He doesn't even write any more, not even short stories. His publisher is said to have lost patience completely. He said, "Not one more sou until I have

169

the manuscript on my desk." It's tactics to put pressure on poor old Pierre. But Jeanne has to be responsible for the rent and the taxes, food and clothes and insurance. They say Pierre is scarcely ever at home; he's taking part in readings and that sort of thing.'

'Readings?'

'Yes. There are some people, actors and intellectuals, who have decided to put on plays together, art for the masses and so on, all of it free. Jeanne's quite right when she says he can't feed a wife and child on that. According to Eliel, they've been in a fantastic state. He was up there the other day. Jeanne and Marthe hadn't any food even. Now she's delivered an ultimatum and is going home. If he doesn't come to some arrangement with the publisher and finish that everlasting novel of his he'll never see her or Marthe again. Not surprising either.'

'If only he could write in peace—. There are other things he wants to do.'

'It's no damned good sitting down and saying there are other things he wants to do. You have to finish one thing at a time before you start on anything else. Look at most of the people who have been to the war. They take up the threads where they left off and are happy to do so. I'm beginning to think that Pierre is pretty spineless. I used to be sorry for him, but now that I've seen at close quarters how confoundedly difficult it is for Jeanne—. It's no fun to have to go home because her husband can't keep her.'

'It won't be much fun for Pierre either.' Alberta spoke bitterly, angry with herself because she could not defend him any better. Pierre's weakness was only on the surface. In reality he was stronger than any of them, braver, richer in goodness. But how could that be proved?

'Then he'll have to behave like a man, so help me,' Sivert said. 'I must say he's not much of one.'

'He has the *Croix de Guerre*,' replied Alberta in her impotence.

'Ye-es—maybe it's easier to earn that than to face everyday life.' Sivert turned off his lamp.

170

Alberta turned off her lamp too. Almost immediately she turned it on again, grasping for her book as if for a lifebelt. Grumbling, Sivert turned over on to his other side. A moment later he was asleep.

*　　*　　*

'It's me, Albertchen.'

'Come in Liesel. Quietly. Tot's asleep for once. Fetch a chair, we can sit outside. It's mild this evening. Nice of you to come.'

Liesel stood unexpectedly in the doorway, faintly illuminated by the lamp that Alberta had turned on in the corner by the divan. She was so out of breath that Alberta was frightened and said, 'But Liesel! Have you been walking too fast again? You know you shouldn't. Sit down. I'll make some tea. I'm so glad you've come. I'm all on my own—'

'Albertchen, put on your new clothes, your dress, coat, hat, hurry.' Liesel sat down holding her throat as if to release her exhausted breathing.

'But my dear Liesel, I never go out in the evening, you know that. Tot—'

'I'll stay with Tot. Get your things and go.'

'Go? Where should I go?'

'Down to the corner of the Avenue du Maine, Albertchen. Outside the café. Pierre is waiting for you.'

'Pierre? At the corner? Hasn't Pierre left?' asked Alberta foolishly.

'He's there, he's waiting for you. Don't ask me to explain so much; I've got a stitch, I've walked too quickly, as you say.' Liesel put her hand between her shoulder blades and coughed.

'Can't he come here?' asked Alberta severely to cover herself.

Liesel nodded in the direction of the attic, where Tot was asleep. 'He probably wants to talk to you alone. Besides, he wants to take you out. Get yourself ready and go.'

Alberta had already brought down her clothes and was in

171

the process of changing, powdering her face haphazardly in the inadequate light. She had not thought for an instant of refusing to go, but she begged for persuasion as one begs for stupefying drugs. While doing so she attempted to gather her strength, the little she had, searching it out from the corners of her mind and putting it where it would be sorely needed, in her voice, her cadences, her expression. 'What an extraordinary idea. At this time of day.'

'Do you think so? There must be something the matter.'

'The matter? With Jeanne? Or with Marthe?'

'I don't think so. Nor do you. Now hurry. I met him outside the Dôme.'

'I don't want Jeanne to be able to make any more accusations,' began Alberta. She had buttoned several of the tiny buttons on her dress wrongly and had to do up the long row all over again. 'Jeanne takes everything in one way.'

'Jeanne is in Dijon.'

'But Sivert is here.'

'Sivert is at Montmartre this evening with the Swede and Eliel. Don't get home too late, that's all. Don't bother about the buttons, Albertchen, it looks all right as it is. Do you think he'll notice? We could put our clothes on back to front without their noticing. Now go.'

'I am going. Where did I put my gloves? And my handbag? Thank you, Liesel.'

'Is Mama going out?' came a wide-awake voice from the attic.

'It's all right, Tot. *Tante* Liesel is here.'

'Where's Mama going?'

'Out for a little while.'

'Out where?'

'Out for a walk. I stay at home all the time,' called Alberta despairingly. Liesel pushed her out of the door and shut it behind her. She heard the child's voice once more, but could not distinguish the words, and felt torn in two, as she ran across the courtyard and through the shadow of the acacia.

In a strange, high voice she called 'Cordon' to the unsuspecting Madame Morin and was out in the Rue Vercingétorix.

At this time of day it was as strange to her as being on a stage.

Pierre was not standing at the corner. He was a little way beyond the lamp, and so close that it made her start. The man with his right hand plunged down into his pocket so that his raincoat was pulled askew was neither a vision nor an optical illusion. He was walking towards her, passing through the circle of light. His scar was thrown into sharp relief for an instant, as if to emphasize that it was he and no other, the man marked by the war, who could never again become the man he used to be. He took Alberta's hand quickly, squeezed it hard, and kept it, thereby adding to the impression that something unusual was happening. Her whole body was trembling. To hide it, she pulled at her hand and met the darkness in which his eyes lay as bravely as she could. 'Very well, thank you Pierre, and you?'

'I have not asked how you are, Alberta.'

'Haven't you? I thought I heard—' Alberta attempted a laugh. It rang forced and lonely.

'Will you dine with me?'

'Dine? It's after nine o'clock, nearly ten—'

'Well, call it supper if you like. But don't start making objections. I know it's nearly ten. An unheard-of time for someone like you, I know that too. But we never meet. I miss you. Spend this evening with me, Alberta, keep me company for a while.' Pierre spoke impatiently and rapidly. The last words came with a rush, breathlessly, as if he had been running. He led her quickly in the direction of a cab standing at the pavement a short distance away; it seemed to be waiting for them as if they were its masters. The chauffeur leaned out, saw them, started up without waiting for orders, obviously knowing where he was to go. They jolted off so violently over the uneven cobbles that Alberta hit her head on the roof and her hat came awry, making her even more confused. Then they swung out on to the Avenue du Maine, gliding easily and quickly over the asphalt. 'Ah!' Pierre said, as if things were taking the right course. He leaned back, still talking, but more calmly, in a conversational tone. Brokenly and in fragments, like an echo, the sentences reached Alberta through her own inner tumult:

173

'— — busy during the day — — Sivert's new côterie—not my type—suits him and Eliel even less—ought to stick to their art, they understand that — — this Swedish woman—don't like her—a bundle of nerves — — Paris is deluged again with loafers from all over the place — —'

'She paints, Pierre.'

'Of course, it's part of the equipment. *Enfin*—I may well be the one who is impossible—keep out of all that, Alberta.'

'I am out of everything.'

'Hm,' said the echo. 'What about your work?' it said. 'And Tot?'

'Oh heavens, my work! Tot is sleeping better, thank you.'

'Listen,' Pierre moved closer, and began talking so fast he scarcely paused for breath. 'Write a novel "full of action". Have you noticed the bands round the new, uncut books this autumn? "Full of action" is written on every single one of them. Not those of the advance guard—they're digging down in the subconscious, they remind me of people in the old days who came home from expeditions to unknown lands without being able to prove they had been there—those don't have much sale—no, the picked troops, the ones whose editions run into high figures. They're crying out for action, external action, that gets the characters moving so that they run round each other in circles and make scenes. Fires, houses falling down, not business houses, that's passé now, simply houses, avalanches, accidents, wild beasts. All of them are useful. Daring, memorable scenes. The main and the secondary characters must pair off once or twice, so that we know all about it and are present when it takes place; that's what they turn the pages to look for first, the publishers and the purchasers, for the same reasons.'

'This summer, Pierre—'

'This summer I expect I said a good many impractical things. Wise sayings I had stopped paying any attention to myself. This advice is better, remember it and earn money. Raise the temperature of your manuscript to boiling point, add a fire or two, don't take it too seriously, the majority of people read superficially. See to it that it's three hundred pages long. Not

174

any less, then the book will be too thin, and they want something for their money. Not any more, then it will be too expensive. There are limits to what they will pay for that sort of thing. It's just a matter of being industrious, you must never lose sight of that. Yes, Alberta, I'm talking out of sheer impotence.' Pierre leaned back in his corner and fell silent, as if the stream of talk had been cut off with a scissors.

Tired, thought Alberta. Harassed, distressed, one of his bad days.

Without any idea of where they were she looked out at autumn yellow trees in the magic light of the arc lamps, at people walking in and out of the shadows of the leaves as if between the wings of a theatre, at cars, buses, trams, feet moving, leaves falling, all of it against a backcloth of milky night mist. It was like travelling backwards in life, to places she had loved once and which could no longer command her attention. She recognized the large red gladioli round the fountain at the Rue Soufflot, glimpsed the railings of the Luxembourg Gardens behind them, lost the thread. Dark, narrow streets, a growing feeling that something decisive had happened. A thought occurred to her, it was on the tip of her tongue, but she kept silence. She was about to ask after Jeanne, but did not. As if she had done so, Pierre said, 'Jeanne is in Dijon. I suppose you know?'

'I heard she was leaving. How is she?'

'Splendid. She's with her parents. It's the best thing for her.'

'Yes, in a way—'

'In every way. Here we are.'

Alberta got out. The street was quiet, crooked, poorly lit, old. In front of her was one of the usual small restaurants: a few tables between laurels in tubs on the narrow pavement, an awning, coloured electric lights along the edge of the awning, an open door, open windows revealing an empty room where three or four men in eager conversation were putting their heads together over the remains of a meal. A waiter stood listening to them idly. Out of doors the walls were half in darkness. Pierre's hand guided her to a table where there was a view of the laurel trees and the cobblestones in the road.

An unexpected feeling of irresponsibility suddenly took charge of her, soothing anxiety, lifting gravity. 'Where are we, Pierre?'

'Oh, at a small, simple place. The waiter is a friend of mine from the trenches. I've been eating here recently, the food's good. If you'd prefer to go to d'Harcourt it's just round the corner, a couple of blocks away.'

'Of course not!'

'Good. *Good,* Alberta. Read this to me, will you? Let's have a proper meal.' Pierre pushed across the little wooden frame with the menu written in faded blue pencil and leaned his forehead on his clenched left hand. After a while he put his hand on her arm, patting it each time she came to something suitable. She heard herself speaking quietly and evenly, as if she had been reading the menu to him for years.

'We shan't get any of this, Pierre, it's too late.'

'Then we'll have something else. Are you to decide what we shall be allowed to have?'

'Of course not!'

He patted her arm a couple of times more, removed his hand and called for the *garçon,* turning his face towards the window as he did so. The light fell directly on him. Alberta was shocked. She could not help thinking of death: a man torn out of a trance who had seen death. Impulsively she put her hand on his. He took it, kept it, smiled, called once more. She heard the tramping of a wooden leg.

'*Mon vieux!*'

'*Mon vieux!*'

They slapped each other on the shoulder. Pierre was still holding her hand. Everything was magically right, safe and good. It could not last. But it was happening now. It was wrong, but they were in it together. Without really seeing him she nodded to the man with the wooden leg as if he were an old acquaintance. His brief, appraising glance fell naturally into the picture. Their table received special attention; a clean cloth was put on it, a dusty wine bottle and flowers brought out. All the sympathy that every couple, legally united or not, finds in Paris, lapped round herself and Pierre. She listened to the discussion about what they could and could not have,

176

rather as a queen might be imagined to listen to her subjects' proposals: benevolently, somewhat absent-mindedly, raised above the matter, but ready to acknowledge their good-will. The wooden leg tramped in and out. The voices at the table indoors rose and fell. Another couple arrived and sat down between the laurel trees; their faces seemed out of focus, they were deaf and blind to all else but each other. The shadow took them under its protection. Props all of it, good props, true to nature, as if on a stage.

'Pierre, is something the matter?'

'On the contrary, on the contrary.'

'The book's finished!' exclaimed Alberta. The unfortunate thought that had occurred to her just now assumed words on its own, and flew out of her mouth before she could stop it. For a brief moment it seemed to explain so much: Pierre's long absence, his fatigue and weariness, his hunger at an unaccustomed hour of the day, the fact that he took a cab. She was at once given reason to regret her rash remark. He released her hand, drummed on the table, put on his mask and his distant voice, laughed his painful, brusque laugh. 'Correctly put. The book's finished. *Finished.* You always hit the nail on the head. Listen Alberta, I thought you were one of those people who understand things without having it hammered into them verbally. I am mistaken. Time after time I am mistaken. It's just that I haven't seen you for so long.'

'It was stupid of me, Pierre.'

'It was stupid of me too. I ought not to have carried you off like this, since I cannot manage to be different. *Pardon* Alberta. You look pretty in that coat and hat. It's nice to see you in clothes that suit you.' Pierre gave Alberta's hat a little push, so that it sat more crookedly. '*Voilà.* That's how it should be worn. You haven't even got sufficient sense to put your hat on right. Never have I seen a person get in her own way to such an extent.'

'Am I to be scolded for that too? I know how it should be worn. But here you come in the pitch dark, at night, and drag me out. We only have the one lamp; you saw yourself how

177

far that reaches. I have to carry it with me all over the studio. I had to hurry. The car jolted—'

'I scold you from habit. I always feel like scolding you. Heaven help us, you were sitting out there with your damned sewing the other day. I almost took it away from you and tore it up. You look ridiculous with it. Comic. Deplorable. You can't sew. I can sew better. And yet you sit there as if bound and gagged with thread. You are in Paris, and not of it. You live as if you're in the back of beyond. Everything passes you by. You hear nothing, you see nothing, you take part in nothing. You remind me of the bricklayer's wife; yes, Alberta, the bricklayer's wife in Brittany. You are no idiot—'

'Nice of you to say so.'

'Listen.' Pierre fumbled for words, then spoke rapidly again. 'There's something I'd like to show you some time. I've thought it out. Today's Tuesday. Come with me to Montmartre when we've finished eating. Not to the foreigners' Montmartre, the Rat Mort and the Moulin Rouge. To some friends of mine. You'll see new people, hear music too, all sorts of things. I think you'd like it. Please don't mention Tot or Sivert. Liesel is with Tot. It's all arranged. I'll take her home afterwards.'

'I'm not saying a word.'

'But it's on the tip of your tongue. I know you. Tot, Sivert, washing, sewing, Tot, Sivert, washing, sewing. One could set it to music.'

'What do you want me to do, then?' exclaimed Alberta, laughing aloud for joy because she was being scolded in the old, proper way, because they were both talking at once, because Pierre was looking at her as he had done in Brittany, and on the train, because his hand was on hers; because he had said she was pretty. A message that she must get a grip on herself passed through her brain. For the image of him had been taken from her, she had been freed of it and made too light. Visible and tangible, fully materialized, he sat there, resembling and not resembling the memory she had kept of him. His mouth was mobile; it was defiant and sad and patient, sometimes smiling. Something behind the mask that

178

no cuts and scars had defeated, came out in flashes, blinding her, so that she had to look away. His scar was worse than she had remembered. There were dark flecks, that she had not noticed, in his grey-brown eyes; they were visible whenever he turned towards the window.

'Yes, what are you to do?' Pierre paused. 'What are we to do? One of us is looked after too much, and the other too little. What are you laughing at now?'

'At ourselves. We're so peculiar,' Alberta said, and knew that this was not keeping a grip on herself.

'It's good to see you laugh. Laugh more. It suits you.'

But Alberta was serious again. She must watch herself. Currents from reality had reached her. She was back in the studio, where perhaps the boy was asking for her and could not sleep, where perhaps Sivert had come home. She also heard a voice from the morning of time, distant and oracular: 'Laugh my girl, you look attractive when you laugh.' Mrs. Buck, Beda's mother. She had always made Alberta retreat into her shell, if she had dared to come out of it for a moment.

'I mustn't be late, Pierre.'

'I know you mustn't,' said Pierre, in a cadence that blocked any approach to him, releasing her hand. There she sat. It is woman's lot when she has had a child to act as a damper on man's happiness, a brake on his initiative. The one who can at all times throw off her ties and be ready for his every whim is a lantern unto his feet and a light unto his paths; not she with the sewing, beside the cradle and the cooking pots.

The wooden leg came tramping back with soup tureen, bread, plates, all of it skilfully balanced along one arm, up to the elbow. He looked searchingly from the one to the other, and then began to talk at random, as if engaged to do so. 'We ought to have gone to Berlin. That's what I've just told those fellows in there. Yes, *mon vieux* Cloquet, yes. The Boch signed the Versailles Treaty. Good. We know what that means. Signatures? Paper, *mon vieux*, paper. When it suits them they call it paper openly. No, we ought to have gone to Berlin. Or at any rate as far as the Ruhr.'

'Hold your tongue, Michaud. You talk like an old maid.

You're always so warlike—you have nothing to sacrifice. One would think you had been there. Give me more soup and hold your tongue. You can't see farther than your nose.'

Michaud shrugged his shoulders and ladled out the soup. 'Here's your soup. It's one of your bad days, I can see that. Nothing to bother about, Madame. Fine fellow, Cloquet, as I should know. Carried me in his arms like a child to the rear, when I lay there with my foot just about cut off. Under enemy fire, Madame. But he has not seen his village wiped off the face of the earth as if it had never existed. He does not have his old parents sitting on sugar crates in a house made of corrugated iron. Fine fellow, Cloquet, but he has his bad days, and he doesn't really understand all that sort of thing. One just has to pretend not to notice. Is the soup good, Madame? Sufficiently seasoned? I added a little lemon when I warmed it up, just a *soupçon*. I'm afraid it was perhaps a trifle green. The proprietor has gone to the cinema with his wife.'

'Now listen, Michaud—'

Alberta noticed Pierre's spoon lying abandoned in his plate and felt his impatience quiver in her own nerves. At the same time she saw a vision: gun smoke, whining bullets, one soldier carrying another, the scar in his face, the crooked jaw. Life's hard journey, man's toil and danger. Michaud, the average type with the ordinary face, who had come as a boy from his village, a little stunted by his early uprooting, a little narrow-chested, was no longer a nobody from out there, one of the many anonymous men with wooden legs. He was a part of Pierre's background, a necessary part that it was good to know about. She looked up at him and said, 'Delicious soup, thank you, really delicious.'

'More bread, Michaud. We're hungry. Come up one evening to the Rue Gabrielle and air your thoughts a bit. I've told you so before. Be off. Now then, Alberta, why aren't you eating?'

'But I am eating.'

'You're waving your spoon about like a child who has not learnt table manners. There, you spilt some too. *Enfin*, you're laughing. Good.'

'And you carried him, Pierre? Under enemy fire?'

'Nonsense. There wasn't a shot. They were retreating. Besides, the stretcher-bearers were coming. And he was unconscious, he knew nothing about it. He gets on my nerves with his chatter. Once he starts—'

'I feel sorry for him.'

'He's a good boy! One of the innocent pawns in the enormous game. He attached himself to me like a dog out there, God knows why. Puts many of us to shame; he manages in a way, as long as he's allowed to talk. I expect things would be better for a good many of us if we stood up and talked. We're always quarrelling, he and I. If we never stop looking backwards we shall never move from the spot. I should have kept away from here this evening, we ought to have gone somewhere else. But it's difficult to keep away from war comrades. We seek each other out as sheep seek out the flock. I found this place by accident one day as I was going past. He's kind, takes everything in good part.'

'It was the right place to go.' Alberta recklessly emptied her glass as if it contained water.

'Oh?' Pierre stared at her. 'What's that you're bringing, Michaud? Roast veal?'

'You *asked* for it, Cloquet. It's cold, but here is mayonnaise. There's the bread.'

'I *asked* for it? All right. Now look after that couple over there. They've forgotten what they came for.'

Pierre was over his ill humour. He ate and talked as if it were a long time since he had indulged in either. 'When you've shared the same trench you go on doing it, you don't float up again. You fight for years in groups and crowds, and then all of a sudden you have to sit alone at a desk and concentrate on things of the mind. It's no good, Alberta, it's no use trying. You have to go on fighting. People can't be put back like clocks. You have to find your place in the ranks. The damnable thing is that if you want to give a good account of yourself, you must first of all be self-supporting. That's why I tell you: write thus and so, earn money. I tell myself the same thing. Not to mention everything Jeanne says.' Pierre's voice became monotonous, his expression blank. 'Poor Jeanne.'

Alberta picked at the veal, got nothing down, gulped her wine carelessly instead, found nothing to say, but felt her eyes widening. Her thoughts touched on the unfortunate novel, and Pierre said suddenly, 'The novel has form too. You set people in motion who use three hundred pages to express what one normally could explain to the world in twenty. Belles lettres, as it's called. It takes a great deal of time and energy to produce it in such a way that people don't notice they're swallowing pills. If they do, it's called tendentious and it's not asked after any more, nobody reads it. If you've seen reality from the wrong side, seen how much drudgery the world is still in need of, you no longer have the patience necessary for such extraneous work. You have to attack directly. I don't know what will become of me, Alberta. I've written a few short articles; I suppose I must write in spite of everything. I'm not fit for anything else.' Pierre smiled crookedly. 'I even got a fee today.'

'Did you?' Alberta turned her head away. For the wine she had drunk so thoughtlessly suddenly inundated her brain, placing everything strangely at a distance. Pierre's voice seemed to be packed in wadding. Her own was independent of herself and had to be kept under strict control. Let Pierre talk. He needs to. He can't mention these things to Jeanne.

From an immense distance she heard him saying '. . . good to be with you, Alberta. You're quiet. You talk with your eyes, not your mouth. All these words destroy me. Why are you looking away? Are you tired? Would you prefer to go home?'

Alberta shook her head, smiled, guarded her tongue, looked away again. She felt secure, as if wrapped up and protected. Pierre wished her well. It was good that somebody did. Faces that once had sought hers gathered in the air, looking at her. They had not simply wanted to own her and take her to bed with them and have her to cook their food. One had scolded her because she did nothing, another was scolding because she did too much. Once one of them had scolded because she had said nothing, though goodness knew why; she had not quite understood and was afraid of misunderstanding. At any rate, it seemed that one should stick to the people who scolded. One of them had died. Her sorrow afterwards now seemed like an illness that she had survived. The pain had been terrible, she knew, but she could no longer remember how it had felt. And Sivert? Of course, she had been alone, that was how it was. The fate of many. Liesel's too, although she had managed to deck it up well. What Liesel had said was true: we want to love the person it happens to be. Alberta had decked it up a bit at times herself. Subjection was not always caused by love . . . mysterious things in life . . .

'. . . besides I'm a man,' said Pierre's voice. 'We men are always faithless to something. Only women are capable of being faithful. When I was supposed to be studying law I wrote novels, and now when I'm supposed to be writing novels—'

'But Pierre.' Alberta summoned up her strength. It was no longer easy to speak.

'Now don't say, but you do write. Don't say it ever again. Do you know what I did today? Now, a short while ago? I've put an end to my sewing, Alberta. I had some sewing too, it was called a manuscript. It exists no longer. Burnt up. Gone I was struggling with a pile of papers and now I've mastered them.' He gripped both her hands, gathering them into his single one.

Now we're both drunk, thought Alberta. Very drunk. Poor Pierre, he hasn't eaten properly today, that's what it is. I must hold his forehead, then he'll feel better. She freed a hand, reached his face, he caught it, pressed it against his cheek, his deep-set eyes were large and close, his mouth trembling. 'You think it was a novel, far advanced? The part I had written before was an attempt at least, a collection of persons who had begun to behave, in the innocent way people did behave at that time. As for the rest—a cock-and-bull story, pages full of disconnected type, *empty* pages. They filled out the pile well enough. It looked as if there really was something lying on the desk. I had it to hide behind. I locked it away in my suitcase when I went out and took the key with me. I shammed illness too; at least I didn't contradict them when they said I was ill. I'm not ill. I'm different. For a long time I hoped it would not be for ever, and that they were right when they said everything would improve when I had published my work. I let myself be put to sit at the desk; I sat there, I waited, I tried. One wants to, you see; one tries to settle down again. Jeanne had done so much for me, and now she believed this book meant the whole world. I should have spoken out at once— I should have said, I am not the man you think I am any more. Besides, none of us are the same, Jeanne's not the same either. The Jeanne I was in love with as a boy was not like this. The war has changed her too. It has been hell, Alberta. If only I had completed my studies or could master a proper trade.'

Pierre removed his hand, laid it flat on the table, and contemplated it. 'There are plenty of people who have to manage with one hand now,' he said.

'So unlike Sivert's,' Alberta heard her voice say in the distance. She studied his hand too, and had to make an effort to do so, frowning. She was suddenly so tired that she could scarcely hold her head up. Nevertheless everything Pierre had said was stored away clearly in her mind for later use. In a while her fatigue would overwhelm her. While she was still capable of it she must tell Pierre that she had understood, and then she would go to sleep. As loudly as she could in order to make it clear, making an effort before each word as if clearing hurdles, she said: 'I understand everything, Pierre. Everything. You could not bear the manuscript any longer, there are other things you want to do. Something to do with social— questions. It's difficult to understand, heaps of things one has to know and read.' She unexpectedly caught sight of a word which seemed to her to be deficient, but unavoidable. 'Statistics,' she said, and repeated it a couple of times. 'Statistics.'

'But Alberta?' An amazed, amused, rather touched expression had come into the face in front of her. That was what happened sometimes, men did get strange expressions, it didn't matter, it would pass. Alberta nodded seriously to the strange face. Her own sank lower and lower towards the table. Then suddenly an arm was holding it, her hat was taken off, and she was leaning on Pierre's shoulder. 'Never mind about statistics. You're drunk, *ma petite*. And I never noticed. I ought to have been looking after you. What are you bringing, Michaud? *Ananas au Kirsch*? Take it away! Give us mineral water and strong coffee. As quickly as you can, Madame is not well. Off with you.'

Alberta felt somebody stroking her head. Michaud was laughing. She was standing a short way away, laughing too. From even further off there came the voices of a man and a woman: 'Is Madame unwell, Monsieur? There is a chemist on the corner. May we help you to take her there?' 'Thank you Madame, thank you, Monsieur, it's nothing, a little fatigue, it will pass,' said Pierre from somewhere up in the air. He was holding a glass to her mouth, cold water trickled down her throat, she sank down into fog and slowly emerged from it again as if getting her head above water, and felt normal. Now Pierre was holding a cup of coffee to her mouth. 'Here you are, good and strong. It helps. You don't feel ill? No? Only drunk a bit too much? *Ma pauvre petite*. It's no good taking you out. That's right, another sip—and another! Better? Hm?'

'I'm not used to going out, Pierre. It's years since—'

'All my fault. I talk and talk and never give you a thought.' Pierre's voice was hoarse and thick with emotion. He was holding her uncomfortably, using his undamaged hand for the cup and leaning over her with it. For a moment his face was close, very close, the scar, the crooked jaw, the mobile mouth, sad now, the searching eyes, the saucers of shadow beneath the cheekbones and temples. She felt his breath, a good, healthy scent like the fields and woods in spring. Then she turned her head slightly and was free, sat upright, emptied the cup and held it out for more. 'I'm sorry. I can stand so little. It comes all of a sudden but passes quickly too. I heard everything you said, Pierre, even with my head full of wine.'

'Now I expect you want to go home?'

'What's the time? We mustn't forget about Liesel.'

'Liesel, yes. I don't like the look of Liesel these days. She seems poorly. But when we're out together for once— It's just gone half past ten.'

'I suppose you'll be leaving soon, too?' Alberta managed an even tone of voice, innocent and without overtones. Then she remembered what Jeanne had threatened, and was covered with confusion.

'Leave?' repeated Pierre dryly. 'No. The bill please, Michaud.' He rummaged in his pocket. Like most men he carried his money loose, and had to take out pamphlets and brochures before he could find it. She took out her compact, righted her hat and smoothed her hair. They seemed to be the actions of an established couple; it felt both good and bad, filling her with sweetness and giving her support. It was emphasized by Michaud's farewell: *'Au plaisir, Madame.* Now you know the way—.'

The night air lay cool against her face, sobering her completely. She and Pierre walked along together as if they had done so always, rapidly, lightly, with matching strides. The joy of walking with someone whose rhythm was the same as her own increased. She thought of Tot, and Liesel; they seemed to be standing in supplication far away. She turned her back on them. I'm staying with Pierre for a little while— just once.

'It's devilish at home in the empty apartment, Alberta. I go there as late as I can. I don't care for cafés any more either. Thank you for staying with me.' He put his arm under hers, they walked even more comfortably. He hailed a passing cab. Paris, as it is late at night, began to pass by. Pierre talked as if he had forgotten all his anxieties: '—a few soldiers from the front who stick together. They've begun to collect other comrades, play for them, read to them—a way of passing the time together to start with, a continuation of what we did out there when we had the chance. We read something or other. Now we have music as well, lectures. All of a sudden it's developed into full soirées. Soon we shan't have room for everyone. Those who have come once or twice bring others with them: wives, sweethearts, friends, people who haven't the money or the opportunity for expensive entertainment. It's at

186

Larbaud's. He and Suzanne are marvellous, they let us meet in their studio twice a week. We sit on top of each other, there's so little room. We've had an enquiry from trade union head-quarters—whether we'd care to affiliate with them. They have big evening meetings with artistic programmes, a huge orches-tra, turns by first class artistes, all free of course. There's a great deal of interest being taken in these things in artistic circles just now. We don't think we have enough to offer yet, we're not used to appearing on a stage. Though not only minor artistes and amateurs appear at our place. If we're lucky we may hear unexpectedly good turns this evening. We shan't stay long. Just so that you can get an impression.'

Pierre was talking as if he was at last being given the chance to do so. He sat leaning forward crookedly. Light from out-side fell on his face momentarily. He looked as if he were telling her about customs and habits in a land he had visited, far away. That was good, since he was not paying so much attention to Alberta, who sat well back in the corner, weak after her intoxication, dull and a little ashamed, above all unresisting. She had lost her strength; it had ebbed away from her, away from her voice and her face. Each time the light shone on her she felt defenceless, at the mercy of any-thing.

'. . . To stick together,' said Pierre. 'Share with each other. That was what we learned out there besides killing. They ought to be thankful if we manage to drop the latter habit, and if anyone fails to do so, nobody should be surprised. Your career, they say to me. Your name, they say. Your living. You have no time, they say. Once I had time to sit all night long discussing literary problems, and nobody said a word. My living? They don't pay much at my publisher's now, it's true. They can't. New little periodicals championing new things can never pay. But you can't feed a wife and child by sitting like a broody hen on an old novel that never progresses play-ing with dead dolls, struggling with old, worn-out forms that you can no longer fill, searching for conclusions to things one wrote years ago in another world. *Enfin*—I've thrown out the ballast. I'm a villain and a scoundrel. But at least I can begin

187

to look round for new truths, new ways of describing them. And then there's this wind from the east that's begun to blow. How far it will blow me I don't know. Poor Jeanne, she already sees me as a bomb-thrower and an executioner, or put up against a wall and shot. I've become malicious and have several horrid bogeymen to frighten her with: Marx and Lenin, Monatte and Monmousson. She puts her hands over her ears and flees. She has fled all the way to Dijon. Will you be afraid too, Alberta?'

'I know too little to be afraid, Pierre,' said Alberta, and it was true. She felt her eyes were large; it was her way of listening. The world widened. There it was beyond the fence, with possibilities, tasks, demands on her and on everyone mature enough to meet them. Pierre sat simplifying it for her, adjusting down to her level, perhaps a little lower than absolutely necessary. But that was her own fault. She always gave the impression of being more ignorant than she really was. As they passed the next lamp she saw that Pierre was no longer absent. Now he was looking at her.

'If I had any money I'd take up my studies again. That could give me an honest living. A lawyer can be useful. But I have no money.'

'No, money—' said Alberta, feeling her armour grow out again, her strength return. If all other barriers were to fall, this one would remain: money. She might just as well prune her emotions accordingly.

Tobacco smoke met them, hanging like mist under the glass panes in the roof, billowing above a tightly packed assembly sitting with their backs to them in rows. A deep, distinct female voice was clearing a way from the bottom of the room, reaching its goal effortlessly above all the heads, word by word. They came clearly through the quietness and the thick air. Not one of them was lost, not one jarred or struck a wrong note. They were supported by the masterly movement on which they rose and fell, gentle and penetrating. In free verse they discussed what could have made a fifteen year-old into the boy he was, lively, generous, cheerful, industrious, with

188

rich artistic and literary talent. Not the poverty and courage of his childhood alone, but the people who had gone before him: men who came home from work in the evening and perhaps felt a pathos they could not explain when the smoke from the chimney rose up thin and light against the golden sky; women who worked hard, wearing their hands red in cold water, and had no time for anything more; a little girl perhaps, who, stiff from holding a younger child on her lap, sat on the pavement in a dark street somewhere dreaming of green lawns, birds, roses, running water. All of it so that, later in time, this boy might write poetry.

> *. . . Qui sait quel trésor, comme un fruit unique*
> *Mûrit depuis toujours en tout enfant qui passe?'*

The voice changed, and became full of bitterness:

> *'Qu'importe ce trésor o mon ami*
> *Aux trafiquants du monde!*
> *Ils nous ont pris, toi, moi, nous tous,*
> *Hommes parqués, matériel humain,*
> *Comme on prendrait la menue—paille*
> *Pour nourrir un feu,*
> *Prodiguant les poignées après les poignées . . .*

There was a disturbance amongst those sitting nearest to them; room was made for Alberta and Pierre. Several people leaned forward and nodded to him, a couple of them shook him by the hand. Then they turned towards the platform again, towards the voice and the small figure up there in a blouse and skirt, the omniscient face, no longer young, the thin hands, the simply arranged hair.

'Who is she, Pierre?'

'Madame L. of the Théâtre Français. She is reading Vildrac, one of the few who has the ability to express something of what went on out there. It's about a friend who fell.'

Alberta looked about her. Seldom had she seen a more incongruous audience, never one more attentive. There was something hungry about the bent backs, the upraised chins. She recognised eyes that she had seen outside the stations

189

during the war, looking at things they scarcely dared believe. The majority were men, many of them in working clothes, pullovers with patched elbows, frayed collars without ties, here and there an empty sleeve, here and there faces more damaged than Pierre's. But a few were in their Sunday best. An elderly woman and a couple of young girls were dressed up to the nines. Squeezed in among the rest sat unimpeachable ladies and gentlemen in simple, irreproachable clothes. The voice, which for a moment had been interrupted by applause, caught her attention again.

> *Jean Ruet aussi est mort;*
> *Il avait vingt-quatre ans;*
> *C'était un gars de Saint-Ay*
> *Dans les vignes sur la Loire.*

> *Jean Ruet a été tue!*
> *Qui donc aurait pu croire*
> *que celui-là mourrait?*

Jean Ruet's brief fate was presented in verses so blunt, so apparently artless, that the effect was that of a straightforward, accurate report. Jean Ruet had been young, light-hearted, a good comrade, a clever worker; a kind brother, who, himself a dancer, had taught his little sister to dance; a cheerful fellow who took the girls by the waist and kissed them down among the vines.

> *Il était si vivant que c'était plaisir*
> *De le regarder vivre!*

> *Hélas! J'ai vu ses traits*
> *S'amincir et se fondre*
> *Pendant qui'l répétait*
> *L'adresse de sa mère.*

> *Beaucoup d'autres aussi*
> *En France, en Angleterre,*
> *En Prusse et en Bavière,*
> *En Flandre et en Russie.*

> *Beaucoup d'autres Jean Ruet*
> *Qui chantaient sur la terre*

En y plantant la vigne
Le houblon et le blé
Sans penser aux casernes.

There was a moment's silence. Then the applause broke like a storm. Alberta looked at Pierre. He nodded, his eyes blank.

Someone pushed a grand piano forward across the floor. A thin man with a great deal of hair sat down and played with long, supple fingers. And melodies began to trickle into Alberta, a tinkling procession of clear drops. She had not listened to music for a long time. It was like a call from another life. It was good and bitterly painful. She had a sob in her throat. Then she suddenly realised how desperate this music was, how full of anguish and bitterness. It made her feel like the inopportune witness to an outburst of emotion. A voice in the treble was in *extremis*, it insulted, scorned, wounded. Another followed, pleading, anxious, deprived, it too *in extremis*. At her side Pierre suddenly whispered, 'I've written to the publisher. He'll get the letter tomorrow. I've told him briefly—'

Words and music advanced together towards a threat, an imminent catastrophe. 'Yes,' said Alberta, not daring to look at him. Her heart was hammering. Someone must intervene—something tragic would occur!

And it was over. The pianist was sitting wiping his forehead. There was clapping and cries of bravo, he rose and bowed. 'What was it, Pierre? I didn't recognise it.'

'Something by Scriabin. An *étude*.'

But Alberta thought: *Etude*? It ought to be called Shriek, Shriek.

'Have you noticed the audience? They're rather out of the ordinary.'

Yes, they were. Many of these men in dungarees and patched pullovers were sitting with sheet music in their hands, writing notes in the margin, pointing out bars to each other, whispering together. Those without music moved closer and leaned over the others' shoulders. The man at the piano began

191

to play 'The Moonlight Sonata'. The first movement filled the room with heavy calm.

'Look at them,' whispered Pierre. 'Sometimes they bring the whole score with them, though goodness knows where they get them from. We have a string quartet here. They've probably finished already. Have you ever seen people listening like this?'

'No,' Alberta said. She felt lazy and backward, a person who had let everything in life pass her by.

The man at the piano rose. In a flash an eager little fellow with sheets of paper in his hand and one sleeve hanging empty was up on the platform and speaking at a tearing pace in a high-pitched voice: 'The average reader is superficial by nature, thoughtless and lazy. He soon puts down the most talented writing if it demands the slightest effort on his part . . .'

'What sort of a character is this?' 'Where did you find him? What does he want?' 'Get him down. This sounds dangerous.' 'But it's the truth!' Pierre got to his feet. 'Let's go, Alberta, it's late, and this may go on for a long time.' He pushed his way out, making gestures of recognition to right and left, leaning down to listen to whispered explanations: 'He must be allowed to continue, *mon vieux*, he has prepared it so carefully. It's about reading. What can you expect? He has reading on the brain. It's Yence, you remember Yence. He can't keep his mouth shut. He's a good fellow, and no fool. When are we going to hear you, Cloquet?'

'When I have something to say. No, not this evening. I was only looking in—Oh, Suzanne!'

A small, simply dressed person with short, smooth hair and eyes enlarged by spectacles was standing in front of them. 'Must you go, Pierre? Is this the Norwegian friend you told me about? How kind of you to come, Madame. I hope we shall see you here again. We meet again on Friday. Maurice will be sorry not to have seen you, Pierre, but I can't get hold of him now, he's sitting so close to the front. Yence? Somebody Maurice found, one of the ones from out there, as you can see. He must be allowed to have his say. It's his contribution.

He's so fond of speaking, and it does him good. *Au revoir,*
Madame, I mean it.'

'Suzanne Larbaud,' explained Pierre. 'First prize at the Con-
servatory. She's incredible, two children, a home, pupils, plays
in the quartet, plays in the Colonne orchestra, helps Larbaud
with these soirées. If he opened a menagerie Suzanne would
find a way of helping him and find room for it. She's that sort.
But he appreciates her too, they're happy.'

'She's attractive,' Alberta said. Her head was whirling; she
felt paralysed by impressions and unaccustomed fatigue.

'Hey, taxi!'

A cab again, as if they were millionaires. Pierre's face without the mask, leaning forward in the light from an arc lamp
to look at her. 'Sleepy? Not sorry you came? No? You know
all this is still trifling, just a small step, the nearest at hand for
people like myself. A way of keeping up with your comrades.
We will not be divided again into different social classes. You
know, Alberta, when men have shared all kinds of misery, as
we have . . .'

'I should like to come with you again, many times, if I
could, Pierre.'

'What about your concierge?' asked Pierre. 'Is she reliable?
Liesel ought to go to bed earlier. She ought to have been doing
so long ago.'

'Madame Morin goes to bed with the chickens. You don't
think there's anything the matter with Liesel, surely?'

'There might be. She is getting thinner. And Eliel—. They
live in their own world, he and Sivert. Gifted artists. Beyond
that they're not dependable.'

Paris rushed past. A glimpse of the hectic flood of light on
the boulevards, the deserted streets again, narrow and dark,
the Seine reflecting the lights. Pierre was talking about Jeanne.
'She can't stand all this. She wants me back in the circus again,
chasing acquaintances and prizes with my tongue out. If you
knew how many literary prizes we have in this country,
Alberta. It's terrible. A fearful method of rewarding work.
That artists and writers should allow themselves to compete!
Those who don't are always wrong, Jeanne says.'

193

Jeanne! thought Alberta. The book burnt. Jeanne left for good? No, it couldn't be true. It must be more complicated than that.

The corner of the Avenue du Maine. The car suddenly stopping. Pierre helping her out, holding her hand, thanking her for coming, still holding it. Something to the effect that if Liesel did not come within such and such a time, he would take it that she had gone home. 'Be careful in the dark when you cross the courtyard, Alberta.'

'Take something to make you sleep tonight, Pierre. Don't lie thinking about you know what.'

The sound of the bell. Alberta's voice calling 'Madame Ness'. The gate opening and slamming again. The horn of a car far away.

Nothing had happened; much had happened. Alberta's feet felt as heavy as if she had been on a route march. The gravel crunched unnaturally loudly.

Before she reached the door she saw that Sivert was home. His shadow fell for a moment on the curtain across the big window, rose to its full height, and disappeared again. Only the top of his head formed a slight curve along the window sill. He was probably sitting reading. Odd that he had not gone to bed. Her heart thudded as she walked towards the door.

'Good evening, Sivert.'

'Good evening. Well? So you've been out for an airing?'

'As you see.'

She took off her outdoor things and hung them up, then went up to the attic to see to Tot. Her heart continued to thud.

'Liesel sat here?' Sivert's tone was that of a kind cross-examiner and put Alberta immediately on her guard. Was not this the way notorious criminals were led to confess?

'Yes, she did. She was kind enough to do so.'

'It's rather late to be out,' remarked Sivert in the same tone.

'It did get late. I was with Pierre.'

'Oh, were you?'

'He hasn't left yet.'

194

'I can well imagine it. Our good Pierre is not a man of action. Poor Jeanne. The mere fact that she can't get him to meet the kind of people he should, people who could be of importance to him—'

'I know all about that, Sivert.' Alberta prepared herself for bed, coming and going in and out of the shadow in the large room, glad of its protection. She thought: If only you would leave me in peace; I don't attack you. Sivert was reading again.

Then he raised his head from the book. 'Did Liesel say nothing?'

Alberta paused in the middle of the room. Sivert's tone was no longer kind. Now he really was interrogating her; his eyes pierced her through the shadow. 'I'm asking you, did she say nothing?'

'Nothing in particular.'

Sivert slammed the book shut, putting it down so roughly on the table that Alberta involuntarily said, 'Hush, Tot!'

'Worse things can happen to Tot than being woken up.' Sivert was on his feet and was walking up and down. He stood still. 'Women! There's nothing more irresponsible than a woman of that type.'

'What are you talking about now, Sivert?' Alberta's rage was mounting. Sivert's attitude was unbearable. She looked him straight in the eye and did not look away.

'I'm saying that the next time you go out waltzing with Pierre or whoever it may be, I wish to be excused from having Liesel to sit with my boy. It would be infinitely preferable to have nobody. Liesel's lungs are diseased. If the possibility had occurred to me that—'

'The possibility was not so remote,' Alberta heard herself say. She sat down in a chair feeling her fatigue and impotence creeping over her like a flood which she could no longer stave off. It was rising, it would seize her, it was useless to struggle. What had Sivert said? And what had she meant to say herself? It had been something else.

She heard Sivert from an immense distance. His voice

reached her again. 'At last Eliel got her to a doctor the other day. The X-ray came yesterday, there's no doubt about it. And then she comes here and sits with the boy as if there were nothing the matter. Without saying a word. I thought she was at least adult. Eliel, poor fellow—'

'I suppose you pity him most?' Alberta at last found her voice. She held her head, trying to think clearly. It couldn't be true? Not like that? Liesel ill? Really ill? But we've survived everything, she and I. We may feel unwell, but we get over it.

'I do pity Eliel most. If he had not felt responsible, if he had not had so much *sense of honour* . . . This has been going on for years, and I must say he hasn't had much of a life with Liesel. Then it turns out that—God knows what he may not have caught too. She sweats at night until she's wringing wet. He has to get up, help her to change. That was what made him suspect something was wrong. He's a healthy person himself, not used to illness—'

'Stop, Sivert. You are not to talk about it like this. Not like this.' Alberta confronted Sivert and told him so to his face. She spoke so calmly that she scarcely believed it of herself. At really bad moments it was possible to behave like that. 'Now stop talking about it for tonight.'

Sivert answered by immediately turning the lamp right down. In the cold vapour that hung in the air she heard him undressing quickly and without fuss.

She fumbled her way across to the kitchen shelf, found matches, took out two sleeping powders and emptied them into a glass of water. Her heart was cold as a stone, closed and tight. Only in her brain was there flickering movement still: melodies, verses, the after-swell of words, music and wine, vibrations it was not accustomed to and could not shake off. She lighted her way up the stairs, and lay down in the high iron bedstead beside Sivert, while the heavy darkness of the veronal already began filtering upwards from the darkness within her, expunged her and became one with the night.

But in the mysterious no man's land between dark and dark she felt for a moment an arm about her neck, warm breath against her face; a man's voice, slightly hoarse as if talking to a child, asked, 'Better now? Hmm?'

*　　*　　*

It was a quiet, late autumn, mild, with pale sunshine. The flower beds in the Luxembourg Gardens were filled with the wild, hectic splendour that gives warning of frost at night: dahlias, enormous gladioli, defiant and strong with leaves like swords, Michaelmas daisies, golden rod. In amongst the yellow foliage the black outlines of the trees became daily more distinct; the summer's shade beneath them dissolved into airy, blue lattice-work. The sky above and the atmosphere about it all were disquietingly light and soft, as if the scene were painted in pastels and could be blown away. Tomorrow morning the iron hand of winter might have been there, and wrung the world dry and withered, or storm and rain might have ravaged it. Each day might be the last.

Alberta and Liesel were sitting together on a bench just as in the old days, without Tot; an unbelievable situation which even repeated itself, and had in fact done so several times. 'All to the good, as long as we can meet here,' Liesel commented. 'I know Sivert won't let me inside the door. Eliel said so.'

'He can't have meant it, Liesel,' said Alberta in embarrassment. 'Eliel must have misunderstood him.'

'He didn't misunderstand him. They pretend I'm gravely ill, both of them. They're scared to death of me. As if it were something serious. The X-ray? You can find anything on an X-ray. They say they're not at all easy to read. And when I actually feel stronger than before, more energetic . . .'

'But you must follow the doctor's orders now, Liesel.'

'I follow them as far as possible. I take medicine and strengthening things. I ought to rest, go out in the fresh air, eat well, be lazy, all the things doctors always suggest in all cases. I *am* out in the fresh air. I can't *lie* in the studio passage for hours on end. It smells of the w.c. and the sun only comes there for a short while. Besides, the whole house would notice.

197

I've set up a new still-life too, a big one. I must finish it before Eliel starts on something monumental again. He threatens to.'

'What does Eliel *say*?'

'Eliel? He wants me to go home. Where should I go?' Liesel looked up at Alberta. A hectic little red rose flamed in each cheek as she did so. 'You can imagine for yourself, Albertchen . . .'

Alberta could. To go home was impossible. The family in the cabinet-sized photograph were in Germany. Liesel would not fit in with them. *'Sie sind alle furchtbar gut, aber . . .'* She refused to go there. 'Not after all we have gone through on account of that nation, Albertchen. I am sufficiently French, sufficiently Russian. Besides, I can't throw myself on my family. It's difficult enough for them without me.'

'What about the country then, Liesel?' Alberta asked hesitantly.

'Don't mention the word sanatorium. It gives me hysterics. Those places are terrible, worse than prisons for people like us who can't pay.'

'But for a while—only until you were better. I'm sure the doctor suggested it.'

'Yes, yes of course. Hush. I told him I lived in open surroundings, with sun, fresh air and green trees. He wanted to come and see me. We shan't open the door if he does, I shall see to that. Why should I go and catch something *here*?' Liesel touched her shoulder blade. 'It's never happened to us before. We've never *caught* anything, just like that. But if only Eliel hadn't begun nagging and I hadn't gone to the doctor, it would have passed by itself. We wouldn't have known about it. If you want to be made really miserable, go to a doctor, my father always said. He didn't die of any illness, he died after a fall from a horse. At home we were never ill. We slept on a balcony in summer, we children. We heard the trees soughing when the wind blew, we could watch the stars. A big balcony, just like a room. I shall never sleep like that again.'

Liesel tilted her head back and looked up at the sky. 'Eliel doesn't sleep in the attic any more. He stays downstairs.'

'It would be better for you to sleep there. The air's fresher.'

198

'He's arranged it like that. Men always make the arrangements. They talk so much about complexes, he and Sivert. One must not have complexes. It's beginning to dawn on me that often it's simply synonymous with ordinary consideration for others. Besides, it's *his* studio. St Sulpice is striking twelve, Albertchen. You must go in ten minutes.'

'Yes, yes,' said Alberta, pretending there was time enough.

Her whole being longed for the moment when she could get up from the bench and go towards her goal, towards the moment round which all the hours of the day revolved, leading her to it and away from it. The boy was in Meudon with Sivert and the Swedish woman. Sivert had suddenly remarked one day: 'You complain that he never gets any country air and that you never get anything written. I'll take him with me. Then he'll *get* country air and you'll *get* something written.'

'I'm not complaining about anything.'

'It amounts to the same thing. It's always in the air. It will be good for him to come with me for many reasons.'

Country air was good for Tot, nobody could dispute that. With the old, familiar feeling of letting everything slip out of her hands Alberta got him ready every morning, hiding things for him in Sivert's lunch packet and painting equipment: extra stockings to change into if necessary, a jersey, the checked rubber ball, biscuits and chocolate for the afternoon, a bottle of milk, apples. Day after day most of it came home unused, and Tot said, 'Father thinks it's silly to take all that with us. Father laughs about it.'

'Does he?' replied Alberta, feeling that her obstinate nature was not entirely dead and destroyed. 'Well, you're taking it with you.'

'Auntie laughs about it.'

'Then she must laugh.'

But when Alberta sat on the edge of his bed in the evening, and Sivert was at the Dôme, she would ask him deceitful and humiliating questions. 'Tell me, is Auntie nice?'

'Father's nice,' said the boy, going on to tell her about things he had seen and heard in the course of the day, on the train and elsewhere. 'What did you do then?' 'I sat in the grass and

199

watched them painting.' One evening he said: 'Auntie painted me with the ball.'

Alberta leaned forward, just managing to brush his cheek with her mouth. 'Good night,' he said, turning his face to the wall. Her kiss met the empty air. Torn apart by warring emotions she went downstairs and dried her tears in the corner of the divan. The next morning, aching, she watched him disappear through the gate. Then she hurried to tidy up and rushed to the Luxembourg Gardens as if she had wings: to sit on a bench with Liesel; to eat with Pierre at Michaud's. We are two people and more than two: there were moments when she felt her mind to be an ill-lit battlefield, on which a struggle was raging back and forth. There were many people fighting there. One might well ask where what we call ourselves really begins and ends.

'Time to go,' Liesel said laconically.

'Come with us for once, Liesel.'

'I didn't know you were a hypocrite, Albertchen. Besides, the weather may change any day now. Even I can't arrange that for you. Sivert can't take Tot with him when the autumn rains begin, however much he wants to disgust you. For he intends to drive you out. That's how men do it. So that in desperation we take the first step, just as they lure us into carelessness when they want to catch us. That's how they free themselves of responsibility. They're terribly cunning. I believe he's miscalculated with this woman of his, but it's of no consequence. To take Tot with him on his expeditions—a dirty trick, as Potter says.'

Of no consequence? thought Alberta. No, whatever it may be, it's not of no consequence. We are bound to a wheel, he and Pierre and I. It's whirling us round. The way we stand in relation to each other when it stops one day is certainly of consequence.

With a little farewell cough Liesel departed. And it was just as painful to see her go as it had been one morning a few years ago, when she had banged on Alberta's door in the middle of the night because she could not bear to be alone, and had crept under her eiderdown, lying there like a frightened

200

little animal, tossing and turning and groaning. Eliel and Sivert were at the Bal des Quat'z Arts. They had let it be understood that they did not intend to deny themselves anything, if the opportunity chanced to offer itself.

'Lie still, Liesel. You're so restless.'

'I can't sleep.'

'Nonsense. Try.'

'Do you believe, Albertchen—do you believe he would simply . . .'

'No, I can't believe it, Liesel.' Alberta trusted Sivert. She thought it most improbable that a person who shared the good and bad things of life with another should fail her so easily in important matters.

'But if—I'm saying, if—'

'I wouldn't put up with it.'

'No, you wouldn't, would you? But then we'd have to— then it would be . . .' And Liesel wept.

In the morning she had gone home, shattered by sleeplessness, her courage barely reinforced with a cup of coffee. Sivert had not come home. She had suffered bewilderingly and indescribably, such as one only suffers for short periods in one's life; afterwards it is different. She seemed to be transfigured by anxiety and pain. In her rather aggrieved manner she continued to be only fond of Eliel, who had made it clear long ago that he attached no importance to it.

Twice Alberta turned round to watch Liesel, but Liesel did not turn. She disappeared down one of the avenues, her back thin and her shoulders sloping.

And Alberta's feet acquired wings. It was a good stretch from the Rue Vercingétorix down to Michaud's. She covered the distance twice a day, unaware of her feet until she was on the way home.

At the first turning in the little street she would see Pierre's head in the right place between the laurel trees, bent over some reading matter. She might also catch sight of a white napkin gesturing among the tables, disappearing through the door: Michaud.

Then Pierre seemed to feel she was coming; or he became

impatient. He would raise his head. And the new expression, an old one really that had reappeared, would spread across his damaged face, blotting out the traces of war. He would stuff the pamphlets in his pocket. 'Five minutes late. Women, women. Not a thought for Michaud's omelette.' And then: 'I never dare to believe you will come, Alberta, that you will come every day. I have to see you before I can believe it.'

And Alberta's defences, if she had any, would melt away. His arms were about her shoulders, his kiss on her mouth, for all the world and Michaud to see, sealing the fact that this was how it was. She was at journey's end.

The little restaurant buzzed with activity at this time of day. Students with their sweethearts, shop people from the *quartier*, the couple who had been there the first evening, and were habitués by now. The woman nodded protectively, in complicity and complete understanding: We are inside, you and I, we know about life and happiness. Michaud thumped about with only time for a greeting and for taking their order. He just managed to say, 'Ah, there you are, Madame! *Tant mieux.* I began to be afraid somebody might want your place.'

And the moment had arrived when Alberta had taken off her gloves, arranged them with her handbag on the table, righted her hair and her hat, and powdered her nose. She and Pierre sat for a while gazing into each other's eyes, silent and smiling: like other couples, like all couples when they meet.

When they spoke, they did not discuss the impossible. 'Well, everything all right?'

'All right.'

'Still free to come?'

'As long as it lasts. As long as we have this weather, I suppose.'

'Well, it doesn't harm Tot to be out of doors.'

'I don't like this woman, Pierre.'

'Nor do I. A bundle of nerves, hungry for life as they say. Although they seem to limit life to certain particular aspects. I sat listening to her once at the Dôme. She tampers with herself and her mental processes according to the latest recipe. It's the newest vice. It will bring at least as many people out

202

of balance as the church's tampering with souls, but in the opposite way. The triumphs of knowledge are one thing; all these dilettantes who immediately take advantage of them are a different matter. If only they kept to themselves, but they practise vivisection around them too. Personal problems? In nine out of ten cases the person who has found his place in society has solved them. I don't wish anyone back in the trenches, but I wish some of them could be plunged into a slum district. She's supposed to be talented. Very possible. She's not Sivert's type, at any rate, and their taking the boy with them—

'It has one advantage,' Pierre brought his eyes back from the distance; they looked directly at Alberta, full of kindness, irony, tenderness. They studied her and continued to do so. The air around her began to tremble with light. 'You really do squint.'

'I'm afraid so.'

'Afraid so? No, it's amusing, it suits you. I've often wondered what it was about your expression. Now I know. Alberta squints. But only enough to make one feel uncertain about it.'

'Here comes Michaud.'

'Let him come. Besides, I'm sitting as stiff as a ramrod. Do you know what I've been doing today, Madame? I've been sitting here working. All morning. There's always something on one's mind, as long as one casts about a bit and breathes deeply and sweeps away old rubbish. Courage suddenly returns.' Pierre brought a few folded sheets of paper half way out of his breast pocket, then thrust them back again. '*Voilà*. Your move, Madame. I shall expect to see you with some pages too. You're not an experienced gambler, however, it shows in many ways. Put the things down and be off with you, Michaud!'

'If you think I have time for gossip, *mon vieux*—! You'll have the chicken after the oemlette, won't you? I can recommend it.'

'Chicken? Are you mad?' Alberta picked up the wooden-framed menu and glanced over it. 'Stewed veal for two, and nothing else. We aren't millionaires.'

'Very well, Madame.' Michaud winked craftily. "The chicken.'

'I haven't a sou, as usual, Pierre. I don't like this. I can't let you spend so much money.'

'Don't you know how over-confident you become when you have a few lines on paper? There's no limit to what you permit yourself.'

'I know that. But I know too that—' Alberta hesitated. What did she know really? She received confirmation of some of her suspicions when they talked, that was all. 'I know nothing really. I haven't tried it out. Are you really writing something new?'

'It feels like it. We'll see. It will be—will be—well, we'll talk about it one of these days. If we're given more of this weather I shall sit here tomorrow. I feel so damned unhappy in the apartment. The people who are going to have it aren't moving in until the first.'

'No,' said Alberta. Her heart turned over, paused, then began pounding again slowly. Now they were near to all the things it was useless to talk about, which would only make them depressed and silent. She tussled with the wing of her chicken and avoided looking at him. And she was right, he said nothing for a while. When he spoke once more it seemed to be with difficulty.

'See to finishing that manuscript of yours, Alberta. It looked to me as if it was at the point when something ought to be happening. Let it expand to three hundred pages or burn it, so that new blood can flow into you. Mental thrombosis—that can kill you too. I don't know how these things are in your country. Here you can make money out of novels, at any rate to start with, but if you don't follow up with successes, you have to live on charity. But who knows? A few produce happily once a year. Then even scribbling can keep you alive.'

Now they had come to the point where Pierre used to say: You must come to terms with Sivert, assert yourself against Sivert. He said it no longer. He said. 'Sivert's making some strange moves these days. Do you never think of making any counter moves?'

204

'Think of it? I have none to make.' Alberta's heart was pounding again. 'I can't produce once a year, either. I feel it in my bones.'

'You're no gambler, as I said. But perhaps it's not easy to gamble against Sivert.'

'Eliel and Sivert!' said Pierre abruptly. For the first time Alberta detected a trace of contempt in his voice. He had referred to Eliel and Sivert frequently in the course of time, referred to them in a tolerant and quite friendly tone, admiringly too, as long as he judged them by their art. 'But then, I'm no more than a bungler myself,' he concluded. His mouth was defiant, his expression blank.

Michaud served them their coffee. Most of the people at the nearby tables had gone, the happy couple had gone, Michaud was no longer busy. He struck Pierre on the shoulder. 'Out of humour, *mon vieux*?'

'On the contrary.'

'He has his moods, Madame. He has it from out there. It's over, *mon vieux*. We knocked them out. It's not right to present such a face to Madame. It's beautiful weather. You've worked well all morning—'

'If you don't hold your tongue, Michaud, and take yourself off—'

'I am taking myself off. I know you. Don't attach any importance to it, Madame. He's like that. It doesn't mean anything.'

'Pierre snarled after him. Then he said, 'Poor devil. He means well.'

'Yes, he means well,' said Alberta. She remembered that she might be looking at the laurel trees and the cobblestones, listening to the thump of Michaud's wooden leg, getting her coffee put in front of her by his thin, worn hands—red from rinsing glasses and sticking out of sleeves that were too short—for the last time. Was there not a change in the weather, a new quality in the air? Or was it simply a cloud obscuring the sun, a shadow in the mind? She searched for words, for something to say that would chase it all away and remove the sting of Pierre's bitter remark, of the blow he had so unreasonably

205

given himself. Then he hauled a letter out of his pocket. It was from Marthe.

He unfolded it and quoted a few lines. Marthe was at a new school, a difficult transition. On the other hand she was not the kind to let herself be bullied. 'Do you think I lack affection for my child, Alberta?'

The abrupt question confused Alberta. 'But of course not.'

'She belongs so very much to her mother. I've been away so much, it shows. I miss Marthe.'

'It's only natural. You—you notice it when a child turns away from you,' said Alberta bitterly.

'Yes, there's that too. I've been annoyed with Sivert more than once, and I've told him so. You know that.'

'It's no use as long as he has these ideas.' It occurred to Alberta that ideas were weapons that Sivert had forged for himself. Behind them stood Sivert himself, obstinate, strong, difficult to understand; one day he might well seize entirely different ones. Suddenly she shuddered, got to her feet, busied herself over leaving the restaurant. The sun had left the street, which now resembled a shaft. The afternoon approached, long and tenacious. She had to go home, make purchases, prepare the dinner, see to something she had left unfinished. They would come home, he and the boy. The painful feeling of dissolution, uncertainty, false situation, would hang in the air making a dangerous undertaking of every step and every word. Her own feeling of having broken faith, of the lack of firmness and purpose in her life, would be waiting to receive her. The momentary horror at the fact that she and Sivert no longer shared their lives, the curious pity she had for him, similar to the pity one feels for people asleep, lying there at one's mercy, she would be spared none of it. Nor the vague fear. Nor the hurt in the fact that the boy lived at home suspecting nothing, that he turned away from her when she sat on the edge of his bed.

'Are you going already?'

'I feel restless, Pierre.'

'Hm. Hi, Michaud.' Pierre rummaged in his pockets for money, found none, blushed a flaming red, which quickly subsided while his expression turned blank. 'Never mind about that, *mon vieux*. I know all about it. *Ça s'arrange.*' Michaud wiped the cloth with his napkin and shook it out. 'You both have credit here.'

'I honestly forgot, *mon vieux*.'

'Your head is full of other things. One cannot remember everything.'

Alberta fought down an impulse to go up to Pierre, put her arms round him, say something. Instead she pressed Michaud's hand so hard that he looked at her in astonishment. 'But you'll be here tomorrow won't you, Madame?'

'If the weather's fine.'

'The weather? We have excellent tables indoors too. A corner, all to yourselves. If it rains I shall keep it for you.'

'Thank you, Michaud, thank you.'

She heard the thump of his wooden leg a couple of times as they left, and suddenly disliked the sound. It had something final about it, the sound of a club striking. At the corner she paused, turned her face upwards towards Pierre, closed her eyes and waited.

'Here, already? *Mon petit enfant!*'

'Kiss me, Pierre.'

He did so. At the brisk pace Alberta loved, the perfect rhythm that filled her body with joy, they walked through the small streets and the Rue de Tournon, into the Luxembourg Gardens, up into the remote, deserted path towards the Observatory, which was theirs.

'Alberta, you can tell me nothing that I don't already know and understand.'

'Nor you me.'

'All this is so wretched, so petty and stupid. I can't even offer to take you out to a meal without—. My small pension goes straight to Dijon.'

'Don't talk about it.'

'But you'll come tomorrow? We have Michaud, after all.'

'I hope I can, Pierre.'

'The concierge?'

'I daren't.'

'She looks trustworthy.'

'It's not that.'

'If something's the matter—Would Liesel—?'

'Liesel does what she can, she always has.'

'Yes, poor Liesel. I shall never forget that she let me know you were alone nowadays. You have to take the initiative, Alberta, the way things are.'

'We've had a wonderful time together, Pierre.'

'Had?'

'Kiss me, Pierre.'

Today was the first time she had asked him to kiss her, the first time she let it happen without turning her head away again at once as if she had burned herself. Kiss, and the world can collapse, all your strength melt away. Longing becomes more agonizing than ever, everything within you that recognises neither reason nor the law seizes power. Kisses are not playthings; Alberta had never understood how anyone could regard them as such. She was afraid of them, cautious as if dealing with fire. Now they were over her like a storm. She was lost in each of them and woke from each like a new person in a new world. Then something penetrated her consciousness, an ice-cold stream from reality. 'I'm mad, Pierre, we're both mad—standing here in the middle of the path—it's late.'

She was already on her way from him, her feet were moving, the distance was increasing.

He accompanied her for a few paces, still holding tightly to one finger. 'Tomorrow, Alberta? I shall not be able to bear it if you stay away.'

'As long as I'm able to, my love.'

Now her finger was free too. His quiet, concentrated face, the eyes alight, continued to accompany her as she ran uphill.

When she got home the key was in the door. She could see it from the courtyard gate. Her heart beat heavily and painfully.

Sivert was sitting at the table. The small box in which he kept money and papers was open in front of him. 'Well, so you've been out?'

'As you see.' And this time Alberta could very well have pretended that she had only been shopping, for she was carrying her purchases, but she said, 'Pierre wishes to be remembered to you. Did you come home again?'

'Had to turn back, I'd forgotten something. We're going out later. I'm expecting a carpenter.'

'A carpenter?' Alberta did not pay much attention. Something to do with frames, she supposed. She walked about, putting her things down, and went across to Tot, who was sitting on the rocking-horse in his outdoor clothes.

'So Pierre is still here? Is he still harping on those theories of his, the obliteration of the individual and so on? I mean his bolshevism.'

'I've heard nothing about the obliteration of the individual. I shouldn't have thought he would be any more obliterated by being given his share in the good things of life than he was after getting tap water and street lighting. I should have thought it would lead to new freedom, greater freedom.'

Alberta was unused to expressing opinions about such matters and listened to herself in amazement. Where had she found such words? If Sivert had not been sitting there, if he were not the person he was, probably she would never even have thought them. He developed them, as pictures are developed on plates. The plate might well have remained undeveloped.

'Pierre's theories. You're as teachable as a parrot.'

Alberta considered for a moment and was certain that she had never heard Pierre say this. Had he already led her into his way of thinking, so that she continued of her own volition? Or was it because they had both been to the bottom in different circumstances, and seen things from below? Sivert had been to the bottom too.

He was rummaging in the box, lifting out papers and putting them down. 'That's odd, I had a hundred francs in notes here yesterday. Now they've gone.'

'But that's dreadful.' Alberta sat down, thoroughly shocked. A hundred francs was a lot of money, even at the present rate of exchange. 'You must have put them somewhere else, Sivert. They can't have disappeared.'

'They have. They were in here.'

'Have you looked in—?' Alberta paused, racking her brains. There were not many places in which to look. 'Are you sure you took them out of the bank, Sivert?'

'Tot, run across to Madame Morin and ask for the hammer. She borrowed it. I may need it when the carpenter comes.'

Alberta noticed Sivert's clenched fist lying on the table beside the box. Her old anxiety gripped her strongly and without reason. There was something about his voice too. She was flooded with homesickness for Pierre, for kindness and silent understanding.

'Have you looked in your best clothes? The inside pocket?'

'Alberta.' He was standing in front of her. 'You might just as well admit it.'

Alberta stood up, as if Sivert were a wall she had noticed at the very last moment. Her thoughts whirled like lightning in her head: Be careful, don't misunderstand him. And then: You did not misunderstand.

The blood rushed to her head, then drained away. Mechanically she went over to find support in the real wall. Sivert followed her. He followed her!

'Tell me the truth, Alberta. I can see it in your face.'

'Do you realise what you're saying?' The words seemed inadequate, pale, empty, without weight. She could find no others.

'Yes, yes, yes. For your own sake let's get this over before the boy comes back. For your own sake.' Sivert spoke quietly and quickly; his eyes, much too blue, never left her face. Alberta shrank away along the wall. Even her lips felt cold and she had difficulty in speaking. Now she and Sivert were so far down that they would never be able to come up again.

'Answer me, at least. I'm saying that as long as you admit—'

'Admit what?'

'Good heavens, I know women have their little weaknesses. Liesel, for instance. I don't attach so much importance to it, in fact. But I must know where I stand. I can't allow myself

210

to be——. You must see that yourself. What have you done with the money? Is there any of it left?'

'I haven't taken your money, Sivert,' said Alberta, suddenly quite calm and resolute, to this utter stranger who was standing in front of her. 'You're mistaken. You must look again, think again.'

'I have looked and I have thought. I don't ask such questions without reason. Well, here's the boy with the hammer. Here's the carpenter too, at the gate.'

'Carpenter?'

'He's coming to look at the divans.'

Anything wrong with the divans? thought Alberta in bewilderment, on the periphery of her consciousness. She watched the carpenter from further down the street taking off his peaked cap: *'Bonjour messieu-dames'*; watched Tot, immersed in what was going on, circling round him and Sivert; watched Sivert clear away cushions and cover and turn the divan upside down: 'I want one exactly the same as this.'

Alberta had sat down again. She noticed she was sitting with her hat in her hand, and put it down mechanically on to the floor. As if from a blow on the head, she felt immense fatigue and a lack of coherence. There were empty holes in her thoughts, gaps from which she returned as if from the hereafter. In one of them she heard Sivert saying, 'If your terms are reasonable I'll take two. But in that case it must be solid work, strong legs that will stand a long journey, for instance. And first-class springs. I could have gone to the Bon Marché, after all. When can you let me have your estimate?'

A journey? What had Sivert said about Liesel? He had talked about her as well, hadn't he? His money? Two new divans? *Two*? Tot—what am I to do about Tot? Until something has been arranged? Tears began to trickle down Alberta's face. To hide them she went up into the attic and sat down on one of the beds. Her thoughts had frozen into a couple of phrases and failed to free themselves: Nothing is arranged, nothing prepared, nothing is arranged, nothing prepared . . .

Again she heard Sivert: 'A fortnight? Not before? Well,

well, as long as I can be sure of them. Leaving at once? No, in a few months' time. But I may need the divans before then. Hell and damnation—wait a moment!'

There he was coming upstairs, standing in the doorway in his shirt-sleeves and with a foot-rule in his hand. 'Are you there? I just want to make a couple of measurements up here. If you wouldn't mind moving for a minute? Thank you.' Sivert studied the ruler and made notes in his notebook, calmly and impassively.

'Are they to stand here?' asked Alberta dully.

'Here, yes.' Sivert was on his downstairs already. 'Yes, the measurements are all right. There's enough room. You can start on them as soon as you can.'

'Very good.' She heard the carpenter leaving. They discussed measurements and materials all the way to the door. The carpenter said, 'Madame,' into thin air to the invisible Alberta. 'Monsieur,' she called back, with the feeling that her voice did not carry at all. Their footsteps crunched on the gravel outside. They were still talking.

Sivert came back with the boy, who was asking questions eagerly. They clattered crockery downstairs, and Sivert lighted the primus. Alberta got up, weak at the knees, went downstairs like a sleepwalker, crossed the room and picked up her hat.

'We're just making some tea to take with the sandwiches,' explained Sivert. 'It's late, we shan't go far. Probably to the fortifications to do some sketching.'

A little later they wandered off together across the courtyard. Alberta stood back from the door, watching them go. Tot strode along on his thin legs, conscientiously carrying the bag of brushes. In the palm of the hand she was pressing against her cheek she still held the softness and the warmth of his body and his face. She had hugged him before he left as if snatching him to her, and squeezed him close, holding his head against hers for an instant. She seemed to hold vulnerability, innocence and simplicity itself in her hands. She released him, or he twisted away from her. She watched the

212

narrow back, the thin nape of the neck, the dent in it, moving away—

She had to hold on to the frame of the door to stop herself running after him. She thrust her clenched fist between her teeth so as not to scream.

'There, you see, Albertchen. He wanted to disgust you to the point of driving you out. What did I tell you? You've put up with a good deal, but you couldn't put up with this. How could you? Not somebody like yourself. Of course he hasn't lost a sou.'

'He must have done, though I can't think how it happened.'

'Have you written to Pierre?'

'I've sent a *pneumatique*.'

'He won't get it until late this evening, in the middle of the night perhaps. He's scarcely ever at home. What did you write to Sivert?'

'Oh, only a few words. "You have won, I can't stand it any longer." It's worse where Tot is concerned. Just imagine not being able to say good night to him this evening. We must come to some arrangement. I can't bring him here. Do you think Sivert has left him alone, Liesel?'

Alberta looked round her in bewilderment at the depressing little hotel room, where a single candle flickered in its holder and cast shadows up the walls.

'Sivert has got what he wanted, *voilà*. He's quite capable of leaving Tot.'

'Then I must go home at once.'

'Stay here until we've talked to somebody else. I've sent a message to Alphonsine. I sent it when I read your letter. She always has good advice, but she can't get here until tomorrow morning. Nor can Pierre. Sivert won't leave the boy the first evening, not the first. Put on your coat and we'll go out. We'll have a meal and then go to a cinema.'

'A cinema? That's the last place *you* ought to go to Liesel.'

'The air is awful in the small ones, I agree, but the price is reasonable. I go to the cinema nearly every evening. Two hours of oblivion.'

213

'You're worse than a child.'

'The last cigarette, Albertchen, the one they give the condemned prisoner. I don't expect he'd want to do without it.'

'What a way to talk. It's up to you to get well again.'

'I'm joking, I am well, the whole thing's a lot of nonsense. Sivert ought to be horse-whipped, he uses such cheap weapons. I suppose he thinks you haven't kotowed to him enough.'

'Not enough? Have I done anything else? What could I do? We have a child. You have no idea, Liesel, what it means to have a child by the wrong man. But it's my own fault. Do you think he'll leave him? Our little boy?'

'I have a very good idea. No, he won't leave him. And we must come to some agreement before you go home, come to some decision as to what you're to say. You can't stay here tonight; you'll go out of your mind.' Liesel looked about her. 'No electric light even. We lived more elegantly in the old days. What did you want to come to this hotel for?'

'I don't know. I stayed the night here once a long time ago. I had fled from a *pension* and didn't want to go where anybody might recognise me . . . You want a child by Eliel—'

'Not any more.'

'Liesel!' Alberta raised herself on her elbow and reached out her hand in remorse. Liesel took it. 'Put on your coat and come with me.'

'I haven't the money, nor have you.' Alberta thought anxiously of the miserable sum she had hurriedly obtained at the pawnbroker's for her old pieces of jewellery. They had become fewer over the years and their value had not increased with inflation, strangely enough. 'Fetch something from the nearest dairy, and we'll eat here. I believe some of the chestnut men have appeared on the corners.' She looked round for her handbag.

'I help myself to money every day from Eliel's trouser pocket. He doesn't keep count, and doesn't notice if I only take a little at a time. Don't mention chestnuts, please.'

Alberta was sitting upright, staring at Liesel.

'We can't go without,' said Liesel in passionate self-defence. 'Not without anything at all. We clean up around them if

214

nothing else, cook and darn socks and pose if necessary. We must have something in exchange. I've finished with begging, I take it. They go round with money loose in their pockets, they sit for hours at the Dôme every evening, they deny themselves nothing where they and their women friends are concerned. I do it when Eliel has gone you know where; he goes there in his bath-robe. Yes, you can stare, Albertchen. Let me tell you something. Once you've begun to degrade yourself, once you've done it really thoroughly—.' Liesel lost her breath and coughed. 'You make me talk too much.'

'My dear Liesel, I haven't said a word.'

'But you're staring at me. You can stare. If I were certain you weren't afraid of me I'd offer to stay with you tonight. There's infection everywhere; it's one's resistance that's important. Tot—'

'You're to sleep in your own bed, not in discomfort here with me. The sheets are damp too. I remember that from last time. Feel them. I have veronal with me. Now I'm coming.'

Alberta had at last found her voice. Sivert's mysterious remarks about Liesel had been glaringly and unexpectedly illuminated. She had been dazzled and confused for a moment.

'You ought to be careful. Eliel might get suspicious, he might exaggerate its importance.' She picked up her coat, which she had instinctively spread over the doubtful blanket before lying down, tidied herself up, and put an arm round Liesel's sloping shoulders. 'How I should manage without you, I don't know. Do be careful.'

'I *am* careful. If Eliel knows anything—,' Liesel frowned, '—then he knows too that I put the money back as soon as I can. The concierge at Colarossi's has the landscape I painted this summer for sale. We'll go to Baty's. There'll be nobody we know and the food is decent. It has to be if I'm to get anything down.'

'Stop thinking, Albertchen. Eat. Would you like something to drink?'

'No, thank you.' Dully Alberta looked about her at the

215

crowded restaurant. The air was thick with steam and tobacco smoke; conversation was half drowned in the hubbub of voices and the clash of crockery. Baty's must have become fashionable. It was not quiet as they had expected, but jammed with people. Alberta had wanted to leave, but Liesel had pushed her into a seat just inside the door.

Nobody they knew. But types, of the kind they had become used to seeing through the years: Mediterraneans, elderly spinsters, very young models, chic in their touching way, naïve newcomers from Scandinavia, all expectation, Americans, Americans, Americans. A new cast in an old play, that could simply be called Montparnasse, all of it presented as if through water or misty glass, heard as if through a wall. Watching, one can forget one's pain, then feel it again, like a toothache. A little thought whirred mechanically on its own somewhere inside Alberta's head: They have no children—they have no children—

Suddenly she noticed a deprecating, apologetic expression in Liesel's eyes, and then felt a slap on the shoulder. 'Alberta! Where *have* you been all this time? Here in Paris? *Comment*? And we never meet? How stupid! I must sit down. Is it true you have a child, a little boy? Are you still living alone, or—? You don't look very happy? But these things come and go, that's life. *Enfin*—you have a child. They say it brings happiness. I have an aunt and an uncle on my shoulders—the Revolution—got out of the country without a sou—Aunt's jewellery, but nothing else. My work suffers. But I've had something at the Indépendants nearly every year. One must try to keep afloat, *n'est ce pas*? Do you think I have changed much, Alberta?'

'No, of course not,' answered Alberta, bewildered by Marushka's nervous torrent of words. She looked distractedly into her ravaged, powdered little face, that was incessantly nodding and smiling to people round about.

'Duty, family, *oh là là*, I know all about that now. Though they are darlings, I'm fond of them. *Enfin*—to be frank with you, I have a friend, not young exactly, over sixty, but kind.

216

Without him I couldn't manage. I have my good days now and again, go to the Riviera, he's rheumatic. We both enjoy gambling. I always lose, but there you are. That's the place to be; there you can take a holiday from your life. You know, the sun and all that. During the war I worked in a hospital, looking after the wounded—I trained as a nurse once upon a time as a young girl, I know all about it. You came across women who were quite incompetent, who had got in through some connection and only got in the way. They were the despair of the doctors. Women always find a way of flirting—'

'I'll go and pay,' said Liesel, getting up.

Marushka put a hand on Alberta's arm. 'Just imagine your having a child. It's courageous of you, but it pays. I was unlucky too, I don't know how it happened. One is careless sometimes. *Enfin*—I found myself in that condition and had to do the same as Liesel. I took it in time, but still. Filthy business, you're never the same afterwards. But there, it's happened since then too. When you have a run of bad luck . . . That's life, one mustn't take it too seriously. Won't you come up one day? You must see my paintings. Where do you live? You must show me your boy. Potter's back. Short skirts don't suit her. But you don't look happy?'

'No, I'm not happy, Marushka.'

'*Pauvre petite.*' Marushka squeezed Alberta's hand, suddenly and surprisingly resembling her old self. 'Listen—is it money? I can see that it's money. I haven't any at the moment, but one day soon—Rue Vavin 35 *bis. Courage. Au revoir.* You can rely on me.'

'Thank you, Marushka.'

Outside Alberta collapsed into nervous sobbing, her head against Liesel's shoulder. All the way up to the Rue St Jacques she wept, asking jerkily, 'Do you think Sivert is at the Dôme—Tot alone? We must go and see, go and see. Do you think Sivert is at the Dôme—Tot alone?'

But she passively allowed Liesel to guide her, accompany her upstairs, take off her dress and shoes; swallowed obediently the two powders, lay down docile and shivering on her outspread coat with her dress over her—met two lips in the no

217

man's land between dark and dark—they were there, they were waiting for her—and fell asleep at last.

. . . Madame Morin was to be divorced. Alberta helped her with her arrangements, full of understanding for her and for Monsieur Morin, who was dead, it was true, but walked in and out all the same.

The corner grocer was there. He looked different, but it was he. Alberta and he were conversing. Then she noticed appalled that she was saying *tu* to him. He looked at her, calm, serious, sure of himself. And suddenly she felt between them that terrible complicity that can exist between a man and a woman, the physical and mental understanding that defies all reason, all laws. She felt guilty, and at the same time guiltless and in the right . . .

But the child in her arms was struggling and kicking, its mouth sought her breast, it sucked, released it, its downy head sank to one side, its eyes dulled with repleteness and sleep, she was filled with a great peace and gentleness . . .

Then one of Marushka's Hungarians from long ago said: '*Machen Sie bitte den Mund ganz dreieckig—lassen Sie sich doch ein Ei geben.*' Alberta looked down at her salad, she had no money for eggs, and hunger possessed her like a nightmare. In desperation she fled with the child in her arms, but her feet would not move. They would not move, and Sivert wanted another woman—

'Don't cry, Albertchen, don't cry.'

Liesel was bending over her, stroking her forehead. 'You were having a bad dream. You had better wake up. Have some coffee. Alphonsine is here too.'

Alberta looked up. It was day, grey, ordinary day. Bewildered and exhausted she saw Alphonsine standing dangling her lorgnette between two fingers, and for a moment could not distinguish dream from reality. It was all one. Obediently she drank from the cup Liesel held to her mouth and listened to them talking. 'Will you go to the chemist's then?'

'Yes, I'll go.'

A door slammed. Liesel had gone. Alberta returned to reality, to the cruel and difficult condition that is life. Alphonsine had sat down on the edge of the bed. 'Here, wash your face, it makes you feel fresher. I'll hold the bowl. Now we must use our time while we are alone. It's ten minutes to the nearest chemist, and she'll probably have to wait a while. Talk about friendship! She's been sitting here all night. She looks like a ghost. So you've left home, *ma pauvre petite*?'

Alphonsine had put on her lorgnette. It was her habit in decisive moments. She was wearing her big skunk collar, which made her look bourgeois, and had indeed become fatter as Liesel once had said. But her face still kept its firmness and determination. The red hair, painted mouth and green eyes still contrasted violently with her powder-white skin. Her teeth were just as strong. As if in parenthesis she took the tube of veronal from the bedside table and studied the label. 'Too strong. Knocks you senseless. Bromide, valerian, *tisane* are all right. Not this.'

'I need to be knocked senseless, Alphonsine.' Alberta was already longing for the heavy, imageless sleep she knew she had slept before the dream began, for new, profound darkness.

'We must find out what's to be done. So you've left home.'

'He insulted me,' said Alberta evasively. 'I had to get away for a bit, I couldn't stand the sight of him any more, his voice, his—his footsteps. I—I couldn't go upstairs and lie down beside him as if there was nothing the matter.'

Alphonsine looked at her omnisciently. 'You ought to have gone to bed downstairs for the time being. Well . . ! Can you remember my saying once, "Not that one"?'

'I remember.'

'I told Liesel the same. How many times has she come to me complaining, "He's in love again, somebody from his own country is here again. He's ardently in love." I've had to laugh. Herr Eliel ardent? Herr Sivert ardent? They're good artists, that's what they're ardent about. They're ardent about anything that serves their art, *tant pis* for the rest of us. In my opinion Liesel is withering away for lack of ardour, besides lack of fresh air. Men can live in a sculptor's studio, but we

219

can't for long. Now her lungs are diseased. *Enfin*—so you've left him.'

'Yes—for the time being.'

'*Ma pauvre petite*, what do you mean by the time being? That man is capable of using it against you. He has already wounded your feelings.'

'He thought I had taken money,' Alberta said, her lips stiff. Merely saying it was humiliating.

'*Le salaud*! Didn't I tell you he was up to something? I've never liked his eyes. Not honest eyes, in my opinion. You have a child, a little boy. How old is he now—five, six?'

'He'll soon be six.' Alberta suddenly remembered that it would soon be Tot's birthday. The thought plunged her into an abyss of despair.

'Six? Time flies. I've seen him once or twice of course. I lived at Morlaix for a long time, as you know. My friend lay there wounded. We're married now and live at Vanves, Rue Murillo. You must come and see us one day. Now you must go home as quickly as you can, cost what it will. I don't know the law. But children's officers and people like them never see further than the end of their noses, I know that. One hears enough. There's something called abandonment of the marital dwelling. That's serious. And if there's another woman . . .'

'There is another woman.'

Alberta was sitting bolt upright in bed. Her head was heavy as lead and she felt giddy, but one thought cut through, sharp as a knife. She flailed with her arms to get the coat off and Alphonsine out of the way. 'I couldn't bring him here. The boy, I mean. I had to think first.'

She was out on the floor, shivering, unable to find her way into the dress that Alphonsine was pulling over her head, then straightened and buttoned up. 'Fighting over children, I've seen a little of that. Here, wash your face a bit more. Have you a pocket comb? Let me help you. These small hotels—they're a disgrace. Look at the soap dish. I can scrape the dirt off it with my nail.'

'Had to have something cheap.' Alberta was looking stiffly at the door. 'Somebody may be coming.'

'Liesel ought to be back soon.'

'No, somebody else. I've sent a *pneumatique* to someone.'

'Doesn't this person know where you live?'

'Yes, of course.'

'*Eh bien,* anyone who really wants to get hold of you is sure to find you. Here's Liesel. Look, *eau de Mélisse,* a good spoonful. It will calm you.'

Alberta swallowed it. She would have swallowed anything without a notion of what it was. She stared at Liesel, who did indeed look like a ghost and whose eyes were filled with guilt and fear as if a crime had been committed.

'I'm going home, Liesel. If Pierre comes—if Pierre comes, Liesel, say I had to go home. I didn't dare to wait any longer. Greet him for me, Liesel.'

Liesel nodded, clearly prepared to wait for Pierre as long as it might be necessary. It occurred to none of them that they could leave a written message. 'Imagine our not realising,' said Liesel. 'That I could have been so thoughtless, Albertchen. But we'll never be the sort to understand this kind of thing.'

As she spoke there was a knock at the door. 'We'll wait downstairs.' Liesel drew Alphonsine with her. 'Come in,' called Alberta. Involuntarily she breathed deeply, hastily righted her hat and supported herself against the table. Help and consolation were on the way, protection too. An embrace, a kiss, a few kind words are great things. She expected no more than that.

The door was not locked. It opened slowly. Jeanne stood on the threshold. 'It is I,' she said, nodding absently at Liesel and Alphonsine as they went out.

There is nothing to be done about some things in life. It was Jeanne and nobody else. 'Sit down,' said Alberta tonelessly, feeling her features sag, their tension dissolve. She moved one of the doubtful-looking chairs. Jeanne looked at it, opened her handbag and took out a handkerchief.

'Here's a newspaper.'

'Thank you. These small hotels are dreadful. Well, here I am. Listen, Alberta, I was so nervous out there this summer.

221

So many things made me nervous. We must talk in peace and quiet.'

'Is it necessary?'

'I have the impression that it is necessary.'

'How did you know I was here?'

'Because I have read your letter. I arrived in Paris this morning, I travelled overnight. This was under the door.' Jeanne opened her handbag again and put Alberta's *pneumatique* on the table. 'Pierre has not been home since yesterday. His bed had not been touched. *Where* he has been—.' Jeanne shrugged her shoulders.

Silence. Anger and mortification struggled in Alberta to such an extent that at first she failed to express them. She opened and shut her mouth a couple of times without making a sound.

'And obviously you don't know either.' Jeanne made a gesture in the direction of the message.

'Are you so sure? People do meet. But of course he's been with friends. He finds it difficult to stand it at home.' At last Alberta had found a tone in which to talk: dry, sober, serviceable. If only she could keep it up.

Jeanne made no reply. She sat looking straight in front of her with an expression of utter fatigue. It made Alberta sorry for a moment. The feeling passed when Jeanne spoke. 'I am candid, Alberta. I go straight to the point, so that people know where they are with me. Let me tell you at once that I understand you. As a woman I understand you. You and Sivert are not happy together. Why, I don't know. I find Sivert very attractive, a good artist, a sensible person. I should have thought that it was you who were too—too complicated, too— *enfin*, it does not work. Sivert has begun to take an interest in somebody else—'

'Thank you, Jeanne, but I'm sure we shall cope with that ourselves, Sivert and I.'

'Good. Then let us consider Pierre. He finds it difficult to settle down after all he has gone through. If there is anyone in the world who understands his difficulties, it is I.'

'*Pardon,* Jeanne.' Alberta could not repress a smile and a new ring in her voice. She knew the smile was spiteful and venomous, an ugly smile to which she should not have stooped. It sat on her face like an unworthy, disfiguring mark. 'Please make haste,' she added. 'I am in a hurry.'

Jeanne was unaffected. She continued where she left off. 'No one knows better than I what is the matter with him. Do you think I like being demanding? Don't you think I too would like to ape his views, to be a companion to him in that way? I am doing my utmost to get him on an even keel again, to bring him back to where he belongs, among the top young writers. I try everything, even to the point of leaving him and telling him it's all over if he doesn't follow me and finish his book. I know what that book might be. I know the beginning let alone the part that preceded it. He did not follow me; he stayed here. He doesn't even write to me. It is your fault. And what does he see in you? You are not beautiful. Intelligent—?' Jeanne paused for a moment as if to consider the matter. 'You are probably intelligent. But in any case you are *understanding.* If there's anything men can't resist, it's that. The person who can appear at the right moment and be understanding—'

'Something in Alberta had struggled to the surface, cold and merciless. 'The book has been burned,' she said, in the same tone of voice as if she were saying, 'It's raining.'

'What?'

'I said the book has been burned. It no longer exists.'

Silence. For a second Jeanne looked as if she had been struck, but it passed quickly. 'When did he do that?' Searchingly, but without enmity, she looked at Alberta.

'The other day.'

'How do you know?'

'He told me so himself. He was relieved. It meant liberation. It stood in his way. It was dead, Jeanne, he could not put life into it again.'

'*Mon pauvre Pierre,*' said Jeanne, and all Alberta's cold wrath dissolved. She took out her handkerchief. Tears, no longer rounded or perfect, trickled down her face. Now Jeanne was ravaged by weeping.

Silence.

'Listen, Alberta, I was allowed to do what I wanted, don't you see? To marry the man I loved? He was well received by my family. While he was at the war they helped us, right up to the day when Pierre would no longer permit it. They lost practically everything. My father had put his money into a sugar refinery. In this country the whole of the sugar industry is in the north. You know how the enemy advanced. Everything was razed to the ground, the machinery destroyed. The shares are not worth much at the moment. He has his little country property, vegetables, fruit, milk. He had to cut down the big trees in the avenue and sell them—'

'I've heard about all that, Jeanne.'

'*Enfin*—they did their utmost. Am I to go to them now and say, "Pierre will not keep me, he cannot keep me. You will have to take me back again. Here is the child I had by him."? Besides—' Jeanne moved the chair next to her roughly—'Besides, after a few months, a year to be generous, he would probably want to come back to us again. A marriage is a marriage, the links are too numerous, too strong, you must not imagine—'

Jeanne paused, biting her lips. 'I cannot give Pierre his freedom for your sake. Because he cannot free himself, however much he may wish it. We have a child together.'

'My dear Jeanne.' Alberta's anger had gone. She was merely tired. And if it had been necessary to make her give way, she had already done so. Had she even gone so far as to think about all this? No, she had avoided it as if they were obstacles she dared not face. They *were* obstacles.

Jeanne continued: 'I'd like to see the two of you in a couple of years, you missing your child and he his. Or perhaps you've thought of letting Pierre support Tot too? I don't know how you have thought it out. Pierre and I had a civil marriage. I deferred to his wishes. These things make no difference to me. It would not be impossible for him to free himself, if he really wished. But I should have to insist on support,

224

to begin with at any rate. And he—in his present state, to support two children and two wives—! I look at it from the practical point of view. One of us must. I shall not mention my feelings for him.' Jeanne sobbed a dry little sob and came no further.

'All he needs in his present state is peace. Peace and quiet.' Alberta had a desperate feeling that it was imperative to say what was important, no more. To put an end to it. To get away. A little spite might do Jeanne good; it would do no harm.

'He has these new ideas on the brain. It's not so surprising for someone who has been through the war. But it's a misfortune for him. Who are these people he meets? Oh, good people, I'm sure, I'm no snob. But they're waiters, tailors and shoemenders, a few literati who have never succeeded on their own account. And before? The centre of an intelligent circle, invited all over the place. Yes, you can smile, I don't suppose you have any idea what it means to be the object of attention in a city like Paris, what chances it opens up. Well—you don't understand that sort of thing. But perhaps you do understand what it means to break up a home. The home may have its drawbacks, one may wish it were otherwise. But it belongs to the child, it protects the child. One has no right to—'

'It's quite true, Jeanne. And I had no intention—'

'Perhaps you think, she has lost him all the same. That's not so certain. Just you get out of the way and then we'll see. You're a mother yourself. You must be capable of imagining what it would mean to be left alone with a child. You ought—'

Alberta raised her hand deprecatingly. 'What do you want me to do, Jeanne?'

Jeanne pointed at the blue letter. 'Tear that up. Write another. Tell him that you—are not going to meet him again—for the time being at any rate. Keep away, in other words.'

'I haven't been running after him.'

'No, you don't follow him in the street. But there are many ways of doing it. You go with him to these meetings, you listen to him, encourage him, dine with him. I know all about it. You're doing the very opposite of what he needs. If this were to continue it would lead to misfortune for all of us. It it not far off.'

'Very well, Jeanne.'

'Here's a *pneumatique*. Here's a fountain pen.'

'Thank you.'

Alberta wrote. She wrote in a dream. The words appeared of their own volition, springing out of the paper. 'I have thought things over. We shall not meet again.' She paused for a moment, pulled herself together, and added, 'Pierre' in disproportionately large letters, which wavered in all directions. The signature, 'Alberta', on the other hand, was quite neatly written. Then she folded the letter, stuck it down, wrote the address, gave it to Jeanne and felt her spine sag.

'Thank you, Alberta. This is the best thing for us all. After a time, I'm sure that you yourself . . . Let me give you a piece of advice, stick to Sivert. He's a good man, the father of your child.'

'Is he really?'

'Don't let's part enemies. We're not enemies. We've met at an unfortunate time. If it had not been for this damned war and for all that we've been through—'

'No, of course not. None of this would have happened.'

'That's just what I think. *Au revoir*, Alberta.'

'*Adieu*, Jeanne.'

The door closed behind her. Alberta remained seated for a second, then threw herself across the bed, wept the burning, dry weeping she had experienced before, no more than a grimace. It passed rapidly. The moment to give in to it had not yet come. Quickly she collected her things and went downstairs. Liesel and Alphonsine were waiting in the dark little vestibule. They did not say much, nor did Alberta. Together they took a tram. It was raining outside, windy and autumnal.

Outside the studio she hesitated for a while, looking in through the windows which went down to head level. Sivert and the boy were sitting at the table playing Halma. They moved the pieces with concentration. For an instant Tot

226

glanced over at the window, but turned back again at once.

Alberta opened the door.

'Here's Mother,' said the boy as calmly as if she had left five minutes ago, lifting his head from the game.

'Yes, here she is, I do declare.' Sivert's voice was quite normal too, as if nothing had happened. And perhaps it had not. God knew.

'Is everything all right, Sivert?'

'As you see.'

Alberta had taken off her outdoor clothes. She stood behind the boy with her hands about his face, lifted it towards her, scrutinized it, bent down and hugged him to her. She thought: If I have to live in hell . . . Hack off a heel and cut a toe, the shoe will fit.

In a fit of feverish gaiety she sat down at the table, knocked down the pieces and began placing them upright again. 'Now you shall play with Mother. I'll get something to eat in a minute, Sivert. Look, I'm going to move this one, Tot.'

Her face was burning and she felt unwell and tousled as if she had spent a night sitting up in the train.

The boy was asleep. Sivert had not gone to the Dôme. He was wandering up and down outside with his coat collar turned up against the chill of the evening. It was drizzling and still windy. But the moment had come when matters had to be discussed.

If one gives way to fatigue, it becomes endless. It was no use giving way to it now. Alberta put on her coat and went outside as well. It was too cold to sit. She joined Sivert and they walked up and down. It was some time before Sivert spoke. Each time the light from the lamp on the pavement outside fell on him she glimpsed his face. As so often before it was impossible to draw any conclusion from it.

'It seems there are quite a few things you are unable to put up with, Alberta.'

'It's not so easy. Do you still believe I've taken your money?'

'No, it's not easy,' answered Sivert, obviously knowing a

great deal about the subject. 'But a person ought to be able to defend himself. I thought you had more pride, I must say.'

'Than what?'

'Than to come back, once you had left. As far as the money's concerned, I don't know what to believe. At any rate it's a highly singular story. I could have shown you the door today. As long as the boy was there I didn't wish to do so.'

'You do so now, then?'

'We needn't use words like that.'

'What words have you thought of using?'

Sivert did not reply immediately. They went on walking. It was dark in the studios, a faint light showed through Madame Morin's blinds. Sivert stopped, and glanced at Alberta quickly. The lamplight caught the glitter in his eyes. 'What would you say, Alberta, if I told you that I was in love with someone else?'

Alberta gave a start. These were decisive words, affecting the fate of all three of them. She felt her strange pity for Sivert for an instant. At the same time his silhouette seemed to change as he stood there: look at his shoulders, his legs, the line of his chin, his hat! Is that how he looks? Just as when she had first known him.

'You don't have to tell me that, Sivert.'

'No, no. But what have you to say?'

'I say that we must settle matters accordingly.' Alberta felt as if she were walking on quaking ground. It was impossible to tell if it would hold when she took the next step. How on earth were they to settle matters?

'Yes,' said Sivert. 'That's what I think too. It's fortunate that we're not legally married. Now we shall avoid a great deal of bother. You don't want to know who it is?'

The thought stirred coldly in Alberta: It's none of my business. She said: 'Need I ask about something I know already?'

'I've been meeting a good many people recently.'

'Then perhaps I am mistaken.'

'I don't know if you are. But it's the Swedish painter, in fact.' And Sivert embarked on an account of which Alberta did not understand the half, such a swarm of old and new

228

anxieties were creating havoc in her mind. Nevertheless, she quickly understood, as if with senses other than her hearing, that this had to come about and that it was to a great extent her own fault.

'Yes, yes, Sivert. It may well be so, Sivert.'

He gave a brief lecture on woman as mother and mistress; she was either the one or the other, seldom both. Then there were those who were neither the one nor the other.

Exhaustion drifted through her brain as black patches. Her anxieties reappeared now and again, and thoughts for which she failed to find words immediately: something to the effect that we are not divided into categories, we would like nothing better than to be both. But it takes strength and the right conditions. Not even a plant will develop all its qualities in any kind of soil. It was useless to explain this to Sivert now.

Then he said something that left her wide awake. 'You said, I love you, first.'

'Did I? It must have been at some moment—? It must have been in your arms?' Alberta searched her memory confusedly. When had she said these amazing words? And had it been so wrong? Had he not just accused her of—?

'You did. And it's a mistake. It's the man who should say that sort of thing first.'

Suddenly Alberta did not know whether to laugh or cry. 'You—you ninny!' she exclaimed in despair. It was a word Sivert had taught her. At home they said booby.

'Another expression I shall not forget,' announced Sivert. 'I shall remember that word, you may rest assured.'

But Alberta repeated the word and made matters worse by saying nincompoop. And she left him to prepare herself for the night with clenched teeth. When Sivert came in a little while later she was already in bed, knowing that she had not improved her position in any way. There would be much to negotiate.

Sivert's breathing was as regular as clockwork. Alberta could not sleep. One can be so tired that no powder will help, not even two. Delivered, delivered, delivered, delivered, said

229

her heart, punching out the seconds. Tot tossed restlessly in his sleep as if life itself was too burdensome for him.

The first to say I love you? Yes, there had been times when she had believed Sivert to be different from the man he was. The misleading moment of engulfment. It must have been then.

Sivert did not say such things. 'Hh, Hh,' said Sivert, keeping his words under control—unless he had finally brought himself to say them now. Alberta smiled maliciously at the thought. He would be incapable of it.

She remembered that she had become effusive at times. Perhaps someone who had kept silent for much of her life does so easily. It must be true that it was dangerous to keep silent, as Frederick Lossius had said one summer at home. It did not do to be effusive. It irritated people. They would have none of it. Not Sivert.

There had also been moments when his name had paused on her lips and refused to be spoken, because she really ought to have been saying another name. God knows which of all the names in the world? And moments when she had had the feeling that she had approached something strong and good-natured in the belief that it was not dangerous. Then either its paws or its jaws had engulfed her, and there she was, trapped.

He was right. One came to men like Sivert of one's own accord, once one had laid a hand on the back of his neck. They were charged with the patient waiting of generations for what finally comes of its own accord. They keep to the letter, and have done so for thousands of years.

What had she felt for him? Gratitude because he had broken into her loneliness? Yes, mainly that. Sympathy? Sivert had been alone too. The lunatic feeling of ownership for what one finds it difficult to do without? The feeling the animal has for its master? A brief period of infrequent moments, a hectic blaze of body and mind, a wave of passion which had more to do with the two strong arms round her in the darkness, the mysterious proximity of another living being, than Sivert himself.

230

And yet—as her antipathy had thawed there had come a blind faith, an unconditional surrender in those strong arms. When she had struggled incompetently to produce meals, clumsily and arduously patched and darned, sewn her unsuccessful creations, fought with dust and fleas, it had been for Tot's sake and out of fear; but also out of tenderness. In order finally to experience a little tenderness.

Anything that she had got out of it had really come from her own hungering blood, her indomitable determination to experience happiness.

Why had they stayed together? In the first place because they had to. There had been no other way out, though Sivert seemed to have found one now. In the second place out of the urge to create continuity, to complete what has been begun; out of egoism, fear of loneliness, a desire to share one's life with whoever it turns out to be. If he does not answer to one's original ideas, one makes a fantasy picture and glues it on to the outside. It will serve for a while.

Supposing the war had not come? It was useless to contemplate. Who can tell how things would have turned out if everything had been different?

Alberta sat bolt upright in bed. One thing had struck her with fearful clarity: Sivert had not abandoned her when she was pregnant. He had not acquired anything so burdensome as a bad conscience. He had plodded on with his burden. But one must not demand more than patience in such cases, it seemed. Sivert had been patient. Sivert had done his duty. The fault was hers, for not having found herself a livelihood. There was the hitch, there the stumbling-block. She was the debtor. She lay down exhausted and dared not think further in any direction.

The following evening Sivert prepared to go to the Dôme. Alberta threw on her coat and went with him outside. 'There's one thing we must discuss, Sivert, the sooner the better.'

'Well, what is it?'

And Alberta got it out, the most difficult, the most burning of all questions. 'Have you thought about us?'

231

'About you?'

'Yes, Tot and me? What arrangements are we to make?'

'Of course I have.'

'Yes, and—?'

'I shall have to take the boy.'

'You?'

'Yes, I. I can support him. You ought to be quite glad to be free, so that you can finally devote yourself to what you want to do. Besides, after what has happened— You simply left. If you had any rights, you lost them then.

'You're not really a mother in that sense of the word,' continued Sivert, when Alberta failed to respond.

'You and she?' she said at last, quietly, as if to clarify the matter. 'Have you gone mad, Sivert?' she got out finally, very loudly.

'Mad? No, I'm certainly not mad.'

'I believe you must be.'

'You believe, you believe. I've given up trying to make you see reason, Alberta. During the first years I thought— But that's not the question now. The question is solely the welfare of the boy. He'll have a wise person for stepmother.'

'Stepmother?'

'Stepmother. Can you find another word for it? A wise person, who will know how to bring him up, how to make a man of him. What do you give him? Spoiling and nonsense. Have you ever been *fond* of him, when it comes to the point? You've constantly had something to find fault with. All that talk about mother love is a bit of a fable, I suppose. A stranger may often be just as suitable. You will be given the opportunity to see him, in so far as it's possible. I don't intend to leave you without support. We shall be reasonably comfortable. But of course I don't know what you will decide to do . . .'

All Alberta could feel was a desire to hit Sivert, hit him in the face. At the same time she knew that if there was one thing she must not resort to, it was this. And she knew why she had been afraid of Sivert. This was why. They were standing at the decisive point in their lives. Something had been spinning in secret. Now it was a completed, dangerous web with threads

232

stretching forwards and backwards in time; it was impossible to see the beginning or the end of it. She went across to the wall, to support herself against it.

Fond of her child? She was knotted with anxiety for him; with distress because he was as he was and not different; with anguish in advance on his behalf; with longing for him.

'We must be reasonable,' Sivert said. 'We must think of the boy first. I'm thinking of you as well. You must admit that with your attitude to life this will be the best solution. There's nothing to quarrel about. I have my work, I can support him, not you, not at the moment, at any rate. Legally my right to him is clear. Well, I must go now.' Sivert took out his watch and looked at it in the light from the lamp. 'Besides, did you want a child?'

'I'd have been an idiot to want one, placed as we were. Did you want a child?'

'No. A man doesn't want children as a woman does. But I did my duty towards him. I've supported him for almost six years—'

'Be quiet, Sivert, with your support.'

'There we go again. It's impossible to talk to you. I repeat, I have done my utmost, always my utmost, I have done all that a man *can* do. As for you, were you even capable of dealing with the situation when he came into the world? Most women manage that. But didn't I have to work like a maid? I lost eight pounds. I have never referred to it, but I did. I won't mention my work. Besides, I've provided myself with a book on the law, I know what I'm talking about.'

Alberta stared at him, petrified. Then she heard herself speaking, quietly, coldly, maliciously. 'I don't know how many pounds I lost. I didn't go and weigh myself. But—' And she went over and hit Sivert in the face. Now she had done it. Foolish or not, it was unavoidable.

Sivert flinched slightly. Then his face came into the lamplight, strangely thin at the tip of his nose. His mouth was a line, his eyes seemed nailed in his head by two contracted pupils in porcelain blue irises. The mask dissolved into cold laughter.

Alberta froze. This was Sivert's rage. And his rage was as assured as everything else about him, stubborn, persistent, unlikely to diminish when first awakened. 'We've thought of going home,' he said abruptly and matter-of-factly. 'In the early spring. We may go to Sweden for a couple of years. Now you know where you stand.'

He turned on his heel and left. The gate slammed behind him.

Had she wanted a child? No, she had been afraid, she had not wanted it to happen. Gusts of fear had passed through her when she realised she was pregnant, the fear of being tied, the fear that she might not survive. She knew she would never be able to take it lightly. And besides—take it lightly, in her position? The child would not have survived.

Only one fear had been greater, that of destroying her body, her healthy body which, unharmed, had borne cold and other deprivations and seen her through many situations. Pride and instinct asserted themselves violently. It was not for nothing that she had seen Liesel lying humiliated and destroyed, weeping and bitter.

What had happened? She had been searching for herself. Then the child was suddenly there, and everything in her had fought against it. Could the boy somehow have known, in his mother's womb? But he had smiled at her when he was old enough, and held her tightly in the evening before he went to sleep. With increased longing she remembered how, when he was a little older, he had woken up to be put on the pot. He had thrown his arms round her neck wanting to sleep there, a gesture of ownership as clear as noonday; a gesture too of unscrupulous confidence that had made her feel confident herself. She had arrived at something important in life, and she had arrived there unawares, as we so often do.

There had come a time when she had been opposed, stubbornly and silently. She had not understood what was happening; it had merely been in the air, disquieting and unpleasant. Now she understood. Now she understood a great deal, with stinging, ice-cold clarity. Is there anything a man is incapable of doing? He can take the child out of the womb, physically and psychologically, born or unborn. His is the power.

She had had her way once. Since then it had been understood that beyond this she could not reasonably make any claims.

On the other hand Sivert had bought this and bought that; he had not gained much joy from it all. She wept under the blanket for Sivert and herself. When her thoughts came to Tot she had to stop herself screaming. They went in circles. Somewhere outside the circle, in another orbit, so distant that he could no longer be seen clearly, was Pierre. He was like a dead man, someone whose existence is uncertain, whom one can only miss. She found herself clinging to her pillow, thrusting her head down into it as if it were alive, and capable of giving her protection and warmth.

Some days passed, unpleasant, unreal days, torturing passages between harbours of heavy, artificial sleep. It rained and blew. Tot stayed indoors, Sivert was home some of the time too. Alberta felt as if she were at a railway station. The train would be leaving soon; it was no use embarking on anything. Sivert spoke to her in an ordinary tone of voice about ordinary things and as little as possible, as if at a departure, when all the good-byes have been said and an awkward void has to be filled.

If she took the boy out they only wandered about the streets. Feverishly she talked to him, feverishly she found things to do when they were at home, taking out games in a display of gaiety which she felt she owed him: clumsy instalments on a sum of joy which she had not kept up to date, had been piling up, and could never be paid off. He watched her in astonishment. Sivert's irony hung in the air, but he did not interfere. Every time he came home her heart stood still. If something were to happen she would offer physical resistance, cling to Tot, scream, call to Madame Morin for help, hide in her apartment with the boy. They would have to knock down the door and kill her before they could take the child. She looked at the thin little figure, the strange little face, the dent in the back of his neck, and knew that nothing was of the slightest importance compared with giving him up. Somewhere on the periphery of her consciousness she had vague notions of looking for help, of going to the authorities and putting her case before them. A mountain of money and paper rose up at the very thought, overwhelming her. The idea of going to strangers with all this was also overwhelming.

If she could have known for certain when she would be alone she would have sent a cry for help to Alphonsine. Soon it would be the boy's birthday . . .

One afternoon, when Sivert had said he was going to sketching class and returned home half an hour later, Alberta's heart stopped dead. When he sent Tot across to Madame Morin it pounded in fear. She felt her legs disappear from beneath her. Then she suddenly felt a savage, furious strength, a desperation. She waited.

Sivert paced the floor, paused, resumed his pacing. Alberta held her breath. As if in a trance she repeated to herself: Keep calm, keep calm. As soon as the first words are spoken you will be stronger. Keep calm. She gripped the table, under the leaf.

'The devil take me if women aren't completely lacking in pride,' said Sivert.

'I suppose it varies?' Alberta could hear the hesitation in her voice. What was he getting at?

'I'm damned if it does.'

Silence.

'She's a mystery,' stated Sivert.

'Really? A mystery?'

'A complete mystery. Here we've—here I've—here I finally come and suggest that we get everything settled, so that we can make our arrangements. A man ought to be able to insist on that. She looks at me and she says, "But my dear Sivert, we've had a wonderful time together, we've been such good friends. It's been really beautiful occasionally, you know I think that. I've been very happy during the time we've spent together, but to go on for ever—!" Sivert threw his hands out in a wide gesture. 'Now it's one of the others, of course, that's

236

what it is. *Women!*' He said the word as if conjuring up the devil himself.

And he made to leave, seizing his hat.

'Are you going out?' Alberta fought against an overwhelming exhaustion that made each word an effort.

'I must go and cancel the divans. What else can I do?' Only Sivert could have said such a thing so simply and straightforwardly. He was already out of the door.

Alberta looked about her. It was all more than familiar, yet she seemed to be seeing it for the first time. Look, there's the stove, an unparalleled luxury once upon a time. There it stood, unchanged in its outward appearance, a little rusty here and there. She must get hold of some blacklead, they would have to start the heating again soon.

She bent forward over the table; she whispered, 'If only everything were different.'

The boy entered in his quiet way. Sivert came back. 'What about your leaving, then, Sivert?' She wondered why she said it. Out of malice, perhaps.

'I shan't change my plans. I shall go home in the spring. With Tot. You must do as you please.'

* * *

It was the end of April, mild and still. The twilight was falling, dark with rain. Moist, blue-grey cloud hung in broad, loose layers above the hills, which looked as if they were merely a continuation of the sky. In front of the hills were bare, violet-brown trees, broken here and there by dark firs; in the foreground ploughed land and withered meadows just starting to green, ruts, lanes, one or two houses, stone walls.

It was a mild landscape, without contrasts. A broken-down barn fell in with it as if it had grown up out of the soil. The air was bland, tasting of vegetation, steaming earth and burning undergrowth. Smoke rose up, collected horizontally, lay floating on the breeze or dissolved into formless masses that displaced all outlines. Bonfires, tended by children, were bright in the dusk. There was quiet birdsong from the hedges

237

and the undergrowth alongside the road. The murmur of hidden streams could be heard continually.

Since leaving the town they had followed the same road, edged with stone markers. It went slowly uphill towards the wood. Alberta was sitting up in front with the grey-bearded man who was Sivert's father. He did not look at her, but asked questions and gave answers to the air about him. With some difficulty and strain they exchanged remarks about the journey and the weather. At the back of the cart with the suitcases, the crate of paintings and the rocking horse, sat Sivert with Tot on his knee. Tot was asleep.

Sivert was doing most of the talking. 'Well, would you believe it,' he exclaimed. 'If the Evensens haven't built a glass veranda! And what's that at the side of the house? Surely it's not—?'

'I expect that's the garage,' said old Ness soberly. He shook the reins out of habit. The fallow horse quickened its pace for a moment and then resumed its jog-trot.

'Oh, so he's bought himself a car as well? Whaling certainly pays.'

'He's worth eighty thousand kroner now.'

'Is that so? Is that really so? Well, well. And what's that we can see above the trees? The new chapel? But it looks as if it's finished?'

'It is, more or less. The women have collected most of the money. Now they want an organ. And then the altar hangings. That's what they're busy doing now, Mother and Otilie, getting in money for that too.'

Sivert could well imagine it. Yes indeed, it was to the credit of the women of the village. But what about the altar-piece? Had they got that? Sivert thought an altar-piece was surely the most pressing task.

'Ho, ho, ho, ho,' cackled the old man. 'Yes, I'm sure you think so, master painter that you are. You can ask them, apply through the proper channels, as they say. I can't give you better advice.'

Well, Sivert did not consider the matter to be entirely out of the question. An attractive altar-piece, some well-chosen

238

motif. There was no need to choose the Resurrection, it had become too ordinary, so had the Crucifixion. But the Annunciation, for instance? Or Mary's visit to Elizabeth? The price would have to be fixed remember that it was all in a good cause.

Female models, hammered Alberta's brain. Female models.

She felt dazed and light-headed after the nights in third class carriages and another on deck between Sassnitz and Trelleborg. Sivert had insisted on travelling via Berlin. He had inspected it indefatigably for several hours, right up to the last minute, while Alberta, crushed by exhaustion, lay on a hotel bed with Tot beside her, occasionally glancing up at a red flowered wallpaper and the Kaiser and his Empress framed to their knees, undisturbed by defeat and revolution.

A little sad and heart-sick she sat watching with astonishment the cold northern landscape which takes so long to unfurl into spring coming to meet her, surround her, disappear behind her. This was Norway. An unfamiliar Norway, yet at the same time surprisingly familiar, as if she had seen it long ago or in a dream. The small, round, yellow horse with its black mane and crupper askew, the apron which old Ness had so carefully buckled round her, the air, the colours, the stone markers, it was homelike and it was foreign, different from the glimpse she had once had of the south coast at Grimstad. Nevertheless it was like driving back into early childhood, experiencing afresh something old and forgotten to which she had been disloyal. As recently as in the railway compartment that afternoon she had felt as if she were only passing through, and sat full of sad recognition. Now, in the open cart out under the sky, she felt defenceless, forced to answer for herself, someone who had really forfeited her right to be here and yet came and insisted on it.

She should have belonged to this country. She did not do so. All the time she was here she would carry with her the smart in her breast, a kind of painful tenderness she could not take into consideration, could not bother about. She was doomed to long to get away again. That was her nature. That was the nature of life.

'Do you feel cold, Alberta?'

'No, of course not.' Alberta drew her coat up round her throat, realising as she did so that she was freezing. But it had been kind of Sivert to ask.

It was almost dark. They were driving alongside a fir hedge, naked and plucked at the bottom, overgrown and far too thick at the top. Alberta could not help thinking that one would have to search for anything more depressing than such a hedge, and that it had better not be here. Suddenly they swung in through an opening. 'Well, here we are,' said Sivert. Alberta remembered that the place was called Granli after the firs, and shivered more than ever.

From an old photograph in Sivert's pocket book she recognised the white house with its veranda and gables and the contours of the two women who were coming down the steps to meet them. The kerchief of the one and the apron of the other gleamed white through the dusk.

Day by day it slowly became greener round the black circles in which the fruit trees stood. Day and night there was the smell of burning undergrowth, that smell which had caught up with her year after year and was the same everywhere, on walks in the mountains at home up north, on the outskirts of Paris, in the garden of a farm down by the fjord. Once it had been a joyous sign of spring, intoxicating, liberating; now it had acquired a tinge of admonition and reckoning, surprising her in the wrong places and in the wrong circumstances, filling her mind with irritating unrest: How far have you come since last year? What business have you here? It was carried up from the garden, where Alberta and Otilie constantly had a small fire going; or it came drifting from somewhere else.

When twilight fell, tartly cool, bordering on frost, other fires showed bright in other gardens and out in the fields. Tranquil blue columns of smoke rose from them. Two lines of verse freed themselves from the chaos of memory and pursued Alberta with the persistence of music: 'The land stood dressed in bud, fragrance flowed from the leaf, Abel's thank-offering rose to the sky.' The transparent Norwegian spring with its strong scent of growth and burning was in them, as blood is in the body. Who wrote them? Björnson.

One morning it was raining, a silent, mysterious rain, full of promise, that had begun in the night and continued hour after hour. The earth greened intensely and magically fast, so fast one could watch it, round the beds in the garden; a garden which was far too cut up by its narrow, curving paths, where no one ever seemed to set foot except when they had to be levelled once a year. Meaty and red, naked and immodest, the rhubarb suddenly shot up out of the dark soil. The gooseberry bushes bristled with a pale mist of countless minute buds along the branches. When the weather cleared towards evening a chuffing sound came up from the invisible fjord, and old Ness took the pipe out of the corner of his mouth and nodded wisely. 'The first motor boat this year. Wonder if it's Even-sens'?'

Alberta was exhausted and bewildered by spring. It was the second she had experienced within a short period of time. It had been over where they had come from. There it had been summer.

'I hope you're going to call me Mother.'

The clear, pale eyes were deep-set in the old woman's thin face under the kerchief, which kept slipping backwards and had to be retied. Cheerful and frank, but searching too, they looked at Alberta. 'It would be a pity if you didn't call me Mother.'

She put her hand on Alberta's and dropped her voice. 'What do you feel about sharing Otilie's room? She's kind, Otilie, not a scrap of badness in her. But she is *odd,* you know. She is *odd.* I wanted you to have the room to yourselves, you and Sivert and the boy. Then the rest of us could have slept downstairs. But no, she would have none of it. She's not married, that's the trouble. She doesn't understand. She can't understand. And perhaps it won't be for so very long, so we let her

241

arrange it as she wanted. So that there should be no *bad feeling*. She thinks it's grand to have you up there in her room, you see.'

The dry, rough hand, so worn with age and work that the veins lay above it unprotected like roots on a forest path, shyly patted Alberta's, then suddenly withdrew, afraid of having dared to go too far. 'The time will soon pass, you'll see. If Sivert gets this bequest he's applied for I suppose you'll all be off again. And that's right and proper. Married folk must be on their own, not hanging about the old folk. I still understand that, old as I am. But you did us a kindness to come home while Father and I were still alive; and it would please us to see you happy the little while we have you.'

'Of course we're happy,' managed Alberta. She also managed the strange, very difficult word, 'Mother', and found the hand that had withdrawn. She smiled. 'I'm glad you asked me here and that I've come to know you,' she brought out. But that was all. Her lips closed tight.

She would have given much to be able to be truly honest in such moments, to be the simple, reliable person whom everyone finds straightforward; a person who, from the moment she had joined forces with him and to the end of her days, was securely and inevitably fond of Sivert.

'You come to me, if there's anything wrong,' said Sivert's mother softly, giving Alberta a little nudge. 'Come to me. And you know it would please Father if you were to *call* him Father.'

Alberta promised. And that obstacle was out of the way. But there were many more. God knew how it would go with them?

They were sitting on the kitchen steps, Old Fru Ness and Alberta. It had come about that they sat there together now and again, almost surreptitiously, even though they were visible from all directions. They did so when Otilie had gone down to the store, or down to the quay, or to town, and Alberta had avoided going with her.

If there were time, Fru Ness would bring out something to eat: jam and biscuits, glasses of cream that had been put

242

aside for Alberta and Tot. The sun was warm at midday, shining directly down on them. Sivert's mother talked about her life, her marriage. From the time when, as an eighteen-yearold serving maid in the town, she had met Sivert's father, she had lived through everything in the unshaken certainty that he, who had first of all gone to sea as a carpenter for many years and then put all his savings into the farm, was the person whom she should accompany and to whom she should accommodate herself in matters large and small.

Over by the steps of the wooden storehouse, where the grindstone stood, Tot was busy. He had established himself, with the box full of objects he had collected, in a safe spot under the stairs. From there it was only a few steps across to the stable where the rocking horse stood in its stall beside Blakken, as was only right and proper. There he waited for the exciting moment when something had to be sharpened and the stone began to turn. He had begun to come over to them of his own accord when he saw there was something to be gained by it; he no longer had to be fetched and forced or persuaded to come. Sometimes he would stand watching Fru Ness and Alberta with his profoundly blue eyes; sometimes he would look round at all these new things and say to himself, in French: 'It's Norway.'

'Yes, it's Norway.' Alberta spoke only Norwegian now, and the boy understood it or should have been able to. But he seemed to be half-heartedly protesting against it all by keeping to the foreign language. 'We shall be friends,' said old Fru Ness. 'We shall be good friends, as soon as he settles down. I must say I think he's thin, Alberta, though he has put on weight. I was frightened the first evening, he looked so poorly compared to what we're used to here. But I expect he was thoroughly tired after the journey, as you said. I'm wondering what we shall do with him when school begins in the autumn. If you're here then, of course.'

'We must put his name down,' Alberta said.

'You must talk to Sivert. He will have to decide. If you're leaving again soon, then—'

'But he must go to school, wherever we are. He must start—'

243

'You talk to Sivert. He knows best how it should be.'

'Yes,' answered Alberta tamely, but without rebellion. There was something disarming about Sivert's mother. She preached the doctrine according to which she lived, no more and no less.

Alberta was sharing Otilie's room. They were up in the north gable, in a large room with two brown-painted beds, a wash-stand, Otilie's chest of drawers with a mirror above it, and a table in front of the window. The air, which never felt the sun, hung full of a sweet, enclosed smell impossible to disperse. It was supposed to be a temporary arrangement. Part of the house was being rebuilt with an eye to summer visitors, and the south gable was uninhabitable for this reason. Sivert was sleeping on the sofa in the sitting-room and had put up a camp bed down there for Tot. Out of doors the brittle spring continued, slightly more advanced, but still tinkling with last night's ice.

The very first evening Alberta had felt suffocated. There are many kinds of nakedness: Otilie's was the unhealthy kind, un-aired and distasteful, never completely unclothed. When she took off her dress and stood there in her old-fashioned corset, with ugly, bare arms which were too thick at the top and wrinkled at the elbows, and assumed a different expression from her usual one, she seemed to Alberta to be an outrage against all modesty, something impure from which she would have liked to turn away, but which she was forced to look at; let alone when Otilie washed herself in the morning, with her clothes turned down to her waist.

Her washstand was crowded with half empty medicine bottles, old pots of ointment, and vaseline. There was a greasi-ness and dustiness about them that permeated the air. That un-pleasant smell one often associates with elderly, rather fat women, accompanied Otilie and all her belongings. If Alberta was forced to undress or dress in her presence, she did so with cunning. She slipped quickly in and out of her clothes as if attempting to vanish. The simple, natural action of splashing water over herself, upright and unclothed, was impermissible up here in this room; it had to be filched briefly and in bits and pieces. Gritting her teeth, Alberta defended her body so that Otilie should not get a glimpse of it.

The Bible lay on the table beneath the window. It had the funereal trappings of the Lutheran Bible Society, a coal black cover, with a cross on it, its mere appearance evoking images of graves, crumbling bones, the corner of the churchyard at home where withered flowers lay rotting in a heap. When old Ness brought out his downstairs in the sitting-room and leafed through it with coarse, careful fingers to find a text, the impact was quite different. But when Otilie sat by the window, which was hermetically sealed against the evening twilight, in grey felt slippers, a shawl over her bedjacket, muttering as she read, turning the pages and sighing over text after text, Alberta crept under the eiderdown so as not to die of mental and physical nausea.

She told herself that Otilie could not help it, that life had made her as she was, that she ought to be sorry for her, and that their stay here would not last for ever. Once again, here was one of those tracts in life that had to be traversed holding one's breath and shutting one's eyes. Time after time she had run into them and coped with them by going at half-speed, sometimes switching to another track and steaming away along that. The days might encircle her like a vice. Then the only thing to do was to keep calm, not lose her head and make everything worse by ill-considered action. Tot slept with Sivert downstairs and was dressed and undressed by him. Tot got air through an open window. That was a big thing, the most important of all.

'Hew down the tree, and cut off his branches . . . nevertheless leave the stump of his roots in the earth, even with a band of iron and brass, in the tender grass of the field; and let it be wet with the dew of heaven, and let his portion be with the beasts in the grass of the earth . . . and let seven times pass over him. They shall drive thee from men, and thy dwelling shall be with the beasts of the field, and they shall make thee to eat grass as oxen, and they shall wet thee with the dew of heaven, and seven times shall pass over thee, till thou know that the most High ruleth in the kingdom of men, and giveth it to whomsoever he will.

'And whereas they commanded to leave the stump of the tree roots; thy kingdom shall be sure unto thee, after that thou shalt have known that the heavens do rule.

'Let not mercy and truth forsake thee: bind them about thy neck; write them upon the table of thine heart.

'Our Father, Which art in heaven . . .'

Alberta's thoughts were suddenly released from the mumbling, monotonous voice, and were again on their own somewhere, half overcome by sleep: Thy kingdom shall be sure unto thee, after that thou shalt have known that the heavens do rule . . . Let not mercy and truth forsake thee: bind them about thy neck; write them upon the table of thine heart . . .

This was what men had had to impose on one another. There was nothing inevitable about life. Thy kingdom shall be sure unto thee, after that thou shalt have known that . . . thy kingdom shall be sure unto thee . . .

Outside an enormous soughing passed through the wood. The wind was rising, fresh and free. Seven times have passed over me, she thought. And seven times seven . . .

An old man with a white beard and spectacles, dressed in a grey habit, staff in hand. He put down his staff and spectacles. Kindly and calmly, but with decision, he took a pen and writing materials from Alberta and put them to one side on a desk. 'There, there,' he said, in a voice like a schoolmaster's.

'Who are you?' asked Alberta dispiritedly.

'I am Time,' answered the man. He picked up his staff and spectacles, and left slowly, unhurriedly . . .

A fearful emptiness spread in and around her. It had all gone, the desk with the things on it, the old man. She was alone in the universe, dispossessed of a good of which she had no understanding.

It was irrevocable. It could not be put right again.

* * *

'Some people use unbleached material for kitchen curtains,' said Otilie. 'It's not a bad idea.'

246

Unbleached? Yes, unbleached—Alberta's thoughts took a daring turn and lighted on the word domestic. God knows why? Probably her inner defences were functioning. She said it in desperation. But it happened to be right. Otilie nudged her playfully in the ribs. 'Domestic, yes indeed. You're not so wide of the mark when it comes to the point. Be a dear and run down to the store for me. It's good for you, you're the one who's married and a housewife.'

Every now and again Otilie made it plain that she did not take Alberta's married status very seriously. It was plain from her questions: 'Do you make much jam in the autumn? I suppose there's plenty of berries and fruit down there? Do you send out *all* the washing, Sivert's shirts too? But my dear, don't you even wash *them* yourself? It must be an expense for him?' She looked suspicious when Alberta offered brief, hesitant explanations. The question as to how far she and Sivert really were married hung in the air. A marriage performed by a French mayor was clearly more than questionable to Otilie.

Alberta went over to the store, uneasy and unused to it all. Housewives from the nearby farms stood with their baskets in front of the counter, studying the shelves with calm, clear eyes, knowing precisely what they wanted and did not want. The verger's wife and the doctor's wife might be there, poking expertly at the meat, turning over the various pieces, connoisseurs. They remembered last year's prices for porridge oats and sugar, and would remark, 'Fancy, it's going up again, two øre the kilo, it's all money after all,' considering whether they should buy any at all under such circumstances.

Alberta always forgot to ask what anything cost. It never occurred to her to ask for cardamom by weight because it was more expensive in small packets. Her blind eyes failed to notice that the price per kilo was very different when sold this way. 'But mercy me!' exclaimed Otilie when Alberta came home with a neat little packet. 'Work out what it would come to if you had bought more. Are we to *give* that money to Larsen? No fear!'

And although Otilie was just about to start baking, in an enormous apron, and had flour lying in heaps on the pastry

247

board, she took off the apron and went to change the cardamom. Clearly Alberta had not been the right person to send. Perhaps spices and so on cost nothing where she came from, in spite of the war. Here they had learned to save during the years when they had eaten whale fat, remember that.

Alberta had to admit that Otilie was right, she was no catch for Sivert. If you undertake to do something you should do it properly, as competently as you can. If you go in for housekeeping you should know how to do it. She looked back with contrition on an endless series of ill-considered purchases. When had she last given a thought to the price per kilo? Her system had been the opposite: What can I buy for the money I have today?

Occasionally the housewives would talk to her as she stood among them, waiting at the counter. They talked about the spring and the summer. It was a busy time for those who had their own homes. No sooner were the spring cleaning over and the summer clothes ready than it was time for making jam and juice, salting beans, canning for those who had the equipment. Some people wrapped hay round the glass jars, that worked too. How did they do things in France? What was that? So much fruit and vegetables all the year round that it was unnecessary? Well, fancy that! They looked at her in disbelief: That *must* be pleasant! As if they were saying: Imagine roast pigeon flying into your mouth. Obviously it was not quite proper that life should be so easy.

It hurt Alberta as if they were prodding her. She would never be purposeful and conscientious as they were. Should she therefore have gone through life alone, without love, without children, without—? Something was wrong somewhere.

She genuinely tried to be of use, offering her services and taking pains. There was nearly always something wrong with the result. In the course of the years she had worked out private little methods which decidedly did not meet with approbation. 'Do you do it like that? Mercy me! Is that French? There are some funny people down there, I must say.' 'It's my way,' said Alberta, so as not to compromise the Republic. If

248

anything succeeded she felt strangely proud and relieved in her degradation, as if she had obtained credentials.

In all this Sivert left her completely alone. Nor could she have expected anything else, she was there on sufferance. Not that he took the side of the others exactly. Sivert was on his own side, that of himself and his painting; he manoeuvred forwards between various obstacles and came out of it with profit. Now here, now there in the terrain Sivert's painting parasol would appear. He might come home with his easel and box on his back, a damp canvas in each hand: violet ploughed land, a patchwork of green fields, a heavy spring sky above, perhaps a rainbow. He had become completely non-cubist again. He would stand by the kitchen steps scraping the thick lumps of the heavy, newly ploughed soil off his shoes, thirsty for coffee, hungrily enthusiastic about Otilie's wheaten cake and doughnuts. With his mouth full he would turn round the canvases, which he had put down facing the wall outside, rub his hands together, continue eating and drinking. Or perhaps he would put on his best clothes, walk the seven kilometres to town, where he had numerous irons in the fire, call on Consul This and Doctor That, full of optimism about selling his pictures. Or he would disappear up into the attic, where he had made himself a studio with overhead illumination from a skylight, and sketch, draw and paint.

Between whiles he would put on his oldest clothes and help old Ness with the rebuilding. They hammered, planed, sawed and measured. Sivert knew how to handle everything; he was not impractical as a result of being an artist. He could even cut panes of glass and fit them into the window frames. Only the doors and the brasswork had to be ordered from town; he and his father coped with the rest. Old Ness had been a carpenter before turning to farming, so he was naturally a handyman. Sivert must have inherited it. When Alberta came and rather awkwardly kept them company for a while in the pleasant scent of sawdust and fresh wood, and stayed making conversation so as not to feel a complete outsider, expressing her surprise at how clever Sivert was, he smiled indulgently: 'I've helped Father since I was a youngster.'

249

'Sivert's very useful to me,' Old Ness said. 'He wasn't much more than a lad when he began helping in all sorts of ways. He was handy on land and handy in a boat. Now I hear he's handy at his painting too. I have to rely on what I hear. The likes of me don't understand that sort of thing. Doesn't surprise me. Sivert has always been clever with his hands.'

'Hm,' Sivert replied .'My hands?'

'Yes, your hands. That's what you do it with, I know that. Of course you have to use your brains as well, as with everything else in this world. I couldn't even saw through this piece of planking without using my brains.'

'You're quite right, Father.'

'You're chaffing me,' snickered the old man, thoroughly pleased with Sivert, whatever he might do. 'But I do know a bit about it. There's more speculation to painting Mary and Elizabeth than to sawing across this piece of planking, I grant you that. Far more. But both of them need brains and deliberation. Look out! Might have expected it—hit your hand that time.'

'You make me think about so much else. Ouch!' Sivert sucked his damaged finger, shook it and laughed. 'All right, Tot, now you shall come with me to see the grindstone.'

He took the serious little boy by the hand. Alberta followed them, embarrassed, at a loose end. Once she had hooked herself on to Sivert; now he was monopolising that part of her which was the boy, drawing her after them, to the grindstone too. She took her eternal sewing with her everywhere, even though Otilie had revealed its shortcomings mercilessly. She had simply taken it away from Alberta one day, held it up for everyone to see, and said, 'Mercy me! What on earth's this? Don't they use sewing machines in France either? This is the oddest way of facing a garment I've ever seen. Whatever you say, you must come from a backward country. Imagine doing that by hand! Now run upstairs and fetch my machine. It's threaded with black cotton so it'll be just right.'

'It's my own way of doing it.' Alberta snatched the garment back again. 'I've sewn a great deal by hand. Sometimes I had the long seams machine sewn.'

250

'You don't say! Perhaps you don't *know* how to use a sewing-machine?'

'No, I don't know how to use a sewing-machine.'

'But, goodness me, you must learn. I'll teach you when I have a spare moment. I've never seen anything so crazy.'

'Let Alberta do things the way she's used to,' mediated old Fru Ness. 'It will be all right, I know. The boy looks very smart, *I* think.'

'That may be so. But we're not living in the nineteenth century. I shall have to run it up for her myself, if the worst comes to the worst.'

In spite of it all Alberta still slunk round with her sewing, her soul numb and dead, in the wake of Sivert and Tot. She felt as if she were back at the beginning, as if life had brought her home again to the place she had come from, in all her uselessness. Only the outer circumstances were different. Incredibly she was married and had a child. And she had relatives in Kristiania who did not even know she was here.

Aunt and Lydia, how would they take it all? They would be grateful to Sivert for marrying Alberta. They would have as little to do with him as possible, but insist: 'The best thing that could happen. I'm sure he's a good fellow.' They would be lady-like and distantly gracious when they met him, were he the devil himself. They would present him with ashtrays and ties; and sigh with relief when he and Alberta left. They were not going to meet him, as long as it was up to her. This relationship was not one to be displayed. Emergency measures seldom are.

Day and night she could feel her heart beating, always more strongly at night. Her sleep was no longer loose and ragged; she lay tossing in the stuffy atmosphere. Torturing restlessness jerked her limbs, her heart tried to hammer its way out. If she finally did fall asleep, it was only to struggle vainly and in desperation with mysterious vague objects. One night she was climbing up a ladder to an attic. It was narrow and in disrepair, grey with spiders' webs, in some places quite shaggy. She had to bend double to pass under beams. Occasionally

251

she struck her head against them and hurt herself. Twice she called out, loudly and complainingly.

A short distance in front of her went the person who was showing her the way, a young, girlish figure she only glimpsed before she disappeared round the curve of the stairs. When Alberta called the second time, an answer came from above: You have arrived.

Stumbling, she reached a wall. In a corner there was a black hole, just big enough for her arm to pass through. She put it in, groped in the empty air inside, understood nothing, called again, heard her own voice in a cracked howl.

Then an answer came from the other side of the wall: You must break through.

I can't!

You must break through. The voice died away like the wind dropping. Silence fell.

She was gripped with boundless fear and uncertainty: her grey, narrow surroundings, the impossibility of going forward, the impossibility of going back. She screamed aloud—

'Alberta!'

Otilie was standing over her, Sivert was in the doorway.

'This is terrible, Alberta,' he said. 'We'll all end up in the madhouse if you go on like this. What's the matter with you? Are you ill?'

'I was dreaming.' Alberta felt as if she had been torn up by the roots, and that they were hanging naked in the air. If only Otilie had not been there. But there she stood in her slippers, wearing a skirt under her bed-jacket and the big, grey check shawl round her shoulders, looking down at Alberta, shaking her head. 'There is only One Who can help here, Our Saviour Jesus Christ. For nervous distress is distress of the soul, after all. None will make me believe otherwise.'

'Yes, yes, yes.' Sivert spoke impatiently and brusquely, nodding at the other bed. 'Go and lie down, Otilie, will you? I'll sit here for a while.'

He crossed the floor and sat on the edge of Alberta's bed. He had put on his trousers and vest over his nightshirt, his

252

chin was unshaven, and he very much resembled a shoe-mender. 'Are you ill, Alberta? Do you feel any pain any-where?' He took her hand. 'Then what is it? This is the second time you've screamed like this in the middle of the night. What's the matter with you?'

'Nothing. Nothing, Sivert.' Alberta turned her face to the wall.

'You must realise it's disturbing for the rest of us.'

Alberta stubbornly contemplated the wall. After a while she said, 'I shan't sleep any more tonight. Just go to bed, both of you.'

'Go to bed!' exclaimed Otilie. 'Easier said than done!'

'Go outside for a moment, will you, Otilie, so that Alberta and I can talk?'

The door opened and closed.

'I agreed to bring you home,' began Sivert, 'because I realised that the boy was of great concern to you.'

Silence. Alberta could not utter a word.

'I have said nothing to anyone here that was not to your advantage. It's entirely up to you if everything is to seem all right between us. I think I have been as considerate as possible, done my duty, behaved—'

'Like a man of honour,' suddenly came from Alberta, quite involuntarily. She had not the slightest intention of being spiteful.

'Put it like that if you wish. I suppose it's your way of being witty. I recognise it. However, you are staying here, with your child. It should in a way be pleasant for you. You can have nothing to criticise Father and Mother for. Otilie has her peculiarities—'

'I've—become fond of your father and mother, Sivert.'

'That's good. We do our best. This is no mansion—'

'Sivert!'

'All right. But you must do your best too. Pull yourself together. Or you'll have to go somewhere else. Tot is happy. I was beginning to think that you too . . . It's healthy here and—'

'It's true, Tot's happy.' Again Alberta glimpsed the ray of

253

hope that put everything else in shadow. Sometimes she was blind to it. 'I will pull myself together, Sivert—go for long walks, to help me to sleep. Things will be better. I'll—I'll do my utmost.'

'If only the room in the south gable were in order, you could perhaps—do your scribbling there. If it would help. But it will be some time before—'

'Go to bed now, Sivert. This shan't happen again, I promise you.' Alberta turned back to the wall, heard Sivert sigh and go, Otilie come in, cough and get into bed. They exchanged a couple of phrases in the doorway, but Alberta could not make out what they said.

Longing which she had learned to suppress because she had to, because there had been no other solution, was suddenly alive in her, as if she had been plundered at that very moment. She murmured her incantation: 'Tot's happy, Tot's happy,' trying to concentrate her thoughts on it.

'Break through.' The words from her dream came to her, linking themselves with the others, threading themselves between them: 'Break through, Tot's happy, break through, Tot's happy . . .'

Alberta felt her eyes widen. She raised her head slightly from the pillow.

* * *

The road which wound past the farm between two stone walls took one further into Norway.

After ten minutes' walk the structure of the landscape changed and became all uphill and down, the fields on each side billowing and advancing, a sea of curving lines in violent movement towards each other, the foreground of round, rich forms in green and violet in full uproar. Down in the hollows were old barns, fences, aspen trunks the colour of plane-trees, firs, young birches white as chalk marks. Furthest away and eternally blue were the hills. But the houses people lived in lay always on the crest of a wave.

Perhaps as in the old pictures God's finger would one day

appear out of the thin layer of cloud, pointing down at a ploughed field. Here and there a band of boys might come into sight, in bright blue shirts and dark red jerseys, colours which would clash horribly anywhere else. Here, with budding alder bushes for background and a purple haze farther off they acquired a mysterious depth and richness, melted down and became priceless as inlaid stones. An extraordinary country, thought Alberta, struck. Is it surprising that every other person here is an artist?

She met children on the road. 'G'morning,' they said, even if it was afternoon or evening. They looked at her frankly, without shyness, their eyes clear under sun-bleached hair. They looked amazingly secure and sure of themselves, talking loudly together in the strange, rather rough melody which is the Norwegian language.

At the top of a steep slope the wood began. A path, brown with pine needles, curved away between the tree trunks. Blue hepatica grew in bouquets amongst the dead leaves. Rolled up like brown hair in curling rags the ferns stood in groups, still with a long way to go. On the south side of the pine trees the ants had been building: enormous old heaps and small new ones, ceaseless traffic. It is concentrated where Norway's stone skeleton lies bare.

One day the ferns had raised their heads and stood with tall, swaying necks, making her think of sea-horses that stand upright in the water. There were catkins on the birch tree. The aspen had them too, and the tree was so splendid that one might imagine oneself at the Mediterranean. It was purple and chenille, with a smooth strong trunk, southern in colouring; Alberta could find no other words to describe it. It was a miracle standing against the blue sky.

She walked this way every day and sat on a tree stump, letting the sun sift down on her through the branches, noticing what had happened since yesterday, reading a little, busying herself with the manuscript she had smuggled out under her coat. It was uncomfortable balancing it on her knees. Piles of straying pages would constantly slide away from her and have

255

to be collected again. But when had anything been comfortable? She thought of the past winter and admitted that quiet, woodland air, mild warmth, security for the boy, were in fact comforts of the first order. If it were a Sunday morning and the wind was in the right direction she could hear the chapel bell, hoarse and mocking. Tot went with the others to church. He submitted for the sake of the ride, so that he could hold the reins going uphill, when Blakken was walking. Godless Alberta was nowhere to be found when the cart was ready to leave.

The manuscript lay in its folder, dead, roughly drafted and loosely written. She had to breathe life into it, or at least pretend she was doing so; or die herself, slowly perhaps, but surely. There was *one* way out, *one* possibility, and four points on which it depended: get it finished, write out a fair copy, not allow herself to be halted by doubt, keep her head high as long as possible if there should turn out to be no other solution.

Her thoughts continually stole away and had to be caught again. Time and again they sought sanctuary in the letters from Liesel that had come from Königsberg.

Liesel had been forced to leave Paris; it had been that or the hospital. There had been two of them to persuade her, a young, energetic doctor, and Eliel. One windy day in March Alberta had accompanied her to the station with one of her sisters, who had come to fetch her. The sister was not at all like Liesel; she was short, fair-haired, plump, primly and unattractively dressed, and wore steel-rimmed spectacles. She spoke only Russian and German and looked at everything about her with suspicious eyes. Liesel had moved to a hotel, and lay weeping and coughing on the bed in a comfortless room, pretending that she had always lived in this way. She had refused to go to the Hôtel des Indes.

Eliel had come up to say good-bye. He refused to come to the station for fear of compromising Liesel, thus emphasizing his delicacy of feeling. He had brought a little statuette with him. It had been standing on the bedside table when Alberta came up for the last time, and tears had come to Liesel's eyes when she looked at it. Otherwise she had been surprisingly calm. Not a tear, very few words. But when the train began to move and she was forced to let go of Alberta's hand they had both cried openly.

The tram on the way home had been halted by a modest funeral, a slow little procession of black-clothed people on foot behind the simplest kind of hearse. Among them was a woman in a long veil, supported by other women. Behind them, on top of the coffin, was a wreath: its broad ribbons flapped, were borne outwards by the wind, floated on the breeze for a moment and fell again. Alberta was just able to read: *A mon mari*. In spite of the words she was left with the painful feeling that she had been watching Liesel's funeral.

But Liesel wrote: 'I shall recover. I am still in bed, but the fever is dropping, I can knit, sew and write letters. Everyone is kind to me. Nobody has commented on the fact that I didn't become a painter. As long as you stop wanting things for yourself, I suppose you can live anywhere, Albertchen. It's bourgeois and terribly anti-French here. I shall not be able to say a word when I have to go to coffee parties later on. I shall not attempt to describe how they dress. It was a good thing you went home; otherwise you would have caught some illness or other too. The artistic, poverty-stricken life isn't much fun in the long run. The men can do it, but not us. After all, you always wished Tot could live in the country.'

In one of her letters she said: 'If I believed that powers who might help could hear me I'd call to them to make me get well more quickly. I need to so that I can start earning. I've thought of starting as a dressmaker when I get up. Do you remember, I used to sew quite neatly? It's no use painting here, and I no longer have any talent. I had once, but it has disappeared. I don't believe anyone is listening, Albertchen. Sometimes I imagine how it would be if an atom in my body began calling to me from its point of view, and how impossible it would be for me to do anything for the atom personally, even if I heard it. Do you think me stupid? You see, they talk to me so much about God. It's so difficult when they give this personal name to something so completely unknown. It's a kind of capsule

257

into which they put it and then expect you to swallow it whole. I've heard from Eliel a couple of times. It's nice of him, but he seems like a stranger. He was really very patient with me all those years, and I really loved him right to the end, although I was often malicious. But now it's all so far away. He says Pierre is back in Paris. He has left Jeanne for good and is living with a Russian woman, a communist, somewhere on the Boul' Mich'. You will hear about this through Sivert in any case. Pierre is supposed to be trying to start a newspaper, but has no money.'

At this place in Liesel's letter Alberta felt the same painful stab each time. Nevertheless she re-read it. Pierre's calm face with the light in his eyes, as she had seen it the last time, became overwhelmingly distinct. She knew that he had gone to Dijon with Jeanne. They said that Jeanne had taken Marthe by the hand and fetched him from Michaud's. He spent his time there, and nobody knew where he lived.

Deep in her mind Alberta kept a secret certainty: Whatever may happen, it doesn't matter. Something *must* happen; life never stands still. We shall not meet again, but if we were to do so everything would be just as it was that day and the rest merely in parentheses. His kisses were branded on her mouth indelibly. Down at Granli her knowledge of it retreated; it avoided Otilie's room as all winter it had avoided the studio and Sivert's presence. Up here in the wood it turned into physical certainty again, mind and body unfurled in burning desire . . .

She bent over her manuscript.

'For heaven's sake, are you writing in the middle of the wood?'

Alberta started, and looked up into a kind, wrinkled face tied up in a kerchief. It looked at her, laughing. She had to laugh back. 'Yes, it is rather absurd, isn't it?'

'Yes, I should think it must be? Not that I know anything about it. And on a tree-stump into the bargain? Have the summer visitors started coming already? They don't usually come before the schools finish.'

'I'm not a visitor exactly. I live at a farm called Granli—I—'

'At Granli? I know all about Granli. I'm a member of the

women's association for that district. The meetings we have there are worth going to. Otilie *can* bake. But for heaven's sake, you're not—you're not Sivert's wife, from Paris?'

Yes, Alberta was.

'Well I never! And here you are, sitting in the wood.'

'It's peaceful and pleasant here.'

'It is peaceful. Yes. I know others who are just the same. My summer visitors, for instance—the husband is always off in the wood. He's an author, he is, writes books and for the newspapers. He gets his ideas in the wood. Then he writes it out up in his room. Are you an author too?'

'No. There are so many kinds of writing.'

'I expect there are. I live over there. Was on my way up from the store when I saw you sitting here. Would you like to come and have a look at it, since you're so near? It's an old farm, over two hundred years old, and run down in some ways, but people say the house is attractive, and the storehouse. The road has disappeared since they made the new rural road twenty years ago. It's often difficult for us when the snow comes in winter, and our horse hasn't ever been outside our land; he just draws the plough and the hay and the muck. And he brings in firewood for us. He's like a child, he's so spoilt. Animals get like that. We're a bit out of the way, we can't get the electric light, though that would make things easier. But you know how it is, when your family has lived for many generations.—But what does Otilie have to say about it? About your sitting up here?'

Her final question decided the matter. Alberta collected her papers and got to her feet. She looked into the many kind laughter wrinkles and laughed herself. 'I don't know what she has to say about it.'

'She is *peculiar*, you know.'

'Perhaps she is a little.'

'She's not married, that's what it is. She ought to have had a man like the rest of us. Then she wouldn't have become so *domineering*. Not that we don't need to be domineering sometimes. The menfolk—but you're still young.'

To this Alberta prudently said nothing.

259

The path broadened into an overgrown road. Shortly afterwards the wood opened out, grass slopes and ploughed land came into view. The farm lay on a ridge: a smoke-coloured log house in a good position, a tumbledown outhouse, leaning and crooked, with an open barn door like a gaping mouth at one end and manure coming out of an opening like an outlet at the other. It resembled other outhouses, but this one was old and done-for. But the buildings stood in the open. The wood had drawn well back from them. An enormous tree stood at one corner close to the wall. When they came nearer, Alberta saw that it was a chestnut tree; the buds were already fat and shining on the branches. A cat got up from a flight of steps, stretched itself, came over and rubbed itself against their legs, purring loudly.

'Well, fancy meeting Sivert's wife! And I go that way so seldom. We have no help on the farm, we plod along ourselves. My husband's up in the woods today. If I'd known I was going to have a visitor I'd have made time to bake some waffles. But you shall have coffee. Well I never, Sivert's wife! He's made a name for himself. Now, you just sit down—

'But the Lord save us, you have a boy too, don't you? Yes, didn't I hear something about it? And you've brought him with you from France? I don't suppose he can speak Norwegian, can he? That must be strange.'

She rattled the rings of the oven that was standing in the fireplace.

Alberta looked round. The walls were built of logs so thick that nothing could hang straight on them, just as in Kjeldsen the smith's house at home in the north. Through the open door she could look across a wide hallway into another large room. A broad flight of stairs with a banister led upwards. 'You have plenty of room,' she remarked mechanically.

'Yes, plenty of room. If there's one thing we do have, it's room. In the summer we take in visitors, as I told you. They have to take us as they find us, a long way from the road and short of water plenty of times. But it's so *peaceful*, they say, so *quiet*. They're the kind of people who like that. But they're not coming until August. He can't take a holiday from the newspaper before then. You shall see their rooms.'

They drank their coffee. The woman studied Alberta over the edge of her cup with intelligent, deep-set eyes. Her wrinkles occasionally contracted, craftily and sympathetically. 'Are you happy to be back home in Norway?'

'Oh, I don't know.'

'You couldn't find kinder people than Ness and his wife.'

'No, you couldn't,' said Alberta honestly.

'So it's Otilie, is it?'

'Yes, it's Otilie.'

'She likes to be the one who makes the decisions. It's often difficult for the old folk, I know that. They say Otilie fell in love with our old vicar. That's what they say. But he came a widower and he left a widower. Would you like to see upstairs? Then you must have a look at the animals. I have such splendid cows too. Balder is up in the woods today with my husband. Balder's our horse. And I have fifty chickens.'

They went to the outhouse and looked at the animals. The cowshed was in good condition inside with panelling everywhere. Alberta politely patted the rump of a cow. Then they went upstairs: a spacious landing, high thresholds over which they had to step carefully, blue-painted log walls everywhere, old, greenish window panes, two big living rooms, one on each side of the landing. In one of them the sun poured in on to a large table standing between the windows. The branches of the chestnut tree swept towards one of the windows on a light current of air. There was simple furniture, an old-fashioned bench-sofa, a four-poster bed bulging with eiderdowns beneath a white bed-cover. Some dried wreaths above the sofa gave out a strong, sweet scent. The farmer's wife went across and let in air. 'I hang these wreaths up in the autumn against the moths. It's almost too much of a good thing.'

But Alberta had, without thinking, put her folder down on the table. There it lay as if it had come home. She almost felt at home herself. The moment had something dreamlike about it.

261

'Is this room left empty?'

'Yes, of course it's empty. Nobody will come here before August.'

'I—I wonder if I might be allowed to sit here for a while during the daytime? I'll pay for it.' It occurred to Alberta that perhaps she might produce short pieces in between and earn some ready money. Now she was gambling high.

'Pay for it? I'll have no payment, not at this time of year.'

'It's—I'd like to keep it to myself—for the present.'

'Come as often as you like, then you won't have to sit in the wood. You shall have the key, then you can go in and out as you like. If I'm away one day, the key to the outer door will be under a stone on the steps. I'll show it to you.'

'You will be doing me a great service.'

'Why not, when it's standing empty? It'll be nice to have you. People must have *peace* for work of that sort, I know that much. Otilie shan't get to hear of it. The men needn't poke their noses into everything either. It isn't always to the good when they do. My name's Lina Haugen. Haugen's the name of the farm.'

'Mine's Alberta Ness. Thank you, Lina.'

Lina laughed with all her wrinkles again, in reality still young, only dried and weather-beaten, as country people are. 'We can fox people too, can't we?'

When Alberta went home she left the folder behind.

She walked down the hill towards Granli. Between the tree-tops she could see the farmyard. Old Ness was pulling Blakken after him. Tot was sitting on the horse's back. He leaned forward and patted it on the neck. As Alberta turned in through the hedge she heard him saying, 'Yes, Blakken, yes, nice Blakken. Gee up, Blakken, gee up.' His voice resembled those of the children she met on the road. The strange, rather rough little melody had become his. His legs pummelled Blakken's sides like drumsticks. The horse was quite unaffected. Ness walked sedately, so did Blakken; neither of them threatened danger to the child on horseback. And the child knew it, and was fearless, safe and secure. When Alberta came over to them and the procession halted, she leaned her cheek against the firm, warm neck of the horse, as if it were Blakken she had to thank for the fact that Tot was turning into a different boy, day by day.

'That rocking horse has had it's day,' whinnied old Ness. 'And of course Blakken's getting on now. He has plenty of sense.'

*　　*　　*

It was almost mid-summer.

It seemed to Alberta that she had never seen such a wealth of leaves and flowers before. The meadow was full of sorrel, heartsease, lady's mantle, herb bennet. Between the rocks behind the storehouse grew limewort in broad purple patches, speedwell, germander bluer than Tot's eyes, cinquefoil and lady's slipper. Above them all rocked the myriad corollas of the wild chervil.

In the wood the pines and firs had bright new shoots. The pines carried theirs vertically, the firs let them hang down in draperies and furbelows.

A black horse was cropping the grass on the bridge to a barn. Behind the horse, the red barn, and the thousands upon thousands of wild chervil heads showing through the grass, it was blue, like deep water. You thought it was water. Then it turned out to be a hill. It was like nothing else, could not be anywhere else in the whole world: Norway.

Alberta saw it all, took it in with her mind, looked at it with astonishment. All the same it did not penetrate. For the first time in her life nature was a frame and a background, not the boasting and demanding thing that makes itself one with you, almost painfully.

She had bound herself to her manuscript like a knot. She felt as if she were in a heated house, in which one exit had been left to her. It was beautiful outside, of course, but . . .

A painful tingling night and day; practically no sleep, a tattered veil that descended on her momentarily, headache, heartache; a strange little boy, who had to be reached from

263

a new angle, along uncertain, untried paths. Keep me away from our child, Sivert, be the one who has the power. Perhaps I shall claim my place before you expect it, by taking a round-about way. Got you, Sivert!

In the garden peonies stood along the wall of the house. Small, hard, opinionated heads on overgrown stalks stuck up above one another and suddenly burst one day into a luxury of silken petals. The mock orange blossom bush by the summer house was covered with buds, making one think of young brides, of everything untouched. They opened, and the intense fragrance contrasted strongly with the bud that bore it; with Otilie too. Alberta picked small twigs in secret, took them aside and inhaled their scent like a forbidden, slightly danger-ous stimulant.

Birds called and answered each other in the wood so pas-sionately that the one had scarcely begun to pipe before the other joined in. Soon after midnight the dawn was reflected in the windows of the neighbouring farm. There was a sound of accordion playing, no one knew where from. One felt there were couples wandering along the paths all night.

If Alberta did manage to fall asleep, she woke again at the first birdsong. Or perhaps Otilie had turned over in bed. Otilie's bed creaked loudly.

Her body felt palsied with fatigue. But her brain teemed. Image succeeded image. Words came to her, inevitable, irres-istable, the only right ones. But if she sat up in bed and reached for the paper and pencil she had hidden under her pillow, the spell was broken. A short while would elapse. Then she would grope her way towards heavy, clumsy sentences, the one piled on top of the other, grating on the ear. And she was afraid that Otilie might wake and notice what she was doing. It did not improve matters.

The result was small pieces of paper, new piles of small pieces of paper which were carried up to Haugen and were the cause of radical changes. It was impossible to ignore them.

Decisive things happened at daybreak. It is then that the birds lay their eggs, birth and death are given release. Then, too, the brain is ready to arrange and put together, to precipitate words with content and significance, part of a sequence. They seemed to Alberta to float up from the mysterious lifestream itself, which, dark and secretive, reaches down into the depths of the mind. They were brewed of bitterness and sweetness. But to reach for them was often like reaching for soap bubbles. When she opened her hand there was nothing there.

At last the time would come when Alberta dared to open one of the windows. Half fainting she got out of bed and did so. It was the evening and night air Otilie was so desperately afraid of; she was less discouraging towards the morning air and sunshine. Alberta lay feeling how the atmosphere in the room slowly became seasoned with the element human beings principally live on and so sorely need.

She must have dozed off again. The next thing she would be aware of was Otilie demonstratively shutting the window because she wanted to dress, her splashing in the washbowl, the emphatic manner in which she put down her mug, a manner full of disapproval.

Not that Alberta's excursions went unnoticed.

'You certainly do go for long walks,' said Otilie. And one day she said: 'It's all very well for those who have the *time*.'

'Alberta needs them for the sake of her sleep, Otilie. And she's on holiday here with us in a way. She's sleeping better now.' Fru Ness nodded at Alberta behind Otilie's back. Her eyes said: You just get away. I'll see to the rest.

Alberta slunk out. She could hear Otilie saying, 'Sleep? I don't know that she sleeps so much better. She's still restless. I repeat, nervous distress is distress of the soul. People who don't even go to church on Sunday . . . '

Sometimes Alberta did not get away. For the sake of peace she had to stay at home and help. Otilie had real talent for starting some enterprise just as Alberta had thought, quite reasonably, that the coast was clear for a while. Cleaning chores that nobody had dreamed of doing were her speciality. Then her cheeks turned red, her false teeth slipped awry, and her shoes squeaked more loudly than usual. Then no one dared argue with Otilie. Fru Ness shook her head in despair behind her back. In the midst of carrying buckets and polishing windows Alberta would be seized with savage, furious longing for the lonely, desultory life of idleness she had once led. Then she simply thought of flight.

Perhaps she would not get up to Lina with her new pieces of paper until the next day. A few of them brought clarity, others nausea and fear, all of them bother and rewriting. She would be seized with hatred of this old manuscript, and a desire to destroy it. Life passes, we alter, we change position in relation to things, seeing them from different points of view. Here lay a pile of paper which it was impossible to revise, there was no time. Alberta was a minute pack animal in front of an enormous load which should have been pulled away a long time ago. The whip lashed, August approached. If the load had not been moved by then it never would be. She saw the future as a hopeless struggle which already made her tired and old. Many manuscripts like this would be required, preferably one a year. Then even scribbling might keep her alive. She felt doomed to the galleys. She wished she could take up dress-making like Liesel. That was work you knew how to do once you had mastered it.

'A luxury for the rich,' Pierre had said once. 'Three hundred pages,' he had said too. As far as Alberta could make out she had many more than that, although she hoped it would shrink in print. Half in delirium she struck out and cut down, took sections out and put them back in again. Sometimes she had the feeling that she was knitting the product, or making a patchwork quilt. Words were added to words and had no more meaning than stitches and rags. Together they would perhaps turn into something one day, but wall after wall of doubt had to be broken down, doubt that this irrelevant story could possibly interest anyone. Alberta knew it all of old. For the first time she was struggling with it under the whip. Sick with anxiety she paced up and down the floor. Her brain stood still.

Then a small incident might occur. Through the open window there would come a sound from the farmyard, calling, footsteps. Lina had let out the cows on to the grassy slope;

266

they would not be allowed into the meadow until after the hay-making was over. Now she was calling from the steps: 'Keep your head to yourself, Beauty! Will you keep your head to yourself!'

Beauty would not keep her head to herself. Undisturbed she cropped at the fresh clover under the barbed wire fence until Lina approached her with uplifted stick. Then she turned and moved away, certain that she would not be seriously chastised.

But Alberta was thinking: What a language! What a concise and descriptive and direct language, full of clarity, clothing thought compactly. My language. And she seemed to feel a flick of the whip. Illumination fell on the many pages. The wheels she had set in motion took purchase in her. Reality ebbed away, she had passed into timelessness. She would hurry back to Granli much too late for something or other and strangely insensitive to this deplorable fact.

One day the meadow was nodding with moon daisies. A warm wind passed through the grass, combing it with its fingers. Everything curtsied after it, now here, now there. 'We haven't had such a fine summer since Sivert sold his big picture,' said Fru Ness.

After sunset the clouds sailed gilt-edged under the light sky. All was abundance, warmth, fragrance and peace.

One day Sivert and his father simply cut down the miracle of flowers in the meadow with their scythes. But in the evenings there was the smell of new-mown hay. Tot went out and rolled in it, shouting aloud for joy.

* * *

The summer was so far advanced that the green had deepened in colour and become monotonous. The willow herb stood in tall, strong clumps. The evenings started earlier, and already had a hint of autumn in them. When it was quite dark an illumination hung above the woods to the south, showing where the town lay.

In the afternoon Sivert sometimes said, 'Will you come to town with me, Alberta?' Sometimes she did so: from old

267

habit, because it was good to walk in company with someone, a change to see different surroundings; perhaps too because it would attract attention at Granli if she did not go.

They did not talk much, and only about neutral topics. Alberta had the feeling of being with a man she knew slightly, no more. Sadness that it was so would flood warmly into her as she watched him disappear into a house with paintings under his arm, landscapes and compositions created by his placid mind and strong, practical hands. He had returned to his former style of painting. The wealth of colouring that had been Sivert's strength and distinguishing characteristic had flowed again. She was glad to see it as one is always glad to see things functioning normally.

She wandered about the narrow streets round the market place while she waited for him, or sat on a bench in the park. If he had collected a fee they would go to a café, and the time would pass pleasantly, as it does at a chance meeting of acquaintances. It sometimes struck Alberta as quite incredible that they should ever have slept together, and that they should be the father and mother of a child. Occasionally Sivert would push money towards her across the table. 'I suppose you need some to throw around too.' 'Thank you, Sivert, I have all I need.' 'You must tell me then, if there is anything.' Sivert would put the money back in his pocket. 'Yes, thank you.'

One day when they were sitting like this, he said, 'I've decided to stay here for the winter. I have orders for a couple of portraits.'

'Have you, Sivert?'

'One of them is of a whaling captain, at least he's gone ashore now. Those people have money. A real character, should be amusing to paint. It's possible that I may be asked to paint the daughter as well. Beautiful girl. Fine-looking. Unusually pleasant too.'

'Oh?'

'I may get the commission for this altar-piece too. It doesn't look entirely out of the question. I shall go to see the vicar one day. It would probably be best to put down Brede for the

268

local school. He can begin there at any rate. It would be too far for him to go to town for the time being. Tot's coming on well.'

'Yes, he is. I'm so happy about it, Sivert.'

'I always knew he'd grow into a fine boy. You looked at the black side all the time. Perhaps mothers are like that.'

'Perhaps so.'

There was no longer any friction between them, only a strange emptiness, a rather distant sympathy; just as when people make brief contact and think: That could have been pleasant, but it can't be arranged. She could sit looking at him as if he were a stranger. A sailor perhaps? Yes. Not the jolly kind with a sweetheart in every port; the tenacious kind, who rows out to fish and drags nets, looks after lobster pots, does his job, in fact. With amazement she remembered how she had alternated in her feelings for him. Many would have called it sensuousness; on the contrary, it had been spiritual, a need to solve the riddle that was he.

When it came down to it it had not been complicated. The solution lay so close at hand that this was perhaps one of the reasons why it had taken her such a long time to find it. Sivert was so completely himself in all circumstances, without any notion that he ought perhaps to behave differently, that such and such would look better. He was not the kind to hide the fact that he was aware of advantages; he was aware of them and said nothing. It was merely that he had a keen eye for business, an instinct as natural as that of a wild animal. 'Yes,' he always said, when Alberta insisted that he had been reasoning again in such and such a way. 'Yes, of course.' And if she were to say to him, 'You wanted to drive me out, Sivert. Liesel was right. I believe you made up all that about the money,' he might well answer, 'Well, yes. What else could I have done to get rid of you just then?'

And the daughter of the whaling captain? Was there anything in the offing as far as she was concerned? If so she must be prepared, so that she could take up the fight over the child on more equal terms. Alberta felt a wild panic, her heart pitched unevenly in her breast. She felt sorry for Sivert too,

269

he was gullible in such matters; he might be disappointed again. Then she thought: Sivert is a wall; I shall demoralize myself in the long run if I go on striking my head against it. I mustn't feel sorry for him. I have enough with my own affairs.

'Won't you buy some little thing for Brede, since we're in town for once? He'd be so pleased.'

'Very well,' said Sivert. 'If there's anything you think he'd like—that isn't too expensive.'

They found something or other. They came home. The boy came running to meet them, full of adventures, full of expectancy. He was handed the little parcel and was obviously and noisily enraptured. He jumped into the air. He had become strong and secure. He rushed about showing everybody what he had been given: in and out of doors, to the kitchen, the stable, the storehouse, the woodshed, eager and at home. Children from the neighbouring farms looked in and asked whether Brede was coming out. Brede answered them in the local dialect, cheekily and loudly. He no longer bothered about his French, although Alberta and Sivert both tried to keep up the language with him.

Alberta felt a bitter happiness at seeing it all. Her laughter at the tricks he played verged on tears; she had to swallow hard on the occasions when he threw his arms round her in new frankness, more friendly towards everyone except Otilie. She sat watching him when he was wide-eyed with concentration on what was going on round him. She thought: Perhaps he will remember this for the rest of his life. A little piece of this moment, the taste of this or that, the smell of it will stay with him down the years: a smile perhaps, the ring of a voice.

He hung about Fru Ness's skirts, calling her Grannie. He followed Sivert and Sivert's father, carrying tools, helping to harness the horse and make hay, sharing actively in the life of the farm. It was evident that this child, who could not thrive in city air or by the open sea, did so in the country a couple of kilometres away from a fjord. But if Otilie tried to take him on her lap and show him the child Jesus in her illustrated Bible he twisted away from her. When he was alone with

270

Alberta he would say, 'Aunt Otilie isn't pretty. Aunt Otilie has ugly teeth.'

'Aunt Otilie is kind,' attempted Alberta.

'No.'

'Otilie hasn't a way with children,' said Fru Ness. 'She means well, but she simply *hasn't* a way with children. Not married, has none herself, that's what it is.'

But Otilie would say, 'Suffer the little children to come unto me. Of such is the Kingdom of Heaven. Who will lead this child to Jesus? Not those whose duty it ought to be, it seems. If he is to come to Him, it looks as if it will have to be through others.'

One evening when the family had gathered on the steps she said, 'I was just thinking. How did you have Brede baptised? After all, they're Catholics down there, as far as I know.'

'Yes, they're Catholics.' Sivert barely glanced up from the local paper, which he read from end to end every evening.

'I suppose you had to go to the consulate, then? Or the legation? Or perhaps there's a Scandinavian church down there? For it seems to me that such a sacred ceremony would not be very dignified in an office. And who were the god-parents?'

'We've wondered about that, I must say.' Old Ness took his pipe out of his mouth. 'Wondered who the godparents were. Here at home those who aren't present can have their names entered just the same. I don't know how things are there. We didn't want to write and ask either. But now that Otilie's brought it up . . .'

Alberta looked across at Sivert. Sivert was reading the paper.

'Brede isn't baptised,' she said. 'He was registered at the mayor's office.'

There was an astounded silence. 'Surely you can't mean—?' began Otilie. Sivert folded up the paper. 'It ought to have been done, of course. Naturally we thought about it, but there was so much else to think about. Then the war came.'

'But gracious me, you're not going to let the boy go *un-baptised*?'

271

'No, no, Otilie, we'll see about it.'

'It would be nice if it were done, I must say,' said old Ness.

'Yes father, yes father.'

Alberta said nothing. She and Sivert had never discussed it, and that was the truth of the matter. For a moment she pictured the boy being led up the aisle, the centre of attention, put on display. Then she thought: As long as I see that it's done quietly, they can do as they like. He's grown strong and boisterous here, grown as I hungered to see him. Everything else is unimportant.

Up at Lina's things went their uneven way. August approached. Lina was already remarking that one of these days she would have to clean the room properly, take out the furniture and bedding, scrub the floors and clean the windows.

Alberta was in a fever. She went to bed and got up in the morning with a burdensome feeling of guilt. In spite of all her work the manuscript was still loose and ragged in many places, vague, insufficiently thought out.

When one day Lina said, 'There's no help for it, you must let me in on Friday at the latest,' panic took her breath away. 'Of course I must,' she replied.

'If they weren't using both rooms—'

'But they do.'

'You can sit here as much as you like during the winter. We have plenty of firewood from our own trees. There's always a lot of snow but I expect you can ski? There'll be plenty happening down at Granli before the autumn. I hear Fru Ness is having the women's association for the first meeting this year, and that will be soon. But you take your time until Friday.'

It was Wednesday. Alberta was half unconscious with anxiety. Without quite knowing what she was about she erased and added. Sentences grated in her ears, flat, empty of content. She caught herself in contradictions and lapses of memory. Fictional characters can die, Pierre had said. It seemed as if Alberta's had never had a spark of life. Hollow exhaustion,

272

the result of revolt against the pressure, threatened time and again to make her impotent. Previously she had sometimes felt that the material evened itself out on its own, when she had laid stone upon stone long enough. The feeling abandoned her when she was in a serious hurry. She could only see an unmanageable chaos, and feel it was too late to do anything about it.

Out in the fields Balder was drawing the plough, turning again and again on a stretch of earth full of heartsease. Behind him came Lina's short, silent husband. Balder pulled when he wished and stopped when he wished. He swished his tail, dragged the reins well forward and made himself comfortable for a while, cropping a few handfuls of grass, setting off again of his own accord after a suitable interval had elapsed. Balder did the work, Balder decided on the tempo, Balder's heart did not beat unevenly. Alberta, who had come beyond exhaustion to a kind of madness when her fountain pen ran away with her, shut her eyes when she raised her head in order to avoid seeing this perfect equilibrium between what had to be done and what the animal thought he could manage.

On Thursday, in a trance, she wrote some final words which sounded sentimental, knowing she would find no others and that no further alterations were possible. She would have to venture it. It was the only card she had to play: a problematic card. She gathered her things together and said good-bye to Lina, who dried her hands on her apron. 'Thank you for everything, Lina. You've been such a help to me.'

'Nothing to thank me for,' said Lina. 'It's been nice having you here. I understand enough to see you're a kind of author too, it's just that you don't want anybody to interfere. *I* shan't breathe a word. My husband never asks about anything.' Lina nodded in the direction of the ploughland. 'He's a bit peculiar too, you know. Well, I'll be coming down one of these days, to the meeting.'

'That will be nice, Lina.'

Before Alberta entered Granli with the folder under her arm she stood for a while watching from the road. Otilie was sitting

273

on the steps, shelling peas. At last she got to her feet and went across to the storehouse.

You can get through a good deal. Even if your mind is raw with anxiety, you finally get through a meeting of forty-five women, presided over by Otilie. If you were being sent to the scaffold tomorrow, you would get through it.

Alberta knew enough about the ways of the world to realise that it was no use embarking on a literary career at the beginning of August. Nobody was at home, everyone on holiday, including the mysterious powers she was about to accost. In a fortnight perhaps . . . three weeks . . .

The moment for sinister schemes was not ripe in other ways either; scarcely was the folder safe in her suitcase before discussion about the meeting began at Granli.

'*We* must have it this time, Mother.'

'It's not our *turn*, Otilie.'

'The doctor's wife is expecting at any time. *She* can't have it. The Evensens have summer guests. Then it's our turn. It's impossible to say no. It's not done.'

Fru Ness righted her kerchief and sighed, not without reason. They could scarcely get away with less than two hundred and fifty *smørbrød*, Otilie had explained that at the start. It was doubtful whether even that would be enough. They had to allow for the fact that almost everyone would come now that it was between the busy seasons. Then there would have to be small cakes and at *least* five big pastries. They ought to have doughnuts too, but those would have to be baked the same day if they were going to be good. That meant such a bother and fuss with all the cutting of bread for the *smørbrød* as well. After a few days of discussion Otilie gave up the doughnuts to Fru Ness's and Alberta's great relief. She did not stop talking about them, however. Although she said it herself, doughnuts were one of the things she really did know how to make.

Alberta felt a kind of armour growing round her. Old emotions from the times when parties had been given at home were renewed in her. 'You'll wear your best, won't you?'

Otilie reminded her. 'And make the boy look nice.' Alberta hastily lengthened Brede's sailor's suit which had become too short.

And the house filled with women. Along all the walls and in all the rooms downstairs they sat, in black dresses with a touch of white at the throat, gold brooches, their hands folded in their laps until their embroidery was brought out as if on command. At the table in the middle were the leaders of society: the vicar's wife, the teacher's and precentor's wives, the wife of the store-keeper, a few whalers' wives. Alberta retreated again and again to Lina and a couple of farmers' wives along the wall, as she had retreated to the potted palm in another life, only to be brought out again. 'Be a little sociable,' whispered Otilie, red spots in her cheeks. 'Tell them what it's like abroad, since you've been there.' Altogether Alberta felt she was the object of considerable curiosity on the part of the centre table, as if she had been engaged for the purpose of entertaining them. Lina nudged her understandingly in the ribs each time she was fetched away. Brede was hauled to right and left and told to bow.

The vicar arrived, went the rounds shaking hands, stood in a doorway, said a few words and prayed a prayer. His wife read about work in the mission field. Old Ness was present in his Sunday best, his beard newly clipped, but Sivert basely stayed away.

The coffee arrived. Alberta, red as a lobster, ran here and there with cream and sugar, cups and saucers. Life repeated itself in an astonishing way. Conversation at the centre table became lively. It concerned prohibition, boot-legging, home distilling, poor relief. Smuggled liquor was being landed at the most incredible places; it was found hidden in the woods and in the homes of completely innocent people who suffered all kinds of unpleasantness. The world's wickedness was endless. The doctor was being called out to people who had drunk the poison and lay at the point of death, having lost their hearing and their sight. Home distilleries were being discovered all over the parish. When the factory ships of the whaling fleet

275

approached the Norwegian coast the boot-leggers' craft were out in swarms, on the watch right up under the ships' sides, silent, quick to make a get-away as sharks. The whalers' wives knew all about it. Then there was the doctor's wife. The voices sank confidentially. Expecting after twenty years of marriage. That would be quite an event. But it was certainly surprising. Most of them had thought she was at the age when—But then it couldn't have been the case, after all.

The group round Lina were talking about animals. Lina and her silent, strange husband had no children. Perhaps that was why Balder, Beauty and Pearl, let alone the cat, had become Lina's main topic of conversation. If Brede was nearby Lina sat looking at him with a quiet light in her small, clear eyes.

Finally Alberta sought refuge in the stable. Brede was there feeding Blakken with pastries. She sat down on a crate, listened to the even munching for a while, and drank in the quiet.

'You're fond of Blakken, aren't you, Brede?'

'No one could help being fond of Blakken.'

'Do you want to stay with Blakken?'

'I'm going to stay with Blakken for ever. No one shall get me to leave Blakken.' The boy turned towards her, and looked her straight in the eyes. Alberta was moved. It seemed as if she were seeing her child's true face for the first time. There was will-power in the face. There was strength in it. The boy had decided to put down roots now. His mother found unexpected mental balance in this sudden overthrow of the guardian element in herself, which hurt for a second, then was good.

Then Otilie's voice jangled across the farmyard. 'Brede! Alberta! Where in the world have you got to now? We're going to draw lots for the quilt. Brede is to draw!'

'Don't let's go,' said Brede.

'We must go.' Alberta quickly took his head in her hands and kissed him. The ring of complicity in her own voice, their swift exchange of whispers, made a moment rich in experience, taking her far back into childhood and at the same time planting her securely in the present. 'We *must* go, Brede.'

She revealed herself in the doorway. Otilie was standing on the steps, flanked by ladies. 'Is that where you are? Come

276

along. You too, Brede. Alberta, how did it go in that story of yours, at the place where it rained so much? I was trying to recall it, but I'm not good at remembering how things go.'

'What do you mean?' asked Alberta.

'Now don't get on your high horse. You know very well what I mean, my girl. It was something about the rain, two people sitting together in the rain. But apparently it didn't come to anything?'

Hatred for Sivert passed like ice through Alberta. He considered her work to be of no importance, but he talked about it just the same. Perhaps they had demanded an explanation of the phenomenon he had come trailing home. It was Otilie who was terrible.

'I don't know what you're talking about. You must have confused things.' With the calm which comes when one least expects it, Alberta walked up the steps, past them all. She laughed a little as she did so, shaking her head, went indoors to sit with Lina, and refused to budge.

She had looked over the boy's clothes and put to rights those that were still usable. The old, peculiar garments she herself had made were far too small for him now. He would need others for school. She pictured Sivert taking him to town, both of them at the draper's. They came out. Brede was wearing ready-made clothes slightly too big for him. Sivert would be sure to leave room for growth. It was painful to handle his clothes and put them away, to know that—no, she knew nothing.

Then one evening, at dusk, something decisive happened. The time was ripe, now or never. They were walking a short way along the path in the wood, she and Sivert's mother, as they often did. Then Alberta said, 'I shall have to go in to Kristiania one of these days.'

'Shall you? Of course, your relations live there. I suppose it's time you visited them. I expect you'll want to take Brede with you?'

'No,' answered Alberta, her mouth dry. 'I'm going alone. I'm not going to my relations. There's something I have to do

277

there. I was thinking—of staying there for the time being.'

'Not to your relations? You'll have to stay in town then?' Old Fru Ness stared at her in perplexity. 'I wonder whether Sivert can manage that,' she added thoughtfully. 'Whether he'll feel he can just now.'

'I shall see to it myself. I mean, I must have money for my ticket. I had thought—'

Alberta paused. This was like throwing herself into the sea. But she had thrown herself into the sea several times before in her life. 'I had thought of asking you to lend me ten kroner.'

Sivert's mother said nothing. Alberta talked on, as one does when a difficult pause must be filled. 'I often think of how it would be if one day I were to be left alone with Brede. I must start doing something, I must find a living. Some people live by writing books. I've written a few trifles and got money for them. Now I'd like to try something a little bigger.'

Old Fru Ness was still silent. She stopped walking; her expression was blank, difficult to interpret. Alberta looked at her standing against the yellow-green evening sky, thin and work-worn, a person who had lived by honest striving for others, without a thought of any reward other than their happiness and progress.

'A novel, you mean?' she finally asked gropingly. 'What they call a novel? I heard you were busy with something of the sort. I didn't like to ask since you hadn't said anything. But it must take rather a long time? But there, I don't know anything about it. Still, it must be very uncertain?' she said, in a more determined tone. 'Wouldn't dressmaking or something like that be better?'

'I can't sew. I can't learn to either. I'm all thumbs. And the novel is more or less finished. I must get it typed, I must do that first of all—'

'You could learn to sew as well as anybody else,' said old Fru Ness, a little sternly this time. 'It's funny what you can do if you really *want* to. But you're not like us, I understand that. I don't mean to scold, I mean that's how it is. And if you have faith in this you must have your ten kroner.'

'Thank you.' Alberta took her veined hands. 'You shall have it back. Soon perhaps.'

But Fru Ness looked at her cunningly. 'So that's what you've been doing up in the wood?'

'Yes, that's what I've been doing.'

'Hmm. Well, Otilie had better not hear about it beforehand, there'd be such a fuss and palaver. I can't quite fathom what we're to do. Have you talked to Sivert?'

'No.'

'You must talk to him. Explain it as best you can.'

'I came to you in order to avoid that. I'd like to manage alone.'

'Hm.'

There was an embarrassed pause. The burden of all the circumstances of life became so heavy for a moment that it took Alberta's breath away.

'I wish I could make out,' said Fru Ness finally, 'I wish I could make out how things are between the two of you. Sometimes I have the idea that there's nothing between you, nothing at all. I've often regretted that Otilie got her way over sharing her room with you. It can't be right when it's like this. If it were not that she's so peculiar—it's not nice to have to say it, but—it's almost as if she *grudged*—grudged you—She's not married herself. It's a misfortune for a person.'

'We understand that,' answered Alberta, in embarrassment.

'Yes, Sivert says the same. And it's as well for the sake of peace. But it's wrong, quite wrong. If I believed you were thinking of staying so long, it would never have been like this. Now Sivert has found so much work here. I shall talk to Otilie.'

'Don't do that,' said Alberta without thinking. 'There'll be bad feeling,' she added, to rescue what was beyond hope.

'I'm sorry for my boy, I am.' Fru Ness was stern now, really stern. 'Indeed I am. What kind of a marriage is this? Has he a wife or hasn't he?'

'He has no wife.'

'That's what I thought, Alberta. Just what I thought. What did you want with each other, then?'

'It's not so easy to explain. We believed—' Alberta threw

279

out her hands helplessly, thoroughly miserable. She had to go through with it.

'Perhaps you'll not be coming back to us?'

'I shall come to see Brede. I am his mother, after all.' In sudden self-assertion she raised her head and looked at Fru Ness.

'*I* think you should stay, and come to an agreement with Sivert. I expect all you need do is give way a little. Goodwill gets one far. That would be the right thing to do, Alberta.'

Silence. Then Alberta said. 'Will you promise to keep Brede here to start with? So that he won't have to change schools and—perhaps have a stepmother.'

'Stepmother?' Fru Ness gave a start. 'Is there any question of a stepmother as well? I've never heard anything to equal it.'

Alberta could control herself no longer. She wept openly. 'I suppose Sivert will want to marry again. It's only natural. And the boy is not to have a stepmother. Keep him here, you and Father—until . . .'

'That's for Sivert to decide.'

'You will decide too, I'm sure.'

'All this is dreadful, just dreadful.'

'We mustn't make it worse than it is. You're a mother yourself.'

'And so you're going out to work, Alberta? For I can imagine it's hard to write too. Are you leaving us tomorrow?'

'Don't talk like that, it only makes me cry.'

Alberta really was crying. After a while she felt the knotted hand on her back. 'Don't take it so hard. As long as we're granted our health. Are you sure you'll get this novel of yours published, though? It's so very uncertain, after all.'

Alberta dried her tears. 'I expect it will work out all right,' she said mechanically, a sentence she had learnt at home. It was useful when things looked most problematic. 'I shall try to get something to do on the side. On a newspaper or something like that.'

. . . Full of people. A small, crowded restaurant with tables outside and laurel trees in green tubs.

'Do you sell it to take out as well?'

'Of course. Here you are, here's the menu.'

'Food . . . I knew French once, now I've forgotten it . . . but it's to be for six persons, cheap and good. It's really cheating to be buying it here. I ought to have prepared it myself. It should have been on the table by now, they're sitting waiting.'

'Roast veal? Cold roast veal? Yes, everyone likes that. Dead, boring, pale-coloured food, sliced corpses, but everyone likes it. For six persons, thank you. Is this the way out?'

I must hurry home and apologise. I shall arrange matters better another time . . .

A door slammed. Alberta sat up. It was Otilie going downstairs. She had decided it was high time Alberta woke up.

She had been asleep, although she had lain awake half the night. She had to collect her limbs and her thoughts piecemeal. It was not a new sensation. But it was new for her to be standing in the middle of the floor as if facing something she had not noticed until it was right in front of her. It was new for her to go across and look at herself in the mirror, examining her face as she had not done for a long time.

What was that? A grey tuft, hidden under the rest of her hair, above her temples. When she swept it back, all at once, it appeared. Look at that, she was greying early like Mama, and like her would probably do so in the manner of nervous people, with sudden white tufts here and there, not evenly and finely distributed like people who are placid. But Mama's hair had been quite fair. It had hidden the grey until she was far advanced in years.

That thin line running downwards from her nose? That too followed a course she recognised, even though it had not come far yet. There was something fateful about it. The rather angular way of walking that she had noticed lately was her own. She had lost her light, easy step, or put it aside on purpose perhaps.

She dressed, packed her smallest suitcase, took out her manuscript and leafed through it for a while. Much of it had been written in panic, and looked like someone else's work. All of it could have been shaped better, expressed better. But each word had come floating up singly from the unknown depths, where the truth hides itself and then rises again, in different guise, unrecognisable as a dream, but irrefutable. That was what she had to support her, to use in her defence, should fate one day demand a reckoning: a new reckoning.

She hid the suitcase under the bed. She would catch a train in the early evening. Immediately after supper would be the easiest time to leave unnoticed. Then Sivert would be reading, old Ness would be reading too. Otilie was going out. Brede —no, she would not be able to wait until he was in bed.

The day passed. She could not have lived through a worse one.

She had smuggled the suitcase downstairs into the garden, under a bush. She came out on to the steps. They were all sitting there, except Otilie. Fru Ness had the boy on her knee. She was telling him a story and he was listening wide-eyed. Alberta came down, paused at the foot of the steps, and found nothing to say.

'Going for a walk?' asked Sivert.

'Yes. Good night, Brede.'

'Good night,' answered Brede briefly. 'Go on, Grannie.'

Alberta stood for a moment irresolute. Then she felt her eyes welling over and ran out of the yard. She heard Sivert say, 'She's in a hurry.'

She had to run, so as not to look back. She thought: If it had been any good talking, Sivert, we'd have done so. For a long while she saw Fru Ness's eyes: they had looked right into her own across the boy's head. They had been neither severe nor mild: they had resembled those of fate, or of the blind.

She controlled herself and walked more calmly; she must not attract attention. The evening was similar to the one on which she had arrived. The air was already cool, with the first acrid taste of autumn. They were burning branches in the gardens. It was the kind of evening in early autumn that resembles an evening in spring.

She met people. They were standing in groups outside their

houses or talking to each other over the fences. There were mothers and children, husbands and wives, acquaintances. The peace of evening was on them. They stood at ease, finished with the day, waiting calmly for the night. At least, it seemed so. A few nodded to Alberta. Nobody asked where she was going.

She walked along, certain of only one thing. She had finished groping in a fog for warmth and security. The mist had risen now, there was clear visibility and it was cold. No arms round her any more, not even those of a child: naked life, as far ahead as she could see, struggle and an impartial view. She would go under or become so bitterly strong that nothing could hurt her any more. She felt something of the power of the complete solitary. Then she remembered Brede and knew that she could never be quite so invulnerable after all.

A young mother with a child on her arm took one of its small hands in hers and waved it at Alberta. 'Wave to the lady.'

Alberta nodded and smiled, waving back. The memory of the soft, tender warmth, the easy weight of a child a few months' old remained like deprivation in her arms. She pictured Tot, when, changed and dry, he lay kicking in his clean napkin. Small as he was, he too could be seized with delight, kicking with socks on his tiny feet, and laughing when Alberta caught them.

At the Evensens' the mare had a foal. It followed its mother closely. She was placid, the foal was placid. Everything was as it should be, and no one remarked on it. Alberta clenched her teeth. I'm actually beginning to grow up, she thought.

At moments she felt quite faint. For this might go completely wrong. She would offer her manuscript, ask for an advance, get it copied, look for work on a newspaper. Supposing nobody accepted it? Would she retrace her steps? Would she be capable of doing so if necessary? It must not be necessary. In the worst case she would have to try anything. To stay with Sivert on sufferance led nowhere, not even into the heart of her child. She would have to approach him from another direction: first as the strange visitor, half forgotten,

283

bringing small presents and sweets; later, if fate was kind, as an equal guardian—as his mother.

Did she have any desires? To go out into the world? To find anyone in particular? One does not desire the impossible. The person who has once taken life in the wrong way must finally accept life as it is.

The truth, Pierre had said once. To tell a little of the truth.

AFTERWORD

by Linda Hunt

Reversing the old adage about a prophet not being honored in his own country, Cora Sandel's *Alberta Trilogy* has long been a classic in her native Norway but is nearly unknown in the English-speaking world, especially in the United States. *Alberta and Jacob, Alberta and Freedom*, and *Alberta Alone*, first published in 1926, 1931, and 1939 respectively, were not even translated into English until the first half of the nineteen-sixties when they appeared in England; a one-volume American edition (which contained all three novels under the misleading title of *Alberta Alone*) appeared in 1966 but drew few reviews, little attention, and soon fell out of print. A look at the *MLA Index* for the decade of the seventies shows that numerous critical articles on Sandel, and especially on the *Alberta* books, appeared in the Scandinavian languages but none in English. The card catalogue of the New York Public Library's main branch reveals no holdings in English on Cora Sandel.

For American readers, Ohio University Press in publishing the *Alberta Trilogy* is making an important contribution to what Germaine Greer has called "the rehabilitation of women's literary history." These three feminist novels are so good that along with hailing their recovery one cannot help but feel angry that we in the United States have had to wait so long for the opportunity to experience their excellence.

Alberta and Jacob (1926) is an evocation of one year in the life of a shy, repressed adolescent girl living with her family in a stuffy, provincial town in the most Northern part of Norway during the last years of the nineteenth century. Alberta Selmer's family and their neighbors could be characters out of Ibsen in their bourgeois concern for sexual respectability and the importance of keeping up the appearance of material prosperity. Alberta despairs at the prospect of a life like that of any of the women in her town. If spinsters, they are objects of pity and, actually, objectively quite "odd"; if

285

sexually rebellious, pregnancy tames them. Respectably married, their lives are bounded by food and servant worries, gynecological troubles, and envy of their neighbors. This grim destiny is appropriately emblemized for Alberta by the figure of Nurse Jellum the midwife who keeps reappearing throughout the novel (and indeed recurs in memory in the sequels), "with her terrible bag and her quiescent know-all smile."

Alberta's options are contrasted to that of her brother Jacob who functions as a foil lest we make the mistake of not recognizing that Alberta's troubles are related to gender. While his life in this environment is far from enviable, he is encouraged to stay in school (although he is a terrible student and she is an excellent one), and he is able to find some relief from the stultifying life of the family by carousing with a sailor friend and coming home late, sometimes drunk. His decision to go to sea is a calamity for his caste-conscious parents, but they accept the unavoidable and he makes his escape. Alberta cannot follow Jacob's example and simply leave or even plan eventually to leave because she has internalized the family's assumption that as a dutiful daughter she will sacrifice her own well-being to be a buffer between her wretchedly-married parents.

Sandel expertly uses the frozen landscape of this Arctic town and the frigid interior of the Selmer house as an externalization of Alberta's inner life. The strange, brief summer of Northern Norway with its twenty-four hours of daylight functions as a metaphor for the protagonist's first furtive recognition that there is a world outside of her experience which can offer light, warmth, and happiness.

Alberta and Freedom (1931) begins with its protagonist standing nude, in Paris, posing for an artist. Lest the reader think Alberta has found the freedom and warmth she longed for as a girl and which the title of this volume seems to promise, we are told immediately of the terrible vulnerability Alberta feels, of the physical and mental discomfort of standing in one position for so long, and, inevitably, of the cold-

286

ness of the studio. (External cold and heat are metaphors for Alberta's emotional condition throughout the trilogy.) The Norwegian young woman's parents had died, and she has at last been able to flee to the Bohemian fringe of Paris; it is the period before the first world war when the Left Bank became a symbol of youthful release from restrictive conventions, but, as this novel and its sequel show, the pursuit of freedom is not easy for a woman.

Alberta and Freedom is framed by images of a woman's physical vulnerability and susceptibility to bodily exploitation. The opening scene of Alberta posing, compelled to earn her bread by making a body into a commodity since she has been trained for no profession or occupation, is matched by the closing scene of the novel in which Alberta, unmarried and pregnant, wanders around an exhibition of "man-eating" tribes from Central Africa which has come to Paris. She comes upon a young "Negress" nursing a child; the African woman recognizes Alberta's condition and nods in delighted affinity. The experience releases in Alberta previously pent-up maternal emotions, and yet it is clear from the imagery that for Alberta, both she and the Black woman are, like animals, captives of their bodies, reduced to a bodily existence. The fact that the African mother is being exhibited to crowds for a price serves to underscore the theme of sexual exploitation.

Between the first and closing scenes we read of Alberta's life in Paris: perhaps the most striking thing about this life is its apparent purposelessness; she does make occasional undisciplined, almost furtive attempts to express herself creatively through writing, but it is impossible for her to take herself seriously enough to have genuine literary ambitions. She spends her time wandering around Paris half-starved—on the Metro, on foot, on trams—taking in the human drama all around her but always a stranger at the feast. Unwilling to accept any of the roles society has assigned to women, Alberta, at this stage, is a kind of Underground Woman, "an outlaw" as one character calls her. She is the female counterpart to all those male anti-heroes of modern literature who define themselves in terms of their marginality. Alberta has no analysis of what is wrong with the position of women in society, but all of her instincts are to keep herself a marginal member. As the narrative voice tells us, "She still had only negative instincts just as when she was at home. They told her clearly what she did not want to do. . . . she was left free to reject what she did not want and without the slightest idea of what she should do with herself."

Sandel depicts the circle of Alberta's Montparnasse friends, men and women who have come there from all over the world to be artists. Alberta's closest friend is Liesel, a struggling painter who always spoils her paintings just when they are very good by putting a dab of color where it does not belong or painting in some lines that mar the overall design. Like Alberta but several steps ahead of her since at least she is able to define herself as an artist, Liesel cannot trust her inner vision. She succumbs to a young sculptor, and initially her love affair is joyous, a reproachment to Alberta's loneliness. But Elial, Liesel's lover, determines the conditions of their life together so that his work always takes precedence over hers. Sandel is certainly making a point about the obstacles to artistic success for women since none of the women in Alberta's and Liesel's Paris circle achieve artistic fulfillment, but both Elial and Sivert, Alberta's lover, become quite successful. The women painters as they get older are evoked as "trudging around Montparnasse. . . . they had wrinkles and untidy grey hair, and they dragged themselves around with large bags of brushes over one arm . . . fussing and wearisome, they filled the academies and life-classes . . . they lived on nothing, making tea with egg water. . . . "

In the final volume of this trilogy, *Alberta Alone* (1939), the protagonist's existence is much less marginal as a result of a marriage-like relationship and motherhood. Alberta has backed right into a life not too different from the one she sought to escape. In this book Sandel shows that integration into society for women too often means oppressive burdens: Alberta is encumbered by the endless work and persistent worry that being a mother entails; weighted down by her lack of love for the father of her child, on whom she is financially dependent, and by her developing love for Pierre, another woman's husband. But the relationship with Pierre is different from either of her previous entanglements with men in that he encourages Alberta to take seriously the pile of papers in a folder that Sivert has always demeaningly referred to as her "scribbling." For the first time she begins to think in a positive way about what she might want to do with her life.

In the course of this third novel Alberta becomes increasingly aware that she must find a way to be financially self-sufficient. In the last scene she walks along a road in Norway carrying the completed novel in a suitcase, her aim publication and the beginning of an autonomous and purposeful existence. Because she has left the child behind, everything she sees along the road, a mother and a baby, mare and foal, seem to tell her she is at odds with nature. Sandel defines Alberta's emotional state at this juncture in her life by an image of external cold which by accretion through the three novels has become increasingly powerful: "the mist had risen now, there was clear visibility and it was cold. No arms around her anymore, not even those of a child; naked life as far as she could see, struggle for an impartial view."

Throughout these books Cora Sandel is a fine stylist with a keenly-observant eye and a good ear; she has been well-served by her translator. Sandel's mastery of precise detail and fresh imagery allows her to bring place and character to vivid realization, endowing both with the emotional meaning she seeks. Thus, the coffee pot in the chill, cluttered Victorian dining room in the Selmer home "stood there like a revelation, its brass well-polished, warming, steaming, aromatic . . a sun among dead worlds." Seen through the window of the office where she works, Beda Buck, the girlhood friend who is as free in spirit as Alberta is repressed, "shook her fist through the window at Alberta, because she was wandering about . . . while Beda had to sit indoors." In Paris the cafe awnings, the dry leaves in a hot summer square, the "rusty" voice of a night club singer, the shrouded shapes in a sculptor's studio, all suggest Alberta's melancholy at being alone in the nearly-deserted city in August. In Alberta's down-at-the-heels hotel room mice drown in the wash-bowl. As Alberta and Sivert become increasingly estranged, his eyes are "much too blue," his presence on several occasions experienced as "a wall." Sandel's ear for dialogue is equally evocative.

Moreover, these novels are structured in such a way that form imitates substance. Instead of chapters, we have a series of scenes separated by blank space or blank space with asterisks. Each time the scene changes the reader must struggle, without expository narration, to re-orient herself, to figure out where Alberta is, who the other characters are, what is happening or what the conversation is about. The effect, especially because Sandel's writing is so visual and reliant on dialogue, is almot cinematic. For example, in *Alberta and Freedom*, an early scene opens in a carefully-described studio in a Parisian hotel. Alberta is lying on a bed talking to Liesel whom we are meeting for the first time. The reader wonders: is this where Alberta lives in Paris? Who is this friend? (The room turns out to belong to Liesel.) In having to work out the situation, the reader is experiencing what Alberta continually goes through as she struggles to make sense of a world which is not welcoming and where nothing is easy for her. Like Alberta, the reader feels peripheral to the life which unfolds.

Sandel's skillful experimentation with formal innovation along with her command of language and the importance of her themes certainly should have ensured her an audience and a reputation outside her native Norway. The question remains: why were these novels not recognized for their quality earlier, at least in the sixties when the Elizabeth Rokken translation appeared in England and America? An examination of the reviews from that time reveal some clues. It is apparent even from the positive reviews (and on the whole the novels were well-received) that the specifically female reality Cora Sandel mined, the answers she found to problems of plot and structure endemic to women's fiction, and her feminist themes made sufficient and appropriate appreciation unlikely in the first half of the sixties in England and America. The work done by feminist critics in the last decade has made Cora Sandel's achievement accessible to us in ways it simply was not earlier. (It would be fascinating to know what Scandinavian critics have been saying about her work all along.) The sixties' reviews also show the extent to which bias against feminism and even downright sexism was an obstacle to a fair literary assessment of Sandel's work.

In 1966 an American reviewer (a woman), writing for the *Saturday Review*, enthusiastically compares Alberta with Philip Carey, the protagonist of Somerset Maugham's *Of Human Bondage*. Like Carey, she says, Alberta emerges from a dreary small-town childhood into "pre-war Paris and the brief years of freedom, art, and love, no money, and infinite possibilities." Since this is not what happens at all, we can only assume that the reviewer processed what she read to suit her preconceptions about what the artistic life in Paris was like in those years, preconceptions that had been formed by reading both the literature and the literary mythology produced by men.

Sandel has written these books in part to show us that while Bohemian Paris may have been a moveable feast to male writers and painters, there was no way that Alberta and her friends could have had the same joyous experience. While they do possess talent, they lack the self-confidence, the money, and the freedom from both conventionality and heterosexuality that made it possible for some few women—the likes of Gertrude Stein and Natalie Barney—to establish a woman-loving artistic culture in Paris in this period. As Liesel says in a letter after she has returned home to her fam-

291

ily, "The artistic poverty-stricken life isn't much fun in the long run. The men can do it, but not us."

The reader today finds herself nodding, 'Yes, that's how it would have been for most women.' She is likely to think of Virginia Woolf's hypothetical story, in *A Room Of One's Own*, of what would have happened to Shakespeare's equally-talented sister (if he had had one), if she had tried to go to London to become a playwright. Shakespeare's sister, in pursuit of freedom, adventure, and creative fulfillment, falls victim to, among other things, her lack of control of her reproductive life—as do Alberta and Liesel. But back in 1966 when the *Saturday Review* piece on the Alberta books appeared, few people were reading *A Room Of One's Own*, and literary minds, even female ones, were not sensitized to the fact that reality gets dangerously distorted when we try to fit female experience into a framework of literary conventions made by and for men.

Almost all the reviews from the nineteen-sixties complain that in Sandel's trilogy "nothing happens." The reviewer of *Alberta & Freedom* in the *Times Literary Supplement* (July 26, 1963) asks, "But what about development, action, drama?" Because of the work of such feminist literary critics as Joanna Russ, Annis Pratt, Nancy Miller and Gubar and Gilbert, we understnd that Cora Sandel is avoiding the patriarchal plot-structures that have been recognized as a major obstacle to women writers seeking to express an authentic female point of view. Since women in stories inherited from the male literary tradition have limited alternatives regarding what they can do (fall in love and marry, fall in love and die), Sandel chooses plotlessness, but in doing so she is not choosing lack of form. Joanna Russ would describe the structure of the Alberta trilogy as "lyrical" in that images, events, passages and words are organized around an implicit emotional center, that center being Alberta Selmer's repressed soul and its yearning, as it gropes in the cold and damp of life, for freedom, warmth, and security. Virginia Woolf structures her novels along similar principles.

292

These three novels read together also have another kind of structure which comes from the working out of certain mythic patterns which feminist criticism such as Annis Pratt's *Archetypal Patterns in Women's Fiction* and Carol Pearson and Katherine Pope's *The Female Hero* show us are recurrent in fiction by women. Both of these recent studies stress the importance of the mother-daughter relationship, symbolized in Greek mythology by the story of Demeter, the goddess of the harvest, and her daughter Persephone who is stolen from her side. Just as in the myth the season of cold when nothing grows initiated by the ruptured relationship between mother and daughter can only end when the two are returned to each other, a female hero in fiction often requires reconciliation with her mother or a mother-figure in order to get in touch with her own power and achieve her creative potential.

Alberta's relationship with her mother is already deeply estranged when *Alberta and Jacob* opens. Mrs. Selmer, self-doubting and disappointed with her life, is incapable of nurturing a daughter. Although Alberta is so cold that her skin is perpetually blue, she has to sneak the hot cups of coffee she craves. At the breakfast table Alberta must help herself to food as surreptitiously as possible while Mrs. Selmer loads Jacob's plate with piles of cheese. Alberta's mother is similarly ungenerous on the level of emotions. She tells Alberta repeatedly that she is a disappointment because of her lack of beauty, her shyness, her inability to interest herself in domestic accomplishments, her inexplicable interest in reading "learned tomes," and her refusal to encourage the attentions of her father's clerk.

Mama's inability to provide warmth is largely responsible for Alberta's guilt-ridden and anxious personality; she is so constrained that she feels "she was without the use of speech, she would die of muteness." Always afraid of eliciting her mother's scorn or anger, Alberta can never feel relaxed in her mother's house.

Given the youthful Alberta's fear that she will "die of

293

muteness," we can understand why in later years her writing becomes the key to life for her. Given the lack of ease she feels in the house in which she spends her childhood, Alberta's discomfort in a series of dingy, even sordid hotel rooms and then in Sivert's crowded studio takes on greater poignancy. Even in a pleasant summer cottage in Brittany she is unable to enjoy the beauty of her surroundings because she is terrified that the sea air is dangerous to the health of her delicate little son. Alberta can never feel at home anywhere.

The inhospitability of her environment, wherever she is, is a factor in her failure to impose coherence on her manuscript. We see Alberta wrestling with her "muddle of scribbled papers" in poorly-lit hotel rooms and on the slopes near the beach in Brittany where she must "struggle . . . with the wind for control of her straying papers."

Towards the close of the last volume Alberta is sitting in a wood in rural Norway uncomfortably balancing her manuscript on her knees, desperate to finish, when she is discovered by an old woman with a "kind, wrinkled face tied up in a handkerchief." The woman, Lina, invites Alberta to see her house on a nearby farm. They go upstairs to a room where "the sun poured in on a large table standing between the windows . . . . There was simple furniture . . . Some dried wreaths above the sofa gave out a strong sweet scent. . . . Alberta had, without thinking, put her folder down on the table. There it lay as if it had come home. She almost felt at home herself." The farmwoman allows her to use the room to work on her manuscript, and in it, over the course of a beautiful Norwegian summer, she completes her novel.

Lina's psychic function is to be a surrogate mother to Alberta and, appearing just when the younger woman needs her most (exactly when Pope and Pearson, in their book on the archetypal "journey" of the female hero, say this figure appears), is able to heal the damage done by Alberta's actual mother who had functioned as a "captor." Lina's description fits that of the "wise old woman" whom Annis Pratt tells us is often in women's novels an archetypal guide for the soul as it pursues its spiritual quest. Lina is surrounded by plants and animals and, as the sweet-smelling wreaths in the room demonstrate, has a knowledge of herbs. Married, but very much her own woman, Lina provides a model of calm autonomy. Most important, she not only provides Alberta with the sanctuary in the form of a simple room which Pratt reminds us so many women characters need to get in touch with their power but, like any good mother, she affirms Alberta's gift by recognizing it: "I understand enough to see you're a kind of author too, it's just that you don't want anything to interfere." Again like an ideal mother, she compels Alberta to impose discipline on herself by telling her firmly she must vacate the room by the date summer visitors are due to arrive. In finding a spiritual mother who both nurtures and yet encourages separation, Alberta becomes capable of saving herself through mastery of language, overcoming the "muteness" which was her biological mother's inadvertent legacy.

Alberta can develop as a person only through the kind of inner, psychic experience that reconciliation with a mother figure represents. As the reviewer of *Alberta and Freedom* quoted before complains, she does not develop psychologically very much in the course of the novels. For example, when Jeanne, Pierre's wife, orders her to send him a telegraph terminating their relationship, she simply complies, as much a slave to an authoritative voice as when she was a child who had internalized her parents' values.

Reading Annis Pratt can help us to understand that Alberta fails to develop much psychologically until the very end not as a result of weakness in Sandel's narrative skill but for the same reasons that female heroes in general don't progress towards maturity through action in the social world. The female bildungsroman cannot demonstrate "*bildung*" in the way that male novels of development do because in patriarchal society adulthood for women means neither authority nor autonomy. Unlike the male hero who develops by achieving an adult social identity, for Alberta increasing

295

integration into society only means further entrapment. Like so many protagonists of women's fiction she can "break through" into true adulthood (as she is told to do in a very Jungian dream by the "young girlish figure" who is her guide) only by asocial moments of epiphany such as she experiences in her almost clandestine first visit to Lina's room.

Alberta's reconciliation with the symbolic good mother links the last volume with the bad-mother motif in the first book, *Alberta and Jacob*, providing unity to the trilogy as a whole. Since Lina is encountered in summer, and Mrs. Selmer tyrannizes over the adolescent Alberta predominantly in the dark, freezing depths of winter, it seems possible that Sandel may even have had the Demeter-Persephone myth consciously in mind. Certainly the extraordinary emphasis on the soul-withering Arctic cold in *Alberta and Jacob* suggests the endless winter that results, in the myth, from the rupture of mother and daughter.

Other criticisms of the *Alberta* books in the reviews from the sixties require no response but are interesting because of their naked anti-feminism and sexism. An unsigned review of *Alberta Alone* in the *Times Literary Supplement* (February 25, 1965) dismisses Sandel's concern for the emancipation of women as outdated and complains about the "female narcissism" in the book. This same reviewer finds the character of Alberta insufficiently deep to warrant her position as the center of interest in a trilogy, an opinion he is entitled to, but one is forced to think about his biases when he observes, "This is not *just* to say that women are less interesting than men, and that this is the flaw" [emphasis mine].

The resurrection of feminism in the years since the *Alberta Trilogy* was first published in English has encouraged literary minds both to develop the interpretative skills necessary to understand women's literature and to be on the alert for "lost" books by women. The appearance in America of these three novels by Cora Sandel should be regarded as an important event of literary archeology. However, literature by women has been retrieved in the past only to slip again into

296

obscurity. It is important that people be told how good the novels in this series are and be urged to read them singly and/or as a unit; it is important that these novels be taught and written about. Readers are ultimately the ones who keep worthy "lost" books alive.